Fire
Magic

Three Moon Falls
Book One

Katie O'Connor

Fire Magic

Three Moon Falls Book One

Katie O'Connor

-Fire Magic-

-Three Moon Falls Book 1-

This book is a work of fiction. Names, characters, places, and incidents either are products of the author's imagination or are used fictitiously. Any resemblance to actual events, locales, or persons, living or dead, is entirely coincidental.

Published December 2019 by Snarky Heart Press and Katie O'Connor

(katieohwrites.com)

ISBN: 978-1-9990192-7-3 (Digital Edition 1)

ISBN: 978-1-9990192-8-0 (Other Digital Edition)

ISBN: 978-1-9990192-9-7 (Print Edition 1)

ISNN: 978-1-997548-09-6 (Alternate Print Edition)

Design and cover art by Raquel Lyon, Crooked Sixpence Book Covers

Copyediting by Terri St. Clair

About Fire Magic

He's a professional diver. She's a witch who controls fire. Fire and water don't mix...

Amber Hawk can trace her roots all the way back to the witches of Salem. She's got astounding magical abilities, including the ability to control fire. Something weird is happening in her peaceful hometown of Three Moon Falls, and Amber suspects dark magic is behind it. The only way she can get to the bottom of all the strange happenings is to team up with the infuriating, sexy man who's been making her life miserable.

Kodiak Wilkins doesn't believe in hocus-pocus mumbo-jumbo. He thinks Amber's a bit off her rocker, but against his better judgement, he's attracted to her. Something keeps pushing them together and scary things are happening. He's going to have to swallow his disbelief and help her out of this dangerous crisis. And in the process learn some interesting things about himself.

Can they defeat this evil and keep their lives separate, or is fate going to keep forcing them together until they admit the attraction burning between them?

Dedication

This one is for Mom. She's my number one fan and supports me unconditionally in everything I do. I would never have produced a single story if it weren't for her unwavering support and belief in me.

A super shout out to my unofficially adopted sister, Suzette who cheers loudly from the sidelines of my career.

Contents

Chapter One

"Turn it up! I love this tune," Amber Hawk shouted over her shoulder at her older sister, Lazuli.

"You've got it." Laz stopped hammering and cranked the radio. Her off-key voice joined in with the familiar lyrics, and Amber added her own somewhat more melodic version as she rubbed wax into the antique sideboard destined to become a candle display cabinet in her soon-to-open new-age store.

Her shop, Four Seasons Metaphysical, would be the first of its kind in their tourist-trade driven hometown of Three Moon Falls. Some of the locals were skittish about Witches and Wiccans, but tourists loved eccentric shops. They'd adore the book her family had written about local ghost sightings. People would buy it, thinking it fun and eccentric, not realizing every word was true.

Unable to resist the radio's rhythmic beat, Amber dropped her rag and performed a stumbling pirouette into the main aisle. Arms flailing wildly, she danced and belted out the song at the top of her voice. Laz and their baby sister, Hazel, joined her in a frenetic, energy raising dance. The positive energy they raised would pull good things into their store. Dancing, singing, and music created the best results for working positive magic. White magic.

The music cut off mid-syllable. "Cut the noise, people are trying to sleep," a male voice roared.

Laz and Hazel squeaked in alarm. Amber dropped her hands to her side. Anger overrode her common sense, and she stomped toward the stranger who stood, uninvited, in her store.

"I beg your pardon?" She jabbed him in the chest with one finger.

Tall and broad shouldered, he still managed to appear slim. A scowl turned down the corners of his mouth, darkened his pale green eyes, and created tiny frown lines around them. Even this early in summer, he was tanned a lovely golden brown. He must like to spend his time outdoors; a trait she identified with—she loved the sun. He wore faded jeans and a loose-fitting t-shirt that emphasized his large, well-defined biceps. The man was definitely drool-worthy, despite his angry expression.

"What are you doing in my store, and how did you get in?" They'd locked the doors after Hazel arrived for the work-bee. She threw him her best, *fess up now* look and waited, with her hands on her hips.

"I'm here to shut down this crap. You've been banging away all hours of the day and night for twelve days, and it's going to stop." He crossed his arms over his chest.

Amber almost drooled when his biceps rippled. Those muscles would be solid and strong under her fingertips. Or her lips. Her unwelcome guest was more than passably attractive—he was flat out gorgeous. Sinful even.

"How did you get in here?" she repeated, mimicking his posture.

"I came down the stairwell that connects my apartment upstairs with this space." His eyes narrowed in challenge.

Well, challenge accepted. "That apartment is empty. It's been empty for seven years. Tell me another one, and this time, make it believable." She almost rolled her eyes at her own childish taunt. The truth was, nobody had occupied that suite since the store owner died up there when she slipped over a mop bucket and cracked her skull. "Exactly who are you?"

"I'm Kodiak Wilkins. I rent the suite upstairs. I'm trying to sleep. I have a business to run, and I can't do that if I'm too exhausted to dive."

She blinked and squinted at him, trying to make sense of his words. Sleep and dive? Oh, he must be the new diving instructor who did tours of the lake bottom. It still didn't explain why he was in her store.

"Okay, Mr. Kodiak Wilkins, try again. My landlord never mentioned renting the suite." The rudeness in her voice would set her grandmother off on a tirade about manners. It made her wince; she wasn't like this. She was calm, cool, and collected—most of the time—but she did tend toward impatience, and he was pushing her that way.

"Kody will be sufficient, and if my cousin, your landlord, didn't tell you about me, it's not my fault. But it is typical." He closed his eyes for a second, and the rock-hard muscles in his arms and shoulders relaxed.

She recognized his attempt at calming himself. He was right. Jason Wilkins, landlord and arrogant pig, wasn't much on keeping his tenants informed of anything beyond rent increases. Owning half the town, he pretty much did as he liked.

"Sorry about the noise, Kody. We didn't know you were up there." She waved vaguely at the ceiling. "We'll tone it down a little."

"I let the noise go because I thought it would be a short-term thing. This is getting ridiculous. I don't suppose you can quit working at night?" he suggested reasonably.

"I'd love to, but we open on Monday, three days away, and our grand opening is the next Saturday. If we don't get the fixtures together tonight, we can't stock the shelves." They were fast running out of time to get ready for the opening. If they weren't, she'd happily avoid night work. She'd like to accommodate this handsome man, but they were way too short on time.

"You can't do this during the day?" He massaged his temples with two fingers.

"Unfortunately, we can't. It's a group effort thing, and the only time we can all be here is at night," she offered warily. "We'll turn the music down."

"Thank heaven for that," he exclaimed. "I detest country music." He shuddered. "Is there anything I can do to facilitate and expedite completion?"

"No." She glared. The ridiculously formal words got on her nerves. "There is nothing you can do to facilitate and expedite completion. Thank you." Sarcasm rang from her voice as she spat the words out. She waved her fingers dismissively toward the back room. The man was intolerable; too bad he was so danged good looking. Wasn't there a saying about that? Something regarding kindness and beauty? She'd have to look it up next time she fired up her computer. "Feel free to leave, and I'll thank you to stop entering my store without permission. Breaking and entering is against the law."

"The door was open. There was no breaking involved."

"That's not true," Hazel spewed, striding forward and planting herself, arms crossed, beside Amber in a show of solidarity. "I checked it myself when I brought in the last of the shelving."

"It is true, and I resent you calling me a liar." His face was turning red, and he looked pissed.

Amber needed to put a stop to the argument. "Listen, I'm sorry we disturbed you. We'll try to keep it down."

"Thank you." He nodded briskly and strode into the back room.

"Shut the door behind you," Laz yelled. "Insufferable jerk," she muttered.

"I heard that," he called back.

"Good," Amber returned his volley. Stupid stuffed shirt of a man.

"Women." Exasperation filled his voice, making the trio of sisters giggle.

"Hyacinth should have been here," Hazel declared. "She'd have put him in his place."

She referred to the oldest of the four Hawk sisters. Descendants of the Salem witches, each had their own magical skill. Though she rarely indulged her petulant side, Hyacinth had a gift for bringing pain or healing with a simple look or touch. She'd have given him a magical flick to the backside.

Pleased that he was gone, they shared a high-five and returned to work. Abandoning her furniture waxing, Amber picked up a shelf and attempted to hang it on the shelving wall. It slipped out of her grasp and clattered to the floor with an eardrum breaking clang.

Ten seconds later, before she'd even picked it up, their neighbor was back. "Let me do that," he demanded, gesturing for her to get out of the way.

"I've got it," Amber said. She didn't need his help. She was more than skilled enough to hang a few shelves.

"I'll get it. I'll get them all. The sooner they're up, the sooner you'll be gone." He snatched the shelf off the floor and gently nudged her out of the way. "What height?"

She pointed to the place she wanted the shelf. Who was she to argue? She was fully capable, but her grandmother didn't raise any fools. If he wanted to do the lifting, she was going to let him. He grabbed another shelf off the teetering stack and looked at her with one raised eyebrow.

Hazel and Laz returned to their hammering while Amber and Kodiak hung the rest of the shelves. As he placed the last one, Amber stood back and watched him. The man had the nicest derriere she'd seen in ages. Firm, fit, and encased in snug denim jeans, he was a fantasy come to life. The muscles rippling down his back and across his shoulders weren't hard to look at, either.

Nope. She wasn't interested. He might be helpful now, but he'd blown in like a backdraft, spewing fire and anger. She didn't have time for people like that. They'd have been quiet if they'd known he was around. They were reasonable people, unlike him. A frown creased her forehead. She wasn't usually so judgemental. Gramma Pearl would ask her what was it about Kodiak Wilkins that set her off? No sense fretting over it now. She'd gladly accept his assistance and was grateful for it.

Kody mounted the last shelf and turned to face Amber. His easy grin rocked her to her toes. Wow! The man was beautiful when he relaxed. An answering smile crept over her face.

"Thanks for the help," she said. She offered her hand. "I'm Amber Hawk. These are my sisters." His large hand dwarfed her small delicate one. She looked up at him, trying in vain to ignore the rush of pleasure his firm grip sent cascading through her. "We'll try to limit most of the noise to daylight hours."

"I'd appreciate that. Let me know if you need any more lifting done. I'm free most evenings." He walked out of the room. Pausing in the doorway, he looked back over his shoulder. "Nice to meet you. Maybe I'll get all your names next time. Don't forget to keep your door locked."

The shop's back door closed with a barely audible click, and Amber make a rude gesture toward the ceiling. "Of all the unmitigated gall. How dare he say the door was unlocked?"

"By the Goddess, he was cute," Hazel piped in. "Like man, I could stare at him all day, and did you see those bulging biceps? And that ass?" She sighed heavily. "He's a gift from the gods."

"With an attitude that doesn't quit." Amber shook her head. "That man is entirely too full of himself. He probably thinks his shit doesn't stink."

"And those eyes?" Lazuli sighed. "And that sleep tousled hair? I'd like to crawl into his bed." She hugged herself dreamily.

"Nobody, not any of us, is going to crawl into his bed. Not now, not ever. He's insufferable. He's rude. He's...." She didn't even want to admit that he had reason to be upset, or that he was pleasant when he chose to be.

"Oh," Lazuli sing-songed. "Amber's got it bad. She's drooling over the hot guy upstairs and staking her claim." Lazuli and Hazel high-fived each other.

"Not even," Amber protested. "Sure, he's hot, but he's—"

"A god among men?" Hazel teased. "Too sexy for words. Too hot to handle. He just needs some good loving to calm his inner beast, the Amber Hawk magic touch."

"Get over yourself," Amber protested. "He's a jerk." He was delicious, but she'd be danged stupid to admit her attraction to her sisters. They'd never let her live it down.

Besides, she wasn't looking for a man. She'd set her heart on opening this new-age shop, and she was going to make it work. She didn't have time for sexy divers with rock-hard bodies and bulging muscles. Nope, not interested. Not one bit. She bit down a sigh. She'd never convince them; she couldn't even convince herself. Their neighbor was a man who could fire up her hormones without even trying.

"He might have been rude, but we have been keeping him awake for nearly two weeks. I'd be pissed, too," Hazel said. "Just because we're up late doesn't mean he wants to be. I can do my work anytime. If he's a diver, he needs to be awake and alert underwater. I can't say I blame him for storming down here." She paused thoughtfully. "Although, I know that door was locked. I double checked."

Like her sister, Amber was certain the door had been locked. His claim that it was open didn't make sense. It was definitely closed, and that indicated that people weren't to just walk in like he had. Kody Wilkins wasn't telling the truth.

"Why would he lie about the door?" she wondered aloud.

"Maybe he didn't," Hazel said, her brow wrinkled.

"You said it was closed and locked," Lazuli countered.

"At the very least, he opened it. I checked it when I went to the bathroom an hour ago," Amber stated, hands on her hips. This was turning into the typical Hawk family running discussion with everyone throwing out ideas without listening to anyone else. They bickered for several moments until Hazel thrust her arms up in a stop gesture and gave a piercing whistle.

"Geez." Amber winced. "Don't do that! You're killing my ears."

"Look, I researched this building before you rented it." Hazel grinned.

"And?" Amber and Lazuli chimed in unison.

"And rumor has it," she paused dramatically, "that it is haunted." There wasn't anything Hazel loved as much as a ghost story. She'd spent most of her twenty-three years chasing ghosts.

"You might have mentioned it," Amber said wryly.

"Hells no." Hazel laughed. "A haunted store is the perfect place to sell the book we wrote about local ghosts. I mean, seriously, can you think of a better place? I've even included our resident spooks in the final version of the book. Well, final version until we find more local properties. I've started talking to the owners of some of the places, like Earl Cooper at the bookstore on fifth, about setting up a ghost tour. We'd run them at set times and charge for them. A portion of the money we receive would go to the other venues, or maybe they'd just like the exposure. I'm working out the deets."

"Resident spooks?" Amber sighed. "Is there more than one ghost in here? Thanks for the heads up."

Lazuli laughed.

"Come on, favorite sister, it'll be fun." Hazel hugged Amber. "Besides, I'm sure they're not malicious, or we'd have heard from them before now."

"Malicious?" Amber squeaked. This was getting out of hand. First, a handsome neighbor, then ghosts? What was next? Demons? "And have you tried to connect with them yet?" she asked with a raised eyebrow, mimicking their grandmother's best I-know-you're-up-to-something look.

"Nopers. I thought we'd get all settled in nice and cozy first." Hazel twirled in place, a rapturous expression lighting her face. "I can't wait."

Goddess help her deal with her practical joker sister and her affinity and passion for all things ghost related. Hazel, with her auburn hair and brown eyes, had a lot of Irish trickster in her.

"Just how many ghosts are we talking here?" Amber asked.

"I've found references to two. The lady who ran the drugstore died upstairs and a teenage girl who died of an overdose; she came in for help, but the paramedics couldn't save her. Neither is reputed to be malicious, but they must have put off renters or this prime location would have been snapped up before now. You know how it is when ghosts don't like their neighbors."

"Great." Or not. She had a point about them scaring off renters. What else would deter someone from renting a large store facing the lakefront in an extremely high traffic location? And their store had been vacant for years, until they leased it. Amber had jumped on it when she started searching for a business location. "Weird that I never felt anything when I toured the store, or since we started moving in."

"I think that's because they want us here," Hazel said. "We're great people, after all. I'm sure they recognise our awesomeness."

Amber marvelled at the seriousness of her youngest sister's voice. Ever the lighthearted jokester, there was a strong undercurrent of solemnity to her statement.

"Are they here now?" Amber looked around. "I can't sense anything."

Her gift for dealing with ghosts was weak, despite trying to develop it into a usable skill. The only spirit she'd ever successfully contacted was her maternal great-great-grandmother, Rosemary Jade Hawk. It was tradition that Hawk women kept their family name. They could all communicate with her, though nobody knew why she was hanging around and keeping tabs on the family. It wasn't uncommon for the ancestors of witches to pop in and out of their descendant's lives. Though they steadfastly refused to discuss any aspect of the afterlife, the sisters had chalked the ghostly visits up to a normal occurrence for their family.

Amber and her three sisters had been living with their maternal grandmother since they were teenagers, when their mother and her new husband took off in search of a witch killer. Unlike their great-great-grandmother, they hadn't heard a peep from great-gramma since she died seven years ago. It was unusual for a family member to fail to pop in on occasion; especially around Samhain when the veil between worlds was at its thinnest.

"No sign of ghosts since we started moving in," Hazel declared, slightly exasperated. "I had hoped they'd be around. I'd love to hear their stories."

"Yeah, me too." Laz wiped down a shelf and dropped her wash rag into a bucket. "Do you suppose one of them unlocked the door?" Laz's hazel eyes lit with excitement, and she tossed her long sandy-brown hair over her shoulder.

Amber looked at her sisters; they shared a common bone structure and similar facial features, but their hair and eyes let anyone know in an instant that they had different fathers.

"Why would they unlock the door?" Amber pulled a box knife from the tool pouch around her waist and sliced open a cardboard box. "Oh, it's the candles. Find my clipboard and I'll count while I place them in the display." Hefting the box, she carried it to the sturdy oak shelving unit she'd been polishing earlier, which was positioned as far from the windows as possible to protect the candles from the sun.

She'd use the adorable bay windows to display items less susceptible to the sun's rays, like stones, ritual brooms, wind chimes, and statuary. She could picture it already. Tomorrow she'd take down the paper in the windows and hang the new blinds so she could create displays that would be revealed when they opened their doors to the public for the first time.

She sorted the candles by size, color, and scent. Votives, tea lights, and pillars.

"I don't know why you're stocking commercial candles," Laz complained from across the shop. "You make the best candles on the market. You've got a gift for scent and color, and you know it."

"I do." Amber smiled at the compliment. "But mass produced are cheaper and will appeal more to the general public. My specialty candles have their own place for the serious witch or spell crafter. You know that. Besides, the only ritual candles I'm stocking are mine."

The petite half-inch by four-inch tapers were perfect for rituals and burned quickly for fast results. She created them in a rainbow of colors to suit different purposes, including silver and gold to represent the deities.

Deity. What deity did Kodiak Wilkins believe in? Did it even matter? She wasn't interested in him. Was she? She shook her head to clear her thoughts. She'd better get her act together or she'd never be ready for the opening. She pivoted to check on her sisters. They were giggling quietly as they sorted and placed books on one of the bookshelves that Lazuli, the family carpenter, had custom built to fit across the lower half of one wall. Books were displayed, spine out, below, and other items would be on the upper level. Staples like herbs, incense, Himalayan salt lamps, and rocks and crystals would occupy the shelves in the center of the store. None of the inner shelves were high; instead, Amber planned on hanging decorative items from the ceiling, keeping an open, airy feel.

"How's it going?" She wandered over to the bookcase. She'd love to spend a couple hours familiarizing herself with each and every book.

"Great. So many titles I haven't read. I can see my book collection growing. I get a discount, right?" Laz nudged her with one elbow. "How's it going with you? You sure were lost in thought over there. Dreaming about your sexy neighbor?"

"That's *our* sexy neighbor," Amber corrected.

"So, you agree that he is sexy?" Laz pounced on her slip of the tongue.

"I never said he wasn't." Amber's cheek heated. "Just because he's hot doesn't mean he's a nice guy, nor does it mean that I'm attracted to him," she said stiffly. Okay, maybe she was.

One thing was certain about her sisters—if she ever let weakness show, they'd pounce on it and tease her mercilessly. It was all great fun, and they all did it, but sometimes the teasing got old. She'd avoid giving them the satisfaction. But damn, he was sweet to look at.

Chapter Two

"**D**amn punk kids," Kody groused, pulling his dark blue Ford F150 4X4 into his spot behind the building that housed his apartment. He stared at the barn-red wooden walls of the two-story building. Eventually, he'd build a house, but for now, the small apartment above the unnamed store run by those three hellcats would serve him well enough.

Just thinking of his trio of noisy neighbors banging and thumping around made his headache worse than it already was. Today had been a shit ass day. His second tour group was late and quibbled about paying full price for a shortened dive. It wasn't his fault they were an hour late. With their top of the line dive gear, one would think they'd be experienced or at least have tried diving a few times. Nope. Pampered rich kids getting whatever they wanted without any effort at all.

He'd given them the usual safety rundown and accepted their assurances that they were all set and understood the safety rules. That was his first mistake. It was all downhill, straight to hell, after that, and he'd known better than to take them at their word. Stupid move on his part.

He climbed out of the truck and beeped it shut. Even that noise set the jackhammers off in his head again. No way would he survive another night of hammering. The shop's back door was open. Soft strains of country music filtered out, but the early evening was blessedly free of hammering.

He stopped at the base of the outside stairs to his apartment, one foot on the ground, the other on the bottom step. Pain slammed through his head. This would pass, he knew, but for the love of mud, the pain was crippling. He lifted his right foot onto the second stair, and waves of blackness washed over him. His knees buckled. He swallowed hard. He. Would. Not. Go. Down. Only pussies fainted from a headache. His vision cleared, and he moved one step higher.

"Hi, Kodiak." Amber's cheerful voice slammed into his head.

"Kody, please." He grunted. The staircase blurred, and he staggered into the railing.

"Kody, are you alright?" Her voice rose in panic. She was at his side in an instant.

"No." He was going to say something witty but couldn't find the words. Shit. He wasn't alright, not by a long shot. He was shaking like a dog shitting tacks.

A soft, warm arm wrapped around his waist. "Come on, let's go back down," she urged. "You look wobbly. I don't think it's safe to climb the stairs right now. Come inside the shop and sit for a minute."

He didn't want to; he just wanted something to kill the pain and to sleep for a week. Gently, she turned him on the stair and led him down. As they stepped over the threshold into the shop, her arm left his side briefly. The door closed, and the lights dimmed. The reduced brightness after bright afternoon sun was a blessed relief. He sighed.

"Come on, over here to the couch."

The couch? There wasn't a couch here last night. The room had been filled with boxes. He vaguely noticed the boxes had virtually disappeared. Only a few remained. Slight pressure on his back urged him forward.

"Tell me what's wrong," she whispered as they walked across the room. "Maybe I can help."

"Tylenol? Advil? Something?" He clutched his head in his hands.

She eased him onto the couch, and he leaned back, closing his eyes. His body calmed, and he stopped shivering.

"Hang tight, I've got something in the bathroom." She was back in an instant, thrusting a cool glass of water into his hand and holding out two white tablets. "Take these."

Obediently, he swallowed the pills, mumbled a thank you, and passed the glass back. The couch dipped when she settled at the other end. She shuffled a bit. Not wanting to risk bringing on more pain by opening his eyes fully, he peeked at her from the corner of his eye. She was cross legged, facing him, elbows on her knees and chin in her hands. Her long hair, not quite brown, not quite blonde hung over her shoulders, almost to her lap. She looked like she'd wait there all day, her green eyes patient and caring. She looked like a goddess; some kind of tempting siren destined to lure him to his doom.

"Sorry to disrupt your day." His voice was like kettle drums in his ears.

"No worries. We've been disrupting your nights. Call it Karma. What's bugging you?" She brushed her hand across his arm, her touch was light and calming.

Calming? He wasn't upset. He was just exhausted and mildly oxygen deprived. "Headache, exhaustion."

"That's more than a headache. Do you get migraines? I have a great tea for headaches. Can I fix you some? It might help."

Tea? Coffee was more likely to help. "No, thanks."

"It'll help. I promise."

Something about the soft, earnest tone of her voice convinced him. "Okay." He was too beat to fight her. He wanted this headache gone and some food in his stomach so he could sleep. He'd been a fool, failing to recognize the lies the kids were telling him. Someone could have died today.

"Who could have died?"

He opened one eye. She was perched beside him, paused in the act of getting up. "A client." He hadn't meant to speak out loud. He massaged his forehead, hoping to ease the pain, half of which was mental. His stomach growled.

She laughed lightly. "Okay, tea, then food, and then you tell me about it. Sometimes a burden shared is a load lightened. I'll be right back." She patted his knee and stood.

Was she always this physical? Did she touch everyone? Questions bombarded him, exacerbating the pain in his head. He massaged it with both hands. Water ran, the kettle hit the stove with a soft thunk. The fridge opened and whispered closed. A drawer slid open and eased shut. The sounds were infinitesimal, as if she were trying not to disturb him. They sounded like a calypso band. Paper rustled.

"Sugar? Milk? Honey?" she asked from across the storage room. "Honey would give it the best flavour."

"Fine." He groaned, not caring. The drugs better kick in soon; he was dying.

"Kody? Here, take this tea."

He squinted at her. "Already?"

"You drifted off. The tea's cool enough to drink. I've made you a sandwich."

"Bacon?" He smelled bacon and toast.

"Yeah, bacon and tomato. I hope that's okay."

He struggled to sit up and grab the tea. The pounding in his head had lessened but was still excruciating. He took the warm mug; it was soothing in his hand. He was thirsty, he always was after a dive. He sipped it gratefully. Bitterness scarred his tongue. He nearly spat it out. It tasted like dirt and bark, like the crap his grandmother had made him drink as a kid. "What the hell is this?"

"Herbal tea. I took a risk that you aren't allergic to aspirin; salicin is the medicinal ingredient in willow bark, it converts to salicylic acid...aspirin. There are a few herbs, as well as turmeric, ginger, and cinnamon. It'll help with the headache. Drink up."

"No allergies." If he didn't hurt so damned bad, he'd question the beverage, but all he wanted was relief. He winced but chugged the contents of the mug. "That's disgusting."

Her chuckle danced over his skin, somehow relieving some of the pounding in his head. Setting the mug on a box beside him, he reached for the sandwich. "Thanks. I'm starving."

"That might have contributed to the headache." She waved toward the box. "Drink the water, too. You're dehydrated."

"What are you, a nurse?" How in the world did she know he was thirsty? His mouth was as dry as the Sahara. He chugged the water, and it helped alleviate the bitterness left by the tea.

"Not a nurse, but I have a working knowledge of medicinal herbs. I've taken some classes." She shrugged off the value of her knowledge.

The sandwich's toast was crispy and warm. Fresh tomato and the comforting flavor of bacon with a hint of mayo exploded on his tongue. "Wow. This is delicious."

"Thank you."

He gobbled the sandwich in half a dozen bites. "Why do you have a complete kitchen in your store?" Okay, maybe not a siren luring him to his death, maybe a healing angel. Oxygen deprivation must be getting the best of him—he wasn't normally taken to flights of fancy like this.

"Convenience. I'll be working long hours. It'll be nice to eat healthy and not have to rush out and pick up my meals."

"Wouldn't a microwave work?" He nearly groaned at the inanity of his questions. He sounded like a social reject who couldn't even talk to women. To his surprise, she laughed again. A light, trilling sound that made him think of chirping birds and bells.

"I rarely use the microwave, though I do have one. I prefer fresh cooked foods with veggies right off the vine. We grew the tomatoes in the greenhouse. That's why they're so flavorful. The bacon comes from Evinger's Butcher Shop. They raise and process their own meat."

"The sandwich is delicious, even if the tea is..." He floundered, looking for a way to politely say the tea tasted like mud.

"Vile? I know. It's disgusting, but it works. Just be glad I sweetened it. Gramma Pearl would have made you drink it plain. It's much worse that way. Trust me, I drank it plain for years before I realized I could run a go-round and sweeten it myself." She grinned broadly. "How are you feeling?"

His head ached like hell, but the pain had eased off considerably. "I don't know if it's the drugs, the tea, the food or the nap that helped, but I'm feeling much better. Thanks."

"You're welcome. How did you end up with such a headache? You should have treated it long before you arrived here. Surely, you weren't driving like that?"

Guilt slammed him in the guts. He had driven like that, and he probably shouldn't have. He should have eaten and drank something before getting into his truck. Calling a cab would have been the smartest idea. What if the headache had overcome him on the road? His stomach roiled, nearly sending his meal back up.

"I did drive, but the worst of it didn't hit until I got out of the truck." He sighed. "I just wanted to get home. I forgot my sunglasses after a crappy day."

"All's not sunshine and blue water in the diving business?"

Her questions could have been prying, but they seemed to be coming from a place of honest concern. He didn't mind answering. "Today sucked. I disregarded my intuition and it cost me." She didn't say anything, just nodded for him to continue. "The morning was great. An easy group of moderately experienced divers. No problems at all. We explored the outer caves below the falls. They'll be back later this summer for a longer dive."

"That doesn't sound bad."

"It wasn't; they listened, and there were no issues. My assistant and I ate lunch before the afternoon group arrived. That's when things went bad. Real bad." Memories washed over him, and the blood drained from his face, despite his pounding heart. "Someone could have died."

"Oh no," she exclaimed, settling beside him and patting his shoulder comfortingly. Her hand rested there, like a soft hug, more soothing than it should have been.

"Yeah. I was an idiot. A group of four college kids. All in top of the line gear. I judged their skill based on the equipment. No novice owns gear like that. It runs into thousands of dollars. I mistakenly equated gear with experience. I ran the safety orientation. They joked about a bit, but I'd swear they understood the importance of the orientation. Apparently not."

"What happened?"

He flashed her a look; her brow was furrowed, and her fingers knotted.

"Everything was fine at first, but after the first few minutes, when we were well into the caves, they completely abandoned the buddy system." He leaped to his feet and paced the room, fighting the anger and desperation he'd felt. His head pounded with fresh waves of agony.

"After that, one kid disconnected himself from his tank when he accidentally severed his air hose with a knife that he'd snuck down with him. I can't figure out how the hell he managed to bring a knife." Anger tore through him, firing him up and making his heart pound, aggravating his headache. He dropped weakly back onto the couch. Pacing exacerbated the thunder in his head.

"What would he need a knife for?" She sounded as puzzled as he felt.

"Hell if I know. I don't allow knives on my dives. I carry one for emergencies. Nobody but my assistant is permitted to have them. I made that clear up front. Or, I thought I had. He cut himself badly. Seventeen stiches badly. Thank God this was a lake dive rather than an ocean one. Sharks would have made quick work of him. The damn kid had panicked and almost set off a riot between his buddies. If it wasn't for the quick actions of Bryce, my assistant, someone might have drowned."

Frustration and irritation wracked him. He shivered remembering the panic and fright. At the last second, his training and years of diving kicked in and a measure of calm had come back.

"Bryce corralled the rest of the group and led them out while I dealt with the cut and forced the boy to stop hyperventilating. It's not easy to give commands underwater, and the cave we were in had no airspace. There's a reason why we have orientation. When he got his shit together, I shared my regulator with him on the way out. We were in deep, too deep for their level of experience. I should have asked for proof. I will next time."

"Oh, Kody, that must have been awful. Is he okay?"

"He's fine. I took him to the hospital and stayed with him until he was released. He'll have a wicked scar, but no debilitating damage, and his oxygen levels were spot on. Incidentally, his father is head of Opti-Oil International. I hope he doesn't decide to sue me." He didn't even want to think about the damage a lawsuit could do to his fledgling diving business, ending it before Kody even got started.

"That's terrible. A lawsuit would ruin you."

"I'm hoping for the best, but I'm not holding my breath, which is exactly what I did so he could use my air until we were out of the caves and could surface," he joked lamely. "I let him use my tank. We stopped only when I couldn't hold my breath any longer and I had to use the regulator for two breaths. Toward the end, the kid fainted. From the stress or panic. Probably both. And I had to tow him the rest of the way while he used the regulator. Do you have any idea how hard it is to cover a man's mouth and nose, use the regulator, and then put it back on?"

"Gracious, that must have been awful. I can't even imagine. No wonder you've got a headache. Oxygen deprivation, dehydration, and starvation. It's a wonder you could drive at all. You'll need to sleep and should probably take the day off tomorrow."

"Can't. I have a youth class. Training beginners. Luckily, it's orientation and pool work, not a real dive. But, yeah, I need some sleep. I should go."

"Why don't you nap here for a while? I'll keep one eye on you while you rest, just in case something goes wrong. I don't mind. I'm stocking shelves anyway. Lie down."

"I'll just go upstairs. I'd rather not litter up your back room." She was being so nice to him, despite his pissy mood last night. It didn't make sense. She should be giving him the cold shoulder. He'd certainly think twice about helping a virtual stranger who'd been as rude as he had. "I don't want to impose," he said, struggling to his feet.

The world tipped alarmingly, and he dropped back to the couch. "Or maybe I'll just stay here a while longer, if it's not a problem."

"No problem at all." She rummaged in one of the remaining boxes, pulled out a fuzzy blanket, and tore the tag off it. "Lay down for a while. There's no pillow, but here's a blanket." She held it out to him.

"I can't take your new stock," he objected even as he reached for the moon and stars patterned blanket. "I'll pay for it."

"Only if you ruin it. I needed a display model anyway. Get some sleep. I'll be out front; just give me a shout if you need me." She waited for his agreement before flicking off the rest of the lights and leaving him alone in the soft comfort of near darkness.

The only light remaining came through the open doorway between the front of the shop and the back room. It was a blessing for his pounding head. Out front, the radio volume decreased until he could barely hear it. Amber hummed softly while she worked, a catchy tune unrelated to the radio rhythm. She was virtually silent except for the occasional sound of a sliding box or the slicing of a box cutter. Her presence was strangely comforting.

In fact, everything about her was strange. Her generosity, her humming, the incredibly homey set-up of the back room. A mini-kitchen and couch in the back of a store? And four large workbenches, one with an enormous sink. Celestial patterned fabric and multi-colored yarn spilled out of a box on another workbench. Storage shelves and cupboards lined two walls. It reminded him of his grandmother's sewing room, where she worked diligently on quilts for charity when she wasn't mucking around in the garden.

Amber's quiet compassion made him smile. Her soft sounds lulled him to sleep.

Chapter Three

"I see you've been sleeping on the job."

"What? No." Amber whirled round to face her oldest sister, Hyacinth, as she entered the store from the back room.

"You can't fool me. There's a blanket draped over the couch." Her blue eyes sparkled with mirth.

"Yup. How can you look like a million bucks in a men's flannel shirt and blue jeans?"

As a midwife, Hyacinth was always on the go and consequently kept her wardrobe simple and easy to clean. It didn't stop her from looking like a model. At five foot seven, she was the tallest of the sisters. A natural healer, she was a great midwife, but she also had an annoying gift for sensing untruths being told by her sisters.

Hyacinth shrugged. "I can't help how I look. The Goddess just made me tall and fit; and my clothing fits my profession. I just got back from a delivery. Reesha Tallows had twins. Two beautiful babies, one of each. I can't believe how beautiful African-Canadian newborns are. Not nearly so red and angry looking as some." She grinned at the memory. "Now, stop with the evasion. Tell me why you slept on the couch. I can sense your lie."

"I'm not lying. I did not sleep back there." She crossed her heart and popped a girl guide salute. "Do you want me to pinkie swear like we did when we were kids?" Those were the days; everything was so simple. Nothing to do but go to school, play outside, and practise their magic lessons with Gramma Pearl. Yeah, it had been tough sometimes, and birthdays were rough without her mom and stepdad, but their grandmother made up for it in many ways.

"Okay, not a lie, a partial truth. Who was sleeping back there, and why don't you want to talk about it?" She reached into a box and handed Amber a small statuette of Athena.

Amber priced it and set it in a glass display case with several other goddess statues. A gathering of colorful fairies was poised to dance on the shelf above, dragons guarded the shelf below. "Kody was feeling under the weather, and I let him rest there. Okay." She held out her hand for the next statue.

"Ooo." Hyacinth made the single syllable sound like both an accusation and a wickedly delightful secret. "I heard about him from Laz and Hazel last night."

"Come on, Cynth, it's not like that. He had a crappy day at work. I won't give you details. I won't betray his confidence, except to say there was no way he'd make it upstairs. He probably would have broken his fool neck if he tried. He could barely stand." When had he left? She'd checked on him twenty minutes ago, and he was dead to the world. Why hadn't he let her know he was leaving? Men!

"What was he doing here in the first place? You said he acted like a jerk last night. And now he's visiting?" Her words were a blend of accusation and question. Another statue, this one of Zeus, came out of the box.

"He wasn't. Now that we have a screen door, I was opening the inner door for some fresh air and he was hanging off the railing. I decided it was easier to help him into here rather than hauling his ass upstairs. Why am I explaining myself to you? Nothing happened." She never could lie to her sister. Cynth was only four years older, but sometimes it felt like decades.

Hyacinth held up her arms in mock surrender. "Don't blame me. I'm just watching out for your best interest. Your dating history isn't the best."

"Get over yourself. I only seriously dated two guys. One of which turned out to be a total tool. Everyone makes mistakes. I'm so over him, and his lies. Besides, I'm not looking to date, and if I was, I certainly wouldn't be interested in Kody Wilkins."

"Just be careful, okay? We don't know anything about him, and his cousin Jason is a first-class jerk, even if he is your landlord. Promise me you'll take care and watch your back." When Amber nodded, Hyacinth continued, "I'm going to look around and check out what you've done. It's looking great."

"Help yourself. Don't be afraid to soil those midwife hands and put in a little work. This *is* a family venture after all."

Hyacinth laughed at the light-hearted teasing.

A fresh wave of excitement washed over Amber. She'd been working since her sixteenth birthday. She'd been a waitress, a chambermaid, a hostess at a steakhouse, a cashier, and a volunteer at the hospital. She did tarot and tea leaf readings at the farmer's market every summer. She was more than ready to work for herself and to contribute more to the family coffers. Four Seasons Metaphysical was going to be a huge hit, she could feel it. People were already knocking on the front door, wanting to come in and look around.

She was timing the opening with the first rush of summer tourists. There would be enough business from locals to get by, but the summer and Christmas rushes would be enormous. After two years of online business classes, she was more than ready for this.

Her heart pounded with trepidation, but at the same time, she was deadly calm with certainty; this was the right move. She'd had dreams and visions of this for eighteen months. Now was the time. For her and for her family. They'd each contributed cash for start-up capital and supplies, as well as using their innate skills to create stock.

Tomorrow, she'd bring additional stock from home. Her candles and gemstone jewellery. Hazel was contributing potions, spell kits, soaps, and lotions. Lazuli had a stock of carved wooden boxes and wall plaques. Hyacinth was donating herbal teas and medicinal herbal creams. Grams was creating cloth bags to hold spells and other special items as well as dream pillows. They'd all worked on crocheted pouches and gemstones on macramé necklaces. They grew most of the herbs and dried them for sale.

She was limiting stock to handmade and local artisans where she could. She'd ordered some custom Rune Stone kits from a friend in Saskatchewan. Books were a different matter; they weren't easy to source locally, but she was bringing in titles by the biggies in the genre.

"This is pretty cool," Cynth called from the corner Amber had set up for psychic readings.

Amber wandered over to join her and straightened the star patterned table cloth. "I know. I tried to blend what tourists would expect with a more realistic, serious vibe. Did I pull it off?"

"In spades, baby sister, in spades. I love the crystal ball display and the fringy curtains; they're so Gypsy-chic. You've got a great bohemian vibe without hitting stereotypical bo-ho. Well done. Who's going to do the readings?"

"For now, I'll do tea leaves and palm reading, especially with walk-ins. Lazuli will do most of it, at least those we can schedule in advance. Lucky for us, she's got a flexible schedule as a self-employed carpenter. Once we're up and rolling, I'll be offering basic Wicca and magic classes."

"You're going to be busy. What does your new boyfriend think about all this?" Hyacinth met Amber's eyes with a questioning stare.

"Boyfriend? There. Is. No. Boyfriend. What makes you think I have a boyfriend?" She shook her head in reinforcement of her words. Sometimes, her sister's tendency to step in and play mother was annoying. Other times, it was a downright pain in the ass.

"No? What about Mr. Hot Diver upstairs? You're already practically sleeping with him." This time, there was definite teasing in Hyacinth's voice.

"By the Goddess, you're a pain in the ass. I did the guy a favor. End of story. Now, help me set up or go home." Hyacinth didn't even blink at the familiar family nagging. The four of them had been bickering back and forth since they were toddlers; she knew when her siblings were teasing and when they meant business.

"You're not answering the question. Are you interested in Kody Wilkins?" She sat in the corner chair.

"No. Not my type." Cute, yes. Nice backside, yes. Pleasing personality? Nope. Admittedly, he seemed concerned about the injured boy and had put his own life at risk to save him, but he was angry, too. It was difficult to judge his true state of mind when he was exhausted, hungry, and recovering from mild oxygen deprivation. "Not interested in him at all." Amber settled into the chair across from Hyacinth and pulled a deck of Tarot cards from their protective velvet bag. She shuffled them and passed them to her sister.

"You sure you aren't protesting too much?" Hyacinth asked, dealing the cards out into a twelve-card spread. She scooped them up without looking at them and slid them back into the bag. She dropped the deck on the table and stood to fidget with the display of crystal balls beside the table. She shifted them from their straight-line arrangement to something more artistically random.

"That looks good," Amber observed. Perhaps she could change the subject. "You've got a good eye."

"I've done some research. Kody Wilkins has a good reputation as a diving instructor. He's got the highest possible level of lifeguard training. Nobody in town knows him, except his family. He's been engaged twice, but both breakups have been amicable. One was his high school sweetheart, the other a girl he met in dive school. No details on what broke them up."

"Hyacinth. How could you go prying into my neighbor's background like that? What gives you the right?" She closed her eyes and shook her head. Shame for her sister's incredibly rude actions and anger at her interference blinded Amber. She clenched her fists and blinked back sudden tears. "How could you? What if he finds out? I'd be mortified."

"You are interested. I figured you were. Which is why I checked him out. It wasn't difficult. It's easy to track someone on the internet, especially if you know his address, his family, and his profession. Easy peasy, even if he doesn't have any personal social media accounts, just one for his business."

"Totally irrelevant. Don't ever pry into my friends again. Stay out of my life." She shook her finger in Hyacinth's face. "How would you feel if I snooped on your friends?" Heat rose in her face, and the burn scar on her left shin ached. Oh, this was bad. When her emotions ran high enough to make the ancient wound hurt, someone was in trouble.

Her palms started to tingle. She fisted her hands to still the angry spark growing there. She would not zap her sister with a fireball. She wouldn't, no matter how badly she wanted to.

"Whoa, bank in the fiery anger before you torch the place. Your hands are glowing blue-red. Breathe." Hyacinth threw up her hands in surrender. "I promise I won't do any more research on Kody."

"You do and I'll torch your precious '69 Camaro." The car was her sister's pride and joy. Hyacinth had inherited the green sportscar when her birth father passed away. Their relationship had been a strong one after he discovered she existed—when she was fifteen. The car was her last link to him. It was a gas guzzler, but completely reliable.

Amber hadn't been so lucky. Her father was living in another town with a new family and uninterested in the daughter he fathered unintentionally. He considered his ex-girlfriend a liar and a fake and wanted nothing to do with her or Amber. Neither Hazel nor Lazuli knew their fathers. Both were conceived while their mother was travelling in Europe.

Their mother, Lily-Beth, hadn't been promiscuous. Each child was born out of love. Their mother just declined to marry the men who fathered her children. In the end, the men moved on. Eventually, Lily-Beth had reconnected with Trevor Moon, a member of Three Moon Falls' founding family. They'd fallen in love, married, and set off to hunt down a witch assassin when Amber was ten. No witch was safe until they put a stop to the targeted killing, which meant figuring out what he was gaining from the deaths, or what he was searching for.

"You touch my car and... and..."

"And what?" Amber taunted, rubbing her palms together to suppress the fire she'd generated. "You've got nothing. You're a midwife, a healer. It's not in you to hurt people." Hyacinth was the gentlest of them all, and it took a lot to set her off. Her calm, rational sister had never hurt anyone.

Hyacinth's shoulders slumped infinitesimally. "Sometimes I wish I were."

"Meaning?" Amber asked. "Who pissed you off?"

"Earl Cooper," she spat.

"Earl, four-eyes, baggy britches, Cooper? Where did you bump into him?" She put a hand on Cynth's shoulder to comfort her. How had she gone from the victim to the consoler?

Earl was Hyacinth's nemesis. They'd been butting heads since he kissed her in Sunday school. When they were young, their mother sent them to church thinking a sound grounding in Christian beliefs would help them understand their peers. The experiment only lasted two years, but it had helped them realize why so many people feared them. Hyacinth and Earl had almost gotten beyond the kiss when he discovered she believed in magic. To a good Christian boy, her beliefs were the death knell to his feelings.

"I stopped into the bookstore and bumped into him, not literally. He gave me the cold shoulder. I don't know if it's because I rebuffed him two decades ago, and he never got over it, or because ..." she waved vaguely around the shop, "because we're ... not Christian. I was trying to be civil, and he was dismissive. I think he wanted to throw me out of the shop."

The floor shivered. Anyone else would have attributed it to a passing truck. Amber knew better. "Bank it, earth girl. You're letting your anger out."

Unchecked emotions could be devastating. Amber had fire, and Hyacinth had the power to move the earth. Things could get dangerous if they weren't in control of their stronger emotions.

Hyacinth pressed her palms together and put the tips of her index fingers to her nose. She drew in a deep breath, closed her eyes, and relaxed. "Sorry. I don't know why it bothers me so badly. I knew how he felt. I shouldn't have expected him to change."

Amber hugged Hyacinth tight. "Relax, girl. He's not worth it. No man is worth changing our beliefs. We are who we are. Accept us or leave us. We're strong together, and I've got your back. I suppose your 'research'" she sketched air quotes, "is just you protecting me. But I don't need it. Thanks, though." They touched foreheads together and relaxed.

"Thanks, Amber. I do have one question. Is Kody as hot as Hazel and Lazuli say he is? Laz couldn't stop going on about him."

"Unfortunately, he is. Tall, probably six feet. Green eyes, brown hair. Clean shaven. Nicest butt I've seen in I don't know how long. Yeah, he's hot. But he was so rude. I mean, how were we supposed to know he'd rented the place upstairs? He stormed down here like a tornado, snapped off the music, and started giving us shit." Remembered anger resurfaced. The least he could have done was be polite.

"And yet, you took him in when he needed help. Why did you let him sleep here?" Cynth asked.

"I could hardly let him fall down the stairs. Karma's a bitch, and I'd never ignore someone in need. I let him rest and now, poof, he's gone without even a word of thanks. I knew he was a turd."

"A turd. Wow, such harsh language. You're out of control. You must be really attracted to him," Hyacinth teased.

"Physical attraction is ignorable. Besides, he's probably a witcha-phobe like half this town. Nope, I'll just stay single, thanks." Amber straightened some books that were already perfectly aligned rather than face her sister.

"You know you don't get a choice, right? The heart wants what the heart wants."

"Is that why you're so upset at Earl Cooper? Maybe, even after all these years, your heart longs for your first love. Maybe one sweet kiss stole your heart. Witches only love once, you know."

"Oh, BS. Mom had many loves. At least five, one for each of us, plus Dad." They all referred to their stepfather as Dad.

"She had four long-term relationships, but she only married once, and she'd known him from kindergarten and reconnected later in life,"

Amber corrected, stifling a laugh. Sometimes, it was entirely too easy to get under Hyacinth's skin. "Come on, Cynth. Chill. You know as well as I do that the universe has a way of making things work out. Eventually, you'll find out what's up with Earl; maybe it's fixable." She wandered toward the back room and Cynth followed.

"And maybe Kody is your dream date."

Amber rolled her eyes and laughed. "Not in this lifetime, sis. Not in this lifetime. Who wants to date a guy who can't be bothered to say thanks?"

"You said it yourself; he was exhausted. Maybe he chose to go home to bed rather than disturb you. You won't know until you ask."

"First, you're warning me away, and now you're encouraging me to seek him out? Pick a direction. These rapid switches are giving me whiplash."

Hyacinth laughed. "Never mind. Let's get some work done and go out. I'm dying for pizza. It's been a long day and a difficult delivery, even if the babies were adorable. I need to fuel up and rest before I go check on them tomorrow morning."

"I can get behind food. I fed Kody my supper."

"It must be love!"

Ignoring her sister, Amber returned to shelving statues. "Want to start hanging those bags of herbs? They're already priced."

An hour later, both jobs finished, they headed out for dinner, but not before locking the doors—all three of them: front, back and the stairwell to Kody's apartment—before they left.

Chapter Four

Kody burrowed deeper into his covers. His nose was icy. His apartment was freezing. The temperature in the suite fluctuated wildly. It was as if the thermostat had a mind of its own. He'd checked the setting before he laid down. Maybe the furnace was broken. Something was digging into his abdomen as well. Wasn't he supposed to walk up rested, not frozen and in pain?

He rolled over onto his back and massaged his stomach. He had his jeans and belt on; he was fully clothed. Weird. Memory flooded back to him. Waking up on Amber's strange backroom couch and stumbling upstairs, taking more pain meds, and falling onto his bed. Judging by the dim light filtering through the blinds, he'd slept the night away. Guilt over not thanking Amber tickled his conscience. He'd have to thank her when he got home tonight, if she was in the shop. First, a quick shower and a bite to eat before heading out for this morning's dive. He had just enough time to hit the office and prepare for the day.

He ambled into the living room and checked the thermostat. It was turned down as low as it could go. What the hell? He didn't change the setting. Had someone been in here? He searched for signs of disturbance. Nothing.

No. Wait. The door between his apartment and the shop stairwell was slightly ajar. Anger surged through him, and his pulse pounded, intensifying the tiny remains of yesterday's headache, turning it into a full-blown annoyance. How dare she enter his apartment uninvited! And how the hell did she get in? The door was locked. He checked it every day. First, the damned infernal racket day and night, and now she comes into his suite?

He couldn't wait for this day to be over so he could give her hell. He turned up the heat, locked the door, and pushed a chair in front of it before showering for work.

He fumed all day. He could barely keep his mind focused on work. Amber Hawk was destroying his equilibrium. His job was dangerous enough—he didn't need some sparkly green-eyed, brown-haired woman with a body that didn't quit making it worse.

The shop was closed and dark when he got home. Exhausted, he went straight to bed and returned in the morning. He pounded on the closed front door. The blinds were down. He could see light and motion behind them but couldn't make out anything clearly. Someone was in there, and he wasn't going away until he said his piece. He banged his palm into the old wooden screen, making it bounce in place and thump against the frame.

The blind slats parted, and a single, long-lashed, green eye peeked out at him. It squinted, the blind flopped back into place, and the deadbolt snapped open. The door flung back, and he stared down into wary green eyes beneath Amber's furrowed brow.

"Yes?" she answered mildly, not quite concealing her irritation. "What can I do for you, Mr. Wilkins?"

He opened the screen door and stepped forward. She backed up.

"By all means come on in." Sarcasm dripped from her words.

"I will, thank you. At least I wait for an invitation before entering someone else's space." He spat the words at her. "It's only the right thing to do." He strode past and pivoted to glare at her.

"I'm sorry? Is there something you wanted to say? You seem to be driving at a point, but I'm unclear what it is." She closed the door behind him.

"Nice innocent act. You know what you did, and I want to know why." He was acting like an ass but couldn't seem to help himself. But something about her made him twitchy and out of sorts. It wasn't like him to go off the rails like this; he was losing his mind.

"Pretend for a moment I have no idea what you're talking about and fill me in. You seem upset over something. Did you get sick from the sandwich I made you? Did the tea upset your stomach? Maybe my couch was too lumpy?"

He gaped at her as she listed off the possibilities. She was good—no great—at pretending innocence, as if she had no idea what he was talking about. "Why were you in my apartment?"

"I beg your pardon?" She blinked twice, and the furrows between her brow deepened.

"Why were you in my apartment the night before last? After I slept here? And why did you mess with my heat?" He enunciated each word separately and clearly. How could she misunderstand the question? "My door was ajar, and my thermostat turned down. I damn near froze to death."

"It wasn't me, or any of my sisters. You disappeared; my sister, Hyacinth, and I worked for an hour and took off. We weren't even around. Don't you lock your doors?" She crossed her arms over her chest, and she glared at him.

"I do lock my doors, that's precisely the point. Are you dense?"

"Okay, enough of this crap. What right do you have to come storm-ing into my store and make false accusations against me? If you have an issue with me, take it to the police. I was not in your apartment. Ever. I didn't even look at it when I rented this space. Now, if you please, get out of my store and don't come back." She gestured toward the door. "Oh, and by the way, you're welcome for everything I did for you the other day, although you weren't human enough to bother to thank me." She yanked the door open, grabbed his arm, and propelled him toward it. "Don't let the screen door hit you in the ass on the way out."

Suddenly, he was outside. He swore he hadn't moved. It felt like something hot slammed into his back, and the next thing he knew, he was standing outside the closed door. His back felt warm. He turned and glared at the door.

That hadn't gone as expected. If he didn't know better, he'd almost think she was telling the truth; but if she hadn't been in his apartment, it must have been one of her sisters. He knew the door hadn't opened itself.

"Hey, Boss," his assistant, Bryce, called out as he walked toward Kody. "No sense trying to get in there. They don't open until Monday. I didn't know you were into all that mystical bullshit." There was a question hanging in his words.

"Mystical stuff?" Kody repeated and stared blankly at the lanky blonde twenty-two-year-old.

"Yeah, magic, witches, spells, crystal balls and all the mumbo-jum-bo. Magic... what the Hawks are into. I figured if you were trying to get into the shop you must be into it to."

"What? I mean, I'm not. I don't believe in all that crap. I live up-stairs. I wanted to talk to Amber about something." He didn't need to justify himself to his employee, but he offered the explanation anyway.

"You've met her, then? Hot, isn't she? She was three years ahead of me in high school. All those Hawk witches are hot. They just seem to glow." He laughed. "There's something magical about them." He sobered. "Seriously, though, everyone thinks they are witches and worship the devil. Don't be pissing them off. Weird things happen to anyone who does."

"Amber hardly seems the type to worship the devil," Kody declared. Bryce's ludicrous words took the edge off his anger. Could anyone even tell a devil worshipper just by looking at them?

"Yeah? Ever been inside?"

Kody thought for a moment. "Twice. Why?"

"What did you see?"

The kid seemed to be trying to make a point. "Books, rocks, windchimes. I didn't look around much. Amber was kind to me. I could barely stand when I got home. She took me in, fed me, and gave me tea. I slept on her couch for a while. She seems nice enough." Which didn't align with her sneaking around his apartment. Whatever was in the vile brew of hers sure helped his headache.

Brew? Great. Now Bryce's accusations had him thinking she was a witch. Fat chance. At best she might think she had some kind of magical power. "Come on, kid. Forget all their nonsense. I'll give you a ride to work. My truck's around back."

"Don't discount it. It's real. Weird things happen around the Hawks. Crazy weird shit. Like, weird weather and bizarre winds. The oldest one, Hyacinth, sells herbal medicine and potions. She's a midwife, too."

Kody laughed. "There's nothing strange about herbal medicine or being a midwife. You've got an overactive imagination." His grandmother made her own herbal teas, claiming they'd cure what ailed you.

"Seriously, man. Something's off about them. They're witches. They'll zap your ass."

"Which is it? Is it real? Are they witches, or is it bullshit? You can't have it both ways."

He never would have guessed Bryce had such an active imagination. The kid was taking chemical engineering and didn't seem to be the least bit fanciful. It didn't matter so long as he did his job for the summer. He was an excellent diver with top certification, and he'd worked a miracle when that kid managed to sever his air hose.

"I don't know. Just be careful, okay? They're hot as hell, but they creep me out."

"Thanks for the advice. I'll keep it in mind. If you're walking to work, I might as well drive you. My truck's this way." He waved toward the end of the building. "And thanks for keeping your cool yesterday and leading the rest of the kids out. You saved my bacon. If I don't get my ass sued off, you'll get a bonus at the end of the summer."

Chapter Five

"Hey," Hazel called from the back room. "Why's the door to upstairs open? Were you having a *breakfast meeting* with our sexy neighbor?" The words dripped with innuendo.

"What?" Amber hurried into the back. "The door was closed and locked when I got here. I checked, and I double-checked after he came in accusing me of being in his suite the other night."

"He did what?" Hazel's voice rose in anger.

"I know. It's insane. He said I was upstairs and changed his heat or something. He was pissed off. I don't get it. I never went up there, and the only other person here was Cynth, and we were together the entire night."

A funny looked passed over Hazel's face.

"What? I know that look. You're up to something." Amber groaned. "Oh no, tell me you didn't sneak up there, please."

Hazel laughed. "Not me, but maybe your resident ghosts are up to some tricks. After all, his door was open, our back door was open. It would be just like a ghost to mess things up. I've been checking out their stories. The owner of the drugstore was quite a joker in her time. She might be playing around."

"Great, just what I need, a mischievous ghost. How do I convince Kody it wasn't us? I can't just tell him it was a ghost. Even people who tour haunted places don't actually believe. This is a mess." She closed and locked the door. "I suppose she opened this, too, trying to stir things up." Amber pivoted around; arms outstretched. "Hey, you, ghosts. Wanna lay off the tricks and stop getting me in trouble with my neighbor?"

"You know that's not going to work, right?" Hazel chuckled and flopped down onto the couch. "Put the kettle on, will ya, sis?"

"If you ask nicely," Amber replied, already walking toward the stove. "Hey, it doesn't hurt to suggest it. Although, I'm not entirely sure it wasn't Kody trying to make a point, or something." The tension between the two of them didn't make sense. They'd been at loggerheads since the first time he exploded into the shop, burning any friendship bridges behind him. What would he gain by kicking up trouble with his neighbor?

"Pretty please with sugar on top? You'll be my favorite sister."

"I'm already your favorite sister. Try something with some impact."

"No need, you already turned it on. Do we have any mango-mint tea here? I haven't had any in ages, and I've got a craving."

"I'll check." Amber wandered into the front of the store. She paused a moment to admire the displays. On the south side of the store, to the left of the door near the cash register, was a glass display case filled with bulk tins of tea. There were samples for clients, and they'd put purchases into custom, fold-top paper bags to take home. The tea selections were created in the industrial kitchen, which had been added to the family home to meet the legal requirements for selling food.

She located the flavorful tea and filled the mesh cup designed to fit inside the teapot. Something brushed against her leg. She jerked forward, nearly dropping the tea. "What the?"

"Meow." A filthy black and white cat rubbed against her ankles, weaving back and forth between Amber's legs. The feline was scrawny, but her belly bulged with pregnancy. She had a dark grey stripe running diagonally across her chest.

"Well there, who are you, and how did you get in here?"

"Merwow."

"That's the way it is, is it?" She laughed when the cat chirped in response. "Well then, come on back, and we'll find you something to eat before we decide what to do with you."

"Who are you chattering to?" Hazel asked when Amber re-entered the back room.

"I seem to have acquired a guest." She looked down at the cat trotting at her heels. "How do you suppose she got in? Did you bring her?"

"Nope, not me. How do you know it's a her?"

"Look at her. Half starved and very pregnant. Poor thing. I'm going to find her something to eat. Milk for sure." She poured a few ounces of milk into the bowl and set it in front of the counter. The cat wandered over, sniffed it, and gave a delicate chirp before tasting. Another chirp and she licked the bowl clean.

"Listen to her," Hazel said with a grin. "She's talking to you. Too bad Hyacinth wasn't here to talk back."

Amber laughed. "She does seem to know what animals are saying. Sometimes, I think she should have been a vet instead of a midwife. Which brings us around to you. You've got your bookkeeping certification. When do you get a job?"

"I've applied at like, a thousand places. Zero phone calls. None. Zip. Nada. All I got was one cryptic email to come to the garden center. I did apply there, but I'm not optimistic. They couldn't even call? I don't want to leave town, but I might have to if I don't get this job at the garden center. I'm going to apply at the bar for a waitress job. They'll hire me. They always need help."

"Oh, honey. That's terrible. Someone will call. I know it. I can feel it." Amber poured steaming water over the tea leaves. Hazel wasn't as empathetic as Lazuli, but a bar full of people relaxed by alcohol would give off too many emotions to be comfortable for more than a couple hours. A daily diet of unchecked emotion would be crazy stressful.

"Laz thinks so."

"Then believe her. If Laz has predicted something, you know she's right. She never misses the mark. Nobody does divination like Laz. Cheer up. It'll come."

"I'm glad you agree. It cheers me up. Sometimes, I need reinforcement from someone who won't lie to me. How's the tea coming, and what are you going to do with the cat?"

"Patience. Gramma Pearl says you can't rush a good pot of tea. As for the cat, she needs a bath, and I'll make some posters to hang around town. I'll probably have the vet check her over and see if she's chipped. She must have belonged to someone before she wandered away. What I don't understand is how she got in here."

The store was closed up tight. There was no basement for the cat to hide in. They were careful when they went in and out. Both doors had screen doors; there was no easy way in unless someone let her in. Unless she'd somehow come in from upstairs, there was no logical reason for her to be there.

"Maybe she's Kody's cat. The door was open. She could have wandered down." Amber grabbed two cups and saucers from the cupboard. Gramma Pearl had taught them the only acceptable vessel for tea was a pretty cup and saucer. Their stepfather hadn't been thrilled, he'd preferred a double sized mug, but he'd acquiesced. "Did you check if his door is closed?"

"Nope. The stairwell is all dust and spiderwebs." Hazel shuddered. "No way on earth am I going in there. The only tracks are from where he came and went the night we met him. I figured if there are no new tracks, he can't accuse you of going upstairs again."

"Good point, but it leaves me without an explanation of how she arrived."

"Magic?" Hazel offered seriously. "Stranger things have happened."

Amber wrinkled her nose. "Doesn't seem likely. I'll check with Kody just in case she slipped out on him." She tamped down the perky little thrill jingling through her. She would not let herself be attracted to him. He wasn't her type, and he was a jerk.

What if he was her destiny, though? The thought popped up unbidden. Dang, Hyacinth had planted that insidious idea in her head. She refused to give it any consideration. The Fates wouldn't be cruel enough to inflict him on her. But hot damn, he was sexy.

"Knock, knock," an all too familiar voice came through the screen door. "Can I come in?"

Amber rose her eyes to the sky. Clearly, the universe was against her today. "What can I do for you, Kody?" Amber asked through the screen. Dang, he looked good in his tight T-shirt and snug jeans. Strong and sexy.

"Can I come in?" He tugged experimentally on the handle.

"Fine." She filled the single syllable with as much reluctance as she could muster and flipped the hook and eye at the top of the door. It wasn't much for protection, but combined with the bell she'd put up, she'd know someone was trying to get in. Magical wards and protective bouquets would go up the first chance she got.

The bell jingled merrily when he opened the door and closed it gently behind him. "Has anything weird been happening in here lately?" His voice was gruff, almost accusatory.

Amber and Hazel shared a quick glance and tried to act casual. "No, why do you ask?" Amber sat and sipped her tea.

"My heat won't stay set. It's digital, and it keeps resetting itself. Sometimes up, sometimes down. It's completely random. I swear someone is messing with it." He raised a brow as if accusing them of being in his suite.

That song was getting old, but Amber bit back a sharp retort.

"If it doesn't stop, I'm going to have to find a new place to rent."

"Weird," Amber replied, managing to keep a straight face. There wasn't a chance he'd believe it was ghosts. "Is that what you were rattling on about this morning?"

"Yeah. It's so cold up there right now I can see my breath."

"Is the air conditioning on?" Hazel choked out the question.

"I don't have air conditioning. I'm sure I'll wish I did come August."

Oh boy, the ghost was really going after him. Had he inadvertently annoyed it, or was it up to something? Ghosts were tricky when they wanted to be. "We have air. It's weird that you don't. The landlord added it just before we started moving in."

"Blame my cousin. He's the cheapest man on the planet. It probably would have cost more to separate the two spaces from each other, so he'd skip putting it in for the apartment."

Jason had a reputation for doing the minimum to his properties. He managed the upkeep but never added anything extra. Failing to put air conditioning upstairs would be typical for him. Unfortunately, he was one of the wealthiest men in town and owned the majority of commercial rental space. She'd have preferred to rent elsewhere, but this shop, in the center of the tourist strip, was perfect for her needs. Aside from the ghosts.

"I don't know what to say. Have you gotten an electrician in to check it? Bad wiring? Could it have been bumped? I'm sure there's an explanation. There isn't anything strange going on here. Our heat is fine." It was all fine, except the door opened itself and a random stray cat letting herself in. "Are you missing a cat?"

The cat chose that moment to growl and hiss at Kody's running shoes. He stepped back, his gaze never straying from the cat.

"Nope, it's not mine. I don't have a pet."

He was so vehement, and the sisters laughed. "Don't you like pets?"

"Cats kind of freak me out," he confessed. "They're all sharp claws and teeth. Give me a wiggly puppy any day."

"That's hilarious. You're what? Six feet tall? And you're afraid of a tiny, underweight kitty." A grown man afraid of an eight-pound cat seemed ridiculous. There was no explaining phobias.

"If that thing weighed fifty pounds like a cougar, you'd never let it inside. You'd be calling animal control and running for your life. When I look at cats, all I can think of is being eaten in my sleep." He squinted at the cat. "It's not yours? It's a skinny little thing, isn't it?"

"She's not ours. She just wandered in. She's underfed and very pregnant. The stairwell door was open, so I assumed she wandered down from upstairs." She raised her voice in inquiry but kept her tone carefully blameless.

"I didn't open it. I've added a deadbolt to the upper one. I swear, on my honor, I didn't open it. I haven't set foot in the stairwell since the first time I came downstairs."

"Neither have we." Amber shrugged. "If she's not yours, I wonder how she got in. I suppose it doesn't matter. She's here now. I'll try and find her owners. Though I suspect she's a stray."

"You're not keeping her?" he asked. "Is that a good plan? I mean—"

"I'll try to find her family. If I can't, I guess I've acquired a shop cat." She scooped up the cat and stroked its back.

"Is having an animal in a store even legal?"

Amber and Hazel laughed outright. "It sure is," Hazel piped up. "We don't prepare food here, and our tea service is optional, no charge. Besides, everyone except you loves cats."

His gaze searched the backroom. After a moment, he asked, "What type of shop is this, exactly? I've barely been up front since you woke me from a dead sleep with brutal country screeching."

"Come on." Amber gestured to the front. "I'll show you around."

"I'm out," Hazel declared. "I've got a job interview with a construction company to get to. Later, sis."

"Good luck!" Amber cheered her sister on. "Maybe this is the opportunity Laz was talking about. You've got this. Go knock 'em dead." Hazel left, and Amber walked over to flip the latch on the screen door. "Anyway, come out front."

"So, Bryce, my assistant, tells me this is a witch shop?" Disbelief filled his voice.

Great, another non-believer. Was there no end to them? "It is a metaphysical shop, yes. The sign goes up this afternoon. We've got books, herbs, candles, gemstones, and all the basics for your magical spell work."

"And you believe all that," he waved his arms to encompass the entire store, "mumbo-jumbo? Are you a Satan worshipper?" He took a half step backward.

She chuckled, not at all offended by the familiar question. "Nope. Truth is, most witches don't believe in the devil. We believe good and bad exist within all of us. It's up to us to determine our actions. What I believe in is a power greater than me, the interconnectedness of all living things, the power of nature. I have a built-in moral compass which reminds me I shall harm nobody. My version of a higher power is not masculine, it is a belief in Mother Earth, the Goddess and her consort, the God of Nature and the sky."

He was silent for several long moments. His serious consideration of her explanation impressed her. He wasn't cowering in fear or dismissing her view out of hand. There might be hope for him after all.

"That isn't the picture Hollywood presents," he said at last, glancing around.

"Well, benign, nature-loving witches wouldn't sell many movies, would they?" She laughed outright. "I won't lecture you anymore, except to ask you to keep an open mind. Witch spells are rather like Christian prayers, except with props. We visualize our intent, cast a spell to the universe, then sit back and let it happen."

"Was that a lecture?" he asked, one eyebrow quirked upward and a grin on his face.

"I suppose it was. I'll shut up now." She mimed zipping her lips. "Over here is where we do tea leaf, Tarot, and crystal ball readings," she mumbled through closed lips, and then led him to the divination corner.

"And people believe you?" He sounded less judgemental than when he'd started the tour. "And they pay for it?"

"Some believe, some don't. For non-believers, it's all fun and entertainment. For others, it's a fresh way to look at their lives and problems. They can gain insight into where they want to go, or what caused them trouble in the past."

"Merp?" The cat jumped up onto the small circular table, nearly skidding over the other side, messing up the tablecloth.

Kody jumped and frowned. "The cat is stalking me."

"Don't be such a coward. Maybe she likes you. Let her smell your hand, it's an introduction of sorts, like dogs sniffing each other's butts. Like this." She held out a lightly fisted hand, knuckles up, and let the cat sniff her. The cat obliged and immediately gave her a head butt.

His expression wary, Kody copied Amber, and the cat sniffed his hand. She chirruped, looked up at him, and then rubbed her face against his knuckles. His hand twitched but he didn't move. Amber could tell he was wary, and on the verge of backing away. The cat looked up at him, and Kody lowered his hand. The cat immediately hopped to the floor and wrapped herself around his ankles. To his credit, he didn't flinch or move.

"She likes you. How about that?"

A small smile stole across his face. "I guess she's not all bad."

"I guess not," Amber concurred. "Sorry about your heat issues. Maybe they'll fix themselves." Not likely, but he wouldn't like the truth.

He gave her a quizzical look. "Somehow, that doesn't make me feel better. Are you sure you haven't cast a spell on my apartment?" He sounded dubious.

"Which is it going to be?" she asked. "Either you don't believe it all, or you do? If you don't, how could I have cast a spell?"

"Did you?"

The worry in his voice brought a smile to her face. He was a believer; he just didn't know it yet. "No, I did not, and neither did any of my sisters. I promise you. Why don't you get someone in to check it out, just to be safe?"

"I'm planning to. Thanks for the tour. You have a nice shop; it isn't creepy at all. Bryce said it was going to be strange or worse, but it isn't. It has a nice homey feel and it smells nice. Like vanilla and spice. I hope you do well."

"Thank you. I'm glad you're not freaked out. We officially open at nine tomorrow. Our grand opening is on Saturday. We wanted a couple days to work any bugs out of the system before the official launch. You should come by."

"Which day?"

"Either, both. We'd love to have you. You can sample some of our teas," she offered.

"Are they as vile as the one you gave me the other day?" His nose wrinkled in disgust.

Laughter bubbled out of her. "Of course not. That tea was medicinal. My sister, Hyacinth, is a midwife and herbalist; it's her special blend. We have fruit teas, veggie teas, teas from tea plants we grow in our greenhouse. We've got it all. Every leaf and flower is from our garden or greenhouse. Fruits we source locally where we can." She paused. "I'm lecturing again, aren't I?"

He chuckled. "You are, but I admire your passion. I get that way about my diving sometimes. There's nothing more attractive than someone passionate about their life and hobby." He held up one hand. "I'm not saying this is a hobby...you know what I mean?"

"I do know. So, how about a cup of tea? I started a pot just before you arrived. I thought Hazel was going to stick around, but I guess she forgot about her appointment." More likely, she'd split to leave Amber and Kody alone. There was no way Amber was going to put the idea out in the open. Nope. No way.

He glanced at his watch. "I suppose so."

"Don't sound so eager. It's mango-mint. You might enjoy it. It's great hot, but even better over ice. Come on, I'll pour you a cup."

They settled on the couch. Amber was comfortable with the ensuing silence; she could tell Kody wasn't. He shifted back and forth, his gaze roamed the room, lingering here and there, questions in his eyes.

"What are all the workbenches for?" he blurted.

"Work?" she teased. "We create a lot of our own stock. We'll start doing it here, instead of at home. It's one of the reasons we chose this spot. A big retail area and a nice workspace and the ideal location," she added. "Being close to tourist central is important, too."

"That I understand. I'm looking for the perfect spot for my dive shop. Right on the waterfront would be ideal, but there's nothing available right now. I might end up building in the off season, if I can find a reasonably priced lot. I'm subletting a room above Peterson's Garage."

They fell into a companionable discussion of location and other business needs. Before she knew it, the tea was gone, and he was standing to leave.

"Thanks for the tea, and the conversation. It's nice to talk to a real person rather than a client." He glanced at her for a moment before his gaze danced away.

"It was nice chatting," she agreed. "I suppose I should get back to work. I've got a lot to finish up before tomorrow. My sisters and I are having a work-bee tonight that I have to prep for. We'll keep the noise down."

"I appreciate it, thanks."

She closed the screen behind him and watched him walk away. He sure had a great back view. "Maybe he isn't so bad," she said to the cat sitting at her feet. The cat meowed her agreement and lifted one paw for grooming.

Chapter Six

Amber, her three sisters, and their grandmother stood in a circle in the shop's back room, holding hands. The morning air was still and hot, on the verge of stifling. They had one last chore before the store opened in ten minutes. A simple spell designed to protect them, their merchandise, and their customers.

The scent of melted wax and fresh cut sage surrounded them. Five candles burned merrily; their flames unwavering in the motionless air. A white candle glowed in the north to represent the element of air and winter. Yellow in the east represented fire and spring. South was blue for water and summer. Finally, a red candle burned in the west to represent earth and autumn. A green sage-scented candle burned on a workbench. Known for its cleansing and protective qualities, sage was a part of many of their rituals. At home, they smudged by burning small bundles of dried sage. At the store, they burned a sage candle rather than risk making the store too smoky for customers with allergies.

Gramma Pearl looked at each of the girls. "I'm sorry your parents couldn't be here for this. They'd be so proud of you girls. Especially you, Amber. You've worked hard to make this dream a reality and in just minutes, it will be." A broad smile lit her face. Though salt and pepper hair brushed her shoulders, her face was virtually unlined. She looked closer to forty than her actual sixty. All the Hawk women aged gracefully, a fact Pearl attributed to their magical skills, herbal lotions, and their lifestyle of eating pesticide and herbicide free foods.

"Let's begin." Pearl drew the rune Algiz in the air with her right index finger, a Y with three fork's tines. The Norse rune represented both protection and Heimdal, son of Odin, protector of the gods. Using the rune, they asked for protection for their venture.

The sisters copied the protective motion, nodded, and spoke in unison.

"Mother Earth, Father Sky,
Powers strong we cannot deny.
Protect this space and all inside.
We welcome all, our doors open wide.
Send prosperity, love and cheer,
Deter evil from entering here.
All our powers, all your charm.
Keep us safe from danger and harm."

They repeated the chant three times.

"As we will it, so mote it be."

The cat meowed in agreement and circled them, brushing each woman as she passed. Amber thanked the Goddess and God, and they broke the circle. A soft breeze drifted through the screen, ruffling their hair. The room felt lighter and more carefree.

"That feels better," Hazel declared.

Amber looked at her sisters. They glowed with the power they'd
cast. Many wouldn't see it, even fewer would believe it, but she saw
it. Hyacinth's blue eyes sparkled as her blonde hair lifted in the breeze.
Lazuli's eyes glowed, and Hazel's lit with laughter. Yes, they'd done a
good thing, calling the universe and asking for protection.

A thought hit her out of the blue. "Dang, I forgot the protective
wards, and I didn't get the protective swags up. It totally slipped my
mind."

"Relax," Pearl advised. "We can do it tonight. One day won't matter."

Lazuli shivered. "I hope you're right."

"What does that mean?" Amber asked.

"Nothing. I've been having these weird flashes. Nothing I can put
my finger on. I've tried scrying in water, and used the crystal ball, but
I can't get anything. It's as if I'm being blocked somehow. Except just
now. I saw a man." She paused to think. "Here in the shop. His image
is fuzzy. I can't get anything concrete, but he feels—off, somehow. I
can't explain it. I hope it's nothing, but I sure wish those wards were
up."

Uncertain visions were nothing to sneeze at. They usually foretold
something negative. Perhaps dangerous. Premonition ants marched
down Amber's spine, touring wildly but not giving her a solid message.
Damn.

"Well, we don't have time for wards now. We've got to open. There
are people out front, waiting." Amber tamped down the unease shifting over her. Laz wasn't always right; sometimes, she misinterpreted
things.

In unison, Pearl and Hazel pulled up the front blinds, letting the
sunshine in and giving the waiting customers their first peek. "There
has to be a dozen people out there," Hazel squealed. "I can't believe it.

This isn't even the real opening." She paused. "Oh, would you look at that!" She giggled.

Amber ignored her and flung the inside door open and gasped. The first person in line, holding an enormous bundle wrapped in floral paper, was Kody Wilkins. *What on earth?* "Kody, hi. Come in. Everyone, come in." She pushed the screen door open. Kody stepped inside and allowed the stream of customers to move past him. Amber kept a mental tally as she greeted them. Thirteen! Perfect. Thirteen was her lucky number.

Once everyone was inside, looking around, she turned her attention back to Kody. "Kody, welcome to Four Seasons Metaphysical. I'm glad you came."

"I brought you this." He thrust the package at her. "I was going to bring flowers, but I thought maybe, with your background, you might prefer a plant."

She opened the paper, careful not to damage the contents, and folded it down around a slender trunked, ball shaped lemon tree in a white wicker basket. Pristine green leaves, three tiny lemons, and a dozen flowers adorned the miniature tree.

"It's beautiful, and perfect. I've never had a lemon tree before. Thank you so much."

"The guy at the garden center told me it would grow indoors, or in a greenhouse, but it wasn't zero hardy for this region, whatever that means. But you mentioned having a greenhouse, and the store's got good windows..." he trailed off.

She slipped the tree into the crook of her elbow and placed on hand on his arm. "Kody, relax. It's beautiful and perfect. Thank you so much." She gave him a one-armed hug. Dang, he felt nice against her side, and she fit under his arm perfectly.

A hint of color touched his cheeks. "You're welcome. I can't stay; I have to get to work. I just wanted to stop by and say happy opening.

I hope it all goes well for you. Plus, it's kind of a peace offering for going off half-cocked the other night. It wasn't your fault my cousin didn't tell you I moved in, and I shouldn't have come unglued about the door." He smiled apologetically.

"Consider it forgotten. I'm glad you came. It's nice to have neighbors who care. Thank you for coming and for this beauty." She shifted the heavy plant.

"You're welcome. Bye now."

"Bye." She waggled her fingers in a wave as he turned to go. She stared at the door long after it closed. How sweet—he'd brought a store opening gift. If he didn't watch himself, he'd ruin his grumpy neighbor reputation. She smiled at the plant.

"Who's the major hunk? And why did he bring you a tree?"

Amber looked up into the laughing blue eyes of Mayor Quinton, who was dressed with her usual flair. A bright fuchsia and purple floral blouse topped a purple striped skirt. Hipster sandals covered her feet but exposed her sparkly burgundy toenails. Her grey hair was braided and fell forward over her left shoulder, hanging to her waist. She was always something to look at and strangely eccentric, but she was a darned good mayor, and the townspeople respected her.

"Oh, him? He's Kody Wilkins, Jason's cousin. He's the new diving instructor. He offers supervised dives of the lake and the caves under the falls. How did he slip under your radar?" The mayor was known for being aware of everything going on in her town. She had more than one pair of ears on the gossip grapevine.

"Vacation. I just got home last night. I went to Salem."

"Fabulous, I've always wanted to go there." Amber was a direct descendent of Margaret Hawkes, one of the original accused witches. Somewhere along the line, they'd dropped the 'es' from the end of the name; perhaps to hide their ancestry.

"I can imagine." The mayor grinned and gave her a nudge. Like the Hawk's, the mayor was a witch. Few people realized it, but unlike Amber and her family, Mayor Quinton was still in the broom closet. As a political figure, she couldn't risk alienating half the town because of her beliefs, so she kept a low profile.

"What's he doing bringing you flowers?"

"He lives upstairs. We've talked a few times. I guess he was being neighborly. Let's catch up later, okay? I'd like the chance to talk to everyone." She glanced away from the mayor. When she looked back, the mayor gave her a quizzical look. "Are you coming for the official opening?" Amber asked.

"Absolutely. I wouldn't miss it. Don't I attend the opening of every new business? I can't afford to miss one, people might forget about me." Her deep booming laugh had everyone turning to stare.

"As if anyone could forget you," Amber teased. "See you then. Thanks for coming."

"I'll just pick up a copy of *The Ghosts of Three Moon Falls* before I go. After all, the mayor has to know all about the tourist spots in her town." She winked broadly and walked away.

Amber set the plant on the counter near the till, threw the paper wrapping in the recycle bin, and roamed through the store, greeting people she knew and talking to those she didn't.

At the end of one aisle, a tall, thin man with dirty hair was looking at crystals. He had a dark air about him, which made her uncomfortable. Even his aura was murky, almost black; like he sucked in all light. She shifted from foot to foot, working up the courage to approach him, yet unsure why she shouldn't. This was her store, her domain, after all. She walked up to him.

"Hi, welcome to Four Seasons Metaphysical. Can I help you?"

He turned and glared at her; his red rimmed eyes narrowed menacingly. "No, I've seen all I need to see." He pivoted and stormed out of the store.

She watched him brush rudely past other customers as he stomped out. Weird.

"Who was that?" Hazel asked, coming up behind her.

"I don't know, but he sure was grumpy." Amber turned toward Hazel.

"Grumpy? The guy gave off negative vibes like a mouse at a cat convention. I wonder if there's anything we can do for him?"

"I don't know," Amber replied. "He just sort of growled and took off. But wow, did he feel messed up." Worse, he gave her the absolute creeps. He scared the living hell right out of her. "I can't even explain it; he was dark and angry. It felt like he was drawing the energy right out of me. An energy vampire." She shivered and forced a smile. "It doesn't matter. He's gone now."

Hopefully, he'd stay gone. Long gone. She picked up a small silver bell and gave it a soft shake to relieve the lingering aura of tension where he'd stood. It rang a cheery tune. She rang four others in succession, and the gloom dissipated. Thank the Goddess, music cleared away negativity. The last thing she needed on opening day was negative energy clouding the positive vibes she'd tried to hard to create.

While they weren't part of a formal coven, the Hawk family had a large circle of witchy and magical friends, and dozens of them stopped in with good wishes. They nearly sold out the entire stock of small ritual candles. Thankfully, there were a few boxes of them back at the house. If sales continued, they'd have to make more before the grand opening on Saturday. Amber spent some of her quiet time making a list of items she'd need to reorder almost immediately.

Freshly bathed and checked by both the veterinarian and Hyacinth, the stray cat wandered around the store inspecting the customers.

Nobody had an issue with her being there, most took the time to pet her and say hello.

Danica Maes walked up to the counter; her wild pink pixie cut hair standing up in planned disarray. Shorts and a crop top displayed her fit, twenty-something body to perfection. She glowed with beauty and magic. The cat lay, belly up, in her arms, purring up a storm. "I see you have a mascot. What's her name?"

"She doesn't have one. We're waiting to see if we get any responses from the posters we put up, or from the ad we put on The Ledger." The Ledger was Three Moon Falls buy and sell website. If someone wanted it, or wanted to get rid of it, it was listed there, including a lost and found pets section. "She's not chipped, so we're keeping her here, for now."

"She's adorable," Danica said, stroking the cat's black and white fur. "I love the gray sash across her chest. You should call her Sasha."

"That's pretty unimaginative," Amber teased her witchy friend. "I was thinking something more magical."

Danica shrugged. "At first, I considered maybe Aphrodite, Calista, Eros or a goddess name, but she's too earthy for those. Sasha just seems right." The cat rolled to her feet without leaving Danica's arms. She stretched her neck and bumped Danica's chin with her head. With a soft merp, she settled back in, purring once again.

"Sasha it is." Amber laughed. How could she argue when the cat agreed with her new name? "We're not even sure how she got inside, she just appeared." Amber chuckled. "Who knows what the universe has planned for Sasha and us? We've made her a bed in the back room, a safe place to have those kittens. Hyacinth says they'll be here any day."

"I'll take a kitten. Preferably male." She bent over and set the cat gently on her feet. "Let me know when they arrive, and I'll take pick of the litter."

"I'll do that."

The day passed in a blur for Amber. It was just busy enough to keep them all hopping. By six, customers trailed to a trickle, and she sent her family home. Customers came and went, some made purchases, others just looked around. It was a typical evening in retail. She cashed out at nine and prepped the nightly deposit. She'd hoped for a good day, but her income was beyond her expectations. Thankfully, the bank was only a few doors down, and she could use the night deposit box.

She was stuffing the money into the deposit envelope when a flat-splat sound startled her. She dropped the envelope, and her hand flew to her chest. "What the heck?"

Spinning round, she searched the store for customers. There shouldn't be anyone here; she'd checked before she locked up. She prowled up and down the aisles. A book lay discarded on the floor at the base of the bookshelves. Okay, that was weird. She picked it up and flipped it over. "Seriously?" she asked, looking at the cover. "*Dealing with Ghosts?* Not much on the subtle hints, are you?" She rested the book in her left hand and flipped through it with her right, glancing idly at the pages.

The pages started turning of their own volition, and the book slammed wide open in her hand, as if someone had forced it open. "How do you know if a ghost is trying to give you a message?" She chuckled after glancing at the chapter title. "I get it. I'm not listening to you. I'll get my sister down here as soon as I can, and we'll talk. Okay?" Something tugged on the book, pulling it out of her hands. She watched it float back to the shelf and slide into place.

She knew ghosts existed, and she believed they inhabited her shop, but she'd never had a first-hand encounter with one who wasn't an ancestor. This ghost was strong, too. Only about half of ghosts had the ability to move inanimate objects with that kind of precision. It certainly shed some light onto the matter of randomly opened doors. It did bring up other questions, like why were they opening doors?

And what did they want? Were they okay with her renting the store? If they weren't, what could she do about it?

"Ugh. Ghosts are so not my thing. Where is Hazel when I need her?" Amber peered around the store, hands on her hips. "Okay, my ghost friend, do me a favour and leave Kody alone? I don't need him getting up in my face over your door tricks and temperature changes."

The lights flicked off and came back on. Great. "Was that a yes or a no?" A breeze floated across her skin, and the echo of a distance laugh tickled her ears. "I'm going with no, then. I'm out for the night. Have a good one," she called to whatever entity might be listening. She scooped up the deposit, locked the shop, and headed to the bank.

Chapter Seven

K ody locked the second-floor suite where he stored his equipment. He'd keep it there, above Peterson's Garage, until he found a proper retail space on the lakeshore. Of course, having a shop meant he'd need to hire someone to man it while he was busy with dives. Fortunately, he'd been saving for this day and was prepared to support himself and his business until he'd built up a clientele and reputation. He'd hired a local teen to answer phones and book clients. She started tomorrow.

He climbed into his truck with a smile. Today had been a long day, but a good one. His first diving for children class, held in the local swimming pool, was a huge success. The kids were attentive and well-behaved, much better than he'd expected for a group of eleven and twelve-year-old kids. The high school Phys-ed teacher, whose son was in the group, wanted to get together to discuss the possibility of teaching diving as part of the high school curriculum.

He was riding high on his success as he pulled around the corner to pass the shop on his way home. Amber walked briskly down the street toward the bank. *Amber, perfect.* He felt like celebrating his success. Maybe she'd have a drink with him since they'd reached a truce of sorts.

He parked the truck and jogged around the corner, heading in her direction. "Amber, hold up," he called out.

She whirled round to face him. The bag she carried dropped to her feet, and she held her arms up in a stop motion. Sparks of blue and orange light flashed from her fingertips.

He jumped back. "Whoa!" *What the hell?*

She lowered her hands and scooped up the bank bag. "Oh, sorry, Kody. You startled me."

He stared at her. After a second, he snapped his mouth shut. "What the hell was that?" He made a vague gesture toward her hands.

She hid her hands behind her back. "Nothing."

"Right, those sparks were nothing. Have you got a Taser?" Not that Tasers looked like that, but it was the first thing that popped into his mind. The second thing was even less likely. Magic wasn't real.

She laughed lightly. "Not exactly, no." Her laughed faded, and she scuffed one shoe on the ground, avoiding his gaze. "I'll just throw this in the night deposit." She walked the last few steps, unlocked the depository, dropped the bag in, and closed it.

Okay, she didn't want to talk about the sparks, and he wanted to know what the hell he'd seen. Time for a round-about. "I was wondering if you'd like to get a drink with me. To celebrate your opening and my great day."

"You know, I might enjoy that. I feel like celebrating. Just let me text home and let them know I'll be late." She pulled out her phone from the fire print bag slung crosswise over her body.

He watched her texting. Her fingers moved like lightning over the screen. Her light brown hair was pulled back in a ponytail. It shone in the dimming evening light. He couldn't see her eyes, but her long lashes made crescents on her cheeks as she looked down at her phone. She was pretty in an earthy, casual way. Her clothing reflected her earthiness. Her bright yellow T-shirt proclaimed, "I left my other broom at home." Her jeans were snug and comfortably worn but not shabby. Her runners were black and patterned with golden moons and stars. She didn't fit his image of a witch. He didn't know what he expected, but it wasn't Amber Hawk. He shook the thought off. Her strange flashy fingers were making him crazy. Maybe it was just light reflecting off the rings she had on every finger. She even had them on her thumbs.

"You text your family when you'll be late? A bit old for that, aren't you?" He was teasing, but curious as well. Respect for family was important.

"Not a bit. I consider it courtesy. It keeps them from worrying. Plus, I don't know you well, and I'd never go out with a stranger without telling someone." Her expression was deadpan.

He couldn't tell if she was serious or joking. Hopefully, she wasn't completely without humor. "I guess that's a good policy."

She chuckled. "Gotcha. I can't go anywhere in this town without someone knowing me. If anything happened, someone would know who I was with. I keep my family in the loop; we all do. Where would you like to go?"

He hadn't gone out much since he moved to town, so he asked for her advice. They settled on Flannigan's. It wasn't as loud as Lloyd's Bar, nor as intimate as Illusions, the Italian restaurant.

Flannigan's, a pub, was shockingly busy for a Monday night. "Wow," Amber exclaimed. "It's nuts. Barely any faces I recognize. It's mostly tourists." She waved at a few people and greeted a couple more, introducing him as he followed her to an empty table for two in the back.

Their server, a middle-aged woman who was nearly as round as she was tall, greeted Amber with an enthusiastic hug. Her blue eyes sparkled behind bright red, diamond studded, eyeglasses. "Amber, good to see you. I didn't make it over to your store today, but I'll be there tomorrow for sure. We're short staffed, have been all day. What'll you folks have? Food or just drinks? Who's your friend?"

"Kierra, this is Kody Wilkins, Jason's cousin. He's new to town. Kody, meet Kierra. She and her husband own this lovely establishment."

"Nice to meet you." Kody smiled and offered his hand. Kierra's eyes narrowed, but she shook hands with him.

"Relax, Kierra. Kody's okay. So far, he doesn't show any of the Wilkins' family traits. He's living in the suite above the shop and has been a decent neighbor... most of the time."

He suppressed a wince. She obviously hadn't forgiven him for storming into her shop the night they met. Either that or she was still mad he took off without saying thanks after she let him rest in the back room. "I was kind of a jerk the evening we met," he explained. "I'm trying to do better."

"See that you do, young man. And treat this girl right. She's one of the good ones. Besides, if you hurt her, she'll zap your ass into next week."

"Yes, ma'am." A lame response, but it was the best he could come up with. "I'll have a Pilsner and a plate of nachos, please." Zap his ass? Maybe he hadn't imagined those sparks. He'd taken his cousin's word that Three Moon Falls was a great, friendly tourist town and had moved here. Maybe believing him was a mistake, despite the stunning caves under the falls. This town was weird, too weird. But he'd made his decision, and he was here now. He'd have to make the best of it. Besides, Amber Hawk was one of the most attractive women he'd seen in a long time. Something about her called to him, despite the way they occasionally reacted like fire and water.

He blinked rapidly. Called to him? That sounded like a damned magic spell.

Great, now he was thinking she was magic. He shrugged the thought off. He was letting rumor and an overactive imagination get to him. He must be more tired than he realized.

Amber snapped her fingers under his nose, jerking him back to the present.

"What? Sorry, my brain was miles away."

"Yeah, for five minutes. I ordered my dinner, chicken pot pie, and you didn't even notice Kierra leaving. Your beer is here." She raised her glass in a toast. "To new friends and neighbors."

"To new friends," he echoed, and they touched glasses. "Sorry for drifting away." She looked like she was expecting an explanation. He wasn't going to give her one. He glanced around to ensure nobody was listening. People would think he was crazy if they overheard his next question. "I saw the sparks? The fire? Whatever it was coming from your hands. What is it? A trick?"

"Can we just drop this? Forget you ever saw anything?" She raised one brow and scrunched up her nose. Her hands curled into balls on the table.

"Nope. I saw something. Something weird. I want an explanation, please." He almost felt guilty for putting Amber on the spot. Almost. Bryce had told him her family was into crazy stuff. Witchcraft. Magic. He didn't believe any of it. Or at least, he didn't think he believed. After seeing what happened when he startled her, he wasn't quite so sure where he stood. A logical explanation would help.

"You wouldn't believe me if I told you," she hedged.

"Try me."

Their table was in the corner, nearly shielded from the rest of the pub's patrons. She stood the oversized menu up to further block the view and turned her hands, palms up, on the table between them. "You've been in our store. You know I'm a witch, though you probably don't believe magic is real. I am magic. My entire family is."

He leaned back, involuntarily, and studied her earnest expression. "And?"

"Watch." She waggled her fingers to get his attention. She curled her hands into tight fists. She opened the right. A small spark appeared in her palm.

"Nice trick." He used sarcasm to hide his unease. What the devil? It had to be an illusion. Like a magician could do. A trick of the light.

She opened her left hand, and the spark jumped into its palm. It jumped back and forth between her hands. She closed her hands, and the spark vanished.

"It's something to do with your rings, isn't it?" He couldn't hide his skepticism.

"Fine," she said with a sigh. She slipped her rings and bracelets off and handed them to him. "Hold these." She rubbed her palms briskly together and opened her hands. Both held sparks, one blue, one orangey-yellow. "Believe me now?"

"I see it, but I don't believe it. It's an illusion."

"Magicians rely on sleight of hand. This is real. Hold out your hand."

He eyed her warily. She was up to something. Rather than be labelled a coward, he lay one hand on the table, palm up, between her open hands. "Okay," he said.

The sparks jumped from her palms to his with a tiny snapping sound. Heat blazed in his palm, uncomfortably hot, but not hot enough to burn. He jerked his hand back, and the sparks vanished. "Shit," he exclaimed. "You could have burned me."

She laughed lightly. "I told you it wasn't a trick."

"It was hot."

"I kept it mild. It will burn skin if I'm not careful. Once, I caught a stick on fire and managed to burn my leg badly enough to scar. I was only seven. I hadn't mastered it yet, and I was playing around when I shouldn't have been."

"Your parents taught you to play with fire that young?" He stared at her, unable to fathom why an adult would let a kid mess with fire. For a moment, the reality of what he was seeing disappeared from his mind.

"No. It doesn't work like that. Witches are born with a set of skills. We can learn more, but most have an inborn skill. Mine is fire. I first manifested sparks when I was five and couldn't have ice-cream. I pitched a royal fit and threw sparks. Luckily, no one was hurt."

"Isn't it dangerous?"

"It is. Some families bind their children's magic until they're old enough to learn to use it responsibly. We grew up with magic. My mother, my stepfather, all my grandmothers... magic was all around us. We learned by watching and some special tutoring when the skills appeared."

He couldn't formulate a response. He gaped at her as she sipped her red wine. Kierra appeared, placing nachos in front of him and a steaming pie in front of Amber. She thanked the server, nodded toward his plate, and dug into her meal.

After a few moments, she said, "You should eat those, before the cheese congeals into a solid mass."

"What? Oh, right." His food. He could have been eating old boots for all he noticed. His mind was stuck on what he'd just heard. Kids playing with fire was insane. You wouldn't give a five-year-old kid a jack-knife. Why in the world would you let them play with fire?

"Out with it," she demanded. "What question is burning a hole in your mind?"

"Are you a mind reader, too?" His stomach clenched; the spicy nachos threatened to make a return visit. He didn't want anything to do with a mind reader, no matter how pretty she was.

"Not exactly, no. I can sometimes sense strong emotions, and your emotions are ricocheting like wild. They're going to scorch you if you don't let them out."

He nodded. One bullet dodged; if she was telling the truth. "Okay, then. Here goes. Do all your sisters play with fire?" His rudeness startled him. "I mean—that is—never mind."

"It's okay. It's freaky. I knew about it, and I flipped out the first time I sparked." She patted his hand, and he almost jerked it away.

"I'm the only sister who can cast fire. My grandmother, can. My great-grandmother and great-great grandmother could, before they passed. My mother cannot. She has different skills."

"What about your father's family? Are they fire throwers, too?" Wow. He was having this discussion as if it were all real. Maybe they were genetic anomalies or something. He'd never heard of anything like this, except in the movies.

"No. Magic is passed maternally. Men can be magic, but they can't pass it on to their children. My stepfather does and his mother had skills. She's gone now. Dad can't pass it on, but he didn't have kids of his own anyway. His sister has children, so the magic genes will get passed on through her."

"Just what percentage of this town are magic?" He couldn't keep the fear from his voice.

"Only about a third, maybe half. It's not common knowledge. The non-magicals, the mundanes, are unaware of us. Many remain in the broom closet. There are only a few families, like mine, who are relatively open about our practises. Though, we tend to keep our major skills, like fire casting, a secret."

"But you told me?" She'd probably only told him because he caught her in the act. Knowing there were people with the ability to generate fire made his brain and stomach ache. He massaged his temples, trying to get a grip on what he was hearing. She'd rocked his reality to the edge of insanity.

"I was distracted. Totally unaware of my surroundings. Not a good habit to have. You startled me. I reacted defensively. Most people wouldn't even notice my little slip. Or, if they did, they'd think they were mistaken. A trick of the light. As for this demonstration? I don't know why I showed you. I should have let you think you were crazy."

"How dangerous are you? Are you evil? You don't seem evil." She seemed more like the girl next door than a fairy tale witch. But evil often disguised itself.

"Look at it like this. My family, and most of the magical in town, are considered white magicians, witches, or mages. We believe in only doing good. Much of my family's belief stems from a Wiccan background. Our number one rule is, "Do what you will with harm to none." As I mentioned already, the only person I ever hurt with my fire was myself. I rarely ever use my gift. I use it to light candles. It's kind of a use it or lose it thing."

He shook his head. This was crazy. He couldn't even formulate more questions.

"Stop fretting over it. We're supposed to be celebrating our great days." She raised her glass again. "Here's to friendship and success."

They finished their drinks and food while making small talk.

"Are demons, dragons and vampires real?" he blurted. Heat fused his cheeks. He had to get a grip on his wayward tongue. "What about unicorns?"

"Vampires? I doubt it. I've heard stories of demons, but never met anyone who even knew anyone who encountered a demon, so I doubt they're real. More likely, they're a scare tactic thought up by frustrated parents or churches. Dragons? I sure hope so; I'd love to have a dragon and a unicorn, too."

"This isn't fiction. Be serious."

"I am serious." She laughed. "Mostly." She flashed him a winning grin. "There are more things on this earth than you can imagine. Why is it so hard to believe in dragons, fairies, and pixies?"

His eyes bugged out.

"Oh, Kody. Chillax. It's all good. I'm yanking your chain."

He forced a few calming breaths, like he taught newbie divers to do before they descended. After a moment, he began to relax. Fairy tales of witches who could compel a man to do their bidding swamped him. Was she? Nah. She wouldn't do that.

"Are you spelling me? Making me relax?" he asked, half serious.

"No. *I* don't have that skill. I promise I'll never spell you without permission, which falls under another of our rules."

She put a slight emphasis on the word *I*, leaving him wondering if she knew someone who could compel him to do something. Which brought to mind the fact she never did say what skills her sisters had; she'd just said they didn't use fire. The deception bothered him. A lie of omission was still a lie. He studied her calm, relaxed posture and recalled everything he knew, or believed he knew about her. Amber didn't seem the type to do something nasty. He decided to trust his gut and go with that feeling. His mother, God rest her soul, always told him to take people at their word until they proved themselves one way or the other. He'd take the advice. For now.

Chapter Eight

A mber hugged herself tightly. This was it. Today was Saturday—the actual grand opening of her dream. They'd been open since Monday, and nothing had gone awry all week. This morning, she'd woke before dawn and dressed in her favorite swirl and star patterned dress in blues, navies, and blacks. She slipped on some sparkly silver sandals and loaded up with silver rings. One for each finger and each having a different stone. She added a quartz pendant for protection and slipped a piece of her namesake stone, amber, into her bra. It hadn't come up in her discussions with Kody, but gemstone magic was a favorite of hers, and she excelled at it.

By the time her family arrived for the opening, she had everything ready. Teas to sample. Cookies, cakes, and treats to feed their customers. She'd restocked the shelves and added to her supply order of things they couldn't produce themselves or source locally.

"Sister, darling," Lazuli exclaimed as she breezed into the store with the rest of the family. "You're feeling very optimistic and prepared." She thrust a smoothie into Amber's hand. "Cynth and Haze mixed this bad boy up for you. Full of all the things to cure your ills and prep you for the day." She stood back to study Amber. "Though, clearly, you're fit as a fiddle and ready to go. Your aura is positively bursting with greens, yellows, and blues. You look phenomenal."

"Thanks, Laz. I can always count on you to make me feel good." Amber gave her sister a one-armed hug.

"I brought this, too." She dug into her back pocket and extracted a wooden bangle. "I made this for today. I carved it myself from a piece of rowan tree. It's not tough like hardwood, but it'll bring you luck. I inset some amber for extra oomph."

Amber accepted the bangle and ran it between her fingers. Perfectly smooth and flawless; it was beautifully created. Three pieces of amber were set flush with the surface of the bracelet as the centers to intricately carved daisies. "It's beautiful. You carved this by hand, didn't you?" Lazuli's affinity was for the element of air, but she was unmatched as a carpenter and could carve almost anything. They had one full display cabinet of wooden figures she'd created. Everything from angels to goddesses to dolphins.

With the smoothie crafted by Cynth and Haze, and the bangle from Laz, she had an opening gift from everyone but her grandmother. Gramma Pearl wrapped Amber in a hug and whispered, "You've got this girl. I'm proud of you." She slipped something into Amber's hand.

Amber looked down. A tiny witch's bottle, no more than three-quarters of an inch high, rested in her palm. It held a tiny goddess charm, dried rose petals, and several dandelion seeds. Sealed with red wax, it had the rune for good luck, WUNJO or Wyn, carved into the wax. It had a hook for hanging from a chain if she wished. To the uninitiated, it didn't look like anything important, it resembled a child's craft. But magic wasn't always ostentatious. This was her grandmother's spell, or wish, for financial success, and Amber had just the place for it. Opening the register, she slipped it inside, in the back of the slot designated for twenties.

"Thanks, Grams; I love it. Let's do this." She hurried to the door and opened it.

Again, like their first day open, there was a crowd of well wishers outside. Friends, fellow witches, and neighbors came out to take part in the festivities. At the head of the line was the balloon animal artist Amber had hired to entertain the children of customers.

Business came in waves all day. It was busy enough to keep them hopping, but not crazy enough to prevent taking breaks. At three, she took a short break for tea and returned to the front to make personal contact with her customers. She wanted to make a good impression on those she hadn't interacted with yet.

Rounding the corner near the books, she sighted a familiar but unwelcome face. The man who'd given her chills on Monday stood there; his short black hair was shot through with uneven chunks of grey. It was dark and shiny, like he'd dipped his head in oil. He clutched a copy of their ghost book between his claw-like hands, his dirty dagger nails dug into the cover. Something deep inside her rebelled at the sight of him. It was all she could do to remain motionless and not recoil.

"Hi, welcome back to Four Seasons Metaphysical. I see you've found our book about local ghosts." She swallowed down a lump of anxiety and forced herself to look directly at him. He was out of focus, as if she were looking at him through smoke. Abruptly, she realized his aura was so dark and damaged it covered him like a cloak. It wasn't the darkness of sadness or depression; it was more. He had no ancillary colors, not a hint of anything but black. She was looking at evil. By the Goddess, this man was bad news. Big time.

She reminded herself to be calm. Just because he was dark and potentially evil, it didn't mean he meant her harm. Even evil magical practitioners had to get their supplies somewhere; she'd always assumed they shopped online. How she knew he was magic she wasn't sure; he didn't have the stereotypical glow she often detected. He was more ... all light sucked out and darkness filled.

"Who wrote this?" he hissed, frowning.

The deep, grating timbre of his voice deepened the anxiety rising in her. "My family. It was a group effort, why do you ask?" She'd be polite, even if it killed her.

"It's nothing but fluff. I was expecting more from this shop." The frown between his eyes deepened to crevices and canyons.

What on earth did he mean by that? "I'm sorry to disappoint you," she offered. "Can I help you find something?" *Please be no! Please be no. Just get out of my store.* "We have plenty of other things worth considering if the book doesn't please you." Nausea rolled through her, a thousand wasps stabbing in her stomach. The pain was as real as if she was being swarmed.

He was doing this! He was casting a spell.

Feigning nonchalance, she picked up a large chunk of quartz from a nearby shelf. Its protective aura wrapped around her, blocking some of his power.

He frowned. "So, Miss Hawk, it's true what they say." He dropped her name like an epithet.

"And what do *they* say?" And who the hell were *they*?

"This isn't just a front. You are magical. I didn't actually believe the rumors."

Her shoulders tensed. She planted her feet firmly, ignoring the anxiety. Where the hell were her sisters? Couldn't they feel her distress? What happened to their familial magic connections? "Don't believe everything you hear," she advised.

"Don't bother trying to call your siblings. I can block mind reading and sending." His icy grin was like a punch to the solar plexus. Her whole body screamed out in terror just being near him. She shifted from foot to foot, fight or flight response in full panic mode.

"I don't know why you came here, but I'm asking—no, telling—you to leave. Now." She pointed toward the door.

"Is that any way to treat a customer?" he drawled.

She'd have sworn he hadn't moved, but instantly, he was standing right in front of her, his hand on her arm, claws digging painfully into her skin. The book lay discarded on the floor behind him.

The little voice in her head told her not to panic. He'd gain power if she gave into fear. "Let go of my arm, and get the hell out of my store," she commanded, her voice strong with compulsion.

"I believe the lady asked you to let go of her," Kody's steel-filled voice came from behind her. "Excuse me, Amber. I'll just escort this gentleman out."

He grabbed the man by the arm and herded him outside as if he were an ordinary person. Seconds later, Kody was back. "Are you okay?"

"Um, yeah. I guess." The answer was unsatisfactory, even to her.

"Are you sure?" Disbelief shone in his eyes. His brows pinched together in a frown.

"I will be. I think I need to sit for a minute." She wobbled badly on her feet, nearly knocking over a shelf.

Kody wrapped his arm around her waist and led her to the back. They passed Hyacinth on the way. "I think she needs help; she's had a scare."

"What do you mean she's had a scare?" Cynth scurried behind them.

Amber collapsed on the couch, and her entire body shook with the aftermath of the encounter; her skin crawled where the man had touched her. She was weak, like she'd run a marathon after an all-nighter.

"What the ever-loving demon's breath happened? Her aura is crazy. Grey, brown, black, even spots of washed-out dull yellow. What the hell terrified her?"

"I don't know, some guy. Grubby looking. He was talking to her, and she was upset, but when he touched her, she just froze. I escorted him outside. I hope it's okay."

"Thank you. You kept her from being badly hurt. Can you go get Gramma Pearl and Lazuli for me? Tell Hazel to mind the front."

Amber listened them, and her gaze followed Kody as he left. She wanted to call out to him, to bring him back, but she couldn't find the strength. The room was spinning and out of focus. Something was seriously wrong with her. She tried mentally grounding herself, but couldn't manage it.

Chapter Nine

K ody rushed into the front and grabbed the first sister he came to. "Come to the back. Your sister needs you."

"What? Kody? What are you doing here?" Her words implied a dozen questions; ones he didn't have time to answer.

"Damned if I know. Something's happened to Amber, a woman, your other sister is in the back with her. She said to get you and your grandmother."

"What's this?" An elderly lady hurried up to them, Hazel hot on her heels.

He skipped the question. "Gramma Pearl and Lazuli go to the back room. She said Hazel should watch the store."

"She who?" Hazel asked.

"Hyacinth did," Lazuli flung over her shoulder. "Something is wrong with Amber."

He followed Gramma Pearl and Lazuli, who rushed from the room. Amber reached out for him. He rushed to sit beside her and clasped her hand. Waves of terror emanated off her like a physical thing. "Relax, Amber. It'll be all right. He's gone."

"You should go," Lazuli advised.

"No! I need him." Amber's voice shook with fear.

"I guess you're overruled," Kody stated, gripping Amber's hand between both of his. "She wants me here." He didn't understand why it was so important to stay, but he heeded his inner voice and her pleas.

Her family gathered around them.

Lazuli turned white and swayed on her feet. He leaped up and steadied her. "Sit, you look as bad as she does." He helped her kneel on the floor beside Amber, regrasping her hand.

"I'm okay, just bad vibes."

Gramma Pearl and Hyacinth bantered back and forth, throwing around words he knew but in strange contexts.

"Somebody want to tell me what's going on? What's wrong with them?" he asked.

"I doubt you'd understand," Pearl patronized him. "Don't worry about it. You should go. We've got this."

"No." This time, it was Lazuli who objected. "She needs him here." The words were soft, barely audible, but vehement.

Pearl raised one eyebrow and studied him. "Are you sure you can handle this? It's going to get weird."

Was he ready for this? Doubt plagued him. He nodded. Something had called him back to the store when he was halfway to a meeting with his realtor. He hadn't questioned it, just turned around and came back to find Amber standing off against the guy Kody had chased out. "I'll survive."

"You have to promise, nothing you see here leaves this room. Ever!" Hyacinth demanded.

"Yeah, whatever, just help her."

Hazel rushed into the room. "Store's empty. I locked up. What do we need?" Pearl rattled off a list of things, and Hazel hurried from the room.

"Help me push this couch into the middle of the room," Hyacinth demanded.

Working together, they managed to move the couch without dislodging Amber. Lazuli scooted out of their way. Pearl poured a line of white crystals in an enormous circle around the couch, surrounding them all, leaving an opening on one side.

"Is that salt? Jesus, I've fallen into an episode of *Supernatural*." What the?

Hazel rushed back in and dumped a load of colored crystals in his hands. "A purple at each point on the clock, starting here." She tapped the floor with her foot. "A clear in between, just inside the circle." She took off.

Amethyst and quartz? Amber had a quartz clutched in her hand, too. He looked at the stones. They were the largest crystals he'd ever seen outside of a museum or rock and mineral store. He placed the stones as Hazel instructed, though he didn't know why. She was back almost immediately with an enormous iridescent blue and green stone, which flashed like lightning. He recognized it as Labradorite. Roughly square shaped, it had to be five inches across. She placed it in Amber's lap. Her hands opened to accept it without dropping the quartz she already had. She shivered like crazy, and Pearl dropped a blanket over her shoulders. Her family moved quickly, almost frantically, but with an air of calm. Hyacinth placed lit candles beside each of the quartz crystals.

Lazuli seemed to be recovering from whatever shocked her. Finally, she hugged Amber. "It's okay, sis. We've got this. You'll be clean in no time."

"Clean?" Everyone ignored his question. Okay, he got it. Time to shut up and just be there for Amber. He didn't understand any of this, but it seemed critical he stay close. Every part of his body and soul said Amber needed him, despite his trepidation.

Everyone stood inside the circle, except Pearl. All eyes focused on her. A quick motion of her hands and a match flared to life. She held it against a green bundle until the bundle began to smoke. *Smudging? She was smudging the room? Was this a Native Canadian thing?* He'd been to Native healing smudge ceremonies with a Cree friend. Even so, at this moment, Kody was totally lost and out of his element. He had a thousand questions. He pressed his lips together, holding the words back. The aroma wasn't unpleasant. It was smoky, astringent, and a bit like burning leaves.

Pearl rested the smoking bundle in an enormous shell. Cradling the shell in one hand, she circled the room, brandishing a feather and waving the smoke into the corners, chanting lowly. Hyacinth, Lazuli, and Hazel joined in. She circled the room three times and stepped into the circle of salt. Hyacinth poured salt to close the circle.

He'd seen enough television and movies to know he had to stay inside the circle. *Wasn't this a demon thing?* He was so far out of his element it would have been comical if he wasn't afraid for Amber.

Hazel lit seven silver candles in the center of the circle. Each was bigger than a birthday candle, but not as large as a dinner candle.

"Come, join hands," Pearl instructed.

He kept one of Amber's icy cold hands in his right hand and grasped Pearl's hand in his left. She reached out for Hazel. One after another, they joined hands until the circle was completed with Amber's hand. They all closed their eyes, and he followed suit.

"Mother Earth, evil has entered our domain. It has stained your daughter. We call you now to aid us in cleansing the evil from her," Pearl spoke.

She went on and on, talking to the entity she referred to as Mother Earth. Her words were calm and measured. The air pressure lightened. Though the door was closed, a soft breeze blew through the room, stirring his hair. He stopped listening to the actual words and focused on the changing feel of the room. Slowly, it began to feel—brighter. He hadn't recognized it as dark until it began to change.

He refocused when more voices joined Pearl's. "By the power of Earth, Air, Fire, and Water, Mother Earth, heal your daughter." Someone clapped, loudly, three times. The sound cut through the air like thunder.

Pearl dropped his hand, and he opened his eyes.

Amber opened her eyes. "Thanks," she whispered.

"Thank you, Goddess," Pearl exclaimed to the sky.

To Kody's untrained ears, it was half plea, half thanks, and one hundred percent prayer. Pearl broke the salt circle with her foot. Hazel and Hyacinth carried the rocks to a workbench and set them inside a plastic tub. Lazuli swept up the salt and put it in a small cardboard box. They extinguished all the candles except the seven in the center. Those, they moved to a workbench and left them to burn.

His mind reeled. The ritual, and there was no other word for it, was straight out of a B-grade movie, and yet, it was real. Too real. Amber was slowly improving. Whatever they'd done had worked, and it scared him to think of what else they might be able to do. These women could do some powerful shit.

Chapter Ten

Someone pounded on the back door. The family looked at each other and then at the door. Pearl walked over and opened it. A middle-aged woman in wild clothing stepped into the room. She was followed by an African Canadian woman, and a woman barely out of her teens with screaming pink hair. Two men holding hands brought up the rear. One was tall and thin, the other muscular and shorter. They shut the inner door behind them.

"What's happening in here? I felt it all the way to city hall," the wildly dressed woman demanded, looking around.

"Mayor Quinton, sorry to disturb you," Lazuli exclaimed. "Sorry to bother any of you."

"Hush up, and call me Gloria," the mayor exclaimed. "This isn't city hall, and it sure isn't public. Use my given name, please. Jerry, Mel, and I were having a meeting on their coffee shop proposal when we felt it. We all felt it. It took Mel a while to hone in on the source."

"What happened?" the shorter, more muscular, black haired man asked.

"We're not sure yet, Mel."

"Yes, we are, sort of," Kody broke into the conversation. "I came in and some man was hassling Amber. He touched her, and she went white as a sheet. Strangest damn thing I ever saw. I hauled his ass out of here. She was weak, like she was in a trance—or something."

"He was evil. I've never felt anything so evil," Amber said, her voice shaking. "He wanted something; I could feel it. I don't know what, but he tried to dig into my mind. If Kody hadn't shown up, he might have gotten in."

"What does that mean, gotten in?" Kody stared at them, one person after another. He'd never experienced anything like this, and it sounded like the guy had been poking around in Amber's mind. That couldn't be right, could it? His stomach lurched at the implications, and he choked back a gag. Mind reading wasn't actually a thing.

"Relax, man," the pink-haired woman ordered. "It's all good." She turned to the sisters. "He doesn't know shit about magic, does he?"

"Magic? You're calling poking around in people's minds magic? He made a vague gesture with his hands. "I don't know what the hell it was, but I'm out of here."

Mel and Jerry moved to stand, arms crossed, in front of the door. "Oh no you don't, mister. Not until you give us time to explain."

"Yeah, I don't think I want to do that. I'm just going home, having a drink, and forget I was ever here. I didn't hear anything, not a damned thing." His fingers and toes tingled with an adrenaline surge. His fight or flight response was kicking in in a major way. He had to get the hell out of here.

The pink-haired girl stepped up to him and placed her hand on his arm. "I'm Danica Maes. I work at Bev's Beauty. Relax, take a few breaths." Her voice was eerily calming. "What's your name? I don't think I've seen you around town."

"Kody Wilkins," he answered without meaning to.

"Nice to meet you, Kody. Chill for a minute, let's talk."

"Uh, okay." His mind reeled. He wanted out of here more than anything, but he felt compelled to stay.

"Stop it, Danica." Amber pulled Danica's hand from his arm. "Don't push thoughts into his mind. You know it's wrong. Besides, he came back to help me."

"She what? What now?" he stammered. The world was spinning out of control. This shit only happened in the movies, not real life. Could someone actually put ideas into your head? He looked back and forth between Amber and Danica, who glared at each other. Whatever Amber believed Danica had done must have annoyed her because her squared shoulders told him she was angrier than when he'd stormed downstairs and interrupted their unpacking.

It dawned on him... Danica *had* pushed thoughts into his head, calming him, just like he'd accused Amber of doing only days ago. His teeth ground together, and bunched his arms until they ached. What he didn't understand was why. He'd have to find a way to stop people from poking into his mind. A wave of near-hysteria washed over him. A week ago, hell, earlier today, he wouldn't have believed such a thing was possible, despite Amber telling him it was. Now, he was busy figuring out how to prevent it. His life was unravelling before his eyes.

"Gramma Pearl, can we get something to eat?" Amber asked.

"Gotcha covered," Mayor Quinton declared. "We hit the bakery on the way over. Brew up some restorative tea, Pearl. We could all use a cup while we discuss this."

Before he knew what hit him, Kody had a cup of tea and two cookies in his hands and was seated on the couch between Hyacinth and Amber. He edged closer to Amber, half sensing she wanted him closer.

Folding chairs appeared from somewhere, and everyone sat in a circle. Amber's defense of him stayed his departure when he should have left. He was torn between curious and frightened. One thing he'd learned during his diving training and career was the best way to conquer your fears was to face them, and if you didn't understand, you researched it.

This was research. He was not afraid they'd spell him. Not much, anyway.

"Somebody want to explain all this?" he asked into the silence. "I was halfway to a meeting when I felt compelled to come back. I don't know why. I just knew I needed to come back."

Everyone gaped at him.

"What?" he asked defensively.

"A premonition?" Amber asked, her tone conveying surprise and curiosity.

"No. Yes. Okay, I don't know. I suppose you could call it that." Great, now they had him wondering. His entire life was topsy-turvy since he moved to Three Moon Falls and worse since he encountered Amber and her family when he moved into the suite upstairs. "Does it matter?" he asked at last.

"Probably not." Amber smiled her reassurance. "I'm glad you showed up. He gave me the creeps from the moment I saw him." She shuddered.

Kody squeezed her hand. "He's gone now. You're safe."

"I don't think I am. He wanted something. He was curious about the ghost book, and he implied our store is a front for something else." She swallowed hard. "He touched my mind. I don't know why, but it felt like he was looking for something. I do know he'll be back."

"Why do you say that?" Gramma Pearl asked.

"He knew my name. He knew our family." Her hand trembled, and she dug her fingers into his fist. He reached over to massage her hand with his other hand. Gradually, her fingers relaxed and stilled, though he was pretty sure he'd have bruises from her nails.

Danica looked around. "Didn't you put up herbal wards? Protect the place with sigils?"

Even Kody recognized the astonishment in her questions. "What does that mean?" he asked before anyone else could respond.

Amber blushed. "I planned to, but I got busy and forgot."

"Sweet Earth Mother, how could you be so foolish?" the mayor asked.

"Don't be harsh," Amber snapped. "It's a ton of work to open a store, and who could have predicted someone so evil would show up the moment we opened? I never even imagined he existed, let alone in Three Moon Falls. And knowing who I was? Unthinkable."

Her whole body shook. Whether from anger, or the aftermath of her encounter, he didn't know, but he didn't like the way Mayor Quinton was treating Amber.

"Back off, Madam Mayor. It was an oversight. No lasting harm. Besides, if this guy is going to be a problem, isn't it better to know up front and prevent a sneak attack?" Kody jumped to Amber's defense.

"That actually makes sense," Hazel replied.

Everyone stared at him like he was some kind of exhibit in the zoo, like he was an aberration in their magical group. And now, he was believing in magic. Amber could conjure up fire. Yeah, magic was real. Knowing it was true didn't mean he had to like it. He wanted to know what skills these other people had but suspected now wasn't the time to ask.

"If these, what did you call them? Wards? If these wards would protect against him, shouldn't we be putting them up and not having tea and cookies?" He stared at each person in turn.

"Magic has a price," Amber informed him. "It takes a physical toll on the wielder and the recipient. Fueling the body helps you recover, as does meditation. Meditation will have to wait until the wards are up and I'm at home. You're right, though. We do need to put up the wards."

"Let's do it," Kody declared.

"You want to help? I thought you didn't believe in all this hocus pocus?" Amber's tone seemed to imply she wouldn't think less of him if he didn't want to help.

"Okay, maybe I do now. Besides, I live in this building, too. If weird shit is happening, I'll take any protection I can get."

Chapter Eleven

Amber smiled as she looked around the room. Mayor Quinton, Danica, Mel, Jerry, and Kody were all pitching in to help her, her sisters, and Gramma Pearl create the herbal wards for over every window and door. They reopened the shop, and business was brisk. An enormous portion of the visitors were known witches and Wiccans. While nobody asked about what happened, Amber suspected they must have felt something. Magic left traces, and when big magic was practiced, magicals could often feel it from a distance.

Lazuli and Hazel did most of the shop work. Amber split her time between the store and helping everyone else work on the wards.

She doubted Kody understood the true significance of the work they were doing, but he gave it his all. Initially, he'd been all thumbs and clueless about putting the dried floral arrangements together; he'd crushed a few stems and snapped off three rosebuds before he got the hang of it. Before long, his strong, clumsy hands had gentled, and he worked in unison with Amber.

They began with swags and wreaths formed from Rowan branches. The Rowan tree was sacred to European witches and Wiccans. Here, in Canada, the mountain ash was its cousin and served the same purpose. They added dried snapdragons, sunflowers, angelica, witch hazel, sage, dried roses, and baby's breath. Each flower and herb had a magical purpose. Together with the magic woven into them, the swags and wreaths would help protect the store from unwanted visitors.

"Will these really keep people away?" Kody asked.

"More or less. They'll help dissuade anyone with ill intentions. Highly negative people will feel compelled to walk right by. We're not creating a physical barrier, but a magical one." He looked puzzled, so she continued, "Protective magic is hard to explain. All I can tell you is it works. You're going to have to trust me on this."

"How can I not believe you after everything I've witnessed over the past few days?" He shook his head and laughed nervously.

"You don't have to believe for it to work. Relax, Kody. It'll be fine."

"Hey, Kody." Hazel skipped up to him and thrust an enormous broom into his hands. "Laz and I made this for you."

"A broom?" His voice rose in query. "It looks like something from *Harry Potter*."

Amber chuckled. "Yes, but it's called a besom. It's a magic broom. You stand it with the bristles up in your apartment for protection. Nobody thinks twice about it, because it's just a broom."

"We've hidden some flowers and herbs inside the willow twig bristles." Hazel gestured for him to flip it over and look. "You can also hang it over your front door if you don't want to stand it up. For that matter, you can hide it in a closet, and it'll work."

"I don't see how a broom can do anything. What am I supposed to do, hit the intruder over the head?" His brow wrinkled. He was half serious and half joking.

Amber patted him on the arm. "Relax. If you're right and the broom does nothing, it doesn't do any harm, either." She was used to skeptics. It amused her how people always laughed when she talked about magic. They claimed it wasn't real, but when they found out she was a witch, the first thing they said was, "Don't cast a spell on me." Fear and skepticism of unfamiliar things was commonplace among mundanes.

"Good point," Kody agreed. "It can't hurt to have it in my apartment, even if I don't understand this whole magic thing and how one man can do whatever he did to you. You were so exhausted, you nearly passed out. What happened, and how does that ... ritual help? I don't see how it could, but it did."

"The Goddess has power; she has all the power of the universe. We simply tapped into it. We'll repay her by planting trees, tending gardens, picking up trash. We also use power when we create wards. Like the broom." She gestured to the besom he'd laid on the table.

"Will you help me find the best place for it? If you aren't too tired after your ordeal. I don't understand what happened, but I recognize the cost to your strength. You're stronger now, but still pale and weak."

"I'd be happy to help you. I'm not so tired I can't help a friend, especially one who helped me first." She cast him a wide grin. "Besides, I'll be great once I get a full meal into me. Is now a good time? It's just past five, and we're not going to stay open late." By all counts, they'd only lost two hours of business; they'd reopen tomorrow, and they'd extend the derailed celebration.

"If you need to eat, I can fix something. I'm cooking anyway."

She studied him for a moment, unsure of his intentions. She didn't have Lazuli's gift for reading people, but she trusted him, he'd came back because he though she was in trouble. "Thank you, I'd like that. I'll just do up my deposit and get one of my sisters to drop it off, then I'll wander up. Does that work for you?"

"Perfect. Any food allergies? Anything you don't like?"

"I'll eat anything not nailed down right about now. I'm good with whatever you choose. I appreciate the meal. Is half an hour from now okay?"

R ight on time, she knocked on Kody's door. She stood on the landing of the wooden stairs on the outside of their building and waited for him.

"Let yourself in," he called from somewhere inside. "Leave your shoes on, the floor is freezing."

She opened the screen door and stepped into a small hallway. There was a coat closet on the left, adjacent to a small open-doored laundry room. A deadbolted door stood across the entry to their common stairwell. She wiped her shoes on the mat, turned right, and entered his suite. He stood at the kitchen sink, his back to her, his hands buried in dishwater.

"I brought some wine." She set the bottle on the counter. The kitchen was U-shaped, with the sink nestled under the window and the fridge on the far wall. She walked through the passage between the end of the cupboards and the fridge. Cold air engulfed her. She wrapped her arms around herself and rubbed her arms briskly to warm them up. "What the heck? This whole place is freezing. Turn up the heat, would you?"

"It's up to eighty. It doesn't matter how high I set it, it either turns itself down or doesn't work at all. I mean, look at this." He waved toward the three large windows lining the front of the suite. Sun streamed through all of them. It was eighty degrees outside. With the sun coming in, all the windows open and the heat up, they should be roasting, not freezing.

"Ghosts," she declared.

"Ghosts?" He whirled round, spraying soapy water everywhere. "Did you say ghosts?"

"Yeah, I did. Rumor has it this place is haunted."

He blanched. His mouth opened and snapped shut. Dishwater dripped off his hands, pooling on the floor. "You're telling me I've got witches downstairs and ghosts up here? Tell me again why I left the city to move here?"

She laughed. "That I can't answer, but Three Moon Falls is a great place to live, especially if you like outdoor life. We witches aren't dangerous, and if it's any consolation, the shop shares your ghosts. I had a visit from one the other night."

His brow wrinkled, and he frowned. She realized ghosts were more than he could handle after the day he'd had. Learning magic was real was often more than people could grasp.

He turned back to the sink. "Supper's almost ready. I'm heating a lasagna and garlic bread. Can you grab the salad out of the fridge while I finish scrubbing these bowls, please?"

"Sure thing." She used a tea towel to wipe up the water he spilled, then opened the fridge, grabbed the salad and the dressing. She carried it to the old Formica and chrome table. "This table must be from the original owners of the building." It was in pristine condition. "Mind if I give myself a tour?" she asked.

"Help yourself, there's not much to see."

An enormous living space housed the kitchen, dining room, and living room. One wall was filled with windows overlooking the back alley. The dining table and chairs were a matching set. The living room held a massive television, a stereo, and a threadbare couch in front of a heavy wooden coffee table. There was also a pristine leather recliner. The room screamed masculinity. If one of the ghosts was the former owner of the pharmacy, she was probably miffed her family home had been turned into a bachelor pad.

A hallway led off from the opposite end to the door she'd come in. She wandered down the hall. Four doors branched off it. First, a small but functional bathroom. The fixtures were old, but like the table, they were in good condition. Two doors led to empty bedrooms. The third, the largest room, held a queen-sized bed, without a headboard, and a utilitarian dresser. The room's enormous window overlooked the street and the lake beyond. The view was incredible.

She wandered back into the kitchen; arms wrapped around herself for warmth. This was ridiculous; she was freezing. "Okay ghosts," she called out. "Stop messing with the heat. We're freezing. We get the point. You want attention. We know you're there. Hazel's coming to talk to you, but not today. She's totally wrapped up her job hunt, and she's still working at the shop downstairs. Cut us some slack, would ya?"

A bedroom door slammed.

"Shit. What the hell?" Kody exclaimed. "I nearly dropped the lasagna."

"That was your resident ghost, expressing her displeasure." The furnace roared to life, and blessed warmth rushed into the room. "Thank you," Amber called to the ghost.

"It's that easy? I wish I'd thought of that." He set the steaming pan on a trivet on the table. "Of course, I had no idea I had ghosts."

"Don't feel badly, most people are totally unaware their homes are haunted. Of course, not many ghosts are hell bent on freezing the new occupants out. Wine glasses?" she enquired.

"No, but there are juice glasses in the cupboard to the left of the stove. Wait, I don't have a corkscrew."

"No worries, this bad boy's a screw cap. I was thinking ahead."

"So, you assumed because I'm a bachelor, I wouldn't have a corkscrew?" He laughed.

"I have no idea if you're a wine drinker; thus, you might not have one. Rather than take a chance, I chose accordingly. It's a Riesling. I hope that's okay?"

"Perfect. I do drink wine, but I don't drink alone. Well, at least not often. Maybe a beer or two, and that's only because aside from your family and my cousin, I don't know many people here yet. I haven't had time to get out and meet anyone."

"I can introduce you around. I've lived here all my life. I knew a few guys your age." She stifled a grin at his frown. So, he didn't like the idea of her knowing other men? Interesting.

"Are they all witches?" He winced. "Wow, I sound witchaphobic."

"Relax. It all takes time to get used to. But no, they're mundanes. Male witches are rare."

"Is that what male witches call themselves? Witches?"

"They call themselves whatever they want. Witch, warlock, wizard. Any way you slice it, it's just a label. We were raised to call them witches." She located two glasses and brought them to the table and poured them each a glass of wine.

"Thanks for the clarification." He waited for her to seat herself and joined her at the table. "Um. Another question. I seem to have a lot of them. What about prayer? Like a meal blessing? I was raised in a Christian home, and we gave thanks before meals. I don't do it now, but if you have something, feel free." He waved his hand in permission.

"Thank you." She interlaced her fingers and rested her entwined hands on the tabletop in front of her plate. "Thank you, Goddess, for the food before us and the company I keep."

"That's remarkably similar to the prayers of my youth." His wide eyes and tense jaw showed his surprise.

"Well, most faiths share a common history. There are Christian witches. At family events, we give thanks as a group, and when I'm alone, I do it silently." She was pleased he was trying to be under-standing of her beliefs. Many people were so freaked out, and they panicked and never talked to her again; although, that was rare here in Three Moon Falls. Something about their town seemed to attract the magical. And the more open minded. Perhaps that's why Kody had ended up here.

"Are you attending the Founder's Day events next weekend?" she asked.

"I might, if I had someone to attend with." He smiled winningly at her.

"Are you asking me on a date, Mr. Wilkins?"

He paused with his fork halfway to his mouth and swallowed. "I guess I am."

"Don't sound so certain." She laughed. "I'd love to accompany you to the festivities. As a friend." She didn't know why she added the qualifier, but somehow, the words popped out of her mouth, unbid-den.

He stuck out his hand. "It's a deal, friend."

Chapter Twelve

K ody smiled at Amber.

"This is awesome," she exclaimed. She sat in a collapsible lawn chair beside Kody on the roof of their building. Their hands brushed between the chairs. A jumbo cooler with soda, beer, and food sat in front of them; though they'd yet to delve into the contents. "I had no idea this was even here."

Two feet in from the edges of the building, a low picket fence surrounded the roof. The fence was fastened down, a permanent part of the structure. The area was obviously meant as a substitute for a yard in downtown Three Moon Falls.

"I didn't know it existed, either. I heard a thump yesterday and went looking for the source of the sound. In the third bedroom, what I thought was a ceiling access was down. I climbed up for a look. I'm not sure how it ended up open. I suspect your *friends* did it." Kody flipped open the cooler and offered Amber a beverage. She accepted a beer with a nod.

"Thank you. Why call them *my* friends?" She laughed. "Those ghosts are no friends of mine; though, they don't seem vindictive or mean spirited. I think they have a mission, something they want to accomplish rather than just being mischievous." She studied the roof again. The tar and gravel roof was safe to walk on, solid and well drained. "I wonder if this is to code. We're awfully close to the edge."

"If I continue to live here, I'll check the building and zoning codes as well as the under-structure of the building. I'd love a gazebo and some potted plants up here. Kind of my own private yard. Nothing too fancy, just a nice place to relax and unwind."

"That sounds lovely. I'm glad to have a great view of the parade from up here." Amber popped open her beer and took a long, slow drink. "Perfect. I can't believe how hot it is already, and it's only eleven-thirty."

He grinned. "It's going to be a warm one for sure. I'm glad my house mates showed this to me. Is your family coming?"

"They are. They'll text when they get here so we can let them up."

Kody laughed when Amber's cell phone chimed. "I guess that's them."

"They're in the parking lot."

"Tell them to come up. I'll let them in." He hastened down the ladder to unlock his apartment. As soon as he opened the door, people swarmed through. Hazel toted a cooler, Gramma Pearl had a wicker picnic basket, Lazuli carried chairs, and Hyacinth an enormous bakery box. Kody and Amber helped them lug everything to the roof. It took a lot of maneuvering and effort to get the heavy cooler up the ladder. He'd brought his up empty and filled it afterward.

"Thanks for having us," Laz exclaimed as she reached the roof. "This'll be the best view ever. I kind of wanted to invite our neighbor,

Frank, and his daughter, Rose. She'd love it up here. That girl's got so much energy, and her dad's always so busy. Sometimes, she sneaks away from him and ends up at our place. Either she's bored or she's got a fascination with us."

"By all means, call them. They're welcome to join us." He figured what the heck. Frank was a man; he was a man. Maybe they'd strike up a friendship.

"Are you sure you don't mind?" Amber asked. "I mean, we're already invading your space..."

"The more the merrier. Consider it a chance for me to meet new people. I don't mind a bit." Despite everything he'd seen over the past few days, the ghosts, the weird-ass magic, he was enjoying living here. Both the building and the town. The lake was just an incredible bonus with its series of connecting, underwater caves and the dozen or more sunken yachts. There was even one section near the far end that contained an entire drowned forest where the trees were preserved by the deep, cold water. He'd heard of it in areas which had been flooded for dams, but this was a natural occurrence and was as beautiful as it was eerie. He couldn't wait to explore more and to introduce others to its wonders.

Laz extracted a cell phone from the enormous bag slung over her shoulder and walked away from them. Moments later, she was back. "They're coming. Frank says Rose is thrilled to be invited. They're just down the street. I'll meet them downstairs, if that's okay with you?"

"Go for it."

Three loud gunfire blasts erupted through the air. Kody dropped to his knees, dragging Amber down with him. "What the hell was that?"

Amber laughed and jumped to her feet, brushing dust off her knees. "Thanks for trying to save me. That was the official starter's gun. They blast it off at the far end of town, letting everyone know its parade time. It's a hold-over from the first Founder's Day."

"Doesn't it scare the animals? Every parade has horses, and I saw a bunch of people with dogs gathering near the start line." This town was crazy. Bat-crap crazy.

"Which is why they do it away from the animals. I think Mayor Quinton likes the attention it gathers, you know, fueling the frenzy of excitement to begin."

He recalled the wildly dressed, extremely bossy and enthusiastic mayor from the day Amber was attacked. She'd love the drama of a shotgun start. "Yeah, I can see that. She's something else all right. Should we stand by the fence?"

"Not yet. It'll take another twenty minutes for the first float to come by. That'll be the mayor in a convertible, waving to her fans." Amber chuckled. "She's been mayor for fifteen years; nobody has seriously run against her. She hasn't missed a parade. Not even when she had two broken legs from a hiking accident."

"She's been mayor for fifteen years? Incredible." *How on earth did that happen? Two terms of four years, maybe. Four in a row? Unlikely, no matter what your political leanings. This place just got stranger and stranger.*

"You haven't seen anything yet. Wait until the parade starts," Amber advised with a laugh. She raised her beer can and tapped it against his. "This town is all about strange things."

"I said that out loud? Sorry."

"No need to apologize. I've lived here my entire life, and Three Moon Falls surprises me on occasion." She winked at him.

Her green eyes sparkled with mirth, and a soft smile graced her lips. Were her lips as soft as they looked? He leaned in for a taste. Just one quick kiss. A taste. She tilted her head to the left and inched closer. Hazel's excited, childish squeal burst the moment. He jerked backward. Holy hell, he'd nearly gone there. In front of her family; he'd almost given in to the inexplicable urge to kiss her. Had she compelled him? He eyed Amber warily. She shrugged; a soft smile played over those tempting lips.

Oh yeah, this woman could spell trouble. Big trouble. Spell? Did he even want to start a relationship with a witch? How would that work? He believed in God, and she believed in…? What exactly did she believe in? Surely, someone who could cast fire wouldn't believe in God. Wow. Time to back away; now, before anything even got started. He could easily see himself spending more time with her, but he wasn't certain he should. Maybe this whole group picnic on the roof was a mistake.

A small, black haired girl jumped in front of him, distracting him from his thoughts. Her hair was wildly curly and untamed; her eyes were grey and almost colorless. Her skin was tanned golden. "Hi," she exclaimed. "I'm Rose. Dad says I have to thank you for inviting me."

"You're welcome. Nice to meet you, Rose. I'm Kody."

"I know, silly. Daddy told me." She wiggled around in front of him, like she couldn't keep still. "The parade's going to start soon. Are you excited? I'm excited."

"Okay, munchkin. Give the man a rest." Her father grasped Rose lightly by the shoulders and turned her away. With a little pat on the backside, he encouraged her to step aside. She skipped away to talk to Lazuli. "Hi, I'm Rose's father. Frank Perrum, nice to meet you." The tall, black-haired, blue-eyed man stuck out his hand. His features were vaguely European, maybe Romanian. He had a short, neatly trimmed beard and bulged muscles everywhere. He was mildly intimidating despite his pleasant smile.

Kody rose to his feet and shook Frank's hand. "Kodiak Wilkens. Please call me Kody. Nice to meet you. I'm glad you can join us."

"Thanks. I'm glad Lazuli invited us. It means a lot to Rose. She doesn't get much time with me, and this will make it extra special." His gaze flashed toward Lazuli and back, his brows bunched together.

There must be some history between them. Kody understood mixed emotions. He was torn between liking the Hawk family and being slightly wary of their skills. And, he hadn't even seen what the rest of them were capable of. Heaven only knew what they could do.

Amber rose to her feet and offered her hand to Frank. "Frank. Thanks for joining us. Rose will love it. This is the best place to watch the parade." She waved around downtown. "We've got the only building with a roof-top view."

"I can see that." His gaze tracked his daughter's motions, as he managed to stay focused on the conversation.

While Kody didn't have kids, he'd dealt with enough of them to know keeping one eye on them at all times was critical.

"Oh, look at her. Rose is having a conversation, all by herself." Amber laughed.

Kody pivoted to look. Rose stood near the back railing, arms gesticulating wildly as she chattered away in a low voice. She pointed to her father, then to Lazuli, and kept on talking.

"Again?" Frank sighed. "She's got more imaginary friends than ten kids. Every one of them has a name and occupation. Some are adults, some are kids. Too bad she doesn't have many real friends; they'd keep her out of mischief." He shook his head. "Sorry. Sometimes, my daughter exacerbates me. For months after my wife died, Rose insisted her mother was still around and talking to her."

Kody glanced away from Rose. His gaze caught Amber's. She quirked one eyebrow. Good grief. Was the girl talking to ghosts or was she just super-imaginative?

"I better go warn her to stay back from the edge. Thanks for having us. Nice to meet you, Kody."

"Thanks for coming."

"Weird," Amber said quietly after Frank walked away. "I didn't think their family was magical. Rose's mother never let on that she might be, and I never sensed it in her, despite Celine visiting the house often."

"You can sense magic?"

"Usually, unless the wielder is very talented and can conceal it." She shrugged as if it were of no consequence.

Great, another thing to be aware of, to be wary of. "So, why do you think she has magic? Can you see it?"

"She's got a hint of a sparkle, though she's barely old enough to start manifesting her powers. She's only six. But it does happen. I wonder if she talks to ghosts, like Hazel?"

"This place gets crazier by the minute." Perhaps he should rethink his plan to settle permanently in Three Moon Falls. Maybe the weird outweighed the great diving.

"You need to relax. Just forget about magic. Half the town doesn't know about it, and they're happy enough. This is a great place for both magical and mundane people. You'll fall for it. I promise."

Her enthusiasm for her hometown radiated off Amber in waves he could feel. Hell, he could almost see it. He couldn't help but smile back at her. He was falling alright. Falling for her with all her quirks and sparks.

Rose squealed with excitement. "It's coming, I can see it."

Amber popped up on her toes and brushed a quick kiss on Kody's cheek. "Come on, diver boy, let's enjoy the parade." She skipped off toward the fence, leaving him staring at her very attractive backside.

Yup, he was in trouble. Big trouble. He'd have to be on his guard to keep her from worming her way into his life; not that she hadn't already.

Chapter Thirteen

A mber stood a short distance from everyone else and stared down at the parade, only vaguely aware of the floats. What in the world had she done? She'd kissed him. A virtual stranger. That wasn't like her, no matter how attractive the man was. She was no quivering virgin; she'd been in a couple serious, long term relationships. She'd lost her virginity to her childhood sweetheart, Stevie Avalon, at seventeen. While she'd been wrong, he wasn't her one and only, he'd been sweet, and they'd fumbled their way through it with kindness and caring. It had been, in hindsight, beautiful. Filmore Rathburn the Third had been her college crush; they'd dated for nearly a year. Aside from casual dates, without intimacy, that was her love life in a nutshell. Not stellar, not pathetic. Just about right. Perfect for her.

Hyacinth sidled up and nudged Amber with her shoulder.

"What was that?" Lazuli whispered. "You kissed him? Are you out of your fricken mind? He's a mundane, even if he did have a premonition you needed him. You guys can be friends, but nothing more. You know most mundanes can't handle knowing about magic. What if he freaks out and exposes us?"

Amber edged a few feet further away from everyone else, even though they were wrapped up in the parade and didn't seem to be listening to her conversation with Lazuli.

"I don't know what the hell I was thinking. I guess I wasn't. It just happened," Amber whispered. By the Goddess, she'd be in trouble if she kept acting without considering the consequences and repercussions. She had no time for a boyfriend, even if he was incredibly hot and had saved her from the magical creep. "It's not going to happen again. I guarantee it." No way was she going to mention how close they'd come to kissing before Frank and Rose arrived. Nope, that was just going to remain her secret. "Pay attention to the parade, that's why we're here. The mayor looks great today. I love how her outfit matches the bright pink of the Cadillac. Whose car is it?" She gestured with her hand, hoping to divert her sisters' attention.

"When she heard the forecast was going to be hot and sunny all weekend, she rented it, just for fun. On her own dime, too. The taxpayers aren't paying for it. Our mayor is one of a kind."

"Yes, she is. Oh look, the broom brigade." Amber pointed toward a brigade of black clad children.

Aside from Halloween, Founder's Day was one of Amber's favorite holidays. Three Moon Falls was great about celebrating their diversity, and they acknowledged their magical origins. The Hawk family joined the Moons, the Webbers, and the Castonguays as the town's founding families. The mundanes didn't believe in the magical history, they considered it myth, or just a colorful tale for tourists; but the magicals knew the truth. With every Founder's Day Parade, there was a tip of the hat to the magical past. Groups of children, dressed as stereotypical witches, rode broomsticks while others rode bikes or horses. The horseback riders carried Canadian flags. The cyclists carried Alberta flags, and the broom riders carried Three Moon Falls' own flag—a left-right diagonal split of blue on top and green on the bottom with three golden crescent moons hanging in the blue.

The children were all in costumes. Flowers, clowns, fairies, princesses, and an abundance of witches and wizards paraded down the street. There were favorite characters from *Lord of the Rings*, *Harry Potter*, *Star Wars* and, of course, several Disney princesses. Kids did love to dress up. It was like Halloween in summer.

Amber watched them go by; recognizing the youngest as a six-year-old and the oldest as a girl in her last year of high school. Not all the kids took part; many, especially the youngest, preferred to sit on the sidelines and collect the loot tossed by participants. "Too bad the town wasn't founded closer to Halloween. We could have turned Founder's Day into a great Halloween celebration instead of summer fun."

"Can you imagine more people than this? Look at them all. They're swarming around like ants. No, that's not right, they aren't moving. They're packed in like sardines." Lazuli laughed at her own joke.

"Look at all the out of towners. I guess tourist season has officially started. This is a fabulous turnout. I'm hoping the crowd will translate to sales when the parade is finished. I'm so worried about making Four Seasons Metaphysical a success. I've wanted this for so long."

"I guess so."

"Oh, no. Look!" Amber clutched Lazuli's arm with one hand and pointed with the other. "Over there, in black. It's him. The guy from yesterday." Her heartbeat doubled. She sucked in a breath. Her mind whirled, and her vision wavered. A flock of pigeons took flight in her stomach. For a moment, she thought she'd puke.

He was easy to spot, dressed monotone, in a crowd of festively dressed, summer clad people. In the blazing sun and temperature in the high twenties Celsius, he had to be sweating in long sleeves and dark pants, but he didn't look it. He was stoic and serious and cool. Just looking at him set Amber's nerves on edge.

"Holy crap, he's dark. I'm not even an empath and I can feel it." Lazuli glared.

"I know, right? Shit, he's looking straight at us."

His mind brushed against Amber's before she could react. She slammed up a mental shield, pushing him back. His eyes glowed red, but she refused to turn away. She wouldn't let him control her. Pushing her entire resolve into her stare, she gave him her best glare.

"What's going on?" Kody's voice came from beside her.

She didn't turn to look at him; she wouldn't lose the fight with the stranger. "It's him. The guy from the other day. Over there, in black."

"What's he doing?"

"Staring. He tried to get into my mind again. I won't let him."

"Bastard. He won't get away with this." He sprinted away.

Thirty seconds later, Kody raced into the street. "Oh, Kody's down there!" Lazuli exclaimed. "What's he doing? He's pushing his way across the street."

"What? Why?" Amber didn't dare break her staring contest. An instant of distraction could give him an opening to get in. Her body was rigid with tension, and she couldn't move if she wanted to. Her mind throbbed with the agony of keeping up her barrier. Her strength was slowly seeping away under the mental effort. She was going to lose this fight. She grabbed Lazuli's hand for strength. Extra power flowed through her, bolstering her flagging energy.

Kody entered her line of sight and grabbed the other man's sleeve, jerked him around, tearing his penetrating stare from Amber. She slumped with relief. Legs unsteady, she dropped to one knee, roof gravel digging painfully into her knee.

She couldn't hear what they were saying, but she could feel Kody's anger and the stranger's disdain. More words were exchanged, and the crowd began to notice. Pivoting toward the angry men, they stared, backing slowly away. Even the mundanes knew he was bad news; though they had no idea why.

Abruptly, Kody hauled back and shoved the stranger away from him. The stranger leaped toward Kody, and they went down onto the concrete sidewalk. Amber lost sight of them, and the crowd's wariness gave way to excitement. It rolled over Amber like a wave, pulsing, pounding, scorching. The mob's unchecked emotion was staggering where it thundered against her already flagging mental strength.

"Oh no! What's Kody doing?" She jerked to her feet and raced downstairs, through the building, and across the street. The parade carried on, uninterrupted, but the crowd had lost interest and saw only the brawling men.

She made it to them seconds before Corporal Lee Wong, who was second in command in Three Moon Falls Royal Canadian Mounted Police detachment. He waded through the crowd, grasped the two men by the shoulders, jerked them to their feet, and shoved them apart.

"What's going on here? Why are you disturbing the parade?" He was a tall, muscular man. In his full RCMP, red serge dress uniform, he was extremely intimidating. The crowd took another step back. He looked from one man to the other. Finally, he focused on Kody.

"You go first. Care to tell my why you are brawling in the middle of the street?" His hands hung, relaxed, at his sides, somehow doubling the impression he was ready to react at the slightest provocation.

"He was ... I mean ... He was staring at Amber Hawk," Kody stammered.

"Since when is staring a reason to fight? And where is Miss Hawk?"

"Right here, Corporal Wong." She stepped in front of him, a safe distance away from the other man. Why did it have to be Wong? Several other RCMP members were open to magic, one was even magical. Wong, on the other hand, was a total non-believer. It would be impossible to make him understand the significance of staring. "That man was in the shop, twice now, hassling me. Kody knew about it. He was standing up for me." She flashed Kody a grateful smile.

"And you, sir, who are you, and what do you have to say? You're not a familiar face around here."

"I'm new to town. I don't know what these people are talking about. Yes, I was in the store where she works, but I don't know why they think I was hassling her then or now. I was just standing here, watching the parade."

"It's true." Another man spoke from the crowd. Mr. Keres and I were just standing here, enjoying the parade, when this man attacked him." He moved to stand beside his friend. "We're in town for the summer, vacationing. We've rented a house outside of town."

"Enough." Keres glared at his friend. "They don't need our entire life story." He turned to Wong; his smile sickeningly sweet. "I assure you, officer, we were doing nothing wrong. Just watching the parade and enjoying your lovely little town. I have no beef with this man, nor with that woman, whomever they are. I won't be pressing charges for the assault."

"Are you certain?" Wong rubbed the back of his neck. "I think we should all go down to the station and file some paperwork on this, for the record." He pinned Kody and the other two men with a serious stare. "I won't tolerate this sort of behavior."

"What seems to be the problem here?" Constable Leticia Stone stepped into the fray, her strong voice demanding the attention of everyone involved. She was Wong's superior and head of the RCMP detachment for Three Moon Falls and its surrounding area. She was a sight to behold with her dreadlocks hanging beneath her regulation broad brimmed felt hat. She wasn't as tall as Wong, but her shoulders were nearly as broad, filling out her red jacket completely. The yellow stripes on her dark blue pants emphasized the length and strength of her legs.

Amber suppressed a smile. Leticia Stone was a died in the wool voodoo priestess as well as an extraordinarily competent RCMP officer.

"All right people. Nothing to see here. Turn back to your parade, please," Constable Stone waved toward the street. Obediently, the crowd turned back to the festivities. Stone had put a compulsion to obey into her words. "Miss Hawk, who is your friend?" Constable Stone flashed Amber a wide smile, her pristine white teeth brilliant against her dark skin.

"Kodiak Wilkins. He's new to town. He runs the diving business. He lives above my shop. He's a decent guy." She hoped her endorsement would keep Kody out of trouble.

"And this gentleman?" Stone gestured toward Keres.

"I don't know him. He's been in the shop a couple times. He made me—uncomfortable." She put a slight emphasis on the last word. "This morning, we were on the shop roof watching the parade, and I discovered him staring at me."

"There is no law against staring," Corporal Wong repeated.

"Thank you, Corporal. You've done an excellent job quelling this dispute. I'll handle it from here. Return to your duties." Her subordinate officer looked like he might object; instead, he nodded briskly and walked away.

"Mr.?"

"Keres, ma'am. I'm here on vacation."

"Mr. Keres, you are to remove yourself from the parade route and steer clear of Miss Hawk, her family, and Mr. Wilkins for the remainder of your stay in town. I know I don't need to remind you to keep your stare and your probing to yourself?"

His expression darkened, and his face went red. He nodded unhappily. "I'm on a research trip. I'll be gone as soon as I get what I came for."

"See that you are," Stone said sternly. "I will not tolerate shenanigans in my town. Do I make myself clear?" She raised one eyebrow.

Keres nodded and walked away, his back rigid, his steps angry and stilted. His friend trailed behind him.

Stone turned back to Amber and Kody. "I assume he is *different*?" she asked. She stressed the last word.

"Definitely. He tried, twice now, to get into my brain. I think he's looking for something. He already knew who I was before he came into the shop. Whatever he's looking for, he thinks I have it."

"Any idea what it is?" She crossed her arms, a furrow forming between her brows.

"None. But he gives me the creeps."

"He did something to her the other day," Kody piped up. "He had her shaking and weak. If I hadn't stepped in, I don't know what would have happened."

Stone's face went rigid and angry. "That's serious. I'll ask around, see what I can find out. Where he's staying, who he associates with. Maybe we can figure out what he wants." She turned to Kody. "Thank you for standing up for my friend. Try not to get into a street brawl next time." Her words were chiding, but her tone was light and friendly.

He saluted. "Yes, ma'am. Officer ma'am."

She laughed. "Constable Stone will do nicely, thank you."

"Yes, Constable Stone. You have my word; I'll keep it off the streets."

She eyed him up and down, clearly understanding his veiled intention to finish whatever started without getting caught. She frowned, then nodded. "Catch you guys later. I have official parade duties to get back to."

Chapter Fourteen

The parade was wrapping up by the time they returned to the rooftop vantage point.

"Sorry to ruin your first Founder's Day parade," Amber said as Kody crested the roof ladder behind her.

"Not your fault. I don't know what that jerk is up to, but he better keep his distance." He'd acted without thinking earlier, but he didn't regret it one bit. There was something just plain wrong with a man going around intimidating a woman. Any woman. He didn't know Amber well, but she didn't deserve to be treated that way. Days ago, he would have called anyone who believed in magic crazy. Now, he understood the reality, and the creep had been using it to mess around with his friend.

"I appreciate you standing up for me, but you need to be careful. He's powerful, and I think he's dangerous. You don't have any defences against him. Watch out, okay?"

"What was that all about?" Gramma Pearl asked, walking up to them, her expression serious. "I couldn't hear what was going on, but I could read the tension from here. It was him, wasn't it?"

"It was." Amber wrapped her arms around herself and rubbed her upper arms.

Kody realized she was nervous and scared, no doubt the aftermath of another encounter with Keres. If someone was after Amber, he might be after her entire family. Something needed to be done to stop Keres before someone got hurt.

"We need to do something about him. Something more than just flowers on doors."

"Those flowers are protective wards. They're stronger than you think. But you're right. We need to be more proactive. Family meeting tonight at the house. You need to be there, too," Pearl demanded.

"Me? Why me?" Admittedly, whatever this was, he was in it up to his neck, which didn't mean he wanted in over his head. He was drowning in a problem that wasn't his own; yet, he couldn't swim to safer shores without risking other people.

"Because like it or not," Pearl frowned, "fate keeps pulling you into this. It's crystal clear she wants you involved."

"So, I just give in and let some mythical thing decide my path? Nobody decides my fate but me." His exasperation came through in his voice. He sounded belligerent.

"It's not that simple," Amber said patiently. "It's about the inter-connectedness of everything in the universe. Somehow, you've been pulled into our world. For now, I think it's where you need to be. Maybe for our benefit, maybe for yours. Come over to the house tonight, after I close up shop, and we'll make some plans. Please."

"I don't even know where the house is," he objected lamely.

If he was going to live over her shop, he might as well get used to dealing with her, her family, and whoever was going to stir up shit.

The thought of backing out at this point was unsettling. It reminded him of the time he'd turned his back when a grade six bully was teasing a small kid with big glasses. He could have done something, but he didn't. That small kid had ended up in the hospital, leaving Kody with the worst case of guilt-gut he'd ever had. The kid, Paxton De Bonier, eventually became Kody's best friend. He wasn't about to let another bully have his way; and one thing he was certain of was that Keres was a bully, plain and simple.

"No worries. I'll ride out with you in your truck and guide the way. I needed a ride home from work anyway. I was going to catch a ride home with one of my sisters."

She popped up onto her toes and kissed him on the cheek. "Now, I have to open up shop. Catch you guys later," she called out to her family and climbed quickly down the ladder.

"Turn right, here," Amber instructed. "We're at the top of the hill."

He steered his truck onto a narrow, paved lane and passed between a set of decorative wrought iron gates. "Those are seriously impressive gates." He glanced at them in the rear-view mirror. They were almost seven feet tall and covered with ornate, stylized flowers. They slid silently shut behind them. "Oh, they're automatic."

"Something like that," Amber grinned at him.

He was afraid to ask what she meant. Best to let sleeping dogs lie. Or, in this case, let the mystery and magic remain unsolved. They drove past manicured lawns and at least a dozen flower beds in full bloom. Annuals and perennials, if he judged by his grandmother's gardens. Groves of fruit trees and what looked like hazelnut trees were scattered across the expanse of green. In the distance, he saw a large greenhouse and a couple of well-maintained sheds.

They passed through a thick grove of coniferous trees and rounded a corner, and the house came into view. Two stories tall, with dormer windows in the attic, it had octagonal towering turrets on either end. Flawless white woodwork was balanced with brick trim. A comfortable, welcoming blend of colonial and Victorian styling, it looked as if it had started as one and had been modified later. It should have felt ridiculously out of place in modern Alberta, but if felt like it belonged here, like it was part of the land.

The black shingled roof was curved in what could only be called witch's peaks. The turrets were topped with curving circular roofs swooping down to drainage spouts. They looked exactly like stereotypical witches' hats, without the brims. The dormer windows were floral stained glass. A full, covered porch ran the width of the lower level. A pretty floral swing graced one end of the porch and a cluster of plush-padded wicker chairs sat at the other.

He parked the truck, and they hopped out and walked the short, gravel path to the house. A light breeze carried hints of roses, herbs, and fresh mown grass. Memories of his grandmother's house washed over him like a peaceful wave of contentment. Three all-black cats were perched, one on each step, leading to the porch. If he didn't know better, he'd have sworn they were staring at him. A decorative broom, not unlike the one they'd made for him, sat bristles up, beside the door. He paused, strangely reluctant to go further. The earlier moment of serenity slid away.

"Hi, guys," Amber greeted the cats. "This is my friend Kody."

The cat on the lowest step meowed and wandered over to Kody, wrapping himself around Kody's legs.

Amber laughed. "Go easy on him, Apollo. He's not a cat person. That's Meeka above him and Calista on the top step. Welcome to Hawk's Manor," Amber said.

As if a weight lifted off his shoulders, Kody's reluctance to move forward vanished. "Holy..."

"Yes, the house is spelled to keep strangers away. When I welcomed you, the house accepted you. Hawk's Manor has a mind of her own. I think she's got an actual, magical, personality. Probably from our family performing magic in her every day for over a hundred years."

"It absorbed magic?" Incredible.

"She is incredible." Amber emphasized the pronoun. "Our house is female."

"Duly noted. Hello, Hawk's Manor. Nice to meet you." He greeted the house like a potential new friend, feeling mildly ridiculous as he did so.

The door opened, and Hazel flew out to greet them.

"Whoa, for a second there, I thought the house was opening the door itself." He laughed.

"Stranger things have been known to happen. Come inside. Supper's almost ready. Gramma Pearl is putting it on the table now," Hazel said.

Following Amber's lead, he stepped inside and slipped off his shoes.

The interior of the house was a lot like many others. The foyer flowed into the living area. Family pictures spanning decades lined the walls. Candles of all shapes, sizes and colors sat on every flat surface. Some hung from the walls in decorative holders. The entry had one large, live flower arrangement; the living room had several more. A long hallway led to the back of the house, where he caught a glimpse of the kitchen. A piano held a cluster of crystals and gemstones as well as an enormous glass ball. A crystal ball? Another broomstick, besom, stood in the corner beside a massive fireplace. The room was enormous, big enough to divide into two separate seating areas, one complete with two jam-packed, floor-to-ceiling bookshelves. An avid reader, the books called to him, but Hazel hurried them into the kitchen.

"We're here," Amber exclaimed. "Let's eat. I'm starving."

"Excellent," Lazuli exclaimed. She waved her arms and a brimming bowl of peas floated off the counter and settled itself on the table. Kody stopped dead and stared. He blinked several times and shrugged. How were floating peas any different than a woman who could shoot fire from her fingers? He ignored the weirdness, mildly uncomfortable that the impossible wasn't upsetting him.

"No showing off. Do your chores the proper way," Pearl chided her.

"Magic is not for personal gain," the sisters chanted in unison.

"Pull up a chair, it doesn't matter which one," Amber said. "We don't stand on ceremony here." She picked a basket of buns and a pile of napkins off the counter and walked around to the back of the eight-person round oak table and took a seat.

He followed her lead and sat beside her with his back to an enormous bank of windows overlooking the yard. The kitchen proper was across from him. The center island, containing the stove and one of two sinks, was fifteen feet long. The rest of the counters were U-shaped with a break at the far end for a doorway that led to an entranceway from outside, and beyond that stairs leading up. Whoa! This house was even bigger than it looked from the outside. Normally, he wasn't much into houses as long as they were warm and functional, but this one had him intrigued.

"I love the house," he said. "It's different."

"She is at that," Pearl said with a laugh. She carried a large crockery pot over to the table and set it down. "Hope you like chicken stew." She stirred the pot, releasing the enticing aroma of chicken, broth, fresh vegetables, and herbs.

Hyacinth, Lazuli, and Hazel joined them at the table. Amber said a blessing, and they all dug in. Good natured ribbing broke out over the dinner rolls and peas. They were halfway through dinner before serious discussion started.

"I get the distinct feeling Keres isn't after me, but something he thinks I, or we, have," Amber stated, swirling a piece of her roll in the broth remaining in her bowl.

"Why do you say that?" Kody asked. "Clearly, he was targeting you."

"A hunch, I guess." She didn't sound entirely certain. "He pokes at my mind, like he's trying to discover something. It's all I can do to keep him out. I'm going to have to find a way to strengthen my mental guards, and fast. I've never needed to protect myself, except from Lazuli's snooping."

Laz fired a chunk of bun at Amber's head. Fire flashed from Amber's fingers, and the bun exploded in a shower of ash, drifting to the table like falling rain.

"Oh, gross," Laz complained. "Good thing we're done eating. It's everywhere."

"You shouldn't have thrown it," Amber snarked.

A thunderclap resounded through the room; Kody jerked to his feet in surprise. The girls fell silent.

"Enough!" Pearl demanded. "This is serious business. You're not teenagers anymore. Quit the petty bickering."

"Um? How'd you do that?" Kody stared at the family matriarch and folded himself back into his chair.

Pearl snapped her fingers and a lesser boom sounded. Kody's jaw dropped open. He snapped it shut with an audible clink of his teeth, which jarred his brain.

"Amber, I'll help you with shielding later. What we need to do now is figure out what Keres wants." Pearl looked from girl to girl, expectation in her eyes. "Well?"

"He feels like—like old magic." Amber's hands fluttered vaguely. "I know, that's not much help. But he's powerful."

"What does old magic feel like?" Kody asked. This was so high school Latin class. He'd always been way out of his element, unable to catch up with everyone else. Only now, he wasn't embarrassed to ask questions.

"Different. When you first come into your magic, it's tentative, unstable. As you mature, it evens out and becomes smooth. Grey magic is smooth with bumps. Black magic feels like shards of darkness. Like broken glass, only it doesn't reflect, it sucks in all light." She shook her head as if she couldn't quite find the words to express what she meant. "Keres is a mix of everything. Almost full black, with hints of grey. Some bumps, more shards. Every witch's magic has a certain feel, like a personality. It's difficult to explain, but you'll have to trust me. Keres feels like—like a dozen witches all mixed up. Maybe more. It's the scariest thing I ever encountered." She shuddered. "By the Goddess, it chills me to the bone just thinking of it."

Across the kitchen, a kettle drifted to the sink and filled itself before settling on the stove. The gas burner under it sparked to life. Kody barely paid attention. He was almost past being surprised by this family's skills; he was more concerned with Keres and how to stop him from harassing Amber.

"What could you have that he wants?" An idea hit him. "Okay, I don't know anything about magic, except what I've seen on TV, and I suspect that's more Hollywood than reality. If he feels like a dozen witches all mixed up, could he be stealing magic? Does he want yours? Is it even possible?"

Everyone stared at him. Despite feeling stupid, he met their gazes.

"That's brilliant," Pearl said. "It makes sense. I can't believe that slid by us. Especially with the girls' parents tromping all over the world in search of a witch killer. If someone was stealing magic, he might do irreparable damage to the witch. This could be worse than just a witch killer."

"Maybe..." Amber didn't seem eager to jump on the idea. "I guess that could explain how he feels, but my gut tells me that's not what he's after." She wrapped her arms around herself. "It's like he wants to rifle through my memories until he finds...something. I think. Like he's trying to uncover a secret."

"Do you have any secrets?" Kody asked, deliberately ignoring the cups and saucers drifting onto the table.

"From you, yes. From a powerful witch? I can't think of anything."

Kody ignored the idea that she had secrets from him. It was to be expected. They barely knew each other. "What about the family? Are you a long line of witches? Could someone else have a secret that maybe he thinks was passed on to you?"

"We are a long line. Descended from Salem," Pearl confessed proudly.

"Any big secrets?" Kody pushed. If they were from Salem, and he didn't doubt it for a minute, they could have magic secrets from hundreds of years ago. Who knew what they were hiding? Or protecting. "Can't you search your book of shadows? Or something? Don't all witches have magic books?"

"Some do, some don't," Amber answered as the teapot floated over to the table. Laz and Hazel physically cleared the remains of dinner as the tea poured itself.

"And your family?" he asked.

"We do."

Chapter Fifteen

Amber looked around the table at her sisters and grandmother. The whole thing with Keres had them all on edge. They needed to figure out what he was up to before it was too late. She was half terrified of what he'd try next.

"So, let's get searching your Book of Shadows," Kody said. "Bring it out, and we'll see what we can find."

"First, it's a Grimoire. Book of Shadows is a television invention, though it is catching on," Amber said and sipped at her tea. "Try the tea, you'll like it."

"I'm not much for tea," Kody said and lifted the delicate cup from its saucer.

"Try it," Amber insisted. "You might like it. It's a special blend for warmth, comfort, and protection. Peppermint, lemon balm, raspberry, mint, and orange blossoms." She smiled at him.

He was taking this so well. She'd be out of her mind with disbelief and confusion if she didn't have a magical background. Goddess knows mundanes didn't take magical revelations very well. Perhaps Kody had some magic in him. He'd shown his intuition was spot on, running to save her from Keres when he attacked in the store, which could be an indication of latent magic. It might also explain why she was so attracted to him, despite their rocky meeting. The attraction was deeper than just physical—he called to her body and soul.

Kody sipped the tea. "It's good. I'm surprised. Much better than the poison you fed me in the shop." He winked at her, sending warmth shooting down to her toes, chasing away her chill more effectively than the tea had.

"So, about this, what did you call it, grim...?"

"Grimoire," Amber said. "We have one. It's a record of our magic. It goes back a long way." She almost rolled her eyes. He had no concept of how much information sixteen generations of witches could accumulate. They recorded every spell, charm, and magical recipe they created. Plus, herbal mixtures, tinctures, lotions, balms, teas...the list was endless.

She alone had filled up eight thick volumes since she started recording her path when her magic came in at five. Those first books were created with the help of an adult until her writing skills developed. Twenty years was a long time, and she'd tried a lot of things. Some successful, some not so much, and all of it was in her Grimoire.

"The thing is, a Grimoire contains a lot of personal stuff. It's like a magical diary. We don't let just anyone read them. We don't just open them up to strangers. My sisters haven't even read mine."

Hyacinth snorted and covered her mouth with her hands.

"That's what you think," Hazel muttered under her breath.

Amber glared at them. She'd deal with them later. Now wasn't the time for family disputes. They had real issues to face.

"Could we just look at some of the older ones? You know, from people who aren't around anymore. If you can't think of anything, and Pearl doesn't remember anything, it stands to reason whatever secret he is trying to dig out must be older than you guys. Doesn't it?"

"He makes a valid point," Hazel conceded. "But I'm not sure having a mundane root around in our history is a good idea. What about you guys?"

Amber shared looks with her family. She reached out to them mentally, feeling them out on the idea of sharing their past. She felt very little reluctance to open up to Kody, which was surprising.

The family ability to touch each other's minds was a blessing and a curse. When her sisters or grandmother were spying on her, it was a pain in the backside. But when one of them was in trouble or needed emotional help, it was an entirely different ball of wax. Now, they conferred with images and thoughts rather than actual words.

Kody jerked back from the table. "What the fuck was that?" he shouted, glaring at Pearl. "Did you just poke my mind? Seriously? I'm done. Figure this out yourself. How is you sticking your nose into my brain any better than what Keres did to Amber?" He stood, pushing his chair away. "Sorry, Amber. I'm done. I won't stick around and let your family dig holes in my head. Take care." He stepped aside, pushed his chair into the table, and stormed away.

"Hang on, Kody." She chased him to the foyer. "Don't let Gramma Pearl put you off. She didn't mean any harm. We just have to be sure..."

"Too bad. She could have asked or something." He slammed his feet into his shoes and yanked the door open. "Your grandmother needs to learn some manners. Bye." The door slammed behind him.

She stood, staring at the carved oak panel, tears streaming down her face. He'd abandoned her. Just like that. The nerve. No! The nerve of her grandmother. She had some explaining to do! She stomped back into the kitchen.

"What the hell?" She stood, hands on her hips, glaring at Pearl. "You probed his mind? How could you? That's the epitome of ill manners. You'd zap my ass if I stuck my nose in someone's brain. What were you thinking? I thought you said fate wanted him here?"

Her grandmother looked marginally chagrined. "He shouldn't have even noticed. You can poke around in a mundane's mind without them knowing."

"I don't even want to know how you know that. What about the rules? The laws? Kody's a good man. He rescued me from Keres, twice, and you're messing with his head? I can't even..." She paced the kitchen, grabbing dishes from the table and slamming them haphazardly into the dishwasher.

"Slow up, girl, you'll scrub the pattern right off," Laz complained and removed several glasses from the dishwasher. "They need more space."

Hyacinth's phone beeped. She glanced at it and looked up apologetically. "I have to run. I've got a patient in labour. I have to get rid of the lingering negativity from this fight." She mumbled a few words and a flash of light passed over her. "Okay, good to go. Catch you later. Don't make any rash decisions while I'm gone. And Gramma Pearl, you owe Amber and Kody an apology." She did a quick check of her medical bag, waggled her fingers, and took off. Nobody moved until they heard the SUV she took on calls drive away.

"She's right," Hazel said. "You screwed up badly, Gramma."

"But he wouldn't have even known if he was a true mundane," Laz suggested. "If he was mundane, he'd have been none-the-wiser, but he obviously has some magic, which makes him a potential threat. I think she did the right thing. He accepted our magic without issue. He didn't even blink at the floating peas or the tea pot. What mundane takes all that in stride?"

"Oh. Grr. You make me so mad. It doesn't matter if he's mundane. If it's wrong, it's wrong," Amber grumbled. "Seriously, I did it once when I was eleven and you bound my magic for an entire month. How is this any different?"

"He has untapped magic potential," Gramma Pearl said, sipping her tea. "I had to know if he was just hiding his magic from us. He's got the glimmer. It's almost nonexistent. I doubt you girls can even sense it. I didn't see it myself until he clashed with Keres on the street today. I had to check. I believe he has magical ancestors, close ones, but doesn't know it. I suspect they've been hiding it from him. He's got untapped power. It's weak, but it's there. And," she set her cup down with a flourish, "I can now say for certain he's not a threat to us. He is who, and what, he claims to be."

"Are you shitting me?" Amber snapped. "You break the rules, one of the cardinal rules at that, and you just brush it off? He's my friend, or at least, he was. I like him; and your stupid mind probing scared him away. What if fate thrust him into our world for a reason? What if we need him?"

"If Fate wants him here, she'll bring him back." She stood and cleared away her teacup and saucer. "Now, you girls tidy up here. I'm going to start searching the Grimoires for information. We need to find a way to protect ourselves from Keres, and more importantly, we need to figure out what he's up to. You may join me when you're finished your chores." She glided through the kitchen and up the back stairs toward their magical library.

"Miserable old bat," Hazel muttered under her breath. "Always ordering us around."

"I heard that," Pearl called down the stairs.

"Ouch. She freaking zapped me," Hazel grumbled.

"You did call her an old bat." Amber laughed. She grew serious again. This was no laughing matter.

Pearl had gone way beyond acceptable behavior. She'd broken one of their primary laws, which was: "Do as you will, with harm to none." Even if Kody hadn't felt it, Pearl had been wrong. Way wrong. Amber would never admit it aloud, but she was somewhat relieved Pearl had confirmed Kody was a decent guy. "Let's get the dishes done and start searching. Who knows what's in those old books?"

Chapter Sixteen

K ody stormed upstairs to his apartment. The old woman had some nerve digging around in his brain. He never should have trusted any of them. "What gave her the right?" he muttered, slamming and locking the door behind him. "Seriously, I can't even believe she did that."

Great, now he was talking to himself! Frankly, he couldn't believe it was even possible. He was seriously reconsidering his decision to move to Three Moon Falls. The place was crazy whacked. Totally nuts. Witches, evil witches. "What's next? Vampires?"

"Vampires aren't real," a voice said from the other side of the room.

"What the living fuck?" Kody blurted. Blood pounded through his body. Adrenaline surged, making his fingers and toes tingle. He crouched into a ready position, arms up to defend himself. He stared around the room. Nobody was there. It was empty, except for the cat on the recliner, licking her paws.

"Holy shit! I'm losing my frigging mind." Kody backed up until he hit the wall. He sidled left and bolted for the front door.

"Chill, dude. I'm just a cat. No need to freak out."

"I'm hallucinating. I have to be hallucinating. Must have been something wrong with my oxygen in the dive yesterday. I need to get to the hospital." He fumbled for the deadbolt. "Or those damned witches poisoned me."

"They didn't poison you. Don't be absurd." The cat made a sound that was too much like laughter for Kody's comfort.

"Um. Okay then. How did you get in here?" *God, he was talking to a cat!*

"I let myself in."

"You did what?"

"I let myself in. I come and go as I please. It's a special, magical, skill. And I said vampires aren't real. Any idiot knows that. They're a product of fiction." The cat's mouth moved in unison with the words before it brushed against his legs.

Kody jumped back. "Get the hell away from me you demon spawn."

"Demons are real," the cat offered. "Vampires, not so much."

Kody closed his eyes and counted to ten. Maybe the cat would be gone when he opened them again. He peeked. The cat grinned up at him. He slammed his eyes shut again

"Can you turn up the heat?" the cat asked. "It's freezing in here. You need to find out what the ghosts want so they stop messing with the heat. I'm pregnant; I've got a belly full of babies, and I need warmth."

"Don't you live *downstairs*?"

"Yes. And no. I like it up here. I like your recliner; it's soft and warm. You look like you need company, so I thought I'd join you. Got a problem with that? I'm Sasha, by the way." She lifted one paw, licked it, and stroked it over her ear, the picture of calm disdain. "You coming back in? I could use a saucer of milk, cream if you have it."

"No cream, just one percent. Will that do, your highness?"

"Delightful, thank you."

Kody massaged his forehead and stumbled into the kitchen. He poured the milk and set it on the floor. "Adequate, I assume?"

"I prefer to dine at the table," Sasha replied.

"No. I draw the line there. It's bad enough I'm talking to you, as if I'm not completely bonkers. I'm not giving you access to my table. Eat on the floor. Take it or leave it."

"Who pooped in your sandbox? You're exceptionally grumpy tonight." She ambled up to the small bowl he'd set down and lapped at it delicately.

"You're exceptionally nosy," he replied, leaning back against the counter to observe his unwanted guest. Milk finished; the cat rubbed herself against his legs. He reached down to tickle her behind the ears.

"Cats are good companions. Talking to them helps you work out your problems," Sasha purred delicately.

"And if my problem is the cat talking back?" he asked wryly.

"Not everyone can hear us, and those who can don't usually acknowledge it. Right there...scratch the base of my neck." She arched up against his hand.

"So, why me? Why pester me?"

"These babies are coming, and soon. I need the heat turned up, and I'll need a doctor. And by doctor, I mean one of those lovely witches who have adopted me. I figure you're a smart guy. You can call them for me. Although, frankly, I didn't think you'd be able to hear me."

"Yeah, me either. Talking cats? I've totally lost it."

"Chillax, dude. There are stranger things in this world than talking cats."

"You've got that right." Talking cats, witches who controlled fire. Floating dishes. Is it just this town, or did this stuff happen everywhere? Did he even want to know? He was so far out of his comfort zone it felt like he was deep-sea diving without an oxygen tank. "How close are you? Do you need the vet now?"

"A vet?" the cat screeched. "Vets are for animals. Honey, I need Hyacinth. She's a healer, or didn't you notice?" She glared at him and strode over to the recliner. She hopped up, her heavy belly making the short jump awkward.

"Off my chair." He kicked off his shoes, scooped up the cat, and took over the chair. She immediately jumped onto his lap and settled in.

"You might be an adequate sleeping place. Excuse me while I catch a few winks." She closed her eyes, kneaded his legs twice, and went still. Only the slight rise and fall of her chest showed she was alive.

"Now what?" he mumbled. A talking cat, magic, ghosts, witches. Sasha was warm and cozy on his lap, emphasising the room's chill. He knew the temp should be up. He'd changed out the thermostat and programmed the new one to come on just before he got home in the evening.

"Hey, ghost, do me a favor and jack up the heat, will ya? I'm freezing to death here." Unsurprisingly, no one answered his request, but in a few moments, the heat clicked on. "Thank you," he called out, grateful for the warmth and not caring he was talking to ghosts and cats.

He sat there, cat on his lap, for half an hour, randomly flipping through the channels on television. He'd barely settled on a deep-sea fishing reality show when the cat grew restless. He murmured words of comfort and stroked her side. Her belly rippled under his fingers, and she let out a howl. Her claws dug into his legs. His thighs tensed, but he resisted the urge to pitch her to the floor.

"Okay, call the witches," she hissed.

"I don't have her number." He paused. "I'll call the shop. Maybe there's an emergency number." Moments later, he had Amber on the phone. "Hi, this is Kody. Your cat is in my apartment, and she's in labour. Can you come help her?"

"Help her? Is she in distress? Cats give birth every day without help. I was just getting ready for bed."

Kody pushed aside a mental image of Amber in a slinky nightgown to focus on the issue at hand. "Um. She says she needs you guys," he blurted, feeling like an imbecile.

"She does, does she?" Amber laughed. "Well, if my cat's talking to you, it must be serious. Hyacinth's better with animals than I am, but she's on a call. I'll head over and talk to the cat." The laughter in her voice was unmistakable.

He ignored it. "Thank you. I'll tell her you're coming."

Amber knocked on Kody's door with the toe of her shoe. She clutched a cardboard box full of old towels in one hand and a thermos of tea in the other. The door flew open immediately. She jumped back. "Whoa."

"Sorry. She's driving me crazy. That cat nags worse than an old lady. Thanks for coming. Come in. Let me help." He lifted the box from her arms. "What's all this?"

"A box and bedding for her to have the babies in. Queening, that's what the process is called, is messy. She'll need a safe dry place to birth in, and clean bedding for afterward. I assumed you wouldn't have much since you just moved in."

His face blanched. "Thanks. I don't have to watch, do I?"

Amber laughed. "Of course not. We'll just set up the bed, show her the space, and leave her to it. She knows what to do. It's instinct."

"So, why are you here?"

"You tell me. You called me." Amber laughed at the puzzled look on his face. Was this just an excuse to get her to come over? It felt like a trick. Unease prickled her belly. Visions of high school and being invited to a tobogganing party where no one else showed up ran through her head. The elation at being invited, the worry when she found herself alone. The agony and disillusionment of giving up and heading home, frozen half to death, in the sub-zero December weather. Her brows pinched together.

Sasha let out a howl and lay down at Amber's feet, her writhing belly on full display. She was definitely in labour. Those kittens could come anytime in the next four or five hours. At least he wasn't pranking her for their earlier disagreement.

"Let's get this bed set up. Where would you like it? Some place private is best."

"In your shop would be perfect," Kody suggested. "But she says she wants to be here."

"How did she get here?" Amber asked, ignoring her jealousy that he could talk to cats.

"She let herself in; though, I have no idea why or how. Cat, you should talk to Amber, before she thinks I'm nuts." He glared down at Sasha, who ignored him with typical cat disdain and aplomb. "Let's put it in the spare bedroom. Lots of room for her and for us, if we need to check on her."

Sasha rose regally to her feet and padded off in the direction of the empty guest room. She cast an impatient glance over her shoulder as she disappeared around the corner.

"Did she just tell us to hurry?" Amber asked, following the cat.

They set a large apple box in the corner, padding it with a thick layer of rags. The box was cut low on one side to allow easy access for both cat and humans. Sasha climbed through the opening, walked in circles, stepped out, and grabbed a piece of toweling with her teeth. She tugged it out of the box, walked back, and lay down. She looked at them, and then at the door.

"I guess she's telling us to leave her alone for now." Amber laughed. Sasha blinked twice, closed her eyes, and ignored them.

"I'm telling you, she talks," Kody said as they settled into chairs in the living room. "Full sentences. I'd swear she's human. Can people be turned into cats?"

"Don't be ridiculous. That type of magic doesn't exist. I wonder how she got up here. You sure she didn't slip in when you weren't looking?"

"One hundred percent. She was in the shop with you today. I saw her there. She was there when I left. When I got home, she was sitting on my recliner. She informed me vampires aren't real. Although, apparently, demons are."

Amber laughed nervously. Was he losing his mind? Too much or too little oxygen in his dives?

"You can wipe the skeptical look off your face. The cat talks. She even complains about the temperature. Trust me on this."

The feeling this was all an elaborate set up passed through her mind. It was totally juvenile of him, but she'd humor him for now, at least as long as Sasha was in labor. If he carried this any further, she'd walk out and leave him to his fear of a pregnant cat.

"Whatever you say, Kody. I know some people have a special affinity for animals and seem to understand them. Maybe that's what you're experiencing." She couldn't keep the skepticism from her voice. She softened her tone. "Thanks for letting her birth here. I appreciate it; and I'm glad you invited me to take part. I haven't seen kittens born since I was a teenager."

"Not even the ones I saw on your step?"

"No, they all wandered in as adults. Nobody claimed them, and we kept them. Much like Sasha. A stray looking for a friendly place to hang out. Of course, she's the only one who was pregnant. I just can't resist a stray. Must be why I keep talking to you." She flashed him a grin.

Sasha yowled in the other room. Amber leaped to her feet and hurried down the short hallway. A small, glistening bundle of ebony fur lay in front of Sasha.

"Oh, your first baby," Kody cooed, kneeling before the box. "Can I touch it?" He looked at the cat; she looked away. He stroked one finger lightly down the kitten's back. It mewed and wiggled.

"It's adorable. Well done, mama cat. You have one beautiful baby. There are a few more to come. Keep it up," Amber praised, stroking Sasha on the head. "Should we go?"

"Neoo," Sasha responded.

"I told you she talks." Kody jumped on the cat's response.

"She meowed." Amber chuckled and mock punched Kody on the arm. "Get a grip, man." She leaned back against the wall to wait for the next birth. Thirty minutes later, kitten number two arrived—a perfectly white beauty.

"Oh, look," Amber declared. "It's so adorable. I want to keep both of them. The vet says she's having six. I wonder what the next one will look like."

"I'm hoping for orange." Kody leaned against the wall on the opposite side of the box. "Have you ever been diving?" he asked.

"A few times, actually. I took some beginner diving lessons while I was in college. I enjoyed it, but it was hard to find the time to dive. I had classes and worked part-time to pay my way. I couldn't spare much time to travel out of the city to a lake for practise. I am recreationally certified. I even stood watch on the dive boat a few times for large group dives. I'd love to go again now that everything is up and running. Soon, I'll have an occasional free day."

"I'd be happy to take you sometime," he offered.

"I'd like that. Thanks." They talked quietly about diving for a while. She thought he might bring up Gramma Pearl poking into his mind, of the magic he'd seen, but he didn't, so she let sleeping dogs lie. She was enjoying their conversation and didn't want to ruin it.

A soft meow woke Amber. Sunlight streamed through a gap in the curtains. She bolted upright. Morning? Already? Where had the night gone? She struggled to her feet, nearly tripping over a fuzzy navy and grey fleece blanket. Kody must have covered her up when she fell asleep. A pillow lay where her head had rested. How sweet; he'd given her a pillow and blanket. She didn't even remember being tired. Just talking casually and watching Sasha. Now, she had to face him, despite her chagrin at falling asleep when she was supposed to be watching Sasha.

"Good morning, mama cat. Let me see your babies." She squatted beside the box. The messy birth bedding had been swapped out with the clean towels she'd brought. Sasha rested at the back of the box. In front of her, an all black kitten lay alongside a white one, a grey one, a tabby, and two orange and white fluff balls with longer hair. Genetics made for adorably different kittens.

The scent of coffee drifted into the room, tickling Amber's nose.

"That's my cue. Coffee time." She glanced at her watch. Wow, nearly nine. They must have talked later than she realized for her to sleep beyond six in the morning, and on the floor, too. "I'll check on you later and make sure you have a litter box and food." She stroked each kitten one last time and headed for the kitchen.

Chapter Seventeen

"Where were you last night?" Lazuli teased Amber when she entered the shop.

Laz looked like a breath of fresh air. Her bright, sky blue capris were topped with a cloud patterned T-shirt. Her waist length blonde-brown hair was piled on her head in a messy updo, and she'd traded in her contacts for blue framed glasses that emphasized her laughing hazel eyes. She looked like the air element she channelled. Amber felt dowdy wearing last night's clothing. Maybe she could find time to run home and change.

"Darn. I hoped I'd make it in before you," Amber admitted. "I was helping Sasha give birth." She set the heavy ceramic mug of coffee Kody had given her on the counter beside the cash register.

"Since when does a cat need help having kittens? And how did you know she was having them? Sounds suspect to me. I can't even find her this morning. If she was having babies, where are they, and better yet, where is she?" Lazuli shot the questions out, rapid-fire, barely breathing between them. She stood, hands on her hips, looking more like a disappointed mother than a nosy sister.

"She's upstairs, in Kody's apartment, with six beautiful babies." There was no sense avoiding the questions. Laz would hound her until she got the answers she wanted.

Laz might only be older than Amber by a year, but in terms of dominance, it felt like she was ten years Amber's senior. She had a gift for laying on responsibility, which reacted badly to Amber's already over-active guilt-gut. She shouldn't feel bad about being out all night; she'd done nothing wrong, but somehow, it felt like a guilty pleasure she should keep secret. Curses to feeling double guilt. One dose from their grandmother, the other from their mother. Amber hadn't mastered it nearly as well as she'd like to and was entirely too susceptible to their penetrating, questioning stares.

"Get your nose out of my business. I need breakfast." Amber trudged behind the counter.

"You spent the night with him, and he didn't even feed you? How rude, not to mention pathetic. Lucky for you, Gramma noticed you were away and sent you a slice of bacon cheddar quiche and a bowl of fruit salad. It's in the kitchen. Gramma wants an update on where you were."

Amber rolled her eyes. "Quiche sounds perfect. I'll call her later, after I open the shop, and eat. For your information, he offered to feed me. He did give me coffee." She picked up the black and white mottled mug and toasted her sister with it. He'd fixed it just the way she liked it—piping hot with a shot of milk and two teaspoons of sugar. She sipped the steaming brew, set it down, and unlocked the small safe hidden in the cupboard behind the cash desk. She recounted the day's float and after ensuring it was correct, slid it into the register. "Can you unlock the door and watch the front while I eat? I'd really appreciate it."

"I'll unlock the door and come talk to you while you eat. The bell will tell me if someone comes in. You're not escaping me that easily." She cackled like a cartoon witch and rubbed her hands together.

"Whatever." Amber slipped past her sister and into the back room. Sisters were such a curse. Of course, there were times when they were also a blessing. Like now. She grinned down at the large slice of quiche her sister had left on the table. "Jackpot!"

She slid the plate into the microwave just as Laz entered the room. "Unlocked and ready to go," she declared, sliding into a chair at the small table. "Now, dish. Give me all the deets. Tell me all about spending the night with the delicious Kody Wilkins." She waved her arm impatiently.

"Seriously, there's nothing to tell. We sat and watched Sasha having her babies. We chatted about nothing, and I fell asleep on the floor. Nothing to tell." She paused. "Except he insists Sasha talks to him."

Laz chuckled. "Good one. Though, he could be animal sensitive. Gramma Pearl did say he has untapped magic. This could be part of it."

"I don't know; Hyacinth didn't get anything from Sasha. No hints of chatter, and you know as well as I do, having latent magic doesn't mean you'll ever use it or even realize you have it. In the hundreds of years since magic was an everyday thing, people have forgotten all about it or have labelled it as a frightening fairy tale. Although, if Kody keeps hanging around us, he's in for a rude awakening." Amber touched the top of her quiche; it wasn't quite ready, so she slid it back in the microwave.

"I can't believe Gramma Pearl poked her nose into his head. Seriously, what was she thinking? Mind probing is the ultimate insult. It's a violation. Not rape, exactly, but damned close. She'd have kicked our asses around the block if she caught us doing it, but she went ahead and did it anyway. She scared him."

"Did he say that?" Laz leaned back and put her feet on the table. Amber slapped them off and wiped it down with their custom blend cleaning spray.

"Funny thing is, he didn't mention it last night. I thought he might, but he let it slide. I sure wasn't going to bring it up. Not after he invited me to watch the babies being born. Which reminds me, I have to run up some food and the litter box before he leaves for work."

She gathered the supplies in one arm and tried to unlock the stairwell door with her other hand. The key jammed, and Amber had to wiggle the knob to get it to click free. When the door did unlock, it was wedged tight. Setting the supplies on the floor, she pulled and yanked until the door broke free with an eerie wood-on-wood sound. She grabbed the cat's food and dish, scooped up the litter box, thankfully it was clean, and jogged quickly upstairs, keeping to the side. There were fresh tracks in the thick dust covering the stairs, and she didn't want to mess them up. It looked like someone had come down and went back up. She rapped on Kody's door. It opened almost immediately. He'd changed since she left. Last night's T-shirt was replaced with a crisp plaid button-down shirt. The sleeves were rolled up to his elbows, revealing his muscular tanned arms. She almost reached out to touch their light dusting of hair. Nope. She was not going to touch him.

"Amber, hi. I was just about to come see if you forgot. Let me take that." His green eyes brightened with his wide smile.

Dang. A girl could drown in those eyes. She blinked and handed the items to him. "Hey, have you been using the stairs?" She gestured behind her. "Someone's been up here, and it wasn't me."

He peered around her and blinked rapidly. "They're big tracks, but they aren't mine. Could they belong to one of your sisters? Or your grandmother? Look how they end without touching the top step. Aside from mine from the night we met, yours are the only ones there."

"They're too large to be mine, but I'll double check with everyone. Oddly, the lock was stuck, too, and I tested it the other day, just to confirm it was locked. Today, the door was jammed. I thought I'd have to go around the back way rather than up the stairs."

"I can have a look at it later, if you want. Maybe it just needs a shot of lube. I've got to run now, or I'll be late for my first dive. Oh, I'm holding you to your promise to dive with me, soon." He grinned.

"I don't recall promising to go, but I'd like to. Thanks. Can you let me know when you're home, so I can come check the kittens? Hyacinth will probably want to give them a once over as well, if it's okay with you."

"Sure thing. I'll see you later then." He smiled broadly, and for a moment, she was lost in his eyes. His smile widened, and the corners of his eyes crinkled.

Heat suffused her face, and she glanced away. Good grief, she was staring. "Thanks for looking after Sasha," she mumbled. She pivoted and flew down the stairs. Gracious, his smile made her feel like a schoolgirl, and she was blushing like one, too. She stopped at the base of the stairs to take a few breaths. No sense letting Laz see her all flustered and red-faced. Laz was too gleeful about Amber not coming home last night. No sense adding fuel to the fire.

Thankfully, Laz had disappeared into the front. Amber shoved the door shut, locked it behind her, and went to check her breakfast. She ate quickly, eager to get to work. As always, the quiche was moist and tasty with just the right balance of herbs, bacon, cheese, and eggs. The crust was tender, even after a trip through the microwave. She had no idea what her grandmother's pie crust secret was, but it was one Amber never mastered, despite countless efforts.

Laz was deep in conversation with a fellow witch, Danica Maes. Her bright pink pixie cut had been died in shades of teal and purple, a striking, if somewhat shocking look which suited her to a T. Her gunmetal-black dress was cut high on her tanned thighs. Her sandals were sparkling silver. She looked set for a night on the town rather than a day of haircuts and perms.

"Love the hair," Amber declared, high-fiving Danica. "It suits you."

"Good morning, Amber. I just stopped by to get some willow bark for tea. I was just telling Laz that your front lock is all scratched up."

"What? It is?"

"Didn't your landlord change the locks when you moved in? He should have. Go look at it."

Amber rushed to the door with Laz and Danica hot on her heels. The deadbolt lock was scratched and scraped, as if someone had been digging at it with a sharp instrument.

"That was a brand-new deadbolt. It looks like someone tried to jimmy it. We should call the police." Lazuli glared at the lock.

"I don't know." Amber hesitated. "Can you see the traces of magic?" The deadbolt had a dark shimmer to it; she recognized it as magical remnants. Good magic left a glowing effervescence that dissipated over time. Negative, dark, or black magic left a lingering darkness. The more magic used, the greater the glimmer left behind or the bigger the dark shadow. The lock had the slightest hint of a dark shadow.

Whoever had magicked it hadn't tried very hard, leaving only two possibilities. Either they'd given up and gone away, or they'd made it past the magical, floral wards her family had put up. Whoever had gotten in could have magicked the lock closed when they left.

"I don't like it," Laz said. "Who would want in here? I mean, besides Keres?"

"And why would they lock the door after themselves?" Danica said. She held her hands over the deadbolt, one on the inside, one on the outside, not quite touching it. "I don't get anything from this. Just the magic traces. There's nothing to identify the caster, or the magic's intent. Except, it's dark. I don't like this a bit. We should call the mayor. She might be able to read more."

"What about Leticia Stone?" Amber suggested. As a hereditary voodoo priestess, Leticia had a different type of magic than everyone else, earthier and darker than Amber's, though Leticia only used it for good. Maybe she could see something. "I'll call the station and see if she's in."

"You're right," Corporal Wong said fifteen minutes later. "Someone tried to open this." He squinted narrowly at Amber. "Your family sure seems to keep popping up lately, and I don't like it."

Amber swallowed a snarky comment. She'd asked for Leticia, and instead, dispatch had sent Wong. He wasn't a bad guy; he just had it in for them. Maybe he was subconsciously aware of magic even though he didn't believe. The imbalance would leave him uncomfortable and defensive.

"Sorry. We don't mean to be a bother. It doesn't look like they got inside, the doors were both locked this morning, and nothing is missing." She didn't bother mentioning the strange footprints on the stairs. He'd only blame Kody, and she didn't think it was him. He'd been too surprised to see them, and unless he stepped over the top step, they couldn't be his. Mentioning the tracks would only cloud the issue.

She smiled at Wong. "We just thought the police would like to know someone's trying to get into shops. Maybe some of my neighbors were targeted as well." She doubted it, but it couldn't hurt to find out, and she'd contact them herself once he was gone.

Wong dusted the door edges and deadbolt for prints, found nothing useful, and totally destroyed the magical traces while doing so. The only fingerprints were where Laz had pulled the door open and blocked it. The rest of the door had been wiped clean. Amber wanted to smack her head into the wall in frustration. Instead, she thanked Wong for his time and forced herself to be polite while he wandered through the store, grumbling about nonsense, gullible people, and wasted time. Finally, he seemed ready to leave. She walked him to the door and held the outer screen door open for him.

Movement across the street caught her eye. Keres sat on a bench alongside his friend from the parade. His friend fidgeted on the seat, as if he wanted to be elsewhere. Keres glared at him and turned to face Amber. He smiled menacingly and waggled his fingers in a parody of a wave. A chill ran through her, lodging at the base of her spine. She wanted to slam the door on him and cleanse herself. Instead, she made a moment of small talk with Wong and stepped back into the store, leaving the inner door open and the screen closed to keep insects out.

"I don't care for him at all," she declared, joining her sister and Danica near the register. "He's frustrating to deal with, and his disbelief is annoying." Disbelief was one thing; open mockery was another. Witches faced it all the time, and it never got easier. In Wong's case, it was worse, because he didn't treat them with the respect he was known for on official business. "He's a good cop, but so prejudiced against magicals. I wonder how he even knows about us. I know we're out of the broom closet, but most mundanes just think we're eccentrics."

"Maybe he's sensitive to magic?" Laz suggested.

"Maybe he just listens to the rumor mill," Danica said with a laugh.

"I guess it doesn't matter," Amber added. "He's gone now, and I think I know who it was. Keres and his crony are across the street, watching this place. We have to figure out what he wants."

"I'll keep my ears open at the salon." Danica glanced at her watch. "Shoot. I've got a client, right now. I better grab my tea and scoot."

Amber grabbed her a pre-package brown bag of willow bark. "I'll make a note, and you can drop by later to settle up so you're not late."

"Thanks. Blessed be, and catch you later."

"Blessed be," Amber and Lazuli returned the familiar witchy salutation as their friend scurried out the door.

"Can you believe it's only ten?" Amber asked. "It feels like the day should be half over, and I haven't had the chance to ask you about the stairs."

Laz gave her a blank look.

"When I took the inside stairs up to drop off the cat stuff, there were tracks in the dust. Except the top step. Someone had been up and down the stairs, or down and up. I don't know which. Was it you?"

"No." She strung the work into three syllables. "We made a deal to leave the door locked and stay away from the apartment. Besides, isn't the only key on your key ring? Was Kody sneaking down?"

"He says no, and I believe him. I think. Mine is the only key for the bottom door. Unless Jason has one." She wasn't entirely sure she trusted Jason, but she couldn't fathom a reason why he'd be sneaking around. He didn't even bother visiting his tenants unless they called with an issue.

Amber's cell phone vibrated in her pocket. She pulled it out. "Hi, Kody. What's up?"

"You tell me," he said. "I was prepping for a dive, and I got this feeling you were in trouble again. I called as soon as I had the chance. Are you okay?"

She couldn't help but grin. He was definitely magically intuitive. "It's all good. Someone damaged the store lock. I guess they were trying to get in. I called the police. Everything's good now." She couldn't stop the warm fuzzy feelings encompassing her at his concern, like when her mom texted from halfway around the world for no reason.

"Are you sure?" Doubt edged his voice.

"Well, Keres was outside earlier, but he's gone now. We're going to double-up the wards today, and tonight, we'll be searching the books for information."

"I feel like you need to do more. Don't take Keres too lightly. There's something weird about him." He paused. "Call me if you need anything, okay?"

"Will do. Thanks for calling." After a quick goodbye, they hung up.

"Wow, he's got it bad. Watch yourself or you might fall into something you don't want or aren't expecting." A frown pinched Lazuli's brow together. "We need to do a Tarot spread, see what it tells us about you and Kody."

The bells over the door chimed.

"Don't think you're getting out of it that easily," Laz warned under her breath. "We're doing this. Divination is my thing, and I'll do it. With or without you." She grabbed her favorite deck and settled into the divination corner.

Chapter Eighteen

"Last night's birth was tough. I'm glad both mom and baby pulled through okay. They're doing fabulously today. The baby is thriving, just like those kittens. You should see them, Gramma Pearl," Hyacinth enthused. "They're the cutest kittens I've seen in a while. They're all healthy, and Sasha's a great mother."

Amber echoed her sister's sentiments. The sisters sat in the attic turret room with their grandmother. Each held a grimoire in their hands. They made casual conversation as they flipped through the pages, looking for anything which might lead them to Keres' purpose in being in Three Moon Falls.

"I don't know if starting only fifty years ago is the right action," Amber groused. "I have this feeling we should be looking further back." It wasn't just a feeling; it was stronger than that, but not really a premonition. Her fingertips tingled and her brain felt fidgety, like she needed to be doing something different.

"Watch what you're doing!" Hazel snapped, yanking the grimoire out of Amber's hands. "Girl, you need to pay attention. Look at your fingers. You're going to scorch something."

She glanced down at her hands. Zig-zaggy sparks and lightning encased her fingers in an eerie orange-yellow glow. Closer to her fingertips, the sparks glowed blue. "Holy crap." She fisted her hands to extinguish the unexpected flames. "I didn't damage it, did I?" She tucked her fists under her thighs in her most effective control technique. She'd been squelching her power in public this way for years. It never failed her.

"Why are you sparking now?" Gramma Pearl asked. "You haven't done that since grade school."

"I don't know, I was thinking we were looking in the wrong place and whoosh. Maybe my intuition is trying to tell me something? I don't know. Oh, someone's coming." She couldn't divine who, but she had a sudden image of a vehicle turning into the yard. "We better see who it is. The gate doesn't want to let them in."

She hurried to the attic window and looked out. "It's Kody's truck. He's a friend. Why is the gate blocking him?" She didn't know which of their relatives had cast the spell on the gate to make it actively defensive, but it steadfastly refused to admit people they didn't know, or people with ill intent. The gate blocking Kody didn't make sense.

"He did storm out of here in a huff last night. Maybe he angered the gate," Pearl injected, joining Amber at the window. "I expect the house will be biased against him until he proves himself worthy."

The Hawks' family home sat on a hundred and fifty acres of land their ancestors had homesteaded over a hundred years ago after fleeing Salem. With a continual lineage of magic users occupying the house, it had absorbed untold magical remnants and over time, had become magical in itself. The house had been known to slam doors in front of people, to shut her own windows in a storm, and seemed to require almost no maintenance. The last time they'd done maintenance was when a contractor accidentally dropped a tree on the porch six years ago.

"I wonder what he wants?" Pearl asked.

"I'll go find out." Amber turned to look at her sister. "Hazel, can you cast something to get the gate to open, just this once, so I don't have to run down there?"

Hazel was the most skilled at telekinesis of all of them. She could move things with her mind from further away than the rest of them. Amber expected her to open the gate from here; she'd done it before.

Hazel stood, her arms spread into the air, her body and arms forming a large Y-shape. She closed her eyes and chanted under her breath. Thunder rattled the windows, a single bolt of lightning flashed, and buckets of rain dumped down on the house and yard.

Hazel was also a water witch; her skills were in controlling the motion of water. She could call in a storm strong enough to knock you on your backside, or she could control and direct the flow of water in a creek or river. None of the Hawk sisters used their skills lightly, or without serious thought. Messing with Mother Nature's patterns was never a good idea. The gate creaked slowly open, the screech of metal on metal loud even inside the house.

Magic was costly. It sapped their energy and strength, especially large elemental castings like the storm Hazel had called. Strong but brief, it let the gate feel her intention to allow Kody in. Hazel must have called the storm with a dual purpose, opening the gate and showing off for Kody.

"Damn. It'll never cease to amaze me that you can call rain out of a clear blue sky. Thanks, sis. I actually thought you'd just open it, but a freak storm is awesome." Amber high fived her water-witch sister. "I'll go see what he wants and bring back tea and cookies for you to replenish with."

Despite being raised in a magical family, occasionally, the workings of magic baffled Amber. While always consistent, it wasn't always logical. It didn't make sense that a storm could convey their emotions to an inanimate object, yet somehow, it did. She didn't waste time thinking about it.

Kody drove through and stopped at the top of the driveway. He remained in his truck until Amber appeared on the deck and waved him in.

"That was the freakiest storm I ever saw," he said by way of greeting her. "It came out of nowhere and then was gone just as fast. Crazy."

"Is there something I can do for you, Kody?" she asked politely. Emotionally, she was torn between inviting him in and kicking him out. He had every right to be upset with Pearl, but he'd been rude to them all. Yet, he'd been so nice and had taken care of Sasha.

"I came to see if I can help with the books. What did you call them? Grim—?"

"Grimoires." She studied him. A quick glance behind her revealed the front door remained open. The house hadn't fully accepted him. Yet. "Why?"

"Your shop was broken into, your cat is talking to me, and Keres gives me the creeps. I can't shake the feeling he's up to something, and I want to stop him. I'm not one for believing in the supernatural, or at least, I wasn't." He laughed nervously. "But I've seen some strange crap, and he just feels evil to me. I've read about negative vibes and dark feelings, but I've never felt anything like that before now. Keres is dark, and I don't like it. And...I'm babbling." He dropped his gaze to the porch floor.

Amber couldn't read him, so she shot a quick mental message to Lazuli to see if Kody was on the up and up. Lazuli was their resident psychic. She could read people's intentions; though, she rarely reached out for the vibes people gave off. Lazuli sent back a tentative positive.

"I guess you can come in."

He didn't move, except to look her straight in the eye. "I get it. I panicked and made an ass of myself. I apologize, though I'm still not happy about having my mind read. But if you don't want me here, or if I can't help, just tell me, and I'll go."

Inviting him to help was a big risk. He wasn't family, and witches didn't share their magical secrets and spell books with just anyone. It took a phenomenal degree of trust to do so. Lazuli had given him a conditional pass. Amber herself felt only positive from him. Yeah, he was scared—she could almost smell his fear—and his eyes darted about nervously. Beyond the fear, she didn't sense anything untoward or menacing. The biggest thing coming from him was attraction, to her, and curiosity.

She'd barely finished processing his arrival and emotions before she decided to risk letting him into their family sanctuary and history. "Come on in. Many hands make light work." She walked into the house; Kody followed.

Chapter Nineteen

The door slammed behind them. Kody jumped. "Whoa." He whirled round to stare at the door. "Was that the wind?"

"Yeah, maybe," Amber hedged.

Kody stared at her. It sounded like she was stifling a laugh. What had she said about the house the other night? Oh, yeah, something about the house being magic and keeping strangers away. If it could do that, couldn't it close doors, too? Great, now she had him believing in all this. He almost turned around and left. He wanted to say this was all an elaborate hoax, an illusion or something; yet, part of him was almost certain magic, actual magic, was real. He was living with a talking cat, and apparently, at least one ghost. Were magic houses so unbelievable?

"Are you coming?" Amber asked.

"Sorry, I was a thousand miles away."

She looked beautiful tonight. Her hair flowed loosely around her shoulders, and it glistened in the muted light filtering through the front door's stained-glass windows. Her work jeans were gone, replaced with a flowing, floor length skirt in shades of blue and purple. Not quite flower print, more an abstract look suggesting flowers. She wore a gleaming white tank top that left her tanned arms bare except for silver bracelets that jingled when she walked. Her green eyes shone. Her smile was tentative and beautiful. Her bare feet were adorned with silver toe rings, and a bracelet jingled on her ankle.

Wow. The woman packed a punch. The attraction was at once, both physical and something more. He wanted to talk to her, to get to know her better. He'd seen some strange stuff from her, the whole shooting fire thing was outrageous, but everything he saw and heard made him want to know more and was part of what had driven him to appear on her doorstep, offering to help. He wasn't often indecisive, but it had taken him two hours to work up the courage to climb into his truck and show up.

"Come in. We're upstairs working. Did you want tea?"

"I don't know. Is it going to float over?" he joked. "Because I wouldn't want a pot of tea to *accidentally* dump itself in my lap."

She laughed with him. "That's funny. The kettle's already on. We just need to fix a tea tray and grab a snack."

"Sure, I'd love a cup of tea." He wasn't much of a tea drinker, but it seemed like this family drank a lot of it, and when in Rome...

He followed Amber into the kitchen. The spotless and moderately cluttered house still surprised him. He'd never seen so many candles in one place. Normally, he preferred things clean and neat without much of what his grandmother called bric-a-brac, but the Hawk house was strangely comfortable. At the risk of jumping the gun in an already unsteady relationship, this house felt like home and was vaguely reminiscent of his grandmother's house. Amber filled one tray with an enormous tea pot and cups and saucers. A second tray held cookies, crackers, cheese, sliced fruit, and small plates to eat from. She handed him the fruit tray.

"I can take the other. It looks heavy."

"I'll manage; it's not bad with a bit of a magical lift." Her laughter reminded him of chimes in a light breeze. "Let's head up."

The stairwell was lined with photographs, some ancient, some more recent. Every inch was covered from floor to ceiling, a collage of their family through history. No one in his family was sentimental. Of course, with his family's military history, they'd never stayed in one place more than a few years. His grandmother had some old family pictures but only displayed a few recent ones. When he finally bought a place of his own, he'd hang a few.

"This is it," Amber declared, gesturing to the room with a jerk of her chin.

"Holy shit." Books of every imaginable color and size lined the walls. Only the wall by the door was free of shelves. "I mean, wow. What a library." Heat rose in his cheeks.

"Impressive, right? Our whole family history is here. The oldest are there." She set the tray down and pointed to the top left shelf. "Time-wise, they go across each shelving unit. Left to right. Top to bottom. The next shelf starts again at the top. We have spell books from as far back as 1653."

"That's incredible." The history in their personal records was incredible. A historian would have a field day in here. "Did every member of your family keep journals?"

"Most. Our birth fathers don't have any; they weren't magical, but our stepfather does. Although, they aren't in here. We tend to keep our personal journals to ourselves until we're older. Mine are stored in my room under lock and key to keep my snoopy sisters from reading them. They're part grimoire and part journal. These yahoos," she gestured toward her sisters, "don't need to know my personal thoughts."

"As if we haven't read them anyway," Hazel teased. "You're my big sister. I want to know everything about you. I worship the ground you walk on." Unable to keep a straight face, she smirked and laughed outright.

"Yeah, yeah, laugh it up. We've read yours, too."

Hazel leaped to her feet. "You better not have!"

Amber laughed. "Not so much fun when the shoe is on the other foot, is it?"

"Sit down, Kody. Ignore those girls. We have work to do. Do you know anything about magic?" Pearl asked.

"Frankly, nothing. I've done a bit of reading about Wicca and Paganism, but only in general terms. There's a lot of conflicting information out there. I thought it best to go right to the source, if you don't mind answering questions as we read."

"Humph. You're smarter than I gave you credit for." Pearl nodded sagely.

Talk about being damned by faint praise. He accepted the back-handed compliment, or insult, without comment and sat down in an empty chair. The room itself was an enormous circle twelve feet across. It had three multi-paned stained-glass windows. Six comfortable looking chairs were set in two chair groupings with sturdy mosaic tile tables between each pair. He sat beside a table depicting an enormous tree with roots that mirrored the branches. He'd learned it was a tree of life, and the mirror image represented "as above, so below." A reminder that what you were on the inside was reflected on the outside and vise versa. Again, candles littered every flat surface. Several were burning despite the pole lamps standing between the chairs. The candles must be more for atmosphere than for light.

"Where do I start?" he asked.

Amber handed him a book. "This one's about a hundred and fifty years old. You can start with it. Flip through it. We're looking more for stories than spells, I think. We're trying to find a clue as to why Keres is hounding us."

"That's not much to go on, but I'll look." He stroked the book cover. Butter-soft leather embossed with leaves and flowers and the initials WAH. "Are you sure it's okay to handle them? Don't we need gloves or something?"

"It's fine. They're spelled to resist damage," Amber said, sitting beside him and flipping open her own book.

Another spell. Was there no end to them? Was there nothing they couldn't do? Well, in for a penny, in for a pound. He stroked the leaves with his fingers. They felt almost alive. Right, because it made sense that a book was alive. He was losing his freaking mind. He flipped open the cover. The first page was an intricately drawn picture of a woman standing in the forest with her arms raised to the sky. A full moon peered down at her. The picture covered both the first page and the inside of the cover and was painted with such precision it was like looking at a photograph. Every leaf and flower were perfectly depicted, right down to the veins and shading. Bright light radiated from the moon illuminating the entire scene. It was awe inspiring. The bottom right hand half of the picture depicted a scroll with the name Willow Amber Hawk written in flowing script and the year 1865. He studied the details for a moment before turning to the first page.

July 15, 1886

The weather's been terrible for weeks now. The garden is flooded.

Perchance our rain dance was too strong. The rains came with a vengeance. Too much water, too late. If it does not stop, all my crops shall be lost. I'm going to try another spell. If good fortune prevails, I shall have success.

A simple spell in the same handwriting followed the entry. Curious, Kody read the following entry to see if the author had managed to stop the rain. Four entries later, the rain had stopped, and he was hooked, yanked right into the past. He should have been skimming, but the history in the entries had him enthralled.

"Any luck?" Amber asked.

Kody looked up. Everyone except Amber was gone. "Pardon me?" he asked. He picked up his stone-cold tea. He must have been reading for longer than he realized.

"Are you finding anything? You're turning the pages quickly. You haven't looked up once."

"Nothing here." He nodded at the heavy book in his lap. "Just simple spells and rituals. Lots of information on day to day farm life. They're about to break ground for a new house, this one, I guess. The area is described perfectly. It's been a rough summer; the weather's been erratic. It's fascinating reading, but there's been no mention of anything that might interest Keres. Although, I don't actually know what I'm looking for. Where did everyone go."

"They're taking a break, downstairs," Amber replied.

Kody stood and placed the book on his chair. Twisting left and right, he stretched out his back. "I'm totally kinked up. I won't be able to move tomorrow." He flexed and contorted his body until the ache went away. "Ah. Much better," he exclaimed, bending to touch his toes. "This is incredible. It's like reading fiction, yet it has an amazing ring of reality to it."

"It was reality," she said dryly. "How many times have you seen our magic, and yet you doubt it?" Blue light flickered at her fingertips. She pointed to his teacup. "Drink up. It's warm now."

Steam rose from the surface of his drink. "Wow. That's cool."

"I was going for hot," she joked.

"What else can you do?"

She walked to the table opposite her and replaced a candle that had burned down to nothing with a fresh one. Sparks flew from her fingertip, and the candle's wick burst into flame.

"Wow. If I'm ever lost in the woods, I want you there to build me a fire. I could watch your magic a hundred times and not get bored."

"I don't usually light candles with fire. Mostly, we do everything the normal way. There's a balance to be maintained. Too much magic makes you weak. Too little and the power builds up inside you and can burst forth without warning. It happens most to teenagers. Their emotions are so tumultuous things can go awry if they're not careful."

"Did that happen to you?" He looked her right in the eye. "I mean, if you want to share with me. You don't have to."

"Only once." She looked down at the floor, her cheeks flushed bright pink. "I was twelve and totally in love with this boy. Alexander Granger. He was a total jock. I was a total nerd. I asked him to the Sadie Hawkins Dance, and he laughed in my face. I wasn't cool enough for him."

"He was a jerk." Who did that to a girl? Kody's mom would have kicked his ass. He might have declined, but not rudely. Hell, who was he kidding? If a pretty girl had asked him out, he'd have blundered into a way to say yes. He'd barely dated as a kid. Science club was his world, and girls were strange creatures he didn't understand. Frankly, he didn't comprehend the way their minds worked.

"Thanks for caring." Amber smiled up at him.

"So, what happened after he acted like a total moron?"

"I ran away. I managed not to cry until I got to the woods, by then the hurt was gone, sort of, and I was just angry. I screamed at him, something like, "May you burn in hell, Alexander Granger." The next thing I knew, the dry grass at my feet was on fire. I zapped my emotions into a spell and set the forest on fire."

"Holy hell!"

"It's a good thing Hazel followed me into the woods. She called a flood of water from the river and doused my disaster. It was so dry that summer it was a wonder we got the fire out."

"And the Granger jerk?"

Amber laughed. "I shouldn't laugh; it's not funny." Her eyes sparkled with glee. "He fell asleep beside his parent's pool and got a wicked sunburn. He ended up in the hospital overnight and didn't even get to go to the dance. I, on the other hand, went and had a wonderful time. At least he didn't suffer any long-term damage."

"Sweet victory," Kody enthused. "Does that happen often? Spells going crazy?" Out of control magic would suck. He couldn't even fathom a world where words could create such havoc; yet, he'd seen magic performed several times. The universe was full of strange, fascinating, and frightening things—including Amber Hawk.

"The thing about magic is it's all about intent. You have to be very certain of your intent, and your wording, or you might get something other than what you actually desire. Basically, a spell is like a prayer, often with props. There's a lot of ceremony to go with the words. Sure, you can cast a spell without the ritual, but the strongest spells take a bit of formality. Music, chanting, or bells are often included."

"And poetry, too, from what I've read." Several of the spells he'd read in the grimoire had lyrical poems along with them. "Why is that?"

"Rhymes are easier to remember than plain words. Things are usually repeated three times; rhyming makes it easier to remember."

"Do you mean the rule of three from the movies?" He picked up his book and sat on the edge of the chair, book in his lap. His fear of magic was morphing into fascination.

"Sort of. Our family does have a rule of three, but not everyone else believes in it. What you do, good or bad, comes back to you three-fold. Karma. It isn't a tit for a tat. It's like, if you trample your neighbors' flowers deliberately, you might get into a fender bender. Does that make sense?"

"It does, but it leads to another question. If you have that rule, why doesn't everyone else? I mean, Christians all follow basically the same rules, as do Catholics. So, why not witches?"

"It's complicated." She laughed. "I don't mean to be trite. We're not just witches. We're Wiccan. You and I talked about this, the harm none rule. Not all witches are Pagan, not all witches are Wiccan. Not all Pagans are witches or Wiccan. You can choose to be any combination. Witchcraft is a practice; Paganism is a way of life, and Wicca is a religion. We just happen to be all three." She flipped pages in her book and scanned the text as she talked.

"I'm going to have to do more research. Are there any good books? I like to research new things. I tried the internet, but there's so much conflicting information I don't know what's accurate." He'd spent hours on the internet the past few nights.

Witch sites often lead to some crazy shit, some of it very dark and sometimes evil. Wiccan sites were never the same. He hadn't even tried reading on Paganism. He leaned back and opened the book to where he'd left off. He hadn't even finished his first grimoire, and she had completed seven of them. He'd have to pick up the pace; but this topic was complex, and he was finding it difficult to divide his attention.

"I can send you to a few good sites," Amber offered. She pulled her phone from her pocket. "What's your email?"

She entered the address he gave her and sent him a few links. "These links are trustworthy sites to information on witches, Wicca and Paganism, but it's important to remember, no matter which path you're reading up on there are variations. Take my family for example. We don't worship a god, we work *with* The Goddess and her consort, The Green Man. I call them Mother Earth and Father Sky. My cousins call them Lord and Lady. They aren't actual beings; they are representative of the power residing within everything. The interconnectedness of all living things...like the Force in Star Wars. Although, I doubt Star Wars fans would think it's the same thing."

"Thanks for the references. I appreciate it. I guess I better hurry with this book. I'm falling behind." He nodded to her completed stack.

"Don't worry and don't rush it. The brain needs breaks. Plus, you aren't as familiar with this as I am. If you go too fast, you might miss something. There's no sense rushing through the job if we have to double back and start over. My great-grandmother used to say, "The hurrieder I go, the behinder I get." Kind of a fun way to word it, if you ask me."

"That is fun. I'll keep plodding along." He picked up his cup and carefully sipped his tea, making sure it didn't spill. It would be a shame to damage the book, even if the books were spelled to protect them. This was an historical document after all.

The rest of the family came back from wherever they'd disappeared to.

"I think I found something," Amber interrupted.

"What?" Her sisters crowded around her chair, shoving to get the best view of the grimoire she held on her lap.

"This." She tapped the left-hand page, which was filled with scribbled handwriting, in several different hands, going in all directions, even overlapping. "It's difficult to read."

"What's it say?" Kody asked, leaning over the table between them for a better look.

"Something about a story one of our ancestors told their grand-daughter. Look here." She traced a line of faded, shaky printing with one finger. "*My memory fails, yet I recall bits of my youth where I spent hours with my grandmother. She told a tale of running away from persecution and taking an object with her to keep it safe. I don't remember precisely, perhaps it was just another bedtime story, but many of her yarns held important truths I discovered as I aged.*" Amber paused and looked up at everyone. "It could be a clue to something, don't you think?"

"Maybe," Kody said. "It's not much to go on. Do you think there could be a, what would you call it, a talisman, a relic? Do you think it might exist?"

"I don't know," Hazel muttered. "It sounds more like fragments of an old bedtime story to me. Something to entertain a child. It's too vague to get anything from."

"I don't know. Something about it rings true." Lazuli rubbed her arms. "It makes my skin prickle, like a premonition, but not quite. Keep reading."

"That's just it, there isn't anything else here. I've skimmed the next ten pages and didn't find anything. If I could figure out whose handwriting this is, I'd go directly to their journals. But it's just a random notation on top of a bunch of notes on crystal magic."

"Crystal magic? You can do magic with crystals? Like rocks?" Kody's brow wrinkled.

"You can, and I do. They can be used for a lot of things," Amber said defensively.

"Oh. There's so much I need to research. I've learned some crazy shit reading these books. Now magic rocks? What's next? Sea monkeys?"

"Don't be silly. Sea monkeys are just brine shrimp." Hyacinth laughed and returned to the chair she'd been in earlier. "They are kind of cute though."

"I had no idea," Kody said. "I knew there weren't actual sea monkeys. I just didn't know what they were." He yawned broadly.

"Are we boring you?" Amber said with a wink.

"Not one bit, but I've got an eight-a.m. dive tomorrow." He glanced at his watch. "I better hit the road. It's pushing two already, and I need a few hours sleep. I'd like to come back and help research, if you don't mind?"

Chapter Twenty

"I can't believe this." Amber stared at the back door of Four Seasons Metaphysical. The outer screen door had been ripped right off, leaving splinters of wood poking out from the broken frame. The inner door hung crookedly; the top two sets of hinges busted clean off. A muddy footprint marred the white surface, right below the knob. Lights she'd shut off earlier blazed from inside. "Somebody kicked in my door!"

Her stomach clenched, the contents threatening to come back up. She swallowed hard and wrapped her hands around her waist. Karma was kicking her ass for something. The trouble was, she had no idea what she'd screwed up or when. There was no way this was a random act of violence. It felt personal. Keres not Karma.

"Mine, too." Kody paced back and forth outside where they stood behind the shop. "I called you as soon as I got home, then called the police." His hands fisted and opened and fisted again. His breathing was harsh. Anger poured from him, fueling her own.

Flashing lights heralded the arrival of a police cruiser. The car stopped, and Constable Leticia Stone climbed out. She strolled over to them, one hand on her hip, the other resting on the butt of her Glock.

"Either of you go inside?" she asked, fixing them with a professional stare.

"No. We waited out here for you." Amber rubbed her palms up and down her thighs before thrusting her hands in her jean pockets.

"Did you see anyone?"

They shook their heads.

"Okay, stay out here, I'm going in. Keep clear of the door in case someone bolts out." She waited for their agreement before pulling her pistol and stepping past the broken doors into the shop.

Time ticked slowly by. Two minutes passed. Then three. Finally, she stepped back outside. "Nobody inside. I'll check upstairs. The connecting door is still locked." She jogged up the outside stairs, taking them two at a time, her dreadlocks bouncing against her shoulders with each bound. Her reconnoiter of the apartment was much faster than her search of downstairs.

"All clear." She ambled down the steps. "I'm going to request another officer take some photos and check for prints. I'll take your statements." She radioed in. "Off the record, I suspect this is linked to your altercation at the parade."

"Look, in confidence, Keres is up to something. We haven't figured out what yet. He seems to be after something my family has, or something he thinks we know." Amber puffed out a breath. "We have no idea what, but we think it's magically related."

Stone's eyes widened, and her brow furrowed. "Are you sure this is the best place to discuss this?" She nodded subtly toward Kody.

"Oh, yeah. He's okay. He's been helping us search the family Grimoires." Amber smiled at Kody. "He's been pretty cool with all of this. Even with his ghosts."

Stone laughed. "Let's take this discussion inside, away from the public."

It was late, there wasn't likely anyone around, but caution was always wise. Amber led them inside.

"So, it's true then. This building is haunted?" Stone asked.

"I've had an—altercation or two. The ghost, or ghosts, have a thing for messing with my heat. Although, we've come to an agreement of sorts. They mess with it until I ask them to stop." He sighed. "I never thought I'd see the day when I was rationally talking about ghosts. Don't even get me started on the cat."

"Do I even want to know?" Leticia quirked one eyebrow upward.

Amber chuckled. "The cat talks to him."

"It's a privilege when a feline shares their opinion with you. Not everyone is so blessed." She turned to face Kody. "So, you've got magic then?"

"Um. No." He blinked at her as if startled by the assumption.

"I think he does," Amber disagreed. She was certain he had latent magic. Her intuition told her he had untapped skills, besides talking to cats. She couldn't put her finger on why she felt she was so sure, except premonitions were often a sign of magical skills.

"I heard about his premonition."

"What?" Kody squawked.

"I'm on the Witch's Council," Stone said. "I hear about most things magical around here. Especially unusual things. Any magic in your family?"

"I didn't think magic was real until I bumped into Amber," Kody replied. "The Witch's Council is a thing?" His discomfort was clear in his questioning tone.

"Not just a thing, a very important thing. It's critical we monitor and police magic use. Someone has to watch out for the mundanes and make sure they aren't being harmed. Being head of the RCMP detachment is double duty for me and makes my job easier."

"Oh, Kody." Amber rested her hand on his shoulder. "You look like a deer caught in headlights. You should see your face. It's all a bit much to take in. Sometimes it overwhelms me, and I've lived with it all my life."

"I'm confused. I thought you mentioned three kinds of magic. White, black or dark, and grey. The council polices dark magic?"

"Not exactly. We only monitor magical use and step in where serious harm will come to mundanes. Typically, it's for over the top or critical situations. Dark and grey practitioners will always exist. Nothing can be done about them. Myself, I've dabbled in the grey with some of my Voodoo and Hoodoo work. It all comes down to intention."

"Is there a manual on this? I'm totally lost."

Amber chuckled at his weak joke and threw her arm around his shoulder. "You'll get the hang of it if you stick with me." She'd enjoy teaching him about magic. If they were lucky, she'd be able to bring his out. She'd never had a magical boyfriend before. She frowned at the thought. Kody as a boyfriend. Where had that come from?

Flashing lights shone through the door as a police car pulled into the alley. "Look, before Wong gets here, I want you to know there's no trace of magical residue in there. If this was Keres, he deliberately kept his magic to himself. He could be trying to throw us off his trail. A hired thug? Maybe he broke in himself. I'm not sure but be careful and watch your backs. Warn your family. And you," she frowned at Kody, "you be especially careful. Dark practitioners don't hesitate to bend mundanes to their bidding. Get yourself a protective amulet. I'm sure Amber has them in stock."

K ody stared at Officer Stone. "A protective amulet. Is that like the protective flowers? They didn't work well, did they?" This had been the weirdest damned night. Grimoires, break-ins, Voodoo cops. Magic amulets. On the plus side, Amber wanted to spend more time with him which put the sunshine back into an otherwise gloomy night.

An hour later, Amber and Kody stood inside the shop. Every cupboard had been ransacked. Books were strewn about, herbs ground into the floor, shelves cleared, and statuary broken as if a tornado had blown through. An utter disaster.

Kody groaned aloud. His hands curled into fists. "Is anything missing?" He couldn't even guess how she'd be able to tell; the place was totally destroyed. He waited a moment, and when she didn't answer, he spoke again. "Amber?" he asked softly.

"I don't know." She buried her face in her hands. "Who would do this? Why would they do this? I haven't even been open for two weeks. Everything is ruined."

Her voice rose with each sentence. Kody couldn't see tears, but he heard them in her voice. He was tempted to embrace her, to offer the comfort she'd given him earlier.

She lifted her head and wiped away her tears. "I'm going to have to clean it all up before I discover what's gone."

"I'll help." He couldn't let her tackle this alone. Having your dream shattered was enough to break a person. It was a wonder she wasn't kicking things or screaming.

"I can't ask you to do that. I'll call my sisters. They'll help. You've got a dive tomorrow."

Shit. He'd forgotten about the dive. "It's a pool dive with kids. Bryce and I will manage. I can nap afterward. I don't have a group for the afternoon. I'll be fine. Let's get this cleaned so you can open tomorrow. Whoever did this wants to hurt your business. We're not going to let it happen. Do you want me to call someone to fix the doors?" He pulled out his phone to start searching.

"No. Lazuli's wicked good with wood. If it's made of wood, she can fix it. She installed the back screen. Goddess, I need a drink."

"Wine? Whiskey? Tequila?" he teased, hoping to make her smile.

"I wish. I best keep my head on straight for this. Tea would be best. Can you see if you can find an unopened bag of something? He's dumped all the bulk bins out. I can't use them. Try the cupboards behind the counter, or in the back kitchen, please."

She pulled out her phone and walked slowly through the store, videoing the damage. Her thoroughness was impressive. She didn't miss a single space. She recorded everything on the shelves and floor, commenting on what she was seeing. She could have been emotional or judgemental, but her cool detachment and sticking to the facts impressed him. He'd have lost his shit.

He watched her take two deep breaths before dialing her family. She sketched out the situation in a few brief sentences. Unable to find any unsoiled tea, he waved to get her attention and suggested they bring some along. As she finished her conversation, he formulated a plan for clean up. He picked up the lemon tree he'd given her on opening day and straightened it in its basket. It had a few broken branches and was missing some dirt, but overall, it had fared well, all things considered. A couple of swipes of his hand cleared the herbs off the counter, and he set the plant down.

Grabbing a broom from the corner, he started sweeping the herbs into a pile. When he looked up, she gave him a sad smile, mingled gratitude and defeat. He leaned the broom against the counter and sauntered to her side. He flung his arms open welcomingly. "You need a hug."

She gave a hiccupping sob and rushed into his arms. Trembling, she rested her head on his shoulder, pressing her face into his denim jacket. "Sorry," she mumbled, the tormented word barely audible. She shuddered a few times, faked a laugh, stepped back, and looked up at him. She repeated her apology.

"No need to apologize. I'd be pitching a fit right now. My place isn't bad at all. I guess it's a blessing I live in a bachelor pad."

Sasha ambled into the room and jumped up beside the lemon tree. She sat there; one paw delicately lifted just above the surface as if she couldn't bear to touch it. "Wow, this place is a dump."

Amber stared, slack-jawed, at the cat. "I'm hallucinating, right?" She shook her head in denial. "Sasha, did you just talk?"

"How else am I going to tell you that the butt-wipe who did this was in here before? He's the dog turd that attacked you the other day. You know, the day Romeo here stepped in and saved your witchy ass."

A giggle escaped Amber.

Kody gave a full belly laugh. "I forgot to mention Miss Sasha here speaks her mind and in no uncertain terms. Now, if only it was that easy to have a conversation with the ghost, we could clear things up and set some ground rules." He shook his head at his fanciful thoughts.

"Stranger things have been known to happen." Amber left Kody's side to pet Sasha. The cat paraded up and down the counter, limping slightly to keep one paw off the ground. "Are you hurt? Let me see your paw."

"Not hurt. I scratched that son-of-a-jackal, and I'm saving his skin for you. You witches can do all sorts of crazy shit with DNA, can't you?" she said mockingly. "Can you clean it out from under my nails, please? I need a bath, and even I won't put that in my mouth, and I ate from garbage cans for months."

"Gross." Amber chuckled. "Hang on." She rushed off and returned with her purse. She pulled out an envelope and a nail file. A few quick strokes put all the yuck from under Sasha's nails into the envelope.

"What are you going to do with the skin? Give it to the police?" Kody asked.

"No. I'm not sure yet. Maybe we can use it in a location spell or something. It's useless to the police. Chain of evidence would be a problem. Besides, what court would believe the cat can talk?" She rummaged through a half-empty drawer and extracted some tape. She taped the envelope shut and slipped it back into her purse.

"Thanks, Sasha. I hope this helps somehow." Kody scratched her under the chin.

"You're welcome, human. Now, I need dinner." She sashayed into the back room.

Amber and Kody stared at her retreating form and then at each other. Amber laughed first. "Gracious, what a cat."

Kody shook his finger at her. "And you didn't believe me." He chuckled. "She's something else that cat. If you hear her, too, I know I'm not crazy, and it's probably not magic letting me hear her."

"Don't write yourself off so quickly. I think you have untapped magic. Why don't you tune into it and zap this place clean?"

Her wink sent a zing of pleasure down his spine. He grinned. "Abracadabra!" He flourished his hand like he was waving a wand. "Humph. Nothing. Must be the wrong words."

"Jeepers. Don't you know not to use magic words you don't understand?" She slapped a hand over his mouth.

He couldn't help himself. He puckered up and kissed her palm.

She jerked back and stared at him. "Um. Enough magic, let's start cleaning."

He let her surprised grin go unmentioned. Hell, he was as shocked as she was. "I was thinking I could start picking up undamaged stuff while you sweep and start cataloguing the damage. Do you think insurance will cover all those spilled herbs? Can you clean them up and weigh them to know how much is lost?"

"Good idea. I can compare my weights with computer records of what we had to start, and what we sold. I never would have thought of that. I probably would have just swept it up and tossed it. Thanks. I guess if you start putting things away and don't know where they go, just ask, or put them where you think they go."

"Ten-four, boss lady." He winked at her. Her blush was adorable. "I'll just start over in the corner." He pointed to the table for doing tarot readings. There wasn't as much damage there. He could straighten it quickly and work outward from the corner.

Chapter Twenty-One

A mber smiled at Kody as she picked up a cleaning cloth. Funny how their friendship started off so rocky with the misunderstanding about noise. They reached a truce of sorts then blew up again over magic. Now, it looked like they were friends again. Her heart gave a little pit-a-pat. He'd even kissed her hand. She'd be okay if he wanted to take their relationship further, as long as they went slowly.

"You don't have to help; my family will be here soon, and you do have an early dive." She wiped the herbs off the other counters. Kody had righted the reading table and straightened the cloth and moved on to the first set of shelves.

He picked up some pieces of broken statuary and carried them to the counter. He laid them in small piles. "I think I've got these sorted. Three different figures. I'm not cleaning my own place until my insurance adjustor comes out. I'd likely be up all night anyway. I don't mind helping."

She rinsed the cloth she was using before she spoke. "I don't know why someone would do this, and I don't understand how they got past the wards."

"Did you look at the wards? There's nothing left but stems. All the flowers have crumbled and disappeared. It's like some magical hand crushed the dried blossoms."

She stared at the remains of the ward over the front door. Initially, it had been a full moon shape with a half moon on each side, facing outward. It was the triple goddess symbol. They had studded the grapevine base with flowers and herbs. The base hung there, naked of everything that once graced it, except the decorative ribbons. She gasped. "I knew they'd failed, but how did he do that without leaving magic traces?"

Kody stood below it and stared up at the decimated ward. He reached up and pulled it from the wall. He dropped it like he'd been scorched. "What the hell?"

Amber hurried to his side. "What?" Her gaze flew from him to the ward and back.

"It's hot. Like freaking burning hot. I could barely hold on to it." He glared at the remains. "Whoa." He waved his hands in a no-way gesture. "It's magical shit, isn't it?"

Amber shoved the remains with her toe. It skidded away from her, coming to rest eighteen inches from her foot. She leaped back. "What the hell? By the Goddess, I've never seen magic so powerful. It moved on its own."

"You kicked it." His eyes widened in disbelief.

"No way. That was not me. I barely touched it. I don't understand how it can burn you and move on its own without having any traces of magic on it." Her voice trembled. She wrapped her arms around her waist to still the shivers crawling up her spine. She'd seen some weird and wonderful stuff in her twenty-five years, but nothing like this. Her breath froze in her lungs. Spots danced before her eyes, and she forced herself to breathe. "Gramma Pearl is going to have to see this. I think we better leave it for now."

"I agree wholeheartedly." He made the sign of the cross over his chest and took two steps to the left.

"I didn't realize you're Catholic."

"I'm not." He paused. "But it felt like I needed to do something to keep us safe." He flashed an uncertain smile.

"You do believe in a higher power then?"

"I have no idea what I believe anymore; you're exploding everything I thought I might believe in." He scraped his fingers through his short, brown hair and then rubbed his hands together briskly. "I know there is more out there than I ever imagined. I know there's something bigger than me out there, but frankly, this is troublesome."

"Troublesome?" Amber laughed. "It's scaring the ever-loving shit out of me, and I'm used to it." This was miles worse than her fear of repercussions from accidentally spelling Stevie Avalon. Nobody liked to get in trouble for a mistake. Now, she was afraid for her life. The back of her neck tickled. Premonition ants marched up and down her arms. Her awakening clairsentience, the ability to see past or future events, was picking a crappy time to kick in. She'd almost prefer to be totally ignorant of what was to come.

She didn't know what was coming, but it was not going to be good, and Keres definitely had his hands in it. He was in it right up to his grubby neck. She needed more backup than just Kody. When was her family going to get there? They should've arrived already. She voiced the last sentiment aloud.

"Why don't you call them," Kody suggested. "Maybe they got held up."

"Good idea. I don't know why I didn't think of it." She could barely form a coherent thought, that's why. Her mind raced a million miles an hour; like she was flying a broom two hundred feet above the ground doing Mach three. Or something. No. There was a meme about it. She dug into her memory. Her mind was like a web browser with twenty-five tabs open.

She muscled up some fortitude. "They'll be here when they get here. They wouldn't delay unless they had no choice. I'm going to start picking up books." She nodded decisively. "Back to work."

"Aye, aye, captain. Your wish is my command." Her returned to the statue display. "Couldn't you just magic this back together? Magic does that, right?"

"I couldn't, but Hyacinth might be able to. Her skill is working with earth. Most of those are ceramic, formed from clay or earth. There are even people who can work with metal, to unbend those stepped on. But it's more than that."

"Personal gain? Your sisters mentioned it in the kitchen at dinner the other night. Explain that, please."

His question was a distraction technique, and she latched onto it like a lifeline. "I don't know where the knowledge it was bad to work magic for personal gain originated, but the concept has been drilled into me for forever. Maybe it's superstition, maybe it's fact. Every time I've cast a spell for my own benefit, it's backfired. I'm not talking small things, but big things. For instance, Hazel cast a spell for good luck in getting a job. Nothing specific, just a strong intention and wish to land a great job, with the caveat of harm to none. Therefore, the energy of the universe could assist in landing something. If I cast a spell to repair the damage in here, it would be definite personal gain and would likely backfire."

"Backfire how?"

"That's the thing. It's not a direct correlation. This mess would be gone, but something else would go wrong later." She straightened a few books on the shelf and added two more.

"I don't see the difference between asking for a job and fixing this mess." He sounded bewildered. He shelved a goddess figure and studied Amber.

"I can't fully explain it. It's one of those grey areas. Asking for help with a job puts the decision in the universe's hands. Fixing this is taking over. There's no easy explanation, and every situation differs. When I stand back and look at this mess, it's all I can do not to try and use magic to fix it. Granted, it wouldn't be within my strongest skillset, but I'd love to. I want it so badly it must be totally personal, which tells me I'd be using magic for personal gain."

"But your customers would benefit, too. Think of all the lost tea."

"But we have more tea at home and can grow more herbs to make tea, and once the insurance pays out, if it does, I can replace the irreparably damaged items. As strong as the desire to magic this better is, I'm going to do it the hard way."

"As well you should," Pearl chided, striding into the room.

"I'm still not clear on all this. If Keres did this with magic, how can it be wrong to fix it with magic? And what about the rule of three? Doesn't it come back to him three times as bad?" He shrugged defeatedly.

"I'm with you on that," Hazel piped in angrily. "We've all worked so hard on this, and Keres comes in and ruins everything. It isn't right. He needs a magical ass kicking."

"And he'll get one." Lazuli put a calming hand on Hazel and Kody's shoulders. "It might not be soon, but the universe will send him what's coming to him, in spades. Our duty is to get beyond this, figure out what's going on, and stop it."

A brisk knock sounded on the front door.

Everyone shared a questioning look, and Amber strode over to open it. "Frank? What are you doing here in the middle of the night?"

"Mind if I come in? I was driving by earlier and saw the police. I waited until they were gone to come back. No sense disturbing their work. What's going on?" He looked around the shop. "Sweet Jesus. What in the name of heaven happened in here?"

"We were burgled. Why were you out and about so late?"

"Mom's in town. She's watching Rose while I put in some extra hours at work. I'm behind on paperwork. I was headed home when I drove by."

"The road between your job and your home doesn't run anywhere near here. Try again, cowboy. Nice boots and Stetson, by the way." Hazel teased.

"Okay, I needed a snack and was hitting the drive-through before it closed. I try not to feed Rose junk, and I had a craving. Mom's with her, so no harm done. Right?"

"You're not getting any validation from me," Lazuli quipped.

"Need a hand to clean up? I'm awake now. Too much caffeine."

"The more the merrier." Amber waved him in and shut the door behind him.

"What's with the dead sticks? They give me the creeps." He glared at the discarded ward.

"We're not sure what happened to it. We need to gather up all the—arrangements and put them in a box," Amber declared. "I'll grab a box and some gloves. They've got thorns," she added at Frank's puzzled look. She gave her family a 'don't ask' look. Luckily, they were used to keeping magical secrets and kept their mouths shut. Initiating Kody into magic was one thing; they didn't need to be explaining things to Frank as well. "Hang tight, and I'll grab the box." She hurried into the back room.

Sometimes, having to keep such a big secret was a pain in the backside. She leaned against the wall, beside a workbench. They'd have to analyze the remains of the wards to determine exactly what had happened to them. After that, they'd need to neutralize whatever negativity remained in them so they could be safely discarded, preferably by burning.

Amber and Kody cleaned the back room while Gramma Pearl, Hazel, and Cynth worked out front. Lazuli worked side by side with Frank, recording the damaged items and generating a list of prices and suppliers. The two of them talked quietly between themselves as they worked, heads together. The attraction between them was almost visual.

They took a break at five for coffee and the pastries Lazuli brought from home. When she wasn't busy creating fine furniture and décor items from wood, Lazuli was a whiz at baking.

Amber leaned back against the wall, watching her family interact. Exhaustion swamped her. She could barely lift her coffee. Frank and Kody chatted amicably about lacrosse and the final games from last winter's season. What was it about guys and sports? She was pleased the two men were hitting it off. It could be difficult for an adult with a full-time career to make friends in a new town. Especially when they primarily worked alone, or with someone much younger than themselves, like Kody. Frank was equally busy running herd on his six-year-old daughter and working full time, which was a heavy burden for a widow.

Kody stared at a spot just to the left of Amber. He shook his head and stared again. His forehead wrinkled. He scratched his nose. He excused himself from Frank and walked over to Amber. "Am I nuts, or is there a shadow of an old lady over there, sitting on the workbench?"

Amber's gaze followed his thumb gesture. "I don't see anything." She looked again. The space he'd indicated seemed to shimmer, and for a few seconds, she swore she saw a middle-aged lady in a white lab coat sitting on the bench, swinging her feet like a bored child. In an instant, the vision was gone. "Holy crap," Amber whispered. "I think I did see something."

"It's not just me then?" He sounded relieved. "I thought I was losing my shit. Exhaustion does funny things to a person, but ghosts? Now I've seen everything." He chuckled uncomfortably.

"I better head home," Frank said. "I've got a full day of work, and Rose is off school for a PD day. It makes me crazy. School ends for the summer in less than a week, and the teachers get a day off." He sighed. "Don't get me wrong, they work damned hard, but ... Never mind. Parental gripes. I'm glad Mom's here for most of the summer."

"I'll walk you out." Lazuli gestured toward the front of the store. She chatted quietly as they left the room. Twenty minutes later, she returned to the back room, a big smile on her face, and her cheeks flushed.

"I guess we should tackle these wards." Amber glared at the box.

"I'm not getting anything from it except negative vibes." Hazel trudged to stand beside Amber. "No trace of magic."

"Me either," Lazuli and Hyacinth added in unison.

"I want to get Mayor Quinton and Leticia Stone to check them over," Pearl suggested. "They might pick up on something we can't see. I'm getting a vague sense of something old." She dug into a laundry basket she'd brought with her and extracted a box of sea salt and an enormous bunch of dried sage. Chanting a protective spell in a low voice, she poured a ring of salt and dried sage around the box of wards. "That'll hold it until morning. For now, we should all try and get some sleep. Kody, you come with us. No sense sleeping at your place until we have a chance to clean it out. We've got a guest room you can use."

Amber stared at her grandmother. She'd never once—ever—let anyone who wasn't a relative spend the night in Hawk Manor. Not ever. The invitation was a testament to the gravity of their situation and her grandmother's fears.

"I guess I could," he accepted the offer. "I'd appreciate it. My place is a mess; my sheets are destroyed, and I only have one set."

"Bachelors," Amber teased.

"I'll hold down the fort," Sasha chimed in. Nobody except Kody and Sasha seemed to hear anything beyond a series of meows. "I'll be awake anyway, keeping my children safe."

"You'll be fine here." Amber reached down to pet the cat walking circles around her ankles. "I'll be back in two hours. Crap. I'm gonna be beat tomorrow. I can hardly keep my eyes open as it is. Let's head out. Kody, do you need anything? Clean clothing for tomorrow?"

"I'll just grab a bag and meet you out back once I lock up. Not that locks seems to help much."

Chapter Twenty-Two

The next morning, Amber smiled as she looked around Four Seasons Metaphysical with Lazuli by her side. There was little remaining evidence of yesterday's disturbance. They'd cleaned and tidied every shelf and display. Chin in her left hand, elbow on the front counter, she studied the list of lost and damaged merchandise. She counted her blessings no essential oils were spilled. There were a few things with minor damage, like a statue of the Egyptian cat god, Bastet, with one chipped ear they might be able to sell at a discount, depending on what the insurance company's policy was. Aside from the missing wards, and a couple bare shelves, the shop looked great. No hints of negativity remained, but Amber couldn't shake the unease poking at her usual morning serenity.

"Laz, I don't like this. Can you feel it?" She struggled to put her emotions into words. "I feel like the universe is holding its breath in preparation for an enormous slap-down. Something is going to go wrong. Big time wrong."

"I know. It's hovering there, right outside my perception. It's like having a word on the tip of your tongue. It's so close, but too damned far to catch. I've got psychic alarm bells going off like crazy, and I can't even catch a glimpse of what's going to happen."

"Shit's going to hit the fan for sure."

The two women whirled toward the voice. Amber's heart pounded, and she gasped.

They stared at the faint figure of a woman standing near a display of stones. She wore a white lab coat and bedroom slippers. Her hair was a full grey, shoulder length bob. Her eyes held a glimmer of blue. "What? Haven't you ever seen a ghost before?"

"Aside from our twice great-grandmother? No," Amber replied. "Seeing ghosts is more Hazel's thing." Judging by the perfect hair, the lab coat and slippers, the ghost must have been getting ready for work when she died. A person spent their afterlife in the garments they wore when they passed. Amber made a note to double-check her wardrobe for stains and holes.

"Well, lucky for you, I decided to show myself."

"Yeah, lucky us." Sarcasm laced Laz's reply, and she crossed her arms over her chest.

"You should be nicer to us. We saw the whole thing, you know," Ev, the ghost, declared.

"Us?" Amber asked. "Who exactly is us?"

The apparition chortled. "You Hawks are fairly oblivious. I'm not alone. I've got company in the afterlife. Admittedly, I'd have preferred my husband to a former drug abuser, but I've got no choice, and she's clean and sober now. Though, she didn't have much choice, being dead and all."

"And who exactly is she? And where is she?" Amber gestured around the room.

"Asleep. Upstairs. She'd cozied up in our sexy roommate's recliner. She prefers the bed, but our needs weren't taken into consideration after the trauma we endured yesterday."

"What trauma was that?" Amber asked. How much trauma actually affected a ghost?

"Keres ransacked the store before heading upstairs to Kody's place and trashing it. He put a temporary binding spell on us. There wasn't a danged thing we could do but watch him. He was long gone, an hour or more before the spell dissipated. Never, in all my magical or ghostly days, did I ever hear about a temporary ghost binding spell. The man has skills." Reluctant admiration filled her voice. "Permanent binding, banishing, is common. When I first passed on, I thought I might be banished to the otherworld, but luckily, nobody wanted this old building. We haunted it until the right renters came along."

"Again with the we." Laz raised one eyebrow in question.

"My roommate, Kansas McGuire. She stumbled into our store, drugged out of her mind and deathly ill. I tried to save her. I guess she hung around until I passed, too. She's a sweet kid, if a bit scatter-brained."

"And you are?" Amber asked.

"Evelyn Woods. I owned and ran the drugstore in this building until I passed. My ungrateful nephew sold the building to the Wilkins family for half of its value. Jason Wilkins doesn't know much about people. He's all about himself. I never met a bigger narcissist. His cousin is a much better person. I've watched him helping out around here. He's not much for ghosts, though. He's got no sense of humor about temperature, either. I was worried when he started yelling at you ladies. I thought he was beyond hope. When he stepped in against Keres, I was relieved."

"Yeah, me too," Amber agreed. "What can we do for you, Mrs. Woods?"

"Pfft. I don't stand much on formality since I died. Call me Ev, or Evelyn, if you must." She floated into the back room. The sisters followed her. She sat on the couch with her ankles primly crossed.

"Okay, Ev, if you insist. I'm Amber, and this is my sister Lazuli. What can we do for you? Do you need help crossing over?"

"I know who you are; I've been watching you since you moved in. The question isn't what can you do for us, it's what we can do for you." A proud, slightly devious smile lit her face.

Amber milled the statement around in her mind. Perhaps ghosts could be crazy. She'd always believed ghosts only hung around if they had unfinished business. Her great-great-grandmother believed it was her task to keep watch over the Hawk family. Nobody had seen her great-grandmother since she died nearly seven years ago, leading Amber to study ghosts, but they really were more Hazel's thing. Amber needed to catch up on her reading. There was an endless list of things for a witch to study. Goddess knew they had enough magical record books to keep her reading for the rest of her life.

"What can you do for us?" Laz asked before Amber could formulate a question.

"Normally, a ghost haunts the place of their death, or on occasion, a particular item. You've heard of haunted dolls or furniture. Talk on the other side is if the right spell is cast, ghosts can move freely. We, Kansas and I, believe if you cast the spell, we can follow Keres around and find out what he's up to." She smiled smugly. "Besides helping you, it'll reduce the infernal boredom of hanging out here. Living in one place and never going outside gets old fast. Granted, things have livened up since you girls arrived."

"I think we're going to need time to think about this." Amber shared a look with Laz.

"Certainly." Ev nodded and disappeared.

"Whoa!" Amber laughed. "Ghosts popping in and out will take some getting used to. What do you think? Should we consider it?"

"I don't know. Can we even discuss it freely here? What if this is a trick? She's been trapped here for years. Maybe she just wants whatever freedom she can get. We really have no reason to trust her." Laz interlaced her fingers and tapped her thumbs against her lips thoughtfully. "She's probably listening."

Ev popped back into sight.

"Ha! I knew you were up to something. Listening behind our backs." Laz shook her finger at the ghost.

"I promise to leave until you shout for me, if you promise to discuss it."

"At this point, I'm going to say no. Ghosts stay behind for a purpose, and I don't think we should mess with whatever the universe has in store for you." Evelyn had already proven she couldn't be trusted, and they'd only known her five minutes. The idea of freeing her made Amber's stomach hurt. "Besides, I've never heard of a spell like that." Amber leaned against the doorjamb between the back room and the shop front. She crossed her arms over her chest. She was trying to be rational but probably came off as belligerent.

"From what I've heard, it's old. Some of the ancient magic, dating back to before the travesty at Salem." Ev stomped her foot.

"And how, precisely, do you communicate with those on the other side if you are trapped on this side? Is there a portal?" Laz jumped into the discussion in full accusatory mode.

"You two aren't very bright for witches, especially for hereditary witches. Samhain." She said the sabbat's name in the traditional fashion, sow-in, rhyming the first syllable with cow. "Halloween. All Hallows Eve. Does any of this ring a bell?" She didn't wait for an answer.

"You know, witch's new year, when the veil between the world of the living and the dead is thinnest and souls can pass through both ways?"

"Your sarcasm is both rude and unnecessary," Amber chided. "We are familiar with Samhain and all the other sabbats. Continue your story, please."

"It takes considerable effort to pass through the veil during other times of the year, but it can be done. But at Samhain, it's as easy as pie. Especially if you were magic when you were alive; and I was." She raised one shoulder and tipped her head to the side in a so-there gesture.

"The answer is no. Maybe when this mess with Keres is finished. There are too many questions right now. Like, how do we tie you back down when we're finished, and will we need to? What are the long-term repercussions of doing this? Can we trust you to come back, or do you have a greater motive we're unaware of? It isn't that we don't trust you, Evelyn, it's more because this is entirely new to us and requires research." Amber ground to a halt.

"And, we'd have to locate the spell. I've never heard of it, and I love searching the old grimoires." Laz filled the kettle while she talked. "Lemon mint or chamomile orange?" she asked Amber.

"Orange, please."

"Orange," Ev piped in at the same time. "I adore the stronger scented teas. My sense of smell isn't what it used to be." She floated toward Laz without even bothering to pretend she was walking.

"You'd be less creepy if you walked," Laz said.

Amber stifled a laugh. "She's right. When you move normally, we can almost forget you're a spirit. No offense intended."

"You know, I revealed myself to you to help out, not to take your criticism. If I didn't need company, I'd have kept to myself." Hurt warbled the ghost's voice.

"Sorry, Ev. Dealing with the sort-of dead isn't something we do everyday. We rarely ever hear from great-great-gramma. We'll try to be better, and we do appreciate your desire to help." Amber moved to pull teacups from the cupboard.

"Yes, I can reveal myself to anyone I want, though not everyone I reveal myself to chooses to see me. Jason Wilkins, for example, is a hard-line non-believer. I swear I could strip him naked and he'd still refuse to acknowledge me."

"Ugh," Laz groaned. "Don't even plant the visual in my brain."

Amber laughed. "I'll second that."

"Your neighbor..." Ev grinned wickedly. "He's something else when he's naked. He's got the finest backside I've seen in a long time. He is delish. I like cranking the heat so he strips down. Although, I get more reaction when I freeze him out."

Amber laughed. "You are incorrigible." For an old, dead person, Ev was pretty funny.

"Maybe so, but I dare you to avoid looking at his hind end. I've seen you ogle him more than once. I can almost feel your need to kiss him, too, not that I blame you."

A distant shuddering boom rocked the shop, dropping Amber and Laz to their knees. The teapot bounced off the stove, and Ev vanished.

"What the hell?" Amber's gaze travelled the room, landing on Lazuli's huddled form. "It sounded like an explosion." Her body trembled in the aftermath. She fought the urge to run out into the street to investigate. Her heart thundered in her chest, and her knees shook. She glanced wildly around the shop and bolted for the telephone.

"Couldn't be. There's no blasting scheduled around here. There would have been a notice in the paper. Something must have blown up. We better check in with the fire department." Occasionally, the Hawks pitched in to assist the fire department. One of the local fire fighters was magical and let them know when their elemental skills were required. Thankfully, there were precious few fires in their small hometown.

"Gosh, we haven't been called to help in months." Amber said, rubbing her arms to dispel a sudden chill.

They rarely altered what was meant to be. Laz could blow winds to preventing a fire from spreading to adjacent buildings; while Hazel could call in a rain shower to douse the flames. Amber would use her ability to control fire and snuff sparks before they exploded into full flames. None of them acted without their assistance being requested, and only in dire circumstances. It was always best to let mother nature take her course. Otherwise, the natural balance of the earth was disturbed, which could lead to unknown and unintended consequences. When called in, they made a supreme effort to keep their efforts from being noticed.

Amber flashed a mental thought to her grandmother and other sisters. Each responded with a quick confirmation they were fine. "I better check the front while you clean up the tea. Hopefully, nothing was damaged. The last thing I need is more insurance paperwork." She hurried to the front.

Several items had shifted toward the front of their shelves, but nothing had fallen. The phone rang, and she hurried over to answer it. Call display identified the origin as the police department. Dread clenched her guts. A police call on the heels of an explosion was bad news; there was no way it could be anything else.

"Four Seasons Metaphysical. Amber speaking, how may I help you?" she spoke into the phone hoping it was just Constable Stone ordering something.

"Amber, it's Leticia. We need your family near Raven Falls at the lake. There's been an explosion. We've started the disaster tree call out, but I want you guys at the boat launch near the falls as soon as possible."

Amber didn't bother waiting for an explanation. She agreed to notify her family and get there on the double. "Laz," she hollered as she hung up. "Shut down the shop. We're headed for the falls. It was an explosion."

Her sister bolted into the room; two ghosts materialized beside her with a popping sound. "What?" they all cried in unison.

Amber ignored the ghosts and focused on her sister. "I'll explain on the way. Call the house, tell them to get their asses to the lake. I'll drive." She put a hastily scrawled "Closed for Emergency" note in the window and locked the door. She flashed a hurry up message to Hazel. Her strength was working with water. If there were problems, she might be able to help. Hazel sent back a buzz of affirmation. She was on her way.

"Which falls?" Laz asked as they sprinted for Amber's gold Honda Civic.

"Raven."

Their hometown, Three Moon Falls, was a tourist town in north central Alberta. Tourists flocked from around the world to visit the falls. Three Moon Falls was named for a series of three waterfalls and town founder, James Moon, who built the town with his wife, Clara. The smallest, Chickadee Falls, cascaded one hundred seventy-five feet into a pool on Hawk land, which in turn, fed into Spruce Creek. The creek flowed toward town. The second, Eagle Falls, dropped an impressive two hundred feet into Spruce Creek, which flowed into the pool beneath the largest falls, Raven Falls. The pool was an enormous half-moon shape connected to Three Moon Falls Lake.

They headed toward Raven Falls, about four miles away from their shop. Three Moon Falls' shopping district, ran along Main street which bordered the lake itself. Quaint shops in restored buildings lined one side of the street, a narrow beach lined the other. Four Seasons Metaphysical sat near one end of Main Street, close enough to catch the tourist trade as well as local business, but not close enough to be swamped by tourists.

They skidded into the falls parking lot and slid into the last empty space. All five of the town's police cruisers were there as well as four ambulances. Constable Stone stood under a portable canopy directing volunteers.

"We're not sure what caused the explosion. As a result, we want only experienced rescue personnel in the water. Reports indicate there are at least up to a dozen swimmers missing, and we need to find them. ASAP. You there." She gestured to her left. "You, come here."

Amber followed the motion. Kody stood beside his assistant, watching the action. He gestured to himself. "Me?" He stared at Stone.

"Yes, you. You're a professional diver. I'm going to need you to head the dive rescue efforts until the RCMP dive team arrives."

Chapter Twenty-Three

K ody blinked rapidly. He was experienced, and he'd worked with rescue crews dozens of times, but he'd never headed up a mission. "Okay. I'll need a boat and some assistance. Preferably people with diving experience."

"We've got the police boat. It's moored at the dock by the boat ramp. Gather your people, check in, and get out on the water. Put as many experienced divers in the water as you can safely control."

Fortunately, the room he rented over the garage was only three blocks from the lake. "Bryce, take my truck to the shop and bring back all the full tanks and gear to outfit the divers." He couldn't even guess at wetsuit sizes. Hopefully, some of the divers had their own. He tossed Bryce his keys. "I'll gather the divers, and we'll get started. Drive right down to the boat launch. I'll make sure they're waiting for you."

"Okay. It'll take me a while."

Kody glanced around the busy parking lot for an assistant. Amber and Laz were the first people he recognized. "Amber," he shouted. "Got a second?" They'd talked about her diving experience; it wasn't much, but she'd be able to help on the boat.

She hurried over to him, Lazuli hot on her heels. "What can we do? I hear Stone telling you to head up the dive."

"Lazuli, can you go with Bryce and help him load equipment and bring it back?"

"Sure thing, as long as I don't need to know anything about the equipment. I'm not a diver."

"No problem," Bryce injected. "As long as you can help carry stuff, we'll be good. Let's go." He took off at a fast jog. "Back as quick as we can."

Kody looked at Amber. "How competent a diver are you?" There wasn't time to play nice; they had to get organized and into the water.

"I can dive. I don't have much time in the water. A few shallow dives in Mexico. A couple dozen lake dives here. I'm not qualified to teach, or probably even supervise, but I can hold my own. Why?" Her face went white. "By the Goddess, you aren't thinking of putting me in charge, are you?"

"If I have to, I will. I know you. I trust you. You're responsible, and you can do things other people can't. That's good enough for me. Do you know any divers better than you?" It sounded like he'd use her if he had to but would prefer someone with more experience. Rescue divers would be ideal, but he'd work with what he had.

She walked up to him, gripped his forearm, and leaned in to whisper in his ear. Her breath tickled his neck. "Bring Hazel on the boat. She works with water." She paused. "If you know what I mean. She'll be here right away."

One controlled water, the other fire. She owed him a dozen explanations after this. Water, fire? Why did those words resonate so strongly?

Right. The basic magical elements. Earth, air, fire, and water; he'd read something in their family books and on the internet. That was two of the elements. Four sisters, four elements. Did each of them control one, or was it coincidence? He shook the distraction aside; he didn't have time for it. It was already too late for anyone under water, unless they'd been trapped in an air pocket. Luckily, the caves below the falls were full of trapped air. He'd lead the most experienced divers there and put the others to work searching for drowned victims.

He closed his eyes at the thought. He could barely bear to think about it after nearly losing a diver himself earlier this summer. Today was worse because it wasn't a cocky kid, but innocent swimmers.

"Right then. Get Hazel to join us at the boat."

She nodded and clutched his arm. "You've got this, Kody. We'll find them." Her tone was calm and confident. "I already sent her a message to get her butt down here."

He took a deep breath and forced the tension from his limbs. He'd been nervous before a dive, but never like this. He had to get a grip. "You're right. We can do this." He put a slight emphasis on the pronoun and then hurried past the awning toward the boat.

Constable Stone made an announcement requesting anyone with diving experience was to report to Kody at the police boat. Fifteen minutes and a dozen volunteers later, they pushed off into the water, Corporal Lee Wong at the helm and nominally in charge of the group. Kody and Bryce would each lead a team of three divers in searching the caves. Amber would stay on top, helping prep the others as they switched out after short shifts. They'd work until all the oxygen tanks were dry.

"Listen up, everyone," Kody called from his perch atop one of the rescue cruiser's benches. "The water's going to be filthy. We're going to tether our teams together. Do not, under any circumstances, release the line. If one of you needs to surface, the entire group surfaces. Is that clear?" Nods of agreement met his gaze. "Do not hesitate to call for surfacing if you become disoriented or for any other reason. We don't have surface to water contact, so we'll check in at ten-minute intervals. You each have orange surveyor's tape and stakes. Tie off anything which needs extensive searching. We're looking for survivors in air pockets, nothing more."

He dropped his gaze, then looked up, being certain to catch each volunteer's gaze. "If, God forbid, we find someone we can't save, tag them for later retrieval." He swallowed hard. "This is about saving lives. The RCMP team will recover bodies. That's Constable Stone's directive, not mine. Is that clear?"

Agreement was less enthusiastic this time. He hated to put the idea forth, but there was no way these people could go under unless they were expecting the worst. Pre-conditioning to potentially startling events, particularly death, might prevent the shock from being too much.

The boat slowed to a halt in a relatively smooth part of the lake, near the base of the falls. It was only a short swim to their destination. Wong dropped the anchor into the muddy water. The explosion had stirred up dirt and debris, obscuring vision, limiting visibility to only a few feet.

Kody and his team dove into the water and attached their tethers. Bryce was instructed to wait until they cleared the immediate area before entering the water.

Darkness swamped Kody, almost stealing his breath. He'd dived thousands of times, in waters all across the world. He had hundreds of dives in this lake alone, but he'd never experienced a near-total blackout. Night dives were nothing like this. Drawing deep for calm, he smoothed his breathing and focused on steadying his heartbeat.

He turned in the water, using his headlamp to illuminate his team. One man looked fit to panic. Kody moved closer and met the man's gaze with his own. After a moment, the panic left his face, and Kody gestured them forward. He swam toward the caves, the tension on his tether letting him know his team followed. They kept to the surface, past the rim of the pool, until the low edge of the cave entrance required them to dive deeper.

Moving as a unit, with surprising ease, they dove and swam through the murky water into the first cavern.

There was a large air pocket inside the first cave. They all removed their masks. Working carefully and slowly, they searched the bottom, moving inch by inch in a line until the entire floor was covered. Nothing there but rocks and empty bottles. Anger added to Kody's tension. Litter wasn't acceptable. He vowed to return and clean the caves. It would be a great exercise for a beginning diver's class.

The second had only a sliver of air. He stood, his headlamp sweeping the surface and shining off the damp walls. The water was higher than yesterday but not as muddy as the first cavern. That was a blessing. It boded well for the remaining caves.

Inside the third cave, a hysterical teenage girl stood shivering. She threw herself into his arms the moment they surfaced. "Oh, my god. Thank God you came. I thought I was going to die in here. I don't know how to get out. My light died. I can't find my boyfriend." The words rushed out in a torrent of tears and hiccupping sobs.

"Easy there. We'll get you out of here. It's going to be okay. What's your name? Let me warm you." He reached his hands out. When she didn't shy away, he rubbed them briskly up and down her arms. They'd have to get her topside quickly to prevent hypothermia.

"I...I...I'm Chandra. Tommy's gone," she wailed, throwing herself at him again. "Find him, please." She wailed the last word hysterically.

"We will. I promise. First, we have to take you out of here. Do you have equipment?"

"No, we just swam in."

Her shivering was getting out of control. He had to act fast, before her hysteria peaked and the trauma of being trapped took over completely, adding shock to the mix.

"I'll share my tank with you. Okay?" She nodded, clearly not certain what he was talking about. "I'll let you use it as we travel down the connecting tunnels. You'll breathe with my mask. I'll swim without it. I'm going to tie this rope around your wrist, to keep us from being separated. My team will follow."

Moving through the tunnels with one hand tied to Chandra and on foot attached to his team would hinder his motion, but he could do this. He'd drilled for this, over and over in rescue classes.

"Are you ready?"

She nodded weakly.

"Let's go."

Surprisingly, she was calm as they made their way slowly through the tunnels, pausing in each cave to breathe. The air was growing stale; the explosion must have blocked the natural ventilation holes. An eternity later, ten minutes by his watch, they surfaced in the lake and made their way toward the boat.

Chapter Twenty-Four

Amber stared at the water where Kody's team disappeared. She cast a silent plea to the Goddess and the universe for them to return safely. Preferably with survivors. When Bryce's team disappeared after them, she stood waiting for them to return, too, watching the shoreline.

The police had cordoned off the pathways to the base of the falls. Volunteers in safety vests patrolled the area, keeping spectators at bay. Her stomach clenched when her gaze landed on the top of the falls. The entire shape of the top lip was changed. A large chunk of rock was blown away, giving the roughly crescent shape rough, jagged edges. There was no way the devastation was natural. What she didn't understand was why someone would destroy the falls.

Keres' image popped into her head. Her intuition was poking at her brain. There was absolutely no reason for thinking he was responsible; yet, she couldn't shift her mind from believing he had to be involved somehow. But why damage the falls? What was he after? Speculation wasn't going to help. She searched the water for signs of the divers and refocused on the beach closest to the falls.

Waves of worry and fear emanated from the bystanders milling about. "Do you feel that?" she asked Hazel, who stood beside her.

"The fear? The anger? The banked excitement? Or the hatred and greed?"

Amber recoiled. "Whoa. I wasn't picking it up until you mentioned it." She glanced at her sister and back at the beach. "It's like it's directed right at us. I don't see anything. I just can't shake the sensation we've angered someone, somehow. I don't get it. This feeling makes my skin crawl, like I need to run to be somewhere else."

"I think we need to be careful going forward. It's time for a family conference. We might even need to call in Mom and Dad. Maybe even Aunt Ivy." The Hawk girls' mother, and stepfather were away, following the trail of a suspected witch hunter. While often out of easy contact range, they'd come home as soon as they realized they were needed. Aunt Ivy and her family lived in Newfoundland. Ivy was the family's strongest telepath.

"I think it's early yet," Amber disagreed without taking her eyes off the beach. "But let's keep it in mind for later. You never know what's coming down the pipe next." She flung her arm out in front of her, pointing toward the beach. "Do you see that?"

An area at the base of the falls was shrouded in shadow, as if smoke lingered there. The clear, unhindered view of the falls was disturbed, it wavered slightly as if something walked in front of it. The wavering moved closer to the falls and slowly disappeared; the cascading water parted as the disturbance passed into the space behind the falls.

Cloaking? Precious few magicals could cloak themselves, but what else could it be?

"Keres," Hazel hissed.

Amber and her sisters had played behind those falls on many occasions in their teens. Over the years, the seclusion of the falls provided a not so secret party spot for teenagers wishing for an evening away from prying adult eyes. There was a single spacious cavern behind the water, or there had been. Who knew what damage the explosion had wrought? She'd love to be off this boat and under those falls to see what Keres was up to.

The soft splash of someone surfacing snapped her attention back to the boat.

"Grab her," Kody called, his voice breathless with strain.

Wong and Amber worked together to pull the weak teenager onto the rear platform of the boat. The redhead sputtered and coughed as she huddled into herself. Tears mingled with the water streaming down her cheeks. She was covered in goose bumps. Her teeth chattered as she begged Kody to go back and find her boyfriend.

"She needs to warm up," Kody panted, giving Amber a raised eyebrow look. She nodded her understanding. He gestured to his team, and they took off swimming.

"She needs a blanket," Amber instructed Wong as she helped the teen onto a bench. "She's freezing." He hurried to find one. "Chandra, I'm going to warm you up a bit." She gave the girl a significant look, and Hazel stepped forward to block the view of the others on the boat.

Chandra was from the Agarwal family. Her mother worked in the library, and her father was a city councillor. Her mother was a skilled Chakra healer and yoga teacher. They were well known and accepted by Three Moon Falls magical community.

"I'm going to rub your arms and legs to warm you." Amber looked the exhausted girl right in the eye, letting her know magic was coming.

She rubbed her hands briskly together as if she was warming them. She generated a tiny spark of fire in each, not enough to burn, but enough to heat Chandra's skin and quickly warm her. Not enough warmth to be noticeable, but enough to take off the worst of the chill and halt the start of hypothermia. She rubbed up and down her arms, then her legs and across Chandra's stomach and back where her modest two-piece swimsuit left her skin exposed. By the time Wong was back with the blankets, Amber was done. She wrapped one blanket around her shoulders and covered her legs with the second.

"What happened?" Wong asked with more respect than Amber expected.

"We were checking out the caves. It's only a short swim underwater." Her teeth knocked together. "We're both great swimmers. We had these cool headlamps for seeing underwater. We were in the first cave. Tommy said there are, like ten, caves in a row. We weren't going that far." Tears streamed down her cheeks. "Did they find him? Where is he?" She glanced around frantically, leaning left and right, trying to see past the divers huddled around her.

"Relax, if you can," Wong advised. "There are two diving parties looking for him. Paramedics are on their way to check you over. Your parents will meet you on shore."

Amber didn't even realize he'd been busy contacting anyone. Sometimes, in her frustration with his anti-witch bias, she forgot he was actually a good cop. She'd have to do better to bank her own prejudices.

"But Tommy?" Chandra wailed. "I can't leave without him. He'll be looking for me."

"We'll make sure he knows where you went." Amber patted her shoulder.

"What happened in the caves?" Wong asked.

"I...I don't know. We were in the first cave, just hanging out and like resting. It's not too deep. I can stand up inside it and have most of my chest and head above water. It's super cool. We were standing there catching our breath and there was this huge rumble." She waved her arms wildly, dislodging the blanket. "Then, it was like something was pushing against my legs, and I went down. The water came up over my head. It pushed and pushed on me. I banged into the walls. When I stood up." She gave a hiccupping sob. "When I stood up, he was g-g-gone. I tried to search the cave, but my lamp was gone."

Amber wrapped the blanket around Chandra's shoulders. "It's okay. We'll find him." She cast a prayer to the Goddess, praying Tommy would be found safe, even though she had her doubts. "Then what?"

"When I stopped coughing, because I swallowed water, I walked around the whole cave. Super slowly, using my feet to feel the bottom. I never found him. I don't know where he went," she wailed, her voice rose with each word. She broke down into tears.

"If one cave flows into the next, he might have been washed into the second cave. I know it's hard, but try and stay calm," Amber advised.

Splashing sounded behind the boat. Wong and Amber hurried over to help Bryce's dive team onto the boat. When they were out of the water and he'd caught his breath, he led his second team into the water and back toward the caves.

The paramedics arrived and determined Chandra needed to see a doctor, just to be certain she hadn't taken a blow to the head. Their examination complete, they took her to the hospital.

Chapter Twenty-Five

K ody led his team back into the caves. He knew the caves like the back of his hand. He'd spent hours in here, charting, memorizing. He had to be one hundred percent certain he could get back to the lake without a lamp if he led a group down here.

Moving with precision, they searched and marked any areas requiring digging to ensure nobody had been trapped. The walls had tumbled in three places, these he marked with flags.

In the tenth and final cave, they found someone else.

Kody blanched as he stared at the teenage boy floating face-down in the pool. His blood turned the water as eerie pink. Motioning for his team to stay back, he rolled the boy over. There was a huge gash across his forehead. Knowing it was futile, Kody checked his pulse. Nothing.

Saddened, he shook his head at the team who had removed their masks. Tears rolled down several divers' faces. Maybe if they'd gotten here sooner, the boy might have been saved; but it was doubtful. If the blow that lacerated his head knocked him out, he'd have drowned where he fell. The power of the waves and aftershocks of the explosion must have pushed him through the large tunnels between caves. Standing silently, he mourned the boy he'd never met and made a silent vow to offer more classes geared toward swimmers rather than divers. Maybe some snorkeling classes or guided tours of the caves to strong swimmers. Maybe he could prevent a tragedy like this from happening again.

There was no place for the body to go. The police would return to collect him.

Heartsick and broken, he led his team back to the lake, gathered another team, and helped search the lake bottom.

Four hours after they hit the water, the dive teams were too exhausted to go under safely. Seven swimmers had made it to shore or been located by their families. The RCMP dive team, whose members were scattered across the province, had arrived by helicopter and taken over the search. Amber helped Kody aboard. He trembled with exertion. Twice, he nearly tumbled back into the water.

"What were you thinking?" she chided him. "You should have stopped long ago. You're crazy to risk yourself and Bryce." He'd stopped going down with anyone but Bryce an hour ago. As less experienced divers, they were at increased risk of dangerous, life-threatening fatigue.

"I couldn't just quit if there might be more people in those caves. The deepest ones don't have any air. They're fully flooded now." His teeth chattered.

"Come here," Hazel ordered. He stumbled to the bench and dropped onto it beside Bryce, barely making it before his knees gave out. "Block Wong's view," she ordered Amber. The officer was piloting the boat back to shore now that their part of the search was over.

With a quick wave of her hands, she magically pushed most of the water from their wetsuits and hair.

"Impressive," Bryce whispered.

"You ain't seen nothing, yet," Amber said with a chuckle. "Get out of those wetsuits, and we'll show you impressive."

They helped the men disrobe and piled their equipment to the side. Hazel stood between the helm and the other divers. "Brace yourself," Amber warned. She rubbed her hands together and generated a small ball of fire. "Touch it." She held her hands out to Bryce.

"Hell no." He leaned back; eyes narrowed.

"It's okay, man. If she says it's safe, it's all good." Kody reached out and touched the tiny glowing sphere. "It's warm, but not hot enough to burn."

Bryce tentatively touched the visual manifestation of her power. "Cool. How come it doesn't burn?"

"It can, if I amp up the power. Right now, I'm just going to give you some extra heat. I'll do Kody first." Stepping forward, she stroked her hands just millimetres away from his skin. Up and down his arms, legs, and torso until his shivering eased. "You should eat," she chided gently. "You burned a crap-load of energy down there." She turned to Bryce. "Your turn."

He didn't move away when she stepped closer to him, but he did flinch. "I promise, this won't hurt." She didn't move until he nodded his acquiescence. She repeated the motions she'd used on Kody.

"Holy shit, that's cool." He grinned up at her as the chill escaped his body.

"It is, but it's not something I do lightly, and you can't tell anyone."

He crossed his heart. "I promise. Your secret is safe with me."

"You need to know; I've tamped it down. This can get hot enough to burn. I could start an actual fire if I wanted to." The tone of her words struck her. "Sorry, that wasn't a threat. I was just...never mind."

"It's okay, I get it." He was calmer than she expected. "I knew you guys could do things, but controlling fire? Wicked cool." He laughed.

Amber chuckled along with him and dropped into the seat between him and Kody. "Shoot." Dizziness swamped her. Hazel rushed to her side and shoved a soft drink in her hand.

Chapter Twenty-Six

"**W**hat's wrong with her?" Kody asked. Amber was pale and colorless. She looked like death. He reached out and touched her gently on the arm. She was frigid cold.

"Large magical exertions are exhausting. Drink this." Hazel handed Amber a soda. "It's got sugar and caffeine. I'll grab you something to eat." She rifled through the backpack she'd brought aboard and handed her sister a chocolate bar. "Usually, we eat something nutritious, but I didn't have much time to pack before this *adventure*." She put a wry emphasis on the last word. "Laz said she grabbed what she could from a vending machine and stuffed it into the bag. Amber needs serious, real, food as soon as we hit land again."

"Real food?" Kody struggled into his sweatshirt.

"Something nutritious. Protein, carbs, veggies. The sugar in the soda and chocolate will boost her up, for now, then she'll crash. At home, we'll stuff her with restorative tea."

"How come your magic, moving the water from us, didn't sap you? Look at her, she can barely sit upright." Kody wrestled his legs into his jeans.

"I didn't use much power. Evaporation is a natural process. I just hurried it along. Amber had to build fire from nothing. Controlling fire, keeping the burn from getting out of control isn't easy; it has an enormous physical toll."

Kody looked up; Amber shivered in the bright sunlight, as if she were trapped in the dark, frigid caves he'd just searched. "She's freezing." Jesus, did she risk herself to help him and Bryce? Just thinking about her sacrifice nearly brought him to his knees. He settled beside her on the narrow bench, wrapping his arm around her shoulders. All the blankets were wet; there was zero sense in covering a cold person with a wet blanket. He'd use the body heat she restored to him and give it right back to her. He shifted sideways and flung one leg over the bench. Straddling the padded seat, he faced her and drew her closer until she nestled tightly against him. Silently, he willed his body to ignore the attraction and desire fueled by having her in such an intimate position.

He'd been attracted to her from the moment she stood up to him the night they met. In light of their different upbringings, he'd tried to keep his attraction under wraps. Now, with her cuddled against his body, leaning in to absorb his warmth... Lord, he wanted to kiss her.

The police boat raced toward shore, to return the divers to land. "A command post has been set up in the parking lot," Wong called over his shoulder. "You'll be given food and fluids and checked over by EMS to make sure you're okay to go home. The Three Moon Falls police service thanks you for your assistance."

The words were mechanical, but Kody recognized the heartfelt sentiment behind them. It must have been hard for Wong to supervise and be helpless to assist in the recovery. If Amber wasn't snuggled against him, Kody would have gone to Wong and thanked him for his assistance. Manning the boat and helping with the divers was an enormous contribution. But for now, he was going to enjoy every second of having her in his arms.

He wasn't looking for a relationship; he had a business to run, as did she. But, damn, holding her felt right, even if her fire skills freaked him out a bit. His grandmother had always said, "Son, there are more things in heaven and on earth than you ever dreamed of." Until recently, he'd chalked it up to the musings of an old woman. Now, he wondered if she knew more than she ever revealed. Had she known magic? Could she do magic? He had a million questions for her the next time they talked, especially now that he recalled her special cold and flu tea. The one from an old family recipe she made from herbs she grew herself.

He found himself chuckling.

"What's so funny?" Amber asked, turning to look up at him, her green eyes bright with inquiry, despite the dark bags under her eyes.

She looked exhausted, but she was still beautiful. His grandmother would like her, especially if she was, like he suspected, magical. "I was thinking about my grandmother. I think you'd like her."

"Oh."

"She's coming out to visit next month. You'll probably run into her." He didn't mention he'd only just decided to invite her. He'd call her tonight.

Wong cut the throttle, and the cruiser coasted to the dock, which had been cordoned off from the public. Two RCMP officers stood guard at the barricade. The police presence seemed to have tripled. There were the locals, extra RCMP, Sheriffs, and wildlife officers. Apparently, it was all hands on deck for the rescue and investigation. The small crowd on shore cheered as the searchers disembarked. The mayor herself was the only other person on the dock, her fuchsia and maroon clothing almost blinding to his exhausted eyes.

"I know you're all exhausted. But the police are going to need each of you to file a statement about the search," the mayor proclaimed. In a lower voice, she continued, "If you'll all just board the bus at the end of the dock, we'll take you to the station, avoiding the press. There are reporters here from several major networks, newspapers, and blogs. I've arranged for volunteers to take your vehicles home for you, and police officers will take you home once your statements have been taken."

There were a few groans, but nobody disagreed outright. Kody scanned the crowd. There was, indeed, a large faction of paparazzi milling around outside the police barricade. He wasn't naïve enough to think he'd be able to avoid the press entirely. This wasn't the first search he'd taken part in. He was glad he had time to process the event and the emotions it had stirred up, particularly his deepening attraction to Amber.

Mayor Quinton thanked each diver personally and shook their hands as they exited the boat. Kody waited until nobody remained on board except Bryce, Hazel, Amber, Wong and himself, before he stood and assisted Amber to her feet.

"Amber, your family is at the station. They have food for you. Kody, good work. This town and I are proud of you." She shook his hand and clapped him on the back. "I wasn't sure of you when we met, but you've earned my trust and respect." She started praising Wong, who was the last to disembark.

Amber stumbled on her feet, lurching into his side. He slid his arm around her waist, lifting slightly, supporting her and drawing her close to him. Her body was like ice, even through the sweater he'd given her just before they arrived.

"You're freezing. Come on, let's get you in the bus." Supporting her as much as he could, he led her down the dock toward the bus. Splitting his attention between their destination and Amber, he nearly missed noticing her magical friends, Mel and Jerry, who were handing out blankets to the divers as they reached the bus.

Kody accepted his and draped it around Amber's shoulders.

Mel and Jerry shared a look and smiled at him. "It's like that, is it?" Mel asked, his brown eyes crinkled with mirth.

Kody didn't bother to reply. Let them think what they wanted. Getting Amber warm and fed was his first, and only, priority. He accepted a second blanket and wrapped it overtop the first. Thanks to Amber's earlier sacrifice and the warmth of the sun, he wasn't cold any longer; his body had reached a normal temperature.

Jerry climbed onto the bus ahead of them and turned to help Amber up the stairs. Kody came up behind her, hands on her waist to steady her ascent. Kody helped Amber onto the first empty bench, and Jerry climbed into the driver's seat.

Jerry turned his lanky body around and grinned at the passengers. "Alright everybody. We're out."

A beefy man wearing a private security company uniform pulled aside a barricade and the bus edged forward, past the crowd, and onto the road leading to the police station. Traffic was light, and they travelled without stopping until the bus was secured in the RCMP detachment's underground garage.

Kody, Bryce, Wong, Amber, and Hazel and three of the twelve volunteer divers took the elevator to the second floor. Jerry and the remaining divers would follow when the elevator returned to the parking garage.

Constable Stone met them upstairs and ushered them into a conference room where Amber's family and an enormous buffet waited.

Stone waited quietly until everyone was seated with a plate of food in front of them. "People," she began. "I can't tell you enough how important your contribution was today. There isn't enough gratitude in this world to express Three Moon Falls thanks. Unfortunately, most of my officers are still out searching for survivors or questioning witnesses. The province's top investigative and engineering team is examining the falls to find out what happened."

She hesitated, cleared her throat, and went on. "I've got three officers here, including myself, to take your statements. We'll make it as brief as possible, but it will be thorough. Once you've given your statements, you can go. Volunteers are waiting to take you home, or to your vehicle as you prefer. I recommend you go straight home unless you want to talk to the press. However, I am requesting you keep today's event under your hats until we get to the bottom of the explosion."

And there it was. She definitely suspected more than a natural occurrence.

"If you choose to go straight home, please give your keys to the volunteers, and they'll see your vehicle is delivered to your home. Any questions?" She glanced around the room. "Good. We'll start with you three." She pointed to three men and instructed them to follow an officer to a separate room to be debriefed. As soon as they were gone, quiet chatter about the day's events started.

Hyacinth hurried to Amber's side. "Are you okay?" she asked, casting Amber and Kody both a significant look and raising one eyebrow, indicating her words had a deeper meaning. She slid a mug of tea in front of each of her sisters.

"I'm great," Kody replied. "Thanks to your sisters."

Bryce, who was seated beside Kody, echoed his sentiments.

"Relax, sister," Hazel said, obviously noticing Hyacinth's shocked look. "Nobody else saw anything. There wasn't really a choice. We couldn't let hypothermia put them in the hospital, could we?"

"Dammit," Hyacinth whispered. "This isn't supposed to be public knowledge. Being outed has cost a lot of people their lives."

"Trust me," Bryce said lowly. "Your secret is safe with me. I owe your family my life, and I'll honor that debt."

"As will I," Kody echoed the younger man's sentiments, filling his voice with as much promise as he could. He'd do whatever it took to keep Amber safe.

Chapter Twenty-Seven

A mber's shoulder brushed against Kody's arm in the back seat of Hyacinth's forest green Ford Explorer. She should pull away; instead, she leaned into him, pulling strength from his solid warm. He shifted and slid his arm around her shoulders. Gently, he pulled her closer until she was nestled tightly against his side. She'd climbed into the vehicle first, sliding into the middle rather than across to the opposite door. She felt a little guilty for drawing strength from Kody's nearness, but not guilty enough to distance herself.

She was finally warm and was regaining her balance. The food and Hyacinth's tea had really helped. She'd never admit it aloud, but Kody had given her stability as well. Probably more than he knew. When she was at her weakest, he'd embraced her tightly, and it had been more than just the heat of his body giving her strength. She'd almost swear he'd pushed energy toward her.

Kody Wilkins might just be a descendent of Salem himself. There were at least four Wilkinses among the accusers during that travesty of justice. It wasn't beyond comprehension to think some of them might have been magical. She'd have to ask him about his family history. For now, she was content to be in his arms; it felt like coming home.

He'd agreed, without question, to Gramma Pearl's request to come back to the house for their own debriefing. Bryce and the other divers had all gone home, exhausted, but exhilarated that they'd saved some lives. Officer Wong had asked Kody about diving classes, claiming he wanted to improve his ability to help should another disaster occur.

Inside the sanctuary of her childhood home, the tension slipped from Amber's shoulders. She inhaled a deep, shuddering breath and released it in a whoosh. She didn't want to be this comfortable at his side, but she was, and there was no denying it.

She peered up at him. He was gazing down at her. A soft smile lit his face. "Long day, huh?" she asked.

"Interminable. I'm glad it's over, but I'm beyond grateful we found those people in the caves."

"Yeah," she agreed. "It breaks my heart that two people drowned in the lake. The explosion shook the whole town." She swallowed the lump of sadness clogging her throat.

"We did all we could do. We saved Chandra. Which is nothing to sneeze at," he commiserated. "Something's bothering me though." His brow furrowed as he frowned.

"What's that?" Could he be feeling it, too? From first thing this morning, something had felt wrong. What she'd felt hadn't been a premonition, not exactly, just a sense of something being off. Not quite right. Like the world was holding its breath. Then, an explosion had rocked the town on its foundations. The unease she'd felt had amplified. More than fear, it was dread and anticipation and a certainty something else was going to go wrong.

"This is going to sound crazy." He paused; his arm tensed across her shoulders. "I don't think the explosion was any sort of natural phenomenon. Watching Stone, I believe she doesn't think it was natural, either, and I'd bet my life someone caused it. But who the hell would blow up a waterfall?"

"And why?"

"You think I'm nuts, don't you?"

She pondered his words for a moment. "Actually, no. I've been fighting this feeling all day. I don't understand it, but somehow, I know whatever happened, it wasn't natural."

"You've got that right," Hyacinth added as they turned into the driveway. The gate swooped open and closed silently behind them.

"I'll never get used to that." Kody glared at the gate over his shoulder.

"What?" Amber laughed. "It's an automatic gate."

"Right. It's some kind of magic. I can't deal with what I don't understand, and your gate freaks me out."

Amber patted his knee. It was rock solid under her palm. She let her hand rest there, either to comfort him, or herself, she wasn't sure. "You can deal with me controlling fire, but an automatic gate freaks you out?" She grinned up at him. "You need to relax."

"I, for one, won't relax until we figure out what the heck is going on," Hyacinth chimed in as she put the car into park near the house.

"I second that," Kody said, flinging his door open. With Amber's hand locked firmly in his, fingers entwined, he urged her to follow him. "Let's get this show on the road. I'm not going to rest easy until we figure out what's going on."

G ramma Pearl was pacing the kitchen when they arrived. She already had tea, cookies, and apple pie waiting on the table. "What took so long?" she demanded.

Amber dropped Kody's hand and hurried, barefoot, to her grandmother's side and pressed a kiss against her beautiful cheek. She marvelled at how young her grandmother looked. At a quick glance, you'd almost mistake her for the girl's mother rather than their grandmother. The Hawk family had good genes, which were enhanced by their magical skills. "It took us a little longer to extract ourselves from the station. You made a clean getaway. By the time we left, the place was bustling with officers and the RCMP dive team. Everyone wanted to talk to us."

"I'm just glad we finally got out of there. Hi, Gramma Pearl," Kody greeted her cautiously.

"Relax, boy. I'll stay out of your head. Unless you mess with my granddaughters."

Kody blanched.

Indignation flared within Amber. "Gramma Pearl, you'll stay out of his head no matter what! I won't let you meddle with my friends." She was certain her grandmother was teasing, but then again, sometimes she couldn't quite trust her. She made everyone else stick to high standards of behavior, but as Amber grew older, and wiser, she realized that occasionally, Pearl twisted those rules to benefit herself and to protect her family.

"Is that what he is? Your friend?" Pearl demanded.

"What crawled up your skirt and died?" Amber jabbed a finger at her grandmother.

All three of Amber's sisters gasped at her bravado in calling their grandmother out. Seriously, Pearl was getting out of hand. "Kody is my friend, our friend, and my neighbor. He's been my protector and more. Back off." What in the world was wrong with her grandmother?

Pearl didn't act like this. Yeah, she might be sneaky and poke her nose where it didn't belong, but she wasn't outright rude.

Pearl had the grace to flush. She stared at the tips of her slippers. "Sorry. I'm off today. The tension in this town is out of control. It's not just what happened today. It's more than that. Something sinister is creeping in, and I can't get a handle one it." She dropped into a chair and looked up at them, one after another.

Pearl's face was pale, almost ashen, and at that moment, she looked every one of her sixty years and then some. Amber walked over, patted her grandmother on the shoulder, and leaned over to wrap her into a hug. "It's okay, we all feel it."

"Even I feel it, and I don't have a magical bone in my body." Kody dropped tiredly in the chair beside Pearl. "It's like ... anticipating a disaster, knowing it's coming and not being able to do anything about it. I swear to God Keres is behind this."

Amber stared at him. She'd had the same thought. "Me too. By the Goddess, he's up to something, and we have to figure out why in the world he'd blast the falls." She slid into the chair between Kody and Pearl. Her sisters took seats around the table while Amber poured tea. Everyone took theirs plain; Kody added a generous portion of honey to his. Pearl made a tsk sound.

"Hey," he said with a shrug. "I'm a coffee guy. All this tea drinking is taking some time to get used to. The honey makes it palatable."

"You might have tasted it first." Amber laughed. "This one is already sweet. It's got clover and rosehips in it."

"With healing properties and medicinal value, no doubt." He winked at her.

"No doubt. Have a cookie, they're lemon sugar cookies garnished with edible flowers."

He wrinkled his nose at the brimming plate but took one anyway.

"Don't be such a coward. You might like it."

Two minutes later, he reached for a second cookie. "They aren't that bad," he admitted. He grasped her hand and raised it to his lips for a quick kiss, like a prince paying homage to his princess. Her skin prickled delightfully, and she stared into his beautiful, expressive green eyes. With his green eyes and hers, they'd make beautiful green-eyed babies. Oh, she was not going there. She tugged gently on her hand, trying to extract herself. He didn't release her. He lowered their joined hands to his knee, his fingers curled around hers.

When she looked up, her sisters were staring, open mouthed, at her and Kody, a thousand questions in their minds. She ignored them, it didn't matter what they thought, she liked him. "What's first on the agenda?" Nobody spoke for several long minutes.

Kody broke the silence. "The area under the falls is riddled with caves. I've never seen any kind of geological survey for the area, but it stands to reason there might be other hollows in the cliffs."

"And?" Amber asked.

"If Keres, I'm operating on the assumption it was him, if Keres thought there were more caves hidden there, he might try blasting to open them up."

"Wouldn't that risk destroying whatever he's looking for?" Amber objected. She sipped her tea, trying to moisten her suddenly dry throat. Something about Kody's words struck deeply. The room spun, and her cup clattered to the table. An image of rushing water and a cloth bound bundle exploded into her head, stealing her breath. "Oh." She swayed in her chair. Kody and her grandmother's hands steadied her shoulders, holding her upright.

"What is it?" The concern in Kody's voice jerked her attention back to the kitchen. "Are you okay?"

"I'm—" She cleared her throat. "I'm fine. I just had the strangest vision. Like an out of body experience, or what I always felt one would be like." She shook her head to clear the lingering clouds and confusion. "I saw...that is...there was a..." She blinked rapidly, trying to recall the vision she'd just experienced, even as it faded away. "A cloth wrapped package and rushing water."

Exhausted, she slumped forward and rested her elbows on the table, chin cupped in her hands, eyes closed. If this was what having visions was like, she wanted no part of it. Her developing clairsentience, the ability to sense events from the past or future, could go take a hike if it was going to be this disorienting. "For a moment, it was so vivid, like I was there. I could even smell the water in the air and hear it splashing. Now, it's like a distant memory from dozens of years ago. Does that make any sense?"

"Rushing water? Like the waterfall?" Pearl asked quietly.

"Are you thinking she saw something from the past? Something involving the waterfall?" Kody stroked circles on Amber's back.

Slowly, his touch calmed her, and she relaxed. He was doing it again; only this time, he was feeding her calm rather than warmth. "Thanks." She smiled at him. "That helps." Strange how he was able to shift her emotions. He had to have some kind of magical ability. He probably didn't even realize he was helping her.

"I don't think it was the falls by the lake," Amber muttered. She wasn't even sure what she'd seen had been a waterfall, but it had that feeling. "It could have been a waterfall. Maybe." This was ridiculous and frustrating. If she was going to get an image, why couldn't it be something readily identifiable? She nibbled on her thumbnail and tried to recapture the vision.

"Hey," Kody said softly. "What's worrying you? You're biting your nails to stubs." He met her gaze with an apprehensive glance.

She dropped her hand to her lap and clenched it into a fist. "This whole thing bugs me. The explosion, Keres being in the store and watching me. The stupid vision. I can't make sense of it. It feels like there's something hovering, just outside my mind. Something I should catch. It's like chasing a shadow." She made a frustrated sound and snatched a cookie off the plate. She rolled it around in her fingers until it started to crumble.

"Are you going to eat that or destroy it?" Hazel asked lightly.

"What?" Amber stared at the cookie in her hand. "Eat it, I guess." She nibbled the edge of it and set the rest of it down on the floral-print, cloth napkin beside her mug. She pivoted the still folded napkin in a circle. Around and around. She stared at it, without really seeing it, half mesmerised by the blurring images. She let her eyes lose focus. White roses on a pale blue background whirled together into a blurred mess. She'd never been hypnotised, nor had she ever astral projected herself or had an out of body experience. She imagined they might feel a bit like this.

The conversation around the table faded away as she shifted her awareness to the whirling fabric. She concentrated, without focusing her vision. Around and around it went. She sent a silent plea to the Goddess and her ancestors for help.

Mother Earth, family mine.
Come to me in this time.
Bring to me visions from long gone
Hear me now, heed my song.
Free me from the past's long curse
I beg you with my simple verse.
Danger rears his ugly head
I seek solutions in its stead.
I honor those gone and past
Clear this vision is all I ask.
By earth, air, land, and sea.
As I will it, so mote it be.

Not her best rhyming by a long shot, but it got the idea across to anyone who might be privy to her thoughts. A call to the Goddess was often done in silent rhyme, and more often than not, made up on the spot. Amber's eyes drifted closed, and she stopped twirling the napkin and sat motionless, her palms flat on the table, her bare feet planted firmly on the floor, grounding her.

The earlier vision returned on a wave of dizziness. Dirty, delicate hands frantically wrapped something in tattered fabric and tied it with rough twine. The image faded to be replaced by one of splashing water. The water's source wasn't clear. It could have been a waterfall. Heck, it could have been a close-up of a running faucet. She couldn't tell. All she knew for certain was they needed to find that bundle of fabric.

She opened her eyes and looked around the table. Five sets of eyes stared at her with concerned interest. She cleared her throat. "I can't get a better image. All I know is somehow, we need to find whatever is in the bundle of fabric. It's near, in, or under water. I think. When I see it, I get a sense of urgency. Of a desperate need to protect the bundle. I can't decipher if the emotion is mine, or if it belongs to the person, a woman, I think, who is hiding the bundle. I just don't know what it is or where to look. But we need to keep it away from Keres."

"Anything else?" Kody asked.

"Nothing. My clairvoyant skills are new and sadly underdeveloped. If I had something of his, I might be able to get something off it, but when I focus, even when I ask the Goddess for help, all I see is the bundle, and water."

"We need to find something of his, then?" Hyacinth suggested.

"How do we do that?" Lazuli asked.

"What if we found out where he was staying? We could sneak in and borrow something of his." Kody looked around the room.

"Are you suggesting breaking and entering?" Amber asked, slightly aghast. "We could get arrested." She stared at Kody.

"Only if we get caught," Lazuli reply dryly. "The trick is to avoid getting caught."

"I don't know about this." Unease roiled in Amber's guts. No matter what they thought of Keres and what he might be up to, it didn't sit right to spy on him or steal something belonging to him. Her whole life had been a balance of truth and lies. Fear and mistrust had kept her family from revealing their magical talents. For the most part, that meant being careful and not mentioning it to anyone. To Amber, a lie of omission was still a lie, but at the same time, they didn't dare let the truth out.

Sneaking around behind Keres' back to discover what he was up to smacked of deceit and made her wince. She didn't like it, but no matter how hard she wracked her brain, she didn't really see another solution; and unfortunately, her instincts told her they needed to do this.

"I don't like it." Amber twisted her hands together. "But I don't see any other choice. How do we do this?" So many things could go wrong. She forced herself not to consider the negative possibilities and the chance of getting arrested. Maybe they could find something and point the police toward Keres for the explosion. If they did, he'd be out of their hair, and she could stop worrying about when he'd show up again and what he'd do next.

She wasn't a coward; she could hold her own in most situations, but Keres scared the shit out of her, and she wasn't afraid to admit it. But she wasn't going to jump in blind. She'd meditate and ask the Goddess for help and insight before she did anything. Her family had her back, that was certain. Hopefully, Kody did, too. He'd been by her side since the lake. She liked him, and he seemed to be dealing with her family's magical abilities without issue.

"Maybe I don't need to take something of his," Amber murmured, staring from one member of her family to the other, her gaze finally landing on Kody.

"What do you mean?" He grasped her hand in his, his thumb stroked a soothing design on the back of her hand.

"If I could just hold something...maybe I could learn more that way." She shrugged. "I don't know. I'm not even sure I want to do this."

"Is there an option?" Kody asked. "Could we just find him and have you touch him?" He shook his head. "No, something weird happens when he touches you. It's as if you lose yourself somehow."

Amber gaped at him. "That's exactly it. It isn't like having someone poke around in your brain looking for information. It's more like he's pushing me down, trying to take over my brain. Does that make sense?"

"That sounds so sci-fi," Lazuli answered seriously. "But it makes sense. He probably thinks he can subdue you to find what he wants." She rubbed her hands together in a let's go motion. "Okay guys. When do we do this? The sooner the better, I think."

Amber's heart sank, and a thousand fire ants crawled through her stomach. As her guts burned, she grew cold. She wrapped her arms around herself, tucking her hands under her arms. She didn't want to do this; it went against everything she stood for. Truth, honesty. Live and let live. Mind your own business. For the life of her, she couldn't think of a way to avoid it. This felt bigger than just her and her family. More people were at stake.

"When do we do this?" she repeated Lazuli's earlier question.

Chapter Twenty-Eight

B efore he knew what was happening, Kody stood guard at the end of a long, paved driveway leading to a rental property five miles from the Hawk's home. He scanned left and right, up and down the highway, watching for any signs of motion or vehicle. They'd parked in a clearing just down the road and crept through the bushes. Amber and Hazel had left him at the edge of the highway to sneak up to the house, which was just out of sight, beyond a turn in the driveway. He was to call them if Keres returned before they got back.

He glanced at his phone to ensure he still had battery power. A touch of a button had the screen glowing like a spotlight in the dark. Half blinded, he sighed and slid it back into his pocket.

Officer Stone had assured them Keres was in Flanigan's Pub for a late dinner with his friend. She'd given Gramma Pearl Keres' local address from her files.

Kody was shocked the head of the local RCMP detachment had shared privileged information. As part of the fight against Keres, he was pleased. But as a man who valued his privacy, it rubbed him the wrong way. Weren't the police supposed to protect civilians?

Maybe she thought finding out what Keres was up to was more important than his privacy. Though, she could have sent officers around to talk to him. Did magical cops have different rules than other cops?

Kody shuffled back and forth along the end of the driveway, kicking stray pinecones off the asphalt as he watched and listened for vehicles. He glanced at his watch. Seriously? Only five minutes had passed. It felt like an hour. What was taking them so long?

A dozen uncomfortable scenarios flashed through his mind, up to including the girls being captured and held hostage. Or worse.

"Geez. Get a grip, Wilkins," he mumbled, kicking a small rock, sending it ricocheting off the trees. "There's only one way into this place by car. It's not like Keres is going to walk from town and take the hiking path in. How frigging long does it take to sneak into a house, steal something, and get back out?" He stomped back and forth. "I should have gone and left Hazel here to stand guard." With each step, he punched his right fist into the palm of his left hand. He never should have listened to them just because they have magic. What could magic do that a man couldn't? He should be up at the house protecting them.

Headlights rounded a corner. He dove behind an enormous spruce tree and crouched down. Cell phone in hand, he waited. Time crawled as the car came closer. After a moment, he realized it was going right past, not slowing for the turn. His breath whooshed out in a rush. Damn. That was close. Too close. Where were they? They should be back by now. Before he could move from his hiding spot, another vehicle came barrelling toward him from the other direction. He froze.

It passed by without slowing.

His heart thundered in his chest.

His mouth went dry.

His cramping calves alerted him to the fact he was still crouched behind the tree. Damn. He straightened, relieving the burning in his legs and tangling his short hair in the branches of the tree. He wrestled himself free and resumed guard.

When he was seven, he'd snuck into his best friend, Lance's, kitchen while Lance's mother was answering the door. They'd swiped a generous chunk of chocolate cookie dough and high-tailed it to the garage where they gobbled it up in a matter of seconds, breathless with fear she'd catch them or notice the dough was missing.

If Lance's mother ever discovered what they'd done, she never mentioned it, but he'd lived in fear for weeks until the panicked memory faded from his mind, replaced by other pressing concerns of childhood. He'd forgotten about it until now. The ache in his guts brought the old memory slamming home like a line drive to the stomach. A guilt-gut was a powerful thing, and he hadn't stolen since then. Not even when dared and ridiculed by some of his tougher teenaged friends.

It didn't feel right to be involved in this now; but what choice did he have? He couldn't let Amber and Hazel do it alone, and for all her assistance, Officer Stone wasn't doing anything. With nothing to go on but rumors and the Hawk family's word, there was no action the police could take.

That was why he was out here, in the middle of the night, freezing his ass off. For the middle of June, it was damned cold. Clouds had rolled in since they started on their venture, fully obscuring the moon. He'd never felt so alone and helpless in his life. He should have worn a jacket. Fifteen degrees Celsius wasn't cold by any stretch, but tonight, it felt like sub-zero.

Standing in the shadow of the trees, he fixed his gaze on the road. And waited. He shuffled his feet and rubbed his arms to get warm. When this was done, he needed a good stiff drink.

"Let me try," Hazel hissed in Amber's ear.

"Back off." She elbowed her sister in the ribs. "I've got this." She inhaled deeply and focused her attention on the lock. Moving things with her mind was a matter of practise. It was a skill she'd learned as a kid. But unlocking a lock when you couldn't see the tumblers inside took a whole different level of finesse. "Watch our backs and keep an eye on the window."

"There's nobody inside."

Amber heard her sister's virtually silent steps as she ambled away to peek in the windows to the left of the double oak front doors. This house was huge. An enormous brick colonial, it had three sets of windows on either side of the door. It had taken them several minutes to reconnoiter around the house, peeking into each window to ensure they were alone. The only light on was in the den at the back of the house. Fortunately, the house didn't have motion sensors lights, nor did the yard. Motion sensors would have ruined any chances they had of entering unnoticed.

"Should I make another perimeter check?" Hazel dropped a hand on Amber's shoulder.

Amber jumped, losing concentration and dropping the tumblers she held in place mentally. "Shit. Now I have to start over. No, you don't need to reconnoiter again. I love that word." She chuckled. "I should have brought Kody and left you guarding the road. At least he'd have kept his mouth shut." She focused her attention on the lock.

Luckily, now that she knew the positions of the first three tumblers, setting them was easier.

"We should have kicked in the basement window behind that bush. It would have been faster."

"Shut. Up. Please. We can't leave any trace we're here. Hence, the mental lock picking rather than a lock pick set. Not that either one of us knows how to pick a lock." She tweaked the tumblers until the lock clicked.

She squeezed the tab, and the latch slid back, the sound ridiculously loud in the stillness of the night. Nothing made a sound, not even crickets. The silence was creepy. "Keep your gloves on. No fingerprints," Amber warned and eased the door open. She paused.

No alarms beeped. Nothing broke the endless quiet, except the sound of Hazel's feet, and she urged Amber inside. "Okay, here goes nothing."

They crept inside, closing the door behind them.

"Holy shit, this place is enormous." Hazel's whisper echoed through the cavernous entryway. Nothing marred the pristine walls and marble floors. The only decorative accent was the plush area rug they stood on. The house had an eerie stillness, as if it was holding its breath waiting for something to happen.

"This place is creepy. Can you feel that?" Shivers raced over Amber's skin. She battled the urge to cut and run before they searched the house for signs of what Keres was up to.

"I thought our house was the only one with a mind of its own. This place isn't happy about whatever is going on here. Just being here makes my skin crawl."

"I know what you mean," Amber agreed. "No more talking. Let's stick together." After a quick check for dirt on their sneakers, they moved further inside, peeking their heads in doorways as they passed. A sparsely furnished sitting area and music room containing only a grand piano revealed nothing of interest. They crept forward, down the hall to the kitchen. Dirty dishes littered every surface, and garbage spilled from an overflowing can. The room was silent except for the lazy buzz of flies in the window.

"Ugg. Gross." Amber wrinkled her nose. They passed through the kitchen, the nook, and into the dining room.

Oak dining chairs were stacked haphazardly to the side with only two of twelve remaining at the table. One on the long side, one on the end. An open laptop sat on the table, surrounded by piles of papers. Amber crept around and nudged the mouse beside the computer. "Who uses a mouse when they've got a trackpad?" The screen flared to life. Thankfully, thick curtains draped the windows and blocked the light from anyone outside. "Look, no password." Why wouldn't he have a password? She flipped through the open computer files while Hazel snapped shots of the papers on the table, without disturbing anything.

"I've never seen anything like this," Hazel whispered. "It's some kind of spell, but I can't tell what it is supposed to do. I've never heard of a spell like this. Graveyard dirt, herbs, spices, fresh human blood." She gagged and shivered.

Amber leaned in to read the faded parchment. "It's old, dark magic. Some of it isn't even in English." Just looking at it made her sick to her stomach. It reeked of something evil and sinful. "Snap a picture of it. We'll figure out what it's for later." She turned her attention back to the computer. "He's got no email program, and there's nothing interesting here, except a dossier on our family." She gasped. "Can you believe this? It's got all our birthdays, a family history chart going back at least a hundred and fifty years." She scrolled down in the document. "Shit. It goes all the way back to Margaret Hawkes, in Salem."

"Let me see." Hazel leaned over Amber's shoulder. "Holy crap! We should have brought an external hard drive and taken a backup of his computer."

"We don't have time; he could be back any second. Take a few pictures of this file, and we'll get going."

Hazel obediently snapped shots of the screen as Amber skimmed through the document. They crept through the remainder of the main floor and scurried upstairs. "Shoot, it's way darker up here. The curtains are all cracked open. We don't dare turn on any lights."

Six bedrooms and an entertainment room revealed nothing. One room was littered with clothing. Judging by the styles and size, it must belong to Keres' friend. The final bedroom was filthy. Clothing littered every surface. An empty suitcase perched precariously on the edge of a dark wood dresser. Amber scanned the room from the doorway. The bedside table was the only clean spot in the room. A shiny picture frame stood on it, angled to face the queen-sized bed.

Careful not to step on anything, Amber stepped toward the bed. She picked up the picture in her gloved hand. A beautiful blonde woman smiled lovingly from the frame. Even through her gloves, Amber was rocked by a crippling sense of love and loss. The picture was signed, with all my love, Meredith, and dated ten years earlier.

"Take a picture of this."

Hazel grabbed the frame and went into the adjoining bath, closed the door, and snapped an image. She returned the frame to Amber, who returned it to the exact spot she'd found it. Keres might notice things out of place. Whoever this woman was, she'd been important to Keres, and he missed her. Could she be involved in this mess somehow?

"I have to find something of his to take, something he won't miss. I need more than just two minutes with it. It could take a while to get a clear image from it."

"What about that?" Hazel pointed to a discarded T-shirt. "He's got a lot of them. He shouldn't miss one?"

Amber slipped off her glove and picked up one of several dirty, plain white T-shirts littering the floor. She got an instant sense of Keres. The smelly garment was ripe with his vibes. She gagged and shuddered with the impressions. "This will do." She slipped the shirt into a plastic bag, tucked the bag inside her hoodie, and nodded toward the door. "Let's get out of here before it's too late."

They hurried downstairs and out the door. Amber paused outside the house to mentally lock the deadbolt. When it clicked shut, they raced across the grass. Under the dim moonlight, they travelled under the cover of the trees' shadows, their footsteps silent on the manicured grass. They moved without speaking until they were steps away from an unaware Kody.

"Kody, we're here," Amber said softly.

The voice came out of nowhere.

"What the hell?" Kody screeched. His heart thundering in his chest, he whirled around and dropped to a defensive posture he'd learned in karate class in high school.

Amber and Hazel doubled over laughing.

"Sorry," Amber choked out between chuckles. "I thought you'd hear us coming."

"Hell no." Kody glared at them. "I was focused on the road. There've been a dozen cars back and forth on the highway. I wasn't expecting to be attacked from behind." He sucked in a deep breath. "I'm not cut out for a life of crime. What took so long? Did you get what you need?"

"It took a while to get through the lock. Mental lock picking isn't easy," Amber explained. She patted her zipped jacket. "I grabbed a shirt. It should work."

"Good. Let's get out of here." He paused. He'd seen her shudder when she touched her jacket. "Are you okay? Do you want me to carry it?" It seemed like Keres' shirt made her uncomfortable. Maybe he could relieve her discomfort by carrying it.

"No. I'm okay. Let's get out of here before he does come back."

"I'll second that," Hazel blurted and took off at a slow jog toward their hidden car.

Kody held out his hand to Amber. She grasped it tightly with her own.

"Your hand is freezing. Didn't you wear gloves?" Holy crap, if they'd gone in there without gloves, their prints would be all over the house.

"I did. I took them off when I came outside. I'm chilled. The house was..." She shuddered visibly. "Houses have feelings, they contain or store, I don't know, maybe reflect the emotions of those who live there. I'm sure you felt it in our house."

"I did. Your house has a life of its own." He'd never forget how alive Amber's home felt.

"It's like that, but almost no houses have the magic stored like ours does. This place," she jerked a thumb toward the house they'd just left, "it's got a negative vibe, like it's not happy. It's almost like it's frightened."

Kody stared at her. House vibes he understood. He'd known many places that felt happy and a few which made him uncomfortable. Years ago, he'd visited a home where a former resident committed suicide. It was the saddest place he'd ever been, and the death had been almost a decade previous. But a house being frightened? It defied belief.

"Frightened?" he echoed.

"Yeah, it was weird. It creeped the hell out of me."

Kody grasped both of her hands and rubbed them between his. "It's okay. You're finished in there. We'll have you warmed up in no time."

"Are you guys coming or what?" Hazel hissed, jogging back toward them. "We've got to get out of here."

Headlights flashed down the highway, forcing them to duck deep under the cover of the trees. A branch slapped Kody in the face. He shoved it away and wiped at the sticky residue left behind. "Great, pine sap. That'll never come off."

"Rubbing alcohol," Amber advised. "Let's go. They're gone."

Kody watched taillights fade in the distance. "I can't wait to be as far away from here as I can get. This night has lasted a week at least."

Amber chuckled. "It's not that bad." She grasped his hand and jogged down the trail.

Chapter Twenty-Nine

It was late, pushing midnight, when Amber, Kody, and Hazel arrived back at the Hawk family home. Their mission had started later and taken longer than expected. They hurried into the kitchen where Gramma Pearl had tea and cookies waiting for them. The scent of basil and tomato sauce lingered in the air along with pepperoni and cheese. Pizza was coming. His stomach growled.

Kody was the first to speak. "How do we go about doing this? What happens? What will you learn?" The questions blurted out, like bubbles from a panicked diver's mask.

"Relax. It takes a while," Gramma Pearl advised. "Take a minute to warm up and relax. Then, we'll cleanse ourselves and cast a circle for protection. Sometimes, messing with another person's belongings has unintended consequences."

"And you're just mentioning this now?" His voice rose in alarm. With this family, it was just one thing after another. About the time he adapted to one surprise, they hurled another one at him. If he wasn't coming to care for Amber, he'd cut and run. Walk away without looking back.

"We're prepared. Besides, it isn't likely anything will go awry," Amber reassured him, her hand resting on his forearm. "We just like to be prepared."

"I don't know about this." He squeezed Amber's hand with his, interlacing their fingers. "I'm going to trust you on this, but I have to admit, I'm nervous." He was more than nervous; he was half terrified. He struggled to keep his heartbeat in check. Scared though he was, he wasn't about to be seen as a coward, not in front of all these women who were taking everything in stride. Nope. He'd man up and be tough. Even if it killed him. Crap, this wasn't going to kill anyone, was it?

"If you keep hanging out here, you'll see things you never imagined possible," Pearl warned him, yet again. She squinted at him like a librarian chiding an unruly student, almost as if daring him to stay. Or maybe she was warning him off. A shiver of fear ran through him. If Amber controlled fire and Hazel controlled water, what did the old gal control? He might be in way over his head here. Well, he wasn't going to let her chase him off. She'd done that once already; but he was back, and he was here for the duration.

Locking eyes with Pearl, he lifted Amber's hand with his and pressed a kiss to her soft, vanilla scented skin. Vanilla, how ironic. Amber was the least vanilla person he'd ever met. Pearl frowned at him for a moment and then nodded, leaving him wondering exactly where he stood with her. She certainly was protective of her adult grandchildren. He admired that; despite being intimidated.

The tea was an invigorating blend of orange and mint. The oatmeal raisin cookies were still warm from the oven. Mouth watering pizza followed as idle conversation flowed around the table, touching on anything and everything from the weather to gardening. From movies to fiction.

Abruptly, Pearl stood, rubbing her hands briskly together. "It's time."

Nobody questioned her. They rose from the table, deposited their dishes in the sink, and filed up the back stairs one after another. Amber's hand in his, they were the last up the stairs. Her other hand clutched the unopened plastic bag that contained Keres' shirt.

They passed the library room he'd been in earlier—was it really only a day ago?—and carried on through a doorway and up a flight of narrow stairs. The stairs flowed into an octagonal room nearly thirteen feet across. He paused in the doorway. With the exception of the wall containing the doorway he stood in, every wall was an enormous window. Solid pillars supported the windows in each corner. The room was flooded with moonlight, and through the windows, he could see the full breathtaking vista of the night sky, glittering with stars.

Below the windows, waist high, glass-fronted cabinets containing all manner of jars, vials, and bottles circled the room. If he had ever imagined what a witch's lair looked like, this was it. The room emitted a sense of calm and order, surprising him. It smelled faintly of herbs and wax.

A white circle, nine feet across, was painted on the glistening hardwood floors, mahogany, unless he missed his guess. Amber circled the room, lighting the candles in the sconces on each window support pillar. When she was finished, all eight corners glowed from the three candles in each wrought iron holder.

"Come inside," Amber urged him.

He took a cautious step forward. Reaching around him, she pulled the door shut and flipped a switch. An almost soundless whir tickled his eardrums. An exhaust fan. Lazuli and Hyacinth cracked open two windows on opposite sides of the room.

"Rituals like this used to be performed outside," Amber said. "We work outside as often as possible. Tonight, we'll work here, with plenty of ventilation."

Before he could ask why, Pearl lit a bundle of twine-wrapped herbs on fire. After a moment, the fire faded to glowing embers in her hand.

"White sage and lavender for cleansing. Rose petals for purification," Amber whispered in his ear.

He nodded, strangely loathe to break the silence.

Pearl took a small bundle of ribbon wrapped feathers from Hazel and used it to wave smoke into all corners as she circled the room chanting musically. After circling the room three times, she set the smouldering remains in a large cast iron pot near the open window.

"Step inside the circle," Pearl advised him.

He obeyed, curious as to what came next. Working like a well choreographed group, they lit candles and put down a circle of salt on top of the painted circle. He watched, mesmerized, captivated by the feeling he was witnessing an ancient religious ceremony. He realized, abruptly, it was, indeed, an ancient ceremony, as had been the one he witnessed in the shop the day of their encounter with Keres.

The Hawks walked in a circle, just inside the salt line, chanting and singing. He stepped toward the middle, staying out of their way. His toes tapped to the ancient rhythm. Amber waved him into their line, and he followed, moving in time to the beat, humming the tune until after a moment, he picked up a pattern to the seemingly random syllables.

His heart rate elevated. His pulse thrummed joyfully as they danced around the circle. One after another, the women folded gracefully to sit cross-legged in a circle around the two taper candles burning brightly in the middle, their flames steadying now that the motion had stopped. He dropped into the spot left between Amber and Pearl, mimicking their posture of relaxed alertness.

They sat in silence for three long minutes. The air seemed to shimmer around him, to tingle with electricity. He'd read about raising power, but this was his only first-hand experience. It was—invigorating.

"Blessed Goddess Athena, bringer of wisdom and understanding. Come to us, if you will. Help us in our quest to understand the plans and workings of Keres. Why does he follow our family? Why has he attacked me?" Amber spoke quietly, her words a reverent whisper. "We graciously and gratefully ask for your assistance."

The room rippled with energy. Kody barely contained his gasp. Something was happening here. His heart thundered with excited trepidation.

Amber lifted the bag, which sat between the candles, and held it in her lap. Her fingers trembled as she grasped the top to pull the zip fastener open. She fumbled for a moment, closed her eyes, and took a deep breath. Beside her, Kody felt her searching for calm. He reached out and placed his hand on her knee. She nodded and opened the bag.

She coughed once and wrinkled her nose. Half a second later, the acrid stench of body odor made him gag. Pearl let loose a mild expletive.

Amber withdrew the shirt from the bag and held it between her hands. She coughed again, closed her eyes, and tipped her chin upward. Kody turned his head to see her better. She stayed there, head back, eyes shut, breathing in small gasps. She shuddered once. And again; and pushed the shirt away from her.

Nobody spoke or moved. Kody took his cue from her family and remained silent, despite the myriad of questions rocking him like waves pounding on the beach. He braced himself against their impact, bunching his hands until they ached.

Amber clasped his fist, the one still resting on her knee. He unfurled it and rolled it over so their palms touched.

"I sense great sadness in him. He's lost someone. Perhaps the woman in the photo beside his bed. He's more than sad; he's angry. Part of his anger is directed at the woman. Some to the universe in general. A lot of it is aimed at our family." She drew a shuddering breath.

Kody slid sideways and wrapped his arm around her shoulders. She leaned into his side as if drawing strength from him.

"We have something he wants," Amber declared, looking around the circle at her grandmother and siblings. "I don't know what it is. I don't think he knows what it is. But it's a thing. Something concrete."

"That's not very helpful," Lazuli declared.

"Look, I'm not a great divinator like you are," Amber snapped. "We talked about this. He came after me. We thought I'd have a better chance of divining something. It's not my fault my skills aren't as great as yours." She picked up the shirt and threw it at her sister.

The candles between them would have tipped over when the shirt brushed their holders if Kody hadn't reached out to steady them.

"Relax," he whispered, patting her thigh. "You did your best. I think you got a lot out of it." She smiled wanly at him.

"Ugh. This thing is gross," Lazuli growled. "I can't even stand to touch it." She shuddered.

"Yeah, how do you think I felt?"

Kody stifled a grin at Amber's childish, chiding tone. Sibling rivalry. He and his sister had it in spades until they moved to different cities. They were closer now. It must be tough to live with your family as an adult. He wondered why she didn't move out on her own. Why did they stay together?

"Tell me what you get," Amber said with less spite than before. Her tone turned hopeful.

Laz closed her eyes. Concentration was written all over her face. Everyone was respectfully silent. "She was his wife." A lone tear traced its way down her Laz's cheek. "She died horribly. She was sick for a long time. He's doing this, whatever he's doing, for her. That's all I get. Nothing about us, or about what he might want from us."

"That sucks," Hazel complained.

"It is what it is," Amber said unsympathetically. "Divination isn't exactly a science with rules and regulations. You get what you get. We didn't get much, but it is something." She scratched the back of her neck and smoothed her hair. "I think this all has something to do with her."

They talked quietly about the idea without reaching any conclusion. Kody remained silent, watching the family dynamics. For the most part, they input equally but, in the end, Pearl dominated them all. Not harshly, just a quiet control stemming from years of being in charge. Each woman silently acquiesced to her leadership.

"Okay then." Amber wiggled around. "My butt is getting sore." She closed her eyes and her sisters followed suit. "Thank you, Athena, for being here with us today. Thank you for your assistance in gaining insight into our foe. You honor us with your presence."

A soft wind blew through the window, extinguishing the flames on the two center candles, leaving the others untouched.

"Wow," he whispered.

"You've got that right." Amber laughed and hopped to her feet. "I guess we'll have to hit the books again and see if we can find any clues to what he might be looking for. We need to find out more about that mystery object mentioned in the grimoires."

"But not tonight. I'm beat. Being a lookout for breaking and entering is exhausting. Plus, I've seen a lot of stuff today. Strange things. I need to process."

Chapter Thirty

After seeing Kody out, Amber wandered the house, randomly picking up items, examining them and putting them back down. She stared at a photograph of her parents for ten minutes, wondering where they were and when they'd check in. They were travelling the world, looking for clues on who might be killing witches. So far, their search was coming up with nothing besides information long outdated. "Miss you, Mom and Dad," she murmured as she set the picture down.

Trevor Moon wasn't her biological father, nor was he any of her sisters' father. Her mother had always been a bit of a hippy, giving freely of her love and accepting the consequences. She was happy to raise her children alone; until she met and married Trevor who was the father of their hearts. He had been since he entered their lives five years ago.

Amber straightened a couple candles, pausing to smell their calming lavender aroma. She felt—twitchy—and out of sorts, like she needed to run. One thing her mother had taught her was when she needed to run, she had to listen to your instincts. The goal wasn't to run, but to determine what was disturbing her. It was time to meditate.

She trudged back upstairs to the room they'd occupied earlier and lit the candles in a single wall sconce. She settled, cross legged, onto a yoga mat she extracted from a tall narrow cabinet beside the door. "Okay, Hawk," she encouraged herself, "time to relax." She stretched her arms over her head, pressing her palms together and tensed her entire body before relaxing one muscle at a time and lowering her hands to her knees. She sat with her eyes closed, palms upturned and hands relaxed.

Brick by brick, she built a mental wall, picturing herself on one side, Keres on the other. She stacked and fortified until the wall stood strong and impenetrable. She'd have to rebuild it every day to keep it solid, to keep him out of her mind. She'd practice, day and night, until it held fast against Keres' full might.

A vision of Kody popped into her head. He'd been uncertain tonight, right from the start. Reluctantly, he'd assisted them in getting into Keres' home and then watched while she tried to divine more information from the shirt she'd borrowed. Yes, borrowed. She'd find a way to put the shirt back. Somehow. If only to ease her guilty conscience.

She admired Kody's willingness to take part in their rituals, and to protect her, despite his lack of knowledge. He'd joined right in tonight, dancing and humming along with their chants. When he'd done so, there had been a small surge in energy, more than a mundane would provide. She wondered if he knew his ancestors had been magical.

She pushed thoughts of Kody aside. She needed to relax and let her subconscious tell her why she was fidgety with a fight or flight response. She focused inward, willing her mind to relax and her heartbeat to slow. The thundering ebbed, but her fingers twitched with the urge to create fire. She fisted her hands and brought them to her mouth and blew on them softly, visualizing the fire extinguishing.

"Talk to me ancestors," she whispered. "Grammas, I call you all: Rosemary Jade, Petunia Opal, Ivy Rowan, Calista Rose..." She listed as many of her grandmothers as she could remember. "I ask for help from you and your sisters." The name Rosemond Willow popped into her head. She didn't know all her ancestors' names, not by a long shot. But there was a detailed family tree in their records. She'd search her up tomorrow. Perhaps Rosemond's grimoire could offer some insight into the missing artifact. If, indeed, there was one.

Mollified by having a plan of action, Amber tried to relax. Tension and unease lingered. She leaped to her feet, extinguished the candles, and jogged downstairs. She wasn't going to get any sleep tonight. Not one lick. She might as well be working. The shop needed more ritual candles. She'd head to the store and burn some energy making them.

After all the evening's adventures, Four Seasons Metaphysical had an aura of quiet comfort. Amber breathed deeply, absorbing the peace, letting it flow through her like a cleansing breeze. She tried to think of a fire analogy for the feeling. Her sisters' elements all had one. Like a fresh breeze, new shoots in spring, water washing away negativity. Fire, not so much. She did feel invigorated, like land cleansed by a forest fire, devasted, yet ready to burst forth with new life. Not a pretty analogy, but accurate, nonetheless. Like the lodgepole pine whose cones needed the heat of fire to open, she was invigorated by fire and by the peace found in the store, the sanctuary she created for herself and her family.

She flipped on a single light and gathered the components to create the perfect ritual candle. She knew the recipe by heart but checked her notebook to be certain. No sense ruining a perfectly good batch of wax. She bent to extract the proper size pot from a tall stack of cookware on a lower shelf. She balanced the pile on the lip of the shelf and lifted the top pot to access the one beneath it.

"Meow?"

Amber tumbled backward at the unexpected sound. The pots clattered to the floor. She winced at the sound and glared at the cat.

"Sasha, what the heck? You took ten years off my life." The sneaky animal meowed softly and stroked herself against Amber's side. "Shouldn't you be upstairs with your babies?"

The cat's response sounded more like no than a meow. Apparently, she was choosing not to talk tonight.

Amber's cell phone started to ring. "Great. Now what?" She climbed to her feet and located her phone in the bowels of her purse.

Kody.

"What's up, Kody?" she asked rather than offering a proper greeting. No doubt he'd heard the noise.

"I was just about to climb into bed when I heard a racket in the shop. Do you want me to investigate or should I just call the police?"

She massaged her forehead with her left hand. "No need for either. It was me." She sighed. "I dropped some pots when Sasha startled me."

"What are you doing down there so late? I thought you'd be long since asleep."

"I couldn't sleep. Too fidgety. I'm going to make some candles until I unwind a bit."

"Want company?"

The question startled her. She thought he'd just go back to bed like a normal person. "Um. Yeah. Sure. I guess," she stammered and rolled her eyes at her own lack of coherence. Kody threw her thought processes off better than any person she'd ever met, and he wasn't even trying.

"That's a vague and uncertain answer." He laughed.

His warm chuckle heated her cheeks. "I'll try not to be so noisy so you can sleep. But if you're up, I'd love the company."

"I'll be right down. Pop open the stairwell door, please."

Half a minute later, he stood in the doorway, his smile warmed her to her toes and set an ember of desire burning deep inside her. More than just physical attraction, it was the desire to spend more time with him and learn more about Kody Wilkins.

"Come on in." She waved him in. "It's nice to have company." By the Goddess, she sounded inane. If she didn't sharpen her conversational skills, he'd be back upstairs, and she'd be alone. She didn't want to be alone. Having him here, in her special place, felt right. Comfortable and exciting all at once.

"Hey, cat." He bent down to pet Sasha. "Shouldn't you be with your babies?"

Amber laughed. "I just asked her that. Great minds think alike."

Sasha scratched at the stairwell door. Kody opened it for her. "I left the top door ajar. Let yourself in and watch those kittens," he advised, closing the door behind her. "I don't know why she needed the door open. She comes and goes as she pleases any other time. So, what are we doing?" He rubbed his hands together.

"I'm making ritual candles. You're watching."

"Can I help?"

"Is that a question or an offer?" She chuckled. "It's really a one-man job, but the company is nice." She walked to the pile of pots on the floor and tidied them, setting the one she needed on one side of a dual burner hotplate on the workbench.

"Why don't you use the stove?" Kody leaned casually against the shelf beside her workspace. His arms hung relaxed at his sides; his head tipped questioningly to the left as he watched her work. She snuck a glance at him. Dang, he looked nice standing there.

"Candle making, no matter how careful you are, is messy work. We're keeping the stove for food. This burner is for candles and soaps. We've got a second one for other jobs. It helps reduce cross-contamination."

"I didn't realize you made your stock." He studied the boxes of supplies on the shelf beside him. "That's pretty cool."

"Not all of it. We make our own teas from things we grow ourselves. Some ingredients, like mango, we get from ethical sources. We make candles, balms, salves, bath salts..." She paused. He didn't need the whole list. "Anyway. Tonight, I'm making ritual candles. Pure beeswax from a local beekeeper, a hardening agent, and some coloring. It's not complex but accuracy is important."

"Don't people use paraffin for candles?"

"You can. There's a large list of ingredients you can use. Beeswax is more expensive, but the smell can't be beat. Take a whiff."

He leaned over her melting pot and breathed deeply. "Oh, that is nice. Like honey and wax and sunshine." He chuckled. "Look at me being all poetic."

Amber smiled at him as she stirred. "You've explained exactly how I feel."

"What about scented candles? Are they beeswax, too?"

"Yes, and no. I could go on for hours about candles, but I won't. Can you stick these wicks into the moulds for me?" She gave him instructions on how she wanted it done.

They worked together for an hour, making batches of green, red, blue, and black candles. White was made with a different process, without beeswax, rather than bleaching the color from the natural wax.

"I'm bushed." Amber dropped onto the sofa after they left the candles to cool on the workbench.

Kody sat beside her, sliding his arm on the back of the couch behind her head. She leaned against his arm. He was firm and soft against her. She leaned toward him a bit, and he shifted slightly until she slid into the curve between his body and his arm.

"You smell good. Like fresh cedar and mint."

His chuckle rumbled through her. "Half of that would be toothpaste."

"Well, I like it." She tipped her head and smiled at him. She was tired, exhausted. She wanted to snuggle close and rest beside him.

He moved a fraction of an inch closer and tipped her head up. A soft smile played on his lips. "I think I'm going to kiss you."

She lifted her head a bit more, twisting her body to press her hand to his chest. "I think I'll let you," she whispered.

His lips brushed softly across hers, a featherlight caress. His lips curved in a smile against hers. She inched upward, deepening the contact, inhaling the warm, fresh scent of his skin. He smelled of serenity and peace. She smiled at the whimsical thought.

He leaned back to look at her. "That's a pretty smile. Penny for your thoughts."

She blushed. She couldn't possibly explain what she was thinking, not without sounding half loony. "How about another kiss instead?" she asked.

"Happy to."

She rolled in his arms, swinging her legs up to curl onto the couch and sliding her arms around his neck to kiss him deeply. Warmth flooded through her. This felt so right, so perfect. This was where she needed to be. For right now, and maybe forever.

He returned her ardent embrace with equal fervor before he leaned back. Hurt rocketed through her. She's thought they were on the same page. She slid away from him. He reached out and caught her by the shoulder, gently holding her in place.

"Hold up. Don't go anywhere." It was a request rather than an order.

She stared at the floor, heat suffusing her face.

"I'm not rejecting you. Quite the contrary. I need to know this is you, Amber Hawk, not exhaustion or emotional distress. You've had a tough day. I saw how difficult reading the shirt was." He touched her shoulder and gently turned her back toward him. "Is this you? Because, if it is, I'd love to kiss you again."

She blinked away a tear and returned to his arms. "Honestly, it's me; but I'm not certain there isn't some emotional baggage, too."

"In that case—" He slid his arms her and kissed her long and deep. Soft and tender. He slid sideways on the coach, pulling her into his embrace, her back against his side. He pressed a kiss on top of her head. "Rest, my magical friend. There's time for kisses when you're not overwrought. And believe me, I'll be taking every opportunity I can get. After we've rested." He reached past her and pulled the soft blanket off the end of the couch and covered them up. "I think we both need to unwind."

Chapter Thirty-One

"Well, isn't this cozy."

The voice jerked Kody awake. Lazuli, Frank, and Rose stood in front of the couch, smirking. Lazuli looked like the cat who swallowed the canary and more than a little amused.

"It's not what you think." Amber jerked out of Kody's arms.

He pulled her back to his side. "Sure, it is. It's exactly what it looks like. Two tired friends catching a nap together after a long night of candle making." He brushed his lips across Amber's ear. "Got a problem with that?"

"Maybe." Lazuli frowned. "I'm undecided."

"Why are you kissing? Are you going to get married?" Rose asked.

"I haven't decided yet," he answered honesty. "I really like her. A lot." He hid his smirk when Amber blushed. She was adorable when she was embarrassed. "Do you think I should marry her?"

Rose scrunched up her eyebrows and pursed her lips. "Maybe. My friends think you should. But they're older than me. I'm not sure."

"Who are your friends?" Frank asked his daughter, kneeling down to meet her gaze. "Do I know them?"

Kody doubted the child would recognize the depths of his parental concern, but it was clearly recognizable to an adult.

"Evelyn and Kansas. You don't know them," she replied with childish candor. "They're nice."

"Where did you meet them?" Amber asked, standing to fold the blanket that had covered them, leaving Kody chilled. More from her absence than the lack of a blanket.

"Here. They live here, but they're not here now."

"Kody's the only person who lives here," Frank corrected.

"Yeah, about that..." Amber winced.

"Do I even want to know? Are you putting my child in danger?" He glared at Lazuli and Amber. Frank crossed his arms over his chest and spread his feet combatively.

A jolt of sympathy went through Kody. If he had a child, he'd want to stand guard over her every second. The only time he'd leave her alone was when she was being watched by Amber, her mother.

Whoa!

One night in her arms, a platonic night, and he was thinking about babies. He leaped to his feet and paced the suddenly small confines of the shop's back room. He liked her. A lot. But having babies with her? That implied a whole other layer of commitment. They hadn't even dated. Yet. Maybe it was time to see where their strange friendship was going.

"Tell me about these friends? Does Amber know them? Or Lazuli?" Frank asked. "Can I meet them?" He stroked his daughter's hair reassuringly.

"Oh, Daddy, they're nice." She skipped around the shop and called out, "Come meet my Daddy. He's nice." She stopped, cocked her head as if listening, and stomped her foot. "Come on, he's nice."

Frank was starting to look worried. Truth be told, Kody didn't blame him. He was still struggling with the concept of ghosts himself.

"Sorry, Daddy. They don't want to talk to you."

"Are these more of your pretend friends?" he asked gently.

"No, Daddy. They're real. They're just different."

Frank looked frantically at the other adults in the room. Kody shrugged. He had no useful advice. He barely knew Frank, though he was optimistic they could become friends.

"They're ghosts, Daddy," Rose proclaimed in a small, worried voice. "They're nice ghosts, 'cept they like to tease Kody 'cause he doesn't like Amber enough."

Kody gaped at her. He snapped his mouth shut. Was that what they were up to?

"Honey, there's no such thing as ghosts," Frank said.

"There is so!" She stomped her foot. "You just don't believe me 'cause you're mean." Tears rolled down her face.

Frank huffed out a sigh. Kody felt for him, but he was not going to get involved in this. "You know, Frank, there are a lot of unusual things in this world. Maybe there are ghosts." The words popped out without thought. So much for not getting involved.

"You're kidding me, right?"

"All he's saying is keep an open mind," Amber injected. "Who knows? A lot of people claim to see ghosts."

"And, we even sell a book on the ghosts of Three Moon Falls." Lazuli waved toward the front of the shop. "I can lend you a copy. Plus, there's plenty of paranormal research to indicate ghosts do, indeed, exist."

"You guys are nuts. I always knew you were quirky. But now I'm worried you're actually crazy. Kody, you should probably stop hanging out with them. Come on, Rose. It's time to go." He tugged gently on her arm when she objected.

"I thought we came to ask Kody to go fishing?"

"I'd love to go fishing with you. I don't have any clients booked this morning. If the offer is still available?" He wasn't ready to give up his burgeoning relationship with Amber, nor was he willing to abandon the potential friendship with Frank and his daughter.

Frank paused. "Yeah, I guess that'd be alright. Meet you at the boat launch in half an hour?"

"You better believe it. I'll grab some snacks. Any allergies?"

"None. Come, Rose. Let's go. Kody will meet us there." He turned and rushed his daughter outside.

"Bye," Amber called after them. "Well," she added in a low voice. "That was rude. He's in for one hell of a surprise when he finds out ghosts do exist. I don't suppose you guys could help?" she called to the air. Light laughter followed her words.

"They don't believe in making things easy, do they?" Kody sighed. He didn't know much about ghosts, but he knew for certain they existed, and they liked playing havoc with his life.

Rose dozed under the umbrella her father had lashed to the side of the small aluminum boat they'd rented. "Do you think she's crazy?" he asked out of the blue.

Kody sipped his coffee. "You know, a few weeks ago, I'd have said yes. Now, I'm not so sure. I've seen some strange things lately." No way was he going to go into details. Even he couldn't quite believe them.

"They have a reputation for actually believing the crap they sell. They even had my wife buying into it before she passed. She spent hours on the internet researching, and I have more damn candles than I'll ever use." Frank reeled in his line and cast again.

Kody tipped his head back to enjoy the sun on his face. "Honestly, I'm beginning to believe there might be some merit to what they say." He waved away Frank's objection. "Like the teas they sell. I've been reading about the medicinal properties of herbs. My grandmother made a few special teas. Where do you think a lot of our modern medicine came from? They're just packaging the original versions. There's a ton of scientific evidence to back it up." There was more to it than science. He'd seen Amber control fire and Hazel control water. It added up to a whole new level of reality.

"Herbs are one thing, ghosts are another." Worry filled Frank's voice. He stared at his daughter, his expression torn between confusion, worry, and adoration. "I worry I'm failing her somehow. What if I'm screwing this up?"

"Cut yourself some slack, man. Look at it this way, if ghosts aren't real and she's just playing with her imaginary friends, what harm can it do. Most kids outgrow it, and if she doesn't, you can take her to the doctor. If they are real, they don't seem to be doing her any harm. Why don't you let it ride a bit, see what happens?"

Frank shook his head. "That's a lot to ask." He reeled his line in and dropped the rod to the bottom of the boat. "It would be better if Rose didn't keep sneaking out and ending up at the Hawk place. She's got some kind of weird fascination with the Hawk family. I don't like it."

Kody's line bobbed, and he started reeling it in. "Hey, I've got something." He flashed a look at Frank, who sat staring at his daughter. "I don't know you well, but to me, Rose seems happy and well adjusted. Especially considering she's lost her mother. She's probably drawn to them because her mom is gone. A woman's touch and all that. The Hawks have a reputation around town for being weird, but people accept them and don't seem to think they're doing any harm. Maybe she just needs a woman's influence?"

"So, I'm supposed to get married? Hell no. I'm not even close to dating, let alone replacing my wife."

"What about a nanny?" Kody offered reasonably.

"I've had six in six months. She hates them all. She refuses to listen to them and hides out in her room and sneaks off to see the Hawks." He shook his head. "She baffles me."

"Have you let her help choose the nanny?"

Frank gave him a quizzical look. "No."

"Maybe if she thinks she's picking, she'll act differently." The irony here was killing him. He was half crazy about Amber and had no idea how to deal with his growing feelings and her strange beliefs. He knew less than nothing about kids, and he was offering child rearing advice. "I remember when I was a kid. We used to have this babysitter. I hated her. I don't even remember why. I used to be a total brat. Until she couldn't come, and I suggested the teenage boy down the street. He was way cooler. All into video games and comics. I thought he was a rock star." He chuckled. "Just putting it out there. Maybe she needs to be involved."

"I don't know." Frank scrubbed his face with his hand. "You're really not bothered by what they do?"

Kody chuckled. "God's honest truth, man. Sometimes, they scare the living shit out of me. But they take in stray cats, invite strangers to picnics, they have good rapport with the police. They pitched right in during the aftermath of the explosion. They've treated me respectfully. I'm giving them the benefit of the doubt." He reeled the fish toward the boat.

Frank burst into laughter. He laughed until his face went red. When he finally calmed himself, he chuckled once more. "Benefit of the doubt. Is that what you call what we saw this morning? You all cuddled up with Amber on the couch."

Kody shrugged. He didn't quite understand it himself. His attraction to Amber was off the charts. When he was near her, he felt giddy, a bit like an oxygen high. When they were apart, he wondered what she was doing. She was beautiful, sexy, and despite freaking him out, the whole controlling fire thing turned him on. She had an inner strength and power that drew him like a diver to sunken treasure. "What can I say? She's unique."

"Can I ask you something, man to man? Friend to friend?"

"Sure thing. Can't guarantee I'll answer." Kody netted his fish, an enormous trout, and tossed it into the fish cooler beside Frank's earlier catch.

"Can she do weird shit?"

"Depends on your definition of weird, I guess."

"That's not an answer."

"Why do you ask? You interested in Laz? She's pretty. They all are."

"Yeah, but they're weird." Frank sighed. "You know when my wife and I settled here, I thought we'd be happy together, for a long time. I pictured half a dozen kids, dogs, and cats. White picket fences. But she's gone..."

"And you're attracted to Lazuli, and you feel guilty. Plus, she's different, which scares you. Why not take a chance? Relax and let the universe play out it's hand."

"Let the universe play out it's hand? You sound just like them." He sounded half bitter.

"Yeah, I guess I do. I've spent a lot of time with them. Amber especially. They kind of rub off on you."

Frank laughed at his unintended double entendre.

"Did your wife like them? You mentioned they knew each other." Okay, now he was just prying, not even trying to help his friend. For all his attraction to Amber, doubts lingered in the back of his mind.

"Celine, my wife, and Lazuli were friends. More than neighbors. Best chums, I guess. What do chicks call it? BFFs? They spent hours together. I didn't mind at first, but then, Celine started getting all into gardening and collecting pretty stones. She burned a shit-ton of candles. We'd picked out a name for Rose. We were going to name her after our mothers, but when she was born, my wife insisted on calling her Rose, after Lazuli's dead grandmother."

"I thought Pearl was their grandmother?"

"Great-grandmother, I guess. I wanted to name her for my own ancestors. It rubbed me the wrong way."

"I can see that. But you let her," Kody commiserated.

"I wanted her to be happy." He sighed heavily. "Unfortunately, she died when Rose was three. Rose took to sneaking out to visit them shortly after. Can you even imagine the panic I went through every time? I can't stop freaking out about it, and I can't keep her home."

"That sucks, man." Kody reeled in another fish as Frank re-cast his line. Kody took the helm and motored them slowly to another spot, closer to the reeds. The temperature had risen, and the fish would be hiding from the sun. "But I don't understand why you don't like them."

Frank shrugged. "They seem nice, but their claims of magic go against my Catholic upbringing."

"And if you believe some people, the Bible advises to kill the witches. It's a hard nut to crack for sure." He'd been over this argument himself, more than once. It played havoc with his guts every time, and he was no closer to settling the confusion. Except, he was certain he wanted to follow the relationship and see where it went.

"What's your upbringing? Does it interfere with your ability to see past their weirdness?"

Kody was getting tired of Frank being negative about a family he was rapidly learning to care for. He banked his anger and tried to be rational. "I was raised without any solid belief structure. Mom and Dad went to church. Mom's mom didn't. They, all of them, encouraged me to find my own way. Grandma loved her garden and her teas. I guess, in a way, she's like Amber. I think Grandma would like her." He stopped the boat and dropped anchor. "My assistant, Bryce, warned me away from them. But he didn't hesitate to accept their skills on the lake."

He almost mentioned their magic. He choked it back. It was tough keeping a secret, and he didn't know how the Hawks managed to keep quiet their whole lives. Maybe that was why they opened their store. If people were going to talk, they might as well be labeled as charlatans or crooks.

"Didn't listen to him, did you?" Frank laughed sourly. "You ever think she put a spell on you? Made you like her?" Frank eyed him seriously.

"Nope." He knew they could, and Danica, the pink haired one, had tried to spell him, and Amber had stopped her, but he'd leave that out. For now.

"You think Lazuli put a spell on you?" He made magical woo-woo noises.

"There's no other way to explain it. My wife was so radically different from Lazuli. Short and curvy instead of tall and thin. She was a redhead; she didn't have those shiny golden strands." He groaned. "Now I even sound love-struck."

Kody laughed. "You do. Man, you are smitten. Bitten by the love bug."

"It has to be a spell. She's totally not my type."

"One thing my grandmother always said is you can't control when the love bug will bite." He chortled. "As a teenager, I thought it was a warning against STDs. Now, I think she was bracing me for falling in love out of the blue. I don't have time for a relationship. I'm building my business. And a relationship with a self-proclaimed witch? Never. Yet, here I am." He shrugged. "Shit happens."

"Not to me it doesn't."

"Daddy," Rose said in a shocked whisper. "Kody swored."

"Sorry, Rose. I should know better."

She patted his leg. "It's okay. Everybody makes mistakes. That's what my friends say."

Frank groaned.

Kody chuckled.

While Frank helped his daughter with her snack, Kody continued fishing, barely paying attention to what he was doing. Caught up in thoughts of Amber, her unusual skills and the threat of Keres, he didn't notice he had another fish on his line until Rose shouted at him.

Chapter Thirty-Two

A mber was beginning to fret. What if Keres noticed someone had been in his house? What if he was preparing for a big blow? He was up to something; she could feel it coming.

As much as she'd like to relax, Amber's instincts told her this was the calm before the storm. Her nerves were strung so tight she thought they'd crush her; or she'd go bonkers and start primal screaming at a difficult customer for no reason. She was poised on the edge of insanity; the waiting was pulling out her crazy.

She closed her eyes, centered herself, and reached for calm. Business was steady all day. Tourist season was picking up, and Three Moon Falls' seasonal regulars and newbies alike were excited to check out the new shop and its offerings. In previous years, Amber and Lazuli had done a brisk business with Tarot and palm readings at the summer farmer's market that ran three days a week. Judging by today's readings and bookings, divination in the shop was going to provide a fabulous source of revenue and would help rocket the store into profitability.

After lunch, Amber heard Kody return from fishing. Ten minutes later, he jogged down the stairs and fired up his truck. She banked her disappointment when he didn't stop to say hi. She did her best to shrug it off. They were friends. Granted, she thought it was developing into more. She'd even let him in on some of their family's secrets. Perhaps he'd been in a rush to clean up after fishing. He'd mentioned having dives scheduled for the afternoon and early evening.

Was he put off after spending time with Frank and Rose? They weren't the type to intentionally bias people against others, nor was Kody the type to let new friends influence him against old ones. Still, stranger things had happened. She massaged an ache in her stomach where unease and worry tumbled together in a maelstrom of doubt.

Frank and Rose had a love hate relationship with Amber's family. Rose loved them; Frank, not so much. Frank's wife, Celine, and daughter had been great family friends until Celine had passed. Frank had been civil, but never really friendly. Since Celine's passing, Rose had taken to sneaking over the hill to visit the Hawk family. They always welcomed her, and immediately informed her current caregiver of her whereabouts. With every visit, Frank grew increasingly distant. He'd only accepted their invitation to the Founder's Day parade to give his daughter the best view possible. He wasn't outright rude, just standoffish. Amber recognized part of Frank's issue was his attraction to her sister. Frank watched Lazuli like a starving man staring at steak, like he needed her and couldn't live without her. His attraction made him keep his distance.

Hopefully, his negativity hadn't rubbed off on Kody. It would be a shame if second-hand emotions sidetracked the relationship growing between her and Kody. The funny thing was, she wasn't looking for a man when Kody showed up, but he'd slid into her life like he belonged there. Because she wasn't one to argue with fate, she accepted his presence in her world. She just wished he wasn't so skittish about magic. She shrugged. She couldn't force acceptance on others. She had to wait until he came around on his own, and he was relaxing about the whole thing. She was just impatient.

Perhaps he'd stop by once she closed.

By eight, business had slowed to a trickle, and she was getting antsy. She couldn't shake the feeling something was off. She cringed at her sense of impending doom, like the universe was holding its breath in fearful anticipation. Like there was a spark glowing somewhere, just waiting for a puff of breeze to flare it into life and burn her world to the ground.

She pushed the distressing thoughts away. She was probably just hungry; she hadn't eaten since lunch, and the mind did weird things when it needed food. Wanting to hang around until Kody came home safely, she texted her family she'd be staying late and locked up, quickly completing the nightly close down procedure.

Hunger gnawing at her stomach, she strode into the kitchen and made herself a heaping serving of nachos and cheese with chopped bacon sprinkled on top. With sides of hot salsa and sour cream, she was all set to snack. And wait. Settling into the chair, she mustered her psychic energy and flicked off the lights. Two snaps of her fingers flashed fire and ignited a pair of silver pillar candles on the table in front of her. There was nothing as relaxing as a candlelit dinner—or snack. Reaching across the table, she turned up the radio. The golden oldies station was playing the Eagles. Witchy Woman, one of her favorite songs.

Food temporarily abandoned, she whirled around the room, singing and swaying in time to the music. Her voice was passible. She couldn't hit the high notes, but she could hold her own overall. Probably because they often sang as part of rituals. Practice made perfect. Too bad she couldn't say the same for dancing. She didn't have much skill, but man, she loved to dance.

A soft click sounded, just as the song ebbed to an end, fading into silence. She opened her eyes, expecting to see one of her sisters.

Keres' friend stood in the open doorway to the staircase.

"What the hell? Get out of my store," she demanded. Light and pain exploded in her head, and her world went black.

K ody drove around the corner toward the alley behind the shop and rubbed his head. Sometimes, on days like today, he wondered why he chose this career. Kids were often a challenge, but when adults acted like jackasses, he questioned his sanity. Why was it necessary for people to piss around and pull stunts?

Diving was a pleasure, but it had its risks. If they didn't pay attention to the safety rules, before they got into the water, how could they expect to know what to do in the unlikely event of an emergency? Some people just assumed lake diving wasn't dangerous. It wasn't like deep-sea diving, but it did have its own risks.

After entirely too much foolishness, he'd kicked one jokester out of his class and begun again, ignoring the man's threats to sue. No fear of that happening. Every client signed a waiver agreeing that under certain specified circumstances, Kody had the right to terminate their agreement without penalty. Even the father of the injured boy had dropped his threats to sue. Kody hated to do it, but the man had left him no choice. The rest of the class had gone smoothly, and their initial dive was uneventful, but the day left a lingering bad taste in the back of his mouth.

He pushed out a sigh and refocused his attention on getting home. As he approached the final turn into the parking lot, a white van hurtled toward him, spewing gravel and fishtailing as it exited the lot.

He cussed and slammed on the brakes to avoid being side-swiped. His heart thundered as he watched the windowless van disappear behind him. He exhaled sharply, ran his fingers through his hair, and pulled into his spot. Nothing like adding a near miss accident to an already crappy day.

Oh well. At least he hadn't been hit, just startled.

Dim light shone through Four Seasons Metaphysical's back door. Bonus. Amber was still around. It'd be nice to share a cup of tea with her and unwind. Maybe they'd even share a kiss or two. He grinned and climbed out of his truck, beeping the lock behind him. His day was looking up. An old tune about love and pain flowed into the evening air from inside. He jogged to the back door and knocked.

The screen bounced open.

What?

Amber never left the back door unlocked, not since Keres made his appearance in the store. He flung the screen open and strode inside, calling her name. Candles burned on the table beside an untouched plate of nachos. A steaming cup of tea sat beside Amber's cell phone with the triquetra pattern on its sparkling silver case. The couch was skewed slightly out of position. Unease prickled up his spine. Something wasn't right. He hurried to the front of the store, calling her name. He raced up and down the short aisles and looked behind the counter for her.

Nothing. No sign of her.

He swallowed a ball of unease that settled like cement in his stomach. Pivoting on his heel, he returned to the back. The bathroom was empty, and the door to the stairwell was ajar. She wouldn't be upstairs, would she? She had no reason to go up to his suite.

Thundering up the stairs, he shouted her name, nearly tripping over Sasha, who greeted him with a meow.

"She's gone," the cat declared. "They took her."

He didn't have time to worry about the cat talking to him again. He was getting used to their unusual discussions. "What the hell? Who took her?"

"Those men." She meowed piteously. "He kicked me in the ribs."

"Shit. I've got to find her. I'll get someone to look at you later." Racing from room to room, he searched his apartment. The front door was ajar. Thinking about crime scenes and evidence, he pushed it shut with his elbow. He raced back downstairs and jerked to a stop beside the couch. "No way in hell is Keres doing this to the woman I love." He stumbled a bit. "Damn." He did love her. He hadn't realized it until that moment. He had to find her. "The police."

He whipped out his phone and slammed it back in his pocket. Not just any officer would do. He needed Stone. She understood what they were up against. He snatched Amber's phone and scrolled through the contacts. Thank the Goddess she didn't lock her phone. *Whoa! Now he was copying Amber's speech, as if he believed as much as she did. But then, with all he'd seen and experienced, how could he doubt it.* He pushed the button to call Stone and waited impatiently for her to pick up.

When she answered, he barked into the phone, "It's Kody Wilkins. I'm inside Four Seasons Metaphysical. Something's wrong. Nobody's here." He hurried to explain what he'd found, including the van racing away from the parking lot. Words poured out of him. "Get over here," he demanded. "It has to involve Keres."

"Don't touch anything, I'm on my way."

The phone went dead in his ear. He dialled Hazel and told her what happened. "I think Keres has her. Is there something magical you can do to find her?" He fought the panic pushing him toward random action. The urge to do something, anything was overwhelming. After a moment of panic echoing his own, Hazel assured him they'd search magically for Amber. "I'll keep you posted on this end," he said and disconnected.

Stone must have been close because she arrived after the longest three minutes of his life. Bar none. Gravel crunched in the parking lot, a car door slammed, and Stone burst inside. She was dressed in civilian clothing, her shimmery black dress and heels indicating he'd interrupted an evening out. Perhaps a date.

"Sorry to ruin your night," he offered, not actually sorry at all. His only concern was to figure out what happened to Amber.

"What have you touched?"

"The door and her phone, for sure. I don't think I touched anything else while I was looking for her. That door," he pointed to the stairwell, "was open when I came in. The tea is hot, and those candles were burning. My suite was unlocked, the door open. I know I locked it when I left. Nothing else seems wrong, except the couch is crooked."

She called the station and ordered a team to the shop on the assumption there was a missing person in a potentially lethal situation.

Lethal? Shit. He'd been worried before; now he was nearly breathless with panic. He had to do something. *Okay, Wilkins; focus.* "Amber is gone, the couch is moved. Candles burning, food untouched. It's just not right. The ladies keep things pretty precise."

"Yeah, I've noticed they like things neat and tidy. Everything in its place. Tell me about the van."

"White panel van. No side windows. It had blue lettering on the back panel, but I don't know what it said. I didn't notice the licence plates, why would I? I wasn't expecting anything to be wrong. I just figured it was an asshole driver." He paced around the room, careful not to touch anything. "It was Keres. I know it."

"What makes you so certain? Did you see the driver?"

He hesitated. How could he possibly answer without seeming like a lunatic? He sure as hell wasn't going to tell her the cat told him, which would be a one-way ticket to the nut house.

"What?" she barked. "Spill it. You've got a face like a book. It shows everything. You can't hide from the police."

He winced and shook his head. Nope. He wasn't saying anything.

"Look, I don't have time for timid mundane's bullshit. Spit it out. If you're right and Keres took her, we need to act now."

"He took her." He sighed and scrubbed his hand over his face, then jammed his fists into his pockets. "The cat told me."

"Do you have any idea how rare it is to be able to hear animals talk? Apparently, you aren't a mundane after all. You've got witch blood in your veins, boy. Witch blood. No wonder Amber's attracted to you. I was worried she had fallen for a mundane. I guess that's one doubt put to rest." Leticia chuckled.

He had witch blood? No way. No how. Fear swamped him, stealing his breath. First Amber was missing; now, he was a witch. Could men be witches? He didn't remember what she'd said. His heart thundered in his ears as he paced. His chest was tight. His fingers and toes tingled. His vision dimmed. He sucked in a breath and eased it out. His vision returned. "Okay, breathe, dammit," he whispered to himself. He wouldn't solve either issue if he passed out in panic.

Stone snapped her fingers in front of his face, jerking him back to reality. "Focus. We don't have time to worry about your mundane sensitivities and panic. Get your shit together. I want you to start driving around. Search for the van. I'll get officers on it as soon as I can." She cursed. "Damn budget. I can't order too much manpower without proof she's been abducted. City council will have my badge. Find that van," she repeated. "Don't touch anything. If they're moving, follow at a distance. Do. Not. Approach them. Not under any circumstances. Find them and call me."

She rattled off her phone number, and he entered it into his phone. She was brisk and efficient, completely professional, but behind the façade, he saw the worry in the way she snapped out her words and fisted her hands.

"I'll contact her family. They can start looking for her magically," she added.

"Magically?" He gulped. "How?"

"Scrying with mirrors, a pendulum. Look for her psychically. Cast a location spell. Never mind." She waved her hand toward the door. "We don't have time to teach you all this."

Every bad witch and magical movie he'd ever watched flashed through Kody's head. The old television show, *Charmed,* topped the list. Yeah, the show was fiction. Now, he couldn't help wondering how much of what he'd watched had its basis in reality. He shoved the thoughts aside. He had bigger worries than the potential truth of old television.

"Okay, I'm out. I'll call you if I find anything. Go ahead and check out my suite. Somebody jimmied the outside lock." Keys in hand, he slammed out the door and hopped into his truck.

Knowing Keres would avoid public areas, and probably his home as well, Kody started his search in the industrial area, cruising up and down the streets and alleys, looking for white vans. It was twenty minutes before he spotted anything.

There! In the yard. A white van with blue lettering.

He slammed on the brakes, left the engine running, and hopped out. The yard was gated and locked. Nimbly, he scaled the chain link fence and jumped lightly down into the yard. He scanned the back of the building for motion lights and security cameras. Seeing nothing, he crept forward between wrapped pallets until he was at the side of the van. He snuck around it, torn between optimism and crippling fear. No sign of occupants. He tested the passenger door. Locked.

Same for the sliding side door. He inched his way to the driver's and tried the handle. It opened easily; the vehicle's light flooded the yard. He leaped inside and scanned the back. Jam packed full of boxes, there wasn't room to hide a person. He closed the door gently behind him, being careful not to make a sound, and tried the back door. The boxes in the front continued to the back door.

He couldn't get into the shop itself without breaking the lock, so he made a mental note of the location, he hurried back to his truck and continued down the alley. With every passing moment, his anxiety rose. Acid burned in the back of his throat. He swallowed it down. Time after time he searched. How many utilitarian, white vans could one town have? After searching three more vans, he finished the small warehouse district. He called Stone after each find, giving her the addresses for a proper search inside the buildings.

So much for that idea. He pulled to a stop at the curb at the end of the last street. He had to come up with a plan. Officer Stone's words echoed in his head. *You've got witch blood in you.* Okay, if he had witch blood, and her family could search for her magically, maybe he could, too. Half scoffing at the idea, he closed his eyes and focused on finding her.

He hadn't been in town long, but he was already getting to know Three Moon Falls' layout. He pictured each street, one after another, waiting for a sign or feeling Amber was there. He mentally moved through town, looking, feeling, hoping.

His cell phone vibrated in his pocket, startling him from his mental task. "Shit." He yanked it out. "What?" he snapped into the device.

"It's Stone. I sent a crew to Keres' rental place. No sign of them there. What have you come up with?"

"Aside from too many white vans and not a single lead? Nothing. I didn't break into the buildings, you should send officers there, but I checked inside of each van. It's crazy how many companies forget to lock their vehicles, even when there is merchandise inside." He marvelled at that. He'd lose a fortune if he left his storage space unlocked and someone broke in. How was a van any different?

"I've driven the warehouse area. Now what?" He didn't mention his mental efforts. No sense opening himself up to ridicule, even if she was the one to suggest he could do it.

"Keep driving. They're here somewhere. I've got two units helping out. I'm going to call in a brigade of citizens I can trust. Her family's scanning for her as well."

"Good to know. I'll keep driving." Temporarily forgetting his plan to search magically, he hung up the phone to head for the downtown core Amber had been taken from.

Chapter Thirty-Three

Jackhammers pounded in Amber's head. She lay still, instinctively knowing something was wrong. She tried to ease the ache by focusing her limited healing skills on it. *Dammit. By the Goddess, you should be able to heal yourself.* Of course, it made sense she couldn't. It took energy to heal, which an injured body was already low on. Physics. Or was it chemistry?

Beyond the pain in her head, her wrists and ankles throbbed from being bound. Rope burns. Her shoulders ached where they were yanked behind her back. Keres hadn't taken any risks on her getting free. Her eyes were blindfolded, and she had a weird metallic taste in her mouth behind a foul-tasting gag.

Drugs! They'd drugged her.

Without moving, she focused on listening. Distantly, she heard the murmur of voices. She focused harder, and the pounding in her head intensified. Pushing past the pain, she persisted. She couldn't sense anyone in the room with her.

Where was she? The faint smell of dust was almost overridden by diesel, motor oil, and mildew. A garage, then. Commercial or residential? She reached out again. Agony slammed through her head, and her senses slipped away.

The burning agony in her shoulders woke her. *Okay, note to self. Don't push too hard. Take it slow, and don't overtax your head or your magic.* She reached out carefully, the smallest mental feeler, while asking the Goddess for assistance and hoping her limited psychic skills would kick in. Now would be the perfect time for her gift to blossom.

As near as she could tell, she was still alone, and she'd been here for some time. A long time judging by the pressure in her bladder. Well, she sure wouldn't give Keres the satisfaction of wetting herself. He could just go screw himself if he thought he could shame her. Anger coursed through her veins. Pushing its way to her fingertips. The ache in her brain redoubled.

Shit.

She'd have to go slow. She shifted slightly to ease the agony in her shoulders. Chain rattled. *What the hell? Her feet were chained together? No fricken way! Not happening!*

Sadly, another whisper of motion proved that true. She might be able to muster the energy to burn through the ropes, but chain was an entirely different debacle.

Gramma Pearl had always said she could eat an elephant one bite at a time, a philosophy which could be applied to any insurmountable problem. She reached out psychically, trying to feel her sisters. Crippling fire burned through her brain. Was it her injury, or had Keres planted a spell in her head? Her guards would have been down, allowing him entry. She couldn't risk trying again. If he'd been messing around in her head, her action could alert him to her attempts. She was on her own.

Her guts clenched, and sudden claustrophobia closed in on her. Her breathing accelerated, and her heart pounded until she felt faint. Bile rose in her throat. She gagged on her rising panic. If she puked, she'd die! The gag would hold it in.

No! He wasn't going to win!

She slowed her breathing and pushed the fear back. She had to reason this out. She couldn't do anything until she could see, and no amount of shifting and wiggling loosened the smelly rags wrapped around her head. Okay, then, she'd have to burn through the binding on her wrists. That was risky. She could set the cardboard under her aflame or catch her cotton clothing on fire.

She'd burned herself once on uncontrolled fire. She was terrified of doing it again. One disfiguring burn scar was enough. She shied away from the plan of burning herself free. Maybe Keres would come check on her, and she could escape if he let her loose to go to the bathroom. Fat chance of him letting her go. Her instincts warned when she saw him again, she was in for a world of hurt unless she gave him what he wanted, and aside from a couple unclear visions and hints of an artifact, she had no idea what he wanted. Failing to give him information would lead to him messing around in her brain trying to find what he was looking for. Permanent brain damage was a definite possibility. A probability.

Nope. She wasn't going to let him into her head if she could avoid it.

Maybe Kody had noticed her missing and called the police. But if he'd had a rough day or Frank had put him off, would he even notice the shop was abandoned? Why would he?

Frustration wracked her body. She gritted her teeth and clenched her fists. There had to be a solution that didn't involve risking setting herself on fire.

Her mouth was dry. She scraped her tongue over her teeth and cheeks, trying to dredge up some moisture. It eased the dryness, but she'd need fluids to counteract the residuals of the drug he'd given her and the obscene, oily taste of her gag.

That was something she could do. She couldn't heal her head, but she might be able to push the toxin out. Keres wouldn't expect her to know how. He probably thought she was still sedated, or he'd have her under guard or be interrogating her.

Fire was her element, but she couldn't draw on it for energy. With dry, oily cardboard beneath her, she couldn't reach the earth. Water? No, she already had dry mouth, and the cardboard beneath her was dry but oily. No help there. That left air. The air was rank with diesel and mildew, but if she tried hard, she might be able to draw on the power of air to help herself.

Too bad she didn't have Gramma Pearl's ability to channel all the elements. It would have made her life much easier at this point. Unfortunately, that skill only surfaced every second generation. If she or her sisters ever had kids, one of them would inherit the rare gift.

Her family would be frantic by now. They'd wonder why she wasn't home. When she didn't answer her cell or the shop phone, they'd have gone searching for her. She ached with the pain of not being able to relieve their fears.

Focus! She had to concentrate on getting free and not let important, but petty fears, distract her from the job at hand. She needed to push the toxin from her system.

Air was the key. The air was motionless. There wasn't a hint of a breeze. Although she couldn't see, she scrunched up her already closed eyes and concentrated on the feel of the air against her wrists and on her ankles where her pants had ridden up. Imagining a cool breeze on her face, she mentally called to the element of air, not daring to do so aloud in case Keres was monitoring for sounds of motion.

She turned her imagination to standing in a lush green field surrounded by towering pines and poplars. A light breeze blowing over her, washing away her exhaustion and with it, the poison in her veins. The breeze ruffled the leaves, setting them in motion with a whisper of sound. She took that energy and guided it into her veins, pushing, shoving, and urging the sedative to leave her body. Slowly, the toxin ebbed away, leaving her less exhausted and drugged. The ache in her head worsened, but at least the sluggishness in her body eased. Thank the Goddess for small victories. Now, she could focus on freeing herself. Magic was always easier when she was clear headed and free of emotion.

Emotion was going to be her downfall if she wasn't cautious. She was petrified of Keres and what he might do. She was angry she let herself get captured, both at herself and her abductors. She was worried for her family and her safety. Her head hurt, and her wrists and ankles throbbed. And dammit, she needed to pee.

The silliness of the objection jolted her out of her self-pity. Okay, time to focus. Since she couldn't do magic all riled up, she'd have to let the emotions go or push them back.

Somewhere, nearby, metal scraped against ceramic. A chair moving? She froze, barely daring to breathe. *Okay, I need to think of this as an enormous game of hide and seek with really big odds. I'm hiding, and I have to keep moving so I don't get caught. Game on!*

Heart thundering in her ears, fingers and toes tingling from an adrenaline dump, she inhaled slowly, deeply and let it out over a long count of five. Again. Again, and her heart slowed to something approaching a normal rhythm. Thank her lucky stars Gramma Pearl had taught her so many things about relaxation and self control.

Ignoring the fear and agony as best she could, she wiggled her wrists, searching for any slack in the rope binding her. Finding none, she mustered her courage and called on her magic and trickled a bit of fire out her right middle finger. She was right-handed and her strongest magic was cast with her dominant hand. Slowly, cautiously, she pushed small sparks from her middle finger, the only one that actually reached the rope. The acrid smell of burning plastic scorched her nose. Polypropylene; a mixed blessing. It would melt quickly, but burning plastic could stick to her skin, permanently scarring her. Crap. Natural fiber would have taken longer to get through, but she had the advantage of being able to roll onto her back and extinguish the flame if it got out of control.

No sense fretting on it now. She had work to do. Another small spark. Then another. After every push of magic, she rested. She didn't dare overdo it. Luckily, the plastic melted and stayed melted with each flare.

Her skin burned, and she whispered a curse. A piece of hot plastic must have dropped on it. Her wrists inched further apart as she melted the rope, strand by strand. Even a single strand of polypropylene rope was strong, and she'd have to melt every solitary one, despite the increased pounding in her head.

One last spark and the rope broke, freeing her wrists, just as a door opened and a whisper of a breeze washed over her skin.

Chapter Thirty-Four

Rounding yet another corner in a low rent district, Kody punched the steering wheel. Where the hell was that van? He had to find it. Stopping again, he dialed Hazel.

"Any luck finding her?" he blurted the second she answered.

"None. He must be blocking us. He probably put up a shield against divination. We can't reach her by scrying, telepathically, or any other way we've tried. We'll keep pushing. Any luck on your end?"

"None. Lots of white vans, none of them with any clues. I'll keep driving." He disconnected and sat staring out into the street.

If Keres was hindering the family's telepathic attempts, they might never find Amber. There was no reason for him to block Kody.

He had to try and find her. Too bad he had absolutely no idea how to even begin. He closed his eyes and calmed his racing heart. "Okay, Goddess. I don't know how this works. I'm a total newbie, and I need your help. I'll trust you because Amber trusts you. Keres is up to something, and he's taken Amber. We can't find her. I'm going to concentrate on her, and if you can swing it, could you send me a clue? I'd appreciate it. Thanks."

Not much of a ritual, but the best his inexperience could come up. He never was one for poetry, so he didn't even attempt to rhyme it.

He called up a vision of Amber, her sparkling leafy green eyes with their ever-changing shades. The softness of her sandy brown hair. The way her smile lit her eyes and turned up the corner of her mouth. The way her backside looked when she bent over to lift a shelf the night they'd met. The way her lips felt on his when they kissed. The soft vanilla of her perfume.

West.

His eyes flew open when the single word popped into his head.

"Thank you, Goddess." He jerked the truck into gear and drove west. Hoping for another flash of insight, he followed the highway out of town, past Amber's home, and past Keres' rental property. He pulled into a tiny turnout and stopped to refocus.

A little further. He headed back down the road, moving by instinct, and turned into a driveway that was little more than two tire lanes in the grass. He rolled five hundred meters along, rounded a corner, and slammed on the brakes, jerking the truck to a stop. Up ahead, there was a house with a single light glowing. He shut the engine off and hopped out, closing the door gently behind him.

He shoved his keys in his pocket and rubbed his palms together. He should call Stone, but he didn't want to risk being wrong and wasting her time. He'd go alone. Keeping to the bush-line, he crept closer, working his way past trees and through thickets of wild rose bushes toward the decrepit bungalow. A particularly sharp thorn tore a chunk out his hand. At this rate, he'd need medical attention to extract all the thorns embedded in his arms and thighs. Even his jeans offered scant protection. Prickles stabbed his legs mercilessly, and he forged on. He didn't dare risk walking in the open, and he had to get there. Amber needed him. Now, not when it was convenient to sneak in.

He paused twenty feet from the house. He had no option but to cross the ragged grass and risk being spotted. The lone light inside flicked off, plunging the yard into total darkness.

The front door opened then closed. Two male voices filtered through the night, too low to hear. Cautiously, he squatted in the trees, doing his best to remain motionless as they walked past him. Keres! He knew it.

The duo continued toward the back of the house and disappeared into a path in the woods.

Kody inched upward, stretching his cramping legs. It flashed through his mind this could be a trap, that they might have stopped just out of sight. He froze with indecision.

Nothing ventured, nothing gained.

He sprinted quietly across the yard to the side of the attached garage. He edged past piles of debris and discarded lumber toward the man door, watching every step. He reached for the handle, dropped his hands, and wiped them on his jeans to remove the sweat gathered there. The thorns ached, but his palms were dry now.

Icy knob in his hand, he prayed for success, and turned the handle. The slide mechanism froze and then slid open. He inched into the garage, giving his eyes a minute to adjust. The garage was as cluttered and filthy as the yard. Piles of rubbish and old car parts everywhere.

"Amber?" he whispered.

Someone bolted to a sitting position in the corner. Kody jerked back, prepared to flee.

"Kody?" her incredulous voice answered.

He flipped on the light and rushed to her, dodging piles of junk. "Are you okay? Let me help you. What's that smell?" The acrid odor burned his nostrils.

"Melting poly. I burned my arms free. My legs are still bound."

He dropped to her side. A blindfold hung crookedly on her head. She was filthy. He studied the lock and chain confining her ankles. Nothing he could do about that right now. They'd need tools.

"We have to get out of here," she whispered, ripping at a rag around her neck. She'd been gagged!

"Keres just left. I saw him head out. I'm calling Stone. She's got half the town looking for you." He put in a quick call and handed the phone to Amber. "Call your family. They're frantic."

She was still talking to them when Stone arrived in a blaze of lights and sirens. She peppered them with questions while the rest of her team searched the house and yard for evidence. Sometime during the evening, she'd found time to change into her uniform.

"Can't you just arrest him? You've got both our words. It was Keres," Amber demanded, rubbing her wrists together while Stone worked on picking the lock on her ankle chains.

"No evidence. He'd just walk in court, if it got that far. I know he's guilty, but without proof..." She shrugged.

"Dammit," Amber blurted. Anger rushed though her veins. "This is bullshit. Ugh."

"Total bullshit," Stone agreed. "I'd like to fry his ass, but we have to go cautiously. Mundanes run the legal system. If we act outside the law, there'll be trouble." She flipped the lock open, unwrapped the chains, and slipped them into an evidence bag. "Tell me everything."

"I can't." Heat rose in her cheeks, and she glanced away. "I have to pee."

Stone laughed. "Inside you go. Don't touch anything."

A mber struggled to stand. Pins and needles exploded through her feet, and the cramps in her hips and knees nearly floored her. "I don't think I can walk," she gasped. The floor's chill had seeped through her body into her bones. She'd never feel warm again.

"You were stuck in one position for too long. Let me help." Kody inched past Stone and kneeled beside Amber. He took one foot in his hand and massaged her foot ankle and calf.

"Ouch. Oh. Stop."

He paused. "Trust me, it'll help."

"Fine." She waved him back into action. "Dammit. That hurts. Oh. Ah." Her groans turned to sighs of pleasure as proper circulation returned. "Okay. Enough. Help me up so I can go." Kody pulled her upright and followed behind as she hobbled across the garage into the house. He stood patiently outside the door until she finished and came out.

Stone met them in the kitchen.

"Um. I left a sample in a drinking glass on the counter." She blushed. "You know, for drug testing."

"Smart move. Though, if he has any brains, he'd use something that dissipates quickly. I need you to come to the station for statements. I'll get the full version in my car on the way."

"What about my truck?" Kody asked.

"Leave your keys with an officer, and they'll bring it to the station when they finish up here." She waved them toward the door. "My car's out front. And, by the way, next time you disobey me and head in without backup, I'll lock your ass up. This might be a special circumstance, but I'm still in charge of the safety of all of Three Moon Falls' residents. Not just the Hawk family."

"Yes, ma'am."

Amber stifled a laugh. There wasn't an ounce of apology or remorse in his voice. She slid into the backseat of Stone's Beemer and wiggled to the middle, making room for Kody. He scrunched himself in beside her, wrapping his arm around her shoulders. She sank into his familiar warmth and tipped her head to look at him. "Thanks," she whispered and brushed a soft kiss across his lips.

"None of that," Stone chided with a laugh. "Keep it P.G. How'd you find her anyway?" she asked as they rolled down the drive past Kody's truck.

"Honestly?" He glanced from one woman to the other. "You won't believe me."

"How?" Amber echoed the question. Curiosity had her looking up at him again. She pursed her lips pleadingly.

"It started when I told Stone that Sasha had told me Keres had you. Shit, I forgot to get someone to look at her where he kicked her." He shook his head. "Anyway, Stone said it took strong magic to talk to animals, implying I have some magic buried inside me. She also said your family would try and find you magically. I put two and two together." He shrugged. "I sat in my truck and asked the Goddess for help and pictured you in my mind. Remind me to get a photograph of you to make that easier. Suddenly, I thought west. So, I went west. I had to stop and recalibrate once, but eventually, I ended up at this house."

Amber gaped at him. She'd suspected he was magic, but to find her on his first try was incredible for a novice, let alone an unguided beginner. Hell, a lot of experienced witches would have failed. "That's remarkable." She brushed a kiss on his cheek. "Thanks for trying something so foreign to you."

"I'm getting used to this weird-ass way of life."

Stone laughed. "I inspired you. Boy, I'm impressed with you. You've got balls."

"Um. Thanks." He blushed.

"I gather you burned your way out of those ropes?" the officer asked, glancing in the rear-view mirror at Amber.

"I did. It took a while. What time is it?" She glanced at the growing light in the sky. "Gosh, it's morning."

"Pushing six." Kody hugged her tight. "You had me frantic for hours. Keres nearly sideswiped my truck on his way out. That's how I knew something was wrong. Then you weren't in the shop."

"About the melted rope," Stone persisted. "We're going to have to work our way around that or risk the whole world knowing you can cast fire. The official story is Kody used a lighter to burn you free when he couldn't loosen the knots. And, he found you by sheer luck. Got it?"

Kody saluted. "Yes, ma'am."

Amber agreed reluctantly. She didn't like having to lie, but she understood the necessity. "How do we explain the low levels of drugs in my body. I had to push the sedation away." She shivered and snuggled closer to Kody. He slipped out of his denim jacket and tucked it around her shoulders. Cozy and warm, it smelled deliciously of him.

"Easy," Kody said. "We let everyone assume he didn't give you much of whatever drug he used. How long were you awake before I came?"

She struggled to put things into a time frame. "Hard to say. Honestly, I was terrified. My head hurt like hell, and I was groggy. My head's still killing me."

"There's no avoiding medical help," Stone warned her. "It's protocol. We'll get Doctor Carter to look at you. She's in the know and familiar with what Hyacinth can handle. She'll provide official paperwork that will stand up in court."

"If we get there." Amber sighed sadly.

"When we get there," Kody and Stone replied in unison.

"I hope you're right." Amber closed her eyes and tangled her fingers with Kody's. She wasn't a frail woman and rarely felt out of her element. Today had knocked her sense of mental balance for a loop. She was out of kilter, and he was steady, like a rock or a lighthouse in a storm. He was both comforting and tinder to the dry leaves of her heart.

"Get some rest," he whispered against her hair.

An impossible suggestion. She was too wired, too afraid, and angry. Plus, her head hurt like the dickens, and despite her best efforts, whatever drug she'd been given combined with exhaustion, played havoc with her sense of reality. Things faded in and out. Reality blended with images of waterfalls and mystery packages. She focused on slowing her breathing and clearing her head. The next thing she knew, Kody brushed a kiss on her cheek.

"Hey, sleepyhead. Wake up. We're at the station. Let's get this done so I can take you home."

"Your place?" she muttered without thinking.

"No, your family is chomping at the bit for details and to inspect you and see for themselves if you're alright."

"Bummer." She giggled. "Sorry. I'm punch drunk, exhausted, and still affected by the drugs."

"And the blow to the head, no doubt. Come on, pretty lady. Out you come." He tugged gently on her arm and helped her out of the car.

A few steps later, she stumbled on a small crack in the sidewalk. He scooped her into his arms and carried her inside as if she weighed nothing. "My hero," she whispered as he set her on a chair in Stone's office. "Thank you."

"My pleasure." His smile lit the room, and warmth flooded through her.

"Enough of that, if you please. We have to focus," Stone demanded with a smile, clearly not upset by the growing attraction between them. "Why didn't Keres bind your powers?"

"I've been wondering that myself," Kody added. "He froze you in the shop. Why not last night?"

"Oh, my gosh, I never even thought about it." She shivered, chilled by the idea she'd missed the obvious. "He managed to get into my head while I was drugged. He put up a block to keep me from contacting my sisters." She closed her eyes and focused on her family. Slicing agony carved into her brain. Bile rose in her throat. "I still can't reach them. Even trying hurts like crazy and makes me nauseated."

"There must be a reason he didn't bind all your powers." Stone slapped her hands on her desk in frustration.

"Ouch." Amber winced. "Keep it down, would you?" She really needed a handful of painkillers and a good night's sleep. Or a day of sleep in this case, since it was practically morning. Concussions were a bitch. She'd had one in elementary school when she fell out of a tree spying on a cute boy. She couldn't even remember his name now. This concussion was equally bad, if not worse. The lingering effects of being drugged exacerbated the discomfort. "He's probably already picked my brain, assuming he's got decent psychic skills. He was in there once before."

Keres in her brain, again, was a slap in the face. A brutal violation. He could, if he dug deep enough, learn all her secrets. Hells bells, he was privy to everything she knew about everyone. The man was demon spawned.

Kody sat in the chair beside her and drew her into his arms. "It's okay. We'll get through this."

She shuddered. Tears rolled down her face. A sob caught in her throat. Knowing Keres was in her mind threatened to break her. It was the worst kind of violation. Mental rape. There were no physical symptoms, no way to prosecute him. The law would never understand her agony. Mental trespass was impossible to prove; unless she was willing to let someone else in to snoop around. That's why the witch's council had such stringent rules against it.

"What is it?" he whispered, squeezing her tight.

"If it's any consolation," Stone said soothingly, "I'm taking his actions to the council. They'll have to deal with him."

"What am I missing?" Kody glanced back and forth between Amber and Stone.

"Messing around in someone's brain is rape. Mental rape. He'll have left footprints all over her brain when he was stomping around and might have damaged her." Anger laced Stone's voice. "Amber's undergone a serious trauma, and as the drug wears off, reality is going to hit her. Hard."

"Then let's get this damned interrogation over so I can get her back to her family. They'll know what she needs."

Amber squeezed his hand. Her knight in shining armor. "Thanks." She took a moment to formulate her words; both to clarify her thoughts and to ensure Kody would understand. "It's like this, I think. Keres needs something from me he can't pick out of my brain himself, or he'd have done so. I'm still here, so he didn't find what he wanted. I'm guessing he needs the use of my powers. Though, for what, I have no idea. I'm making assumptions here, until I have something better to go on. If he needs me to use my powers, he can't bind them. He probably thought he'd given me enough drugs to keep me under until he wanted me awake. His mistake is our advantage."

"Could he take your powers?"

Kody's question was a punch to the gut, rocking her already unstable world.

Blood drained from her head, making her woozy. She gripped the table for support, breathing heavily through her nose. In through the nose, out through the mouth, until she regained her equilibrium.

"Yes," she whispered. "He can steal my powers. That's where Mom and Dad are. They're looking for someone who's been stealing power from witches. Only, they don't just take what they want. The victim ends up brain dead or worse. What if it's Keres?" Her head swam, and she wavered dizzily in her seat. Her throat went tight, and she struggled to swallow and breathe. She sucked in a breath and pushed it out, trying not to hyperventilate.

"What the actual hell?" Kody exploded to his feet, nearly unseating Amber as his support left her shoulders. "This is way the hell out of control." He glared at Stone. "You better get your ass in gear and call the damned council, before Amber gets hurt worse than she already is."

Stone stood and leaned forward menacingly; her hands flat on the table. "Get a grip. We don't have time for histrionics. We need to finish taking both statements before the doctor arrives. While he's examining Amber, I'll contact the council. I'll trust Amber to contact her parents. I'll need to talk to them as well. Now, sit your ass down, and we'll get started."

Chapter Thirty-Five

Kody opened the door to Amber's family home. Welcoming aromas of cinnamon, apple, and vanilla washed over him. Beneath it all, deep undertones of sage drifted to him. It felt like coming home. He pushed the thought aside and helped Amber inside. She wavered on her feet, completely done in by exhaustion, drugs, and her head injury.

Her sisters rushed to her side, pushing Kody out of the way and gently leading her to the couch and helping her sit, braced up in one corner. They hovered around her, all of them chattering at once, demanding answers to their questions about what happened and how she was feeling. They sounded like a flock of crows fighting over roadkill. The noise was deafening.

"Shut it," Kody shouted rudely. They all turned to glare at him, mouths agape. "Amber's head hurts, and you guys are deafening. Show a little respect and caring." He shoved his way between Hazel and Lazuli and perched beside Amber. She smiled weakly at him.

"Sorry," Hyacinth said. "We've been worried sick. But you're right. I need everyone to back off and let me in to examine her. We can chat later, after I ease her pain. And you, too, Kody. I'll look after those scrapes on your hands and arms. But Amber comes first." She shooed her siblings away with a wave of her hand. They didn't go far, just a few steps back, but they did remain blessedly silent. At least they knew when to shut up, he thought uncharitably.

Without being told to, he shifted left, increasing the space around Amber but keeping a light grip on her hand, despite the thorns digging into his. He'd tried to pry them out at the police station, but they were buried deep. It didn't matter; Amber was his only concern.

"Where is it the worst?" Hyacinth asked. "We'll start there."

"My head. It's cut and bruised. But the worst is inside, where you can't go."

Hyacinth looked questioningly at Kody.

This wasn't his story to tell, but he didn't give a rat's ass. "Keres messed with her head. Not only did he bash her on the skull, he drugged her." Kody paused. "And he walked through her brain looking for something."

Amber's sisters and grandmother gasped. Hazel cussed a blue streak using words Kody had never heard a woman use before.

"I don't know how bad it is." He glanced from one sister to another, ending at Gramma Pearl. "He blocked her from contacting you, but I don't know what else he did."

"I'm right here," Amber snapped, dropping his hand. "I can speak for myself." She leaned forward, clutching her head in her hands.

"Sorry," he said contritely, guilt blooming in his heart. "I just want to help. You've been through so much." He gathered her hand between his and stopped talking.

Hyacinth examined the large cut on Amber's head. She turned to her sisters and barked out orders to nobody in particular. "I need a garlic, rosemary, and honey antiseptic wash, willow and comfrey for the pain. She needs clean clothing. Sweats or something comfortable." She turned to Pearl. "They both need food and hydration. Make some of that mango-orange juice, add some honey. Make a high protein snack, and then find something sweet to eat."

They snapped to attention and hurried off to follow her orders. She kneeled on the plush carpet in front of Amber. "Truth time. Are you okay? How badly did he mess around in there?" She tapped Amber lightly on the forehead. "Quick, before they come back."

Kody opened his mouth to respond, but her glare stopped him. He snapped his mouth shut. Hyacinth was a force to be reckoned with when she was in healer mode. No doubt, she would be an excellent midwife, not taking any guff from her patients but being understanding at the same time. She reminded him a bit of his maternal grandmother.

A memory of his grandmother forcing him to drink a mug of nasty, bitter tea when he had a fever drifted into his mind. He'd detested it, but it had made him feel better and helped him sleep off the bug. He'd thought it had come from the store. Now he wondered if it was the product of her incredible garden. He'd have some questions for her when he called her on Sunday.

"Take her shoes and socks off," Hyacinth ordered. He hastened to obey, gently removing her filthy sneakers and socks. She'd be upset later, her pink and green star patterned shoes were ruined, covered in filth and grease. He set them aside and stuffed the socks inside them. He helped her out of the jacket he'd lent her earlier.

Hyacinth gently bathed Amber's head wound and washed her arms. A yellow salve, smelling of dandelions, was smeared on her wrists and ankles. Soft cotton bandages covered the salve to keep it from smearing and to protect the wounds.

Amber sat motionless through it all, barely wincing at motions that must have hurt like hell. She wasn't stoic, she was ... beat down and done in. Her detachment wrenched at his heart. Her hand sat limply in his, but he refused to relinquish it for more than a few seconds. He'd help her get through this.

Her sister's external wounds cleaned and dressed, Hyacinth dropped onto her backside and sighed. Her face was pale and colorless. Her hands shook when Pearl thrust a plate of cookies and cheese at her and handed her a steaming mug of tea. She chugged the tea down and devoured the snack before she spoke.

"We need to get some food into you two."

Kody followed Hyacinth's lead and devoured the snack and his tea. Amber stared at hers without touching it. Was this detachment typical for rape victims? Did they retreat into themselves? He couldn't imagine a worse thing to happen to a person. But to have it in their mind where there were no visible wounds and no proof for the authorities? He couldn't fathom the mental anguish she must be experiencing.

He lifted her tea to her mouth. "Come on, Amber, take a drink. It'll help."

Pearl and Hyacinth nodded their encouragement. Sip by sip and bite by agonizing bite, he encouraged Amber to finish her refreshing snack. Despite the mental strain seeing her like this was causing him, the snack had revived him somewhat.

He politely turned his back while her sisters helped her into blue floral yoga pants, a t-shirt, and zippered hoodie.

"Let's get her outside." Hyacinth rose slowly to her feet.

"Shouldn't she be in bed?" he blurted. Outside? What the hell? She needed sleep, not sunshine. These women were crazy.

Pearl rested her hand on his arm. "Trust me, son. This is what she needs. Hyacinth isn't finished yet. She needs the strength of the earth to work her strongest magic."

Right. Hyacinth must be the earth one. Amber was fire. He shook his head in disbelief. He tried objecting again but was overruled.

"It'll be easier if you carry her," Hazel suggested. "We can drag her or support her, but you can just sweep her up and bring her for us. You're strong enough."

He rolled his eyes at the blatant attempt to entice his masculinity and scooped Amber gently into his arms. "Come on, sweetheart. Let's go outside. Maybe some sunshine will help."

Lazuli smiled encouragingly and nodded her approval. She led him through the house and out into the back yard. He carried Amber over the covered porch, down the stairs, and across the grass. His arms were killing him; she wasn't heavy, but he was still exhausted. Hazel led him through a gate into a lush green space surrounded by brilliantly colored flowerbeds back by a thick potentilla hedge.

The center of the space held an enormous star surrounded by a circle made of tiny gravel. The spaces in the star and between the star and circle were plush grass. A pentacle. This must be their ritual space. He doubted many people set foot inside those hedges. He was honored to be here. He might not understand their beliefs, nor was he a full believer, but he recognized the compliment offered him.

"Where do you want her?"

"In the middle, right in the center. Please." Hazel gestured. "Set her down, there."

"Here you go," he whispered against her hair. "Outside in the sun, with your sisters to help."

Hazel waved him away, and he stepped back. Not too far, just far enough to be out of the way but still inside the pentacle's circle. Hyacinth pulled up her yoga pants, exposing her legs, and sat cross-legged on the grass in front of her sister.

The other sisters whirled into action around Amber. Casting a circle of dried rose petals, lighting candles, and calling the Goddess. They worked quickly and acted as if he wasn't there. He held himself motionless; he didn't want to remind them of his presence.

Circle complete, they settled around Hyacinth and Amber.

Pearl spoke first. "Come, join us, Kody."

He hurried to fill the spot they'd left vacant for him. Pearl took his right hand; Hazel took his left. One by one, they joined hands, forming a closed circle around the patient and her healer. Their arms stretched uncomfortably wide to reach.

Pearl began to sing, her voice low and sweet. Moving clockwise around the circle, each woman joined in. When they reached him, Pearl nodded. He didn't know the words, but he joined in humming the simple tune. He was rewarded with smiles all around.

Hyacinth spoke a prayer to the Goddess, ending with, "By the powers of earth, air, fire, and water, Mother Earth, help me heal your daughter."

Kody expected her to take Amber's hands or ankles and heal them. He had no doubt in his mind she could heal with a touch. Instead, she closed her eyes and placed her hands on Amber's head.

Amber slumped sideways. Kody tried to go to her, but Pearl's tight grip held him in place. He stared at the older woman. She shook her head without pausing in her song. Hyacinth talked lowly, too low for him to hear, and didn't lift her hands from Amber's head after easing her onto her back.

He had a thousand questions.

A million questions.

He was scared shitless for Amber, and yet, he knew this was what she needed, what she'd want. Her strange catatonic-like state had frightened him. The aftermath of the night's troubles was too much for her to bear.

Time crept by. They repeated their song. Over and over. And over again; until he recognized the words and began to sing along. Still, they sang. His voice grew hoarse, as did everyone else's. Hyacinth didn't move. She knelt beside Amber, hands on Amber's head, whispering softly. Tension grew within him, threatening to steal his voice and his sanity. He wanted to jump up, grab Amber, and rush her to the hospital. Only the doctor's earlier assurance held him in check. Dr. Carter had repeatedly told him her family could give her everything she needed to get over her injuries. The indignity and shame of rape would take time.

He turned back to humming, his voice no longer able to sing. Sorrow filled his soul. What if she didn't come out of this? What if he'd been too late in finding her? How much damage had Keres done? His snack was like a bag of marbles rolling heavily in his stomach, threatening to come up.

Amber stirred, and his heart soared. He hummed with renewed vigor until Amber struggled to sit up. As soon as she reached a sitting position, Hyacinth slumped sideways, her hands falling from Amber's head. In an amazing turn-around. Amber helped her sister to the ground.

In unison, the family around the circle cried thanks to the Goddess. Kody echoed their cry.

Pearl leaped to her feet with the agility of someone half her age. At the edge of the circle, she cut a box shape in the air with her hand, hurried to the edge of the sacred space, and grabbed a potted plant. She rushed back into the circle and repeated the slashing motion in reverse. Kody recognize the action as opening and closing a magical door in the circle.

Pearl carried the plant to Hyacinth.

Hazel and Lazuli helped Hyacinth sit up. They grabbed her hands and thrust them deep into the pot, holding them there against her weak struggles.

The plant's leaves curled and turned brown. The stalk wizened and dried up until the beautiful flowers were nothing but crisp, dead leaves that crumbled into dust.

"What the hell?" He jumped to his feet.

She'd killed a plant with her bare hands.

His blood turned to ice in his veins. He started to shake. He'd seen some weird stuff around this family, but this took the cake.

He stared at the dead plant and realized the once plush grass in the circle's center was dry and brown. She'd killed it, too. Stolen its life. His heart almost stopped. She could ruin her neighbor's lawn. Did she also possess the power to destroy farmer's crops or ruin forests? Hell, could she end all life on the planet if she took the notion? Maybe not Hyacinth, but in the hands of someone like Keres... Kody couldn't handle the thought of possible magical powers so dangerous and the horrible implications of their wrongful use.

He rushed to Amber's side. "Are you okay?" he demanded.

"Better. I need to sleep," she said, grasping his hand. "Help me inside?"

He scooped her up and rushed toward the house. He'd get her inside, and he'd get the hell out of here now that she was fine.

What kind of family was this?

Magic was one thing, but this? This was beyond everything.

Amber's recovery was a miracle, the rest was living hell.

"Upstairs, third door on the right," she advised him, her voice weak with exhaustion.

He carried her into the room, threw back the covers, and eased her gently into bed. He covered her up and backed away.

"Come sit. I need you." She smiled at him.

"I have to go." He turned and bolted into the hallway, nearly running Hazel down in his haste to escape.

Behind him, Amber called out for him to come back. She could explain.

Now way, no how. He was out of here. If they had that kind of ability, the skill to kill with just a touch, he didn't want any part of it. *Was that what Keres was after? Was he trying to grab that murderous power for himself? What if evil had that power? Then what?* He wanted to be tougher than this, to stand by her side and protect her, but he needed time to think and he couldn't do that near her or her family.

Chapter Thirty-Six

Amber paced the house and yard. Kody wasn't answering his phone. Sasha told her he'd rushed in, made some calls, and packed a duffle bag. He hadn't returned to his apartment since. That had been days ago.

He hadn't called.

He hadn't texted.

He ignored all her attempts to contact him.

She'd even tried having Frank call him. As soon as Frank told him he was calling for Amber, Kody had said goodbye and hung up. A call to his business number reached Bryce, who told her he was running the dives, with Kody's approval, indefinitely.

She hurled a throw cushion against the wall, knocking her grandparents' photograph askew. She wanted to kick his ass. They'd been building something together, and he walked away without even bothering to try to talk things over. Even in her muddled state, she'd recognized his concern for her health. Why didn't he call?

"I know why," she muttered. "They scared the living shit out of him. Why didn't they wait until he was gone to rejuvenate Hyacinth?" A newbie, practically a mundane, wouldn't understand the need to draw strength from the earth after such a strenuous healing. He'd only see the death.

Healing wasn't always like that. Small wounds took their toll. Assisting in labour and delivery a bigger toll. But those could be mitigated with food and drink. This had required more.

Hyacinth had sped up the healing in her head wound. Amber rubbed the wound. It still ached, but it hadn't gotten infected, despite the filth she'd laid in for hours, and it had scabbed over. But the ritual healing had gone deeper.

Her sister had risked her own health to remove the binding Keres had put on Amber. She could reach out for her family again. Tampering with the mind was strong magic and even stronger healing. She'd tried to erase the stain of his presence in Amber's mind. She'd gotten most of it, but small bits still lingered. They always would, but with time, the terror and discomfort would ease. She hoped.

"Dammit." She kicked the pillow and straightened the tilted picture. "If he'd just answer, I could explain. I thought we were friends. I thought we were more than friends." She stomped into the kitchen, upstairs, and back down again. The movement wasn't easing the fire burning inside her. Her fingers sparked. She fisted her hands, sparks leaked out the sides, falling harmlessly to the floor. Except one ember, which left a tiny burn on the hardwood.

"Shit." She scrubbed it with her finger, making sure the cinder was out.

She slammed her feet into a pair of flip flops and stormed outside. If she didn't burn off this tension, she'd accidentally set the house on fire. She jogged across the back yard, past their ritual space, and into the woods to her childhood safety zone.

Gramma Pearl had commissioned a tall, cinder-block enclosure, thirty feet across on each side. Twelve-foot-high walls shielded a sand filled room without a roof. Three solid walls and one with a generous, six-foot-wide opening that served as a doorway. A ten-foot-wide, plant-free gravel border surrounded the enclosure. Amber stepped inside and paused. How many years had it been since she came here to vent? More than she could count. Probably not since high school. Someone had been keeping it weed free. Nothing grew inside the enclosure, and all the trees had been trimmed back to keep them safe from her unspent emotions.

"Thank you, whoever you are."

She kicked off her shoes and burrowed her feet into the sand. She pressed her palms together in front of her face, thumbs on her chin, index fingers against the tip of her nose. A heavy sigh puffed out, fanning cooling air over her scorching fingers.

She swore a blue streak at the indignity of having to vent before she lost control. She felt like a hormonal teenager all over again. She'd achieved full control over her talent years ago, and here she was losing her mind with no option but a controlled burn of emotion.

Her hands fell to her sides, hanging limply until she bunched them into fists. Heat blossomed in the tight enclosures of her fists. Her anger spiked.

Men were so damned irrational. Kody was a freaking scaredy cat.

Sparks spilled out of her fists, dropping harmlessly to the sand.

Screaming, calling him all kinds of stupid, venting her anger, she thrust her hands forward, palms out, blasting fire. Flames shot out of her hands, splashing against the wall twenty feet in front of her. Covering the wall, top to bottom, left to right. Charring the bricks and scorching the sand at it's base.

She screamed again, letting loose another blast.

Again, and again, she berated Kody, careful not to call a curse upon him.

She didn't want him hurt. She was in love with him, even if he was a stubborn jackass.

Rage spent, she dropped to her knees in the sand, buried her head in her arms, and wept. Exhausted, she slept. When she woke, dusk was falling. She grabbed her flip flops and padded, barefoot and contrite, back into the house.

"Done then?" Pearl asked when Amber entered the kitchen.

"For now."

Her grandmother drew Amber into her embrace. The familiar, comforting scent of her hand-crafted cologne washed soothingly over Amber. Lemon, pineapple and sage. Unconventional, just like her grandmother. As it had so many times in her youth, the embrace brought a measure of peace. "Oh, darling. He'll come around. I know it. He came back after I messed in his head, didn't he?"

"I guess." She wasn't convinced, even knowing her grandmother's ability to perceive things. Pearl always claimed her decades of life experiences made her extra wise. Big words for a woman who was only sixty. Still, her confidence was bolstering. "I'd like the chance to talk to him."

"And you'll get it," Lazuli proclaimed, entering the kitchen and snatching a banana chocolate chip muffin from the cooling tray beside the stove. She took an enormous bite. "I can't say how it'll go, but you'll get to talk," she said around a mouthful.

"Gross," Amber declared, momentarily distracted by the mess her sister was making. "Whoa, what?"

"You'll get to talk to him. I asked the cards." Tarot was one of Lazuli's stronger skills. "I couldn't get a read on the result, but you'll definitely talk to him."

"That's a relief. I don't suppose you know when?"

"Nope." She shoved more muffin into her mouth.

"That's disgusting," Hazel groused from the doorway. "Stop hogging the muffins, and I'm not cleaning up those crumbs."

"It's your day on kitchen duty," Laz disagreed.

"You'll clean up your own mess," Pearl injected. She swung sideways so Amber slipped under her shoulder and remained half in her embrace. "Since everyone is stuffing themselves with treats, I might as well cook something more nutritious. Have you eaten today, Amber?"

"Not yet. I'm ravenous."

"Setting half the forest on fire will do that to you," Hazel teased.

"You shut up, or I'll burn your ass," Amber fired back her childhood response.

"The fire was out?" Pearl pulled a ball of pizza dough from the fridge.

"One hundred percent out. I slept for a while. Everything was cool." She'd checked automatically. It had been her ritual for so long, she reassured herself before leaving without thinking. She pulled a package of pepperoni from the fridge and started slicing.

Everyone pitched in to make their favorite pizza. Pepperoni, mushroom, pineapple, and shrimp with heaps of cheese and a homemade sauce. Hyacinth returned home in time to crack open a bottle of their custom homemade wine and join them at the table.

"We should sell this," Hazel declared. "It's delicious."

"Too many regulations. Tea is one thing; alcohol is a whole different ball of string. A million rules and regulations to untangle. The permits are ridiculous. I've checked." Pearl refilled her glass.

"Any thoughts on when you're going after Kody?" Lazuli probed.

"I'm not." Amber crossed her arms over her chest.

"You should."

"I don't know where he is." Amber felt her brows scrunch together and forced them to relax. She wasn't going to let her sister get her goat. That would get them into a fight, and she'd be all riled up again. Venting once was bad enough; there was no way she wanted to do it again. She was still burning inside. The only thing relieving the heat of her emotions would be talking to Kody.

"But you love him, right?" Hazel nagged and glugged half a glass of wine. "Yum."

"Irrelevant," Amber argued. "He bolted. I'm not chasing him. He'll have to come to me." To her dismay, her eyes welled with tears. "Why did he turn out to be a cowardly jackass?"

Lazuli threw her arm over Amber's shoulder and pulled her close. "Love is always worth the fight."

"So says the woman who's half in love with Frank and won't chase him." Amber stuck her tongue out at her sister.

"He's afraid of us. Why would I chase him?"

"I rest my case," Amber said smugly. "Kody is frightened of us. If he can't deal with the magic, I have no use for him." The delicious pizza she'd eaten turned to lead in her stomach. She rubbed the discomfort growing there. What if he was worth pursuing? She could be making a huge mistake in letting him go.

That was neither here nor there. She didn't know where to find him, and if Bryce knew, he wasn't telling. The brief joy of familiar family rituals vaporized like water under fire. She stood and loaded her dishes in the dishwasher. Time to go to bed and hope for the first good night's sleep since he bolted. It was going to take hours of meditation to even get close to relaxed enough to drift off. Not sleeping well made for a long night, and she had to work tomorrow. She'd taken enough days off in her extended pity party. Real life called, even if Kody didn't.

Chapter Thirty-Seven

Kody stared at the familiar façade of his grandmother's house. She called it her little cabin in the woods, but it was more than that. Way more. The three-bedroom log house was two full stories and three thousand square feet. More if he accounted for the addition that connected the main house to her greenhouse. She called it her playroom. It was full of drying herbs and other interesting stuff. Bottles of strange liquids. Stones, candles, powders.

Funny, he hadn't realized how it resembled the Hawk's place with all it's herbs, plants, and candles. He'd assumed they were decorative, but now he wondered.

Grandma's yard was in full bloom. It seemed like it always was. She had bulbs which flowered before the frost left. They transitioned to spring then summer flowers. Then autumn flowers and foliage. There was even a thicket of red osier dogwoods with their bare red branches that colored the winter snow.

The familiar scents of flowers and evergreens rolled through his open window. He breathed deeply, falling into the easy memories of youth. Digging weeds, trimming plants. Bundling herbs to dry. He'd never connected those activities to her teas and balms. He'd been oblivious, until Amber.

He shoved aside the image of her lying in her bed, reaching out to him. Her family was terrifying. He'd come home for comfort, not to think about her. His mind said the word like an expletive. Their tentative relationship had exploded with the revelation that they could kill things with a touch. Magic or not, it wasn't natural, and it wasn't right. His stomach churned.

"You coming in or what?" Grandma called from the front porch.

She stood there, a broad smile on her face but lines of worry on her brow. Her gray hair brushed her shoulders in a blunt cut. The early evening sun set the variety of grays sparkling. There was almost a hint of red to them, reminiscent of her youth. He'd marvelled at those pictures, though he couldn't recall her with any but the color she now had.

He climbed from the truck and trudged toward her. He was thrilled to be here, to see her, but his heart remained heavy with loss.

"I'd say this was a pleasant surprise, but clearly it isn't. Something's wrong." She hugged him tight, resting her head on his shoulder. He remembered the days when she towered over him, and he found comfort against her chest. Times changed, he mused sadly.

"Hi, Grandma. How've you been?" He dropped a kiss on top of her head.

"Fabulous, better than you. I'm learning yoga." She contorted her body into a weird, one-footed twist, astounding him.

"Wow. That's incredible."

"Gotta stay young." She danced toward the door. "Come on, Kody. I've just made lemonade. Must have known you were coming."

"Yeah, about that." He followed her inside.

As always, the lemonade was delicious, but it tasted different today. "You changed the recipe."

"I grew the lemons myself. I've got two lemon trees and one lime tree in the addition. I added lime and some pansy petals. I'm quite pleased with the outcome."

"It's good." He rubbed his fingers up and down through the condensation on the glass before chugging it. "Got any work that needs done?"

"Not much. I've got a handyman now. But we could do some weeding." She winked.

"Weeding sounds good." He stood and placed his glass in the sink. Grandma had a dishwasher she never used, preferring the hands-on method of cleaning her dishes.

"What, no complaints, no sudden appointments?" She laughed.

"Nope. I could use a day of hard labor."

"Your boots are still in the greenhouse. There are gloves there, too." She gestured to the side door, and he led the way out.

They slid into their boots, though her knee-high rubbers had changed to Crocs. She handed him a pair of work gloves. He left them on the counter and headed for the yard. Kneeling between long rows of potato plants, he started pulling weeds barehanded. She teased him for it.

"I thought those hands were too soft for weeding without gloves." She yanked a stubborn weed and tossed it into the weed bucket.

"Thought I'd see what appealed to you about bare hands in the dirt." He avoided her gaze and crawled ahead to a patch of a broad leaf plant. He grabbed the first bunch.

"Whoa. Leave that. It's wild plantain. I'm harvesting it." She gently pushed his hand away.

"It's a weed. I thought we were weeding." He gave her a puzzled look, making her laugh.

"You always did rush the job. I'm trying a new recipe for a salve for insect bites. Wild plantain is the main ingredient. Let it be."

"You make a lot of salves, don't you?" He moved onto a patch of dandelions. "Can I pull these?"

"Yes, I've harvested enough of those for the year. I make a few," she said, answering the first question and tugging at a stubborn patch of clover.

"Not saving the clover," he teased.

"Nope, got a nice little patch in the northwest corner."

Her house sat on a thirty-acre plot of land, miles from the city and a four-hour drive from Three Moon Falls and backed onto crown land. She kept a special area planted in wild grains for the deer, elk, and moose who were frequent visitors to feed on. As a result, they rarely disturbed her extensive gardens.

They fell into silence until they went inside for the evening and a late supper. The bunk beds he'd loved as a child had been replaced by a queen-size box spring and mattress. His trophies lined a high shelf, their plastic cups and metal parts shone in the dim light filtering through the open blinds. The room had changed drastically but still held all the familiar comforts of home. He'd lived in this room every summer he could remember. His sister, Janice, had occupied the room next door. He'd always found refuge here, especially after his parents' accidental death.

Sleep wouldn't come. Amber was heavy on his mind. He missed her. He'd only left her days ago, and he couldn't shake her from his thoughts.

Watching Hyacinth kill the plant and all that grass had scared him spitless. He wasn't one to frighten easily, but he'd been scared and had bolted without waiting for an explanation. Amber used fire, and it stood to reason her sisters had equivalent skills but healing Amber and then killing plants was miles beyond comprehension. His fear had gotten the best of him. He'd grabbed his stuff, turned his business over to Bryce, and hit the highway. After spending two nights in motels, he realized he needed to come home.

He shook off the residual fear tingling along his limbs and climbed out of bed. He couldn't stay away from his life for long, but tonight, he'd escape to the garden. Outside, barefoot, like a child, he strolled up and down the long rows of his grandmother's garden, digging his toes in the earth and smelling fragrant flowers. Her workspace had been a revelation. The closed, locked cabinets were gone. Open shelving filled with dark, glass bottles replaced them. The number of drying herbs had tripled, at least. The gardens were bigger, too. How did a woman pushing seventy-five manage all this?

He strolled, lost in thought, until he found himself at the base of a familiar clump of trees, staring upward. He'd all but forgotten about his treehouse. He'd spent hundreds of hours here with a friend from the next acreage, playing all sorts of games. Pirates had been a favorite. The old rope still hung from the tree. He gave it a tug, and a rope ladder uncoiled before him. A few sharp tugs reassured him of its strength, and he scrambled up into the treehouse that was nestled between four large poplar trees.

The once enormous space seemed cramped now, but the treehouse was pristine. The wood had been stained and the floor swept. Grandma had kept it up for him. Probably in hopes of great-grandchildren. He sighed and settled on the floor in one corner, his eyes on the open doorway. No chance of kids. At least, not yet.

He was still there, awake, when dawn broke.

"Ahoy, the ship," his grandmother called up. "Permission to board?"

"Permission granted." He chuckled at the old ritual, not expecting her to climb up.

Seconds later, a carafe and two mugs preceded her into the tree-house. "Brought you some java. I assume you were up all night." She nudged his legs aside so she had room to sit in the opposite corner. She poured two mugs and handed him one.

He nodded and sipped the brew. "Thanks."

Like old times, she didn't press him for information. She let him sit and stew as he tried to work out his problems. Two cups of coffee later, she broke the pattern. "Are you going to tell me about her?"

Startled, his gaze flew to her face. "There is no her."

"Perhaps not." She nudged his foot with hers. "But there was. You can't fool your old granny. I assume it ended badly."

He nodded. Her ability to divine what ailed him was uncanny.

Or was it?

"You acted like an ass." Her words were as much a question as a statement.

Another nod.

"What are you going to do about it? You can't live in this treehouse forever. Not without paying rent. I've got bills to pay."

"How much is rent?" He tried delaying the conversation, knowing she'd persist. She never gave up when she got a bee in her bonnet. It was one of the reasons why he loved her so much. She persisted and didn't put up with his childish crap.

"More than you can afford." She climbed over to the ladder. "I'm making cinnamon buns. They're ready to go in the oven. Come inside when you're finished with your sulk. I've got the perfect tea to go with the buns." She climbed partway down. A second later, her head popped back in the opening. "They've got pecans."

His favorite. She was pulling out the big guns.

Twenty minutes later, she was pouring tea when he entered the kitchen. "Wash your hands."

He cleaned up and set the table before sitting down. "What kind of tea is that?"

"Oh, a little of this, a little of that," she hedged, sitting across from him and avoiding his eye.

"Your own special blend, no doubt."

Her gaze flicked up in surprise. She grinned. "Maybe."

"How'd you know I was coming?"

She blushed. "I didn't. What's with all the questions?" She pushed the platter of sticky buns toward him. "Help yourself."

"Are you a witch?" he blurted. Surprised he'd spoken the question aloud, he grabbed the platter and busied himself dishing them each a bun and adding generous scoops of extra cream cheese frosting to their plates.

Her laughter startled him. He stared at her. She chuckled until she was breathless. Her cheeks grew pink, and her lips stretched into an enormous smile. Several minutes later, she regained control of herself. "What kind of question is that?"

"One I'd like an answer to." He sliced a piece of roll and popped it into his mouth. Still warm from the oven, it tasted like heaven. Cinnamon, butter, brown sugar, a dash of something he didn't recognize along with pecans and cream cheese frosting danced on his tongue.

"Where are all the questions coming from?" She tore a piece of roll off and stuffed it into her mouth. She waved to indicate she couldn't talk with her mouth full. She was avoiding the conversation. She looked guilty.

He gave her his best imitation of the 'give it up' look she always gave him. The one that demanded instant compliance.

"Everyone knows witches are a myth."

"No, they don't."

"Care to enlighten me about what this is all about? The girl?"

"She'd not a girl. Amber is a woman. A beautiful, talented woman."
He snapped his mouth shut. She'd tricked him into answering her and
managed to avoid the question.

"Ah."

"I asked a question, Grandma. I'd like an answer." He leaned back,
crossing his arms over his chest, virtually daring her not to answer.

"I'm an herbalist." She mimicked his position, tilting her head to
the side defiantly.

"And the Goddess? Do you believe in her?" He dropped his arms
and picked up his fork. Getting answers from her was like hunting for
sunken treasure. He knew what he sought was there but didn't know
how to extract it. He knew she was stubborn, but he had now idea just
how much so.

"You've been studying. Because of her?"

"Her name is Amber," he snapped. "At least use her name." He
slammed his mouth shut with an audible click of his teeth.

"Amber, then. Does she believe in the Goddess? You think she's a
witch."

"Of for shit's sake. Just answer the questions. I'm an adult. You
don't need to hide things from me. I noticed the change in the work-
room. Where is your ritual space?" he pushed, asking question after
question until she sighed and rose from the table.

With a wave for him to follow, she left the kitchen and jogged up the
stairs. She led him into her bedroom, through the walk-in closet, and
into a large room with a skylight. He stared around him in disbelief.
The room was uncannily similar to a couple rooms in Amber's family
home.

"Satisfied?" she asked. "Do me the favour of not mentioning this to
your sister."

"How?" He stared around the room.

"It opens into the space above the garage. Nobody notices it. I designed it that way."

"You designed it." She was shocking the hell out of him. "I thought Grandpa designed this house?"

"I designed it. A rough sketch and he made it work. He was a man of many talents, rest his soul." She leaned against the wall near the door. "Go ahead and look around. I've got nothing to hide." The tone of her voice warned him payback was coming.

"Later. Maybe." He grinned at her. "I have a million questions. Let's go back downstairs and finish breakfast."

They ate and talked, did dishes, and talked some more. Lunch came and went. They were prepping vegetables for supper when she finally pinned him down. "Time's up, Kody. Tell me about Amber and what sent you running home like a dog with his tail tucked between his legs. She must be one hell of a woman."

"She is. She's a witch. She's got some badass, scary skills." He grinned, thinking of her ability to throw fire. Wouldn't that just shock Grandma's sensibilities. "She can trace her family right back to Salem."

"As can you. You're the descendent of one of the Salem accusers. Abigail Wilkins, to be precise, though I'm loath to admit she's my ancestor. She accused others to escape persecution herself. Hide in plain sight by joining the mob if you will."

"Wow." He paused, knife in the air, in the middle of chopping carrots. "I had no idea. I mean, you've said we were related but..."

"Yup." She chuckled.

"Why keep it a secret? I don't understand."

"It's hard to keep things from your family, especially things which are important to you. Your mother was deeply religious. Very Christian. Not that I minded. I'm good as long as you believe in something greater than yourself. But she wanted to raise you with her beliefs and asked me to hide mine. I concurred, reluctantly. I'll stand by my decision. Slowly, over the last few years, since she's been gone, I've been opening up more. Neither you nor your sister noticed." She shrugged.

"I must be blind. Or an idiot."

"Indeed." She raised one eyebrow mockingly. "I've already reached that conclusion."

"Thanks," he said wryly. "Wait! That's how you always knew I was coming and when there was something wrong. You're psychic."

"Nailed it in one," his grandmother praised. "There might be hope for that brain of yours yet."

Over the next few days, they talked about her beliefs and his experiences with Amber. Reluctantly, he told her about the last day and how he'd run. She sat quietly, showing no sign she was distressed by Amber and Hyacinth's powers.

"Chillax. Crap happens. Everyone messes up. If you love her, you'll suck up your pride and go home."

His grandmother had said chillax. Kody laughed. She sure was a pip.

"What's wrong with you? You're fidgeting like you've got ants in your pants."

He'd been at his grandmother's for ten days. This morning, he was up before dawn. He was tense, like there was someplace he needed to be, or something he should be doing. His first thought was that he needed to get back to his company, but a quick call to Bryce reassured him that everything there was under control. Kody tried working in the garden, then cleaned the garage. Now, he was pacing the house, trying to figure out what was gnawing at him. "I don't know. I feel uneasy. Like something's going wrong."

"You know, magical abilities are passed down by the mother, right? Men can be magical but don't have the gene to pass it on."

"And?" He didn't see the point of her spewing random statements.

"Has it occurred to you that you might have some psychic abilities? You did find her using the power of your mind. And you can talk to her cat. Do you have any idea how rare that is?"

"Yeah, I've heard." He stopped pacing and stared at her. "Do you really think I might be picking up something psychically?"

To his irritation, she shrugged. "Who knows? You've never tried to develop your gifts, and you're going to have to work on that. If you marry a witch, your kids will have skills, and you'll need to know how to cope with them."

"I'm not getting married." He shook his head. "Old people."

"Young upstarts," she countered. "Go upstairs, light some incense and meditate. See what happens."

He rolled his eyes.

"Listen to me. I'm done messing around and coddling you. You found a good woman. One who seems to like you, though I don't understand why. Get your head out of your ass and figure out what to do. If that means meditating, then you damn well better get after it."

Sighing, he went upstairs and tried to meditate. Time stretched to eternity; minutes felt like hours. Finally, an hour later, he began to relax. After another ten minutes, tension started to slip back in, but it was different. He was rocked with the sudden, unavoidable feeling that Amber needed him. Now!

He bolted downstairs.

"Grab your shit. We've got to go," he demanded, startling her as she pulled a roast from the oven.

"What?" She set the roaster on the counter and looked at him.

"Something's wrong. Big time wrong. I don't know what it is, but Amber needs me. She needs me, and I need you. Get your shit together." He made a hurry up motion.

Hands on her hips, she pinned him with a chiding stare. "Will you please stop cussing?" She removed her apron. "I'll pack some things. Put supper in the fridge and lock up."

By the time he had the food put away and the doors and windows locked, she'd called her handyman to watch the house, packed a suitcase and another duffle bag, and met him at the front door. "Let's go. I can't wait to meet this woman of yours."

"This isn't a social call." He locked the door behind them and threw her bags into the back of the truck.

"I know it's not; this is serious. Watch that duffle. There's glass inside." She climbed into the truck and fastened her seatbelt. "I trust you'll drive like a civilized human?"

He slammed the truck into reverse and sped out of the driveway, spraying gravel onto the lawn.

"Apparently not," she drawled. "You're cleaning that up when you bring me home."

"I just have to get there. Your lawn is sacrificial. Amber needs me."

Chapter Thirty-Eight

A mber paced the shop. Tingles of unease scurried up and down her spine. Something was up. Even with her limited psychic abilities, she could feel it. There was a storm coming. Whether it was actual weather, magic or something else, she didn't know, but something bad was coming. B.A.D. Bad.

She called each of her sisters, in turn, to assure herself they were okay. No problems there. Pearl was fine as well. Everyone was at home, relaxing, though they were all tense.

Maybe something was wrong with Kody. She called him up in her cell phone contacts and put the phone away. If he didn't want to talk to her, she didn't want to talk to him. Maybe her feelings were a residual effect of Keres' mind walk. Could he have planted some sort of suggestion in her mind that Hyacinth had missed during her medical repairs? She shuddered. Hopefully not; although weird things happening wasn't a good thing, it would be better than stains on her brain.

By the Goddess, she was tired of living in Keres' shadow. She had to find a way to get beyond his violation and move on. She placed her hands on the trunk of the lemon tree Kody had given her, closed her eyes, and slowed her breathing. She needed to relax. A moment of calming meditation would help. Breathe in. Breathe out. Repeat.

Keres popped into her mind. Again. She clenched her teeth and tried to force his image out, to no avail. Yeah, this unease had something to do with him. She knew it, right down to her bones.

She glanced at the clock. It wasn't even six yet, and hours remained until the shop closed. Suddenly chilled to the bone, she made a decision. She was going home. She had to be with her family until whatever was coming happened. She emptied the cash drawer into the safe, put a note of apology in the window, locked up, and headed home. She'd wait this out with her family.

Her call had stirred up her sisters' unease. They met her at the door, each demanding an explanation for her call or the answer to a dozen more questions. She held her hands up. "Stop. Let me get in, and I'll give you the rundown."

They subsided instantly. Two minutes later, they gathered around the kitchen table. "It's weird," she began. "I can't shake this feeling of impending doom. It's like a panic attack, only it's not." She scraped her hair back from her forehead with her fingers. It flopped forward, and she shoved it back again. "All I know is Keres is up to something. I wish these damned psychic skills would kick in. What good are skills if you can't use them at will?"

"That's not the way magic works, and you darn well know it," Pearl chided. "Skill comes with practise, but you can't force a skill to appear on your schedule."

"Well, I wish I could." She was being petulant and couldn't stop herself. "I know Keres is planning something. What I don't get is how I know. It's not a premonition; it's something else. I just knew I had to come home. Whatever it is, it's happening soon." Half of her wanted to delay the fight forever, the other wanted it over and done with, no matter what the outcome.

"Tonight's the first night of the full moon," Hazel offered helpfully.

Traditionally, the moon's power was considered strongest on the three nights of the full moon. The night before, the night of, and the night after the moon was full. These were the nights covens met or when witches practised reduction magic; spells to decrease things, like lowering an attraction to junk food. In some magic circles, the full moon was considered *the* night for all types of magic. The full moon was when anything was possible.

"That explains it. Keres needs the moon's magic for whatever he's up to. Dammit, I just wish I knew what he was planning."

"Can you feel anything, Laz? How about you, Gramma Pearl? Anything?" They both had psychic skills much stronger than her own. Surely, they were feeling something.

"Just a niggling sense of unease like yours," Laz responded. "I've been meditating, scrying, and using my favorite Tarot cards without luck."

"I wonder if he's blocking us somehow." Pearl twirled the remains of her tea in her peony and ivy patterned china cup and flipped it over on its saucer. Amber and her sisters froze in place to concentrate on the cup. If a person focused on a question during a tea leaf reading, the leaves would leave a clue. Everybody was silent until Pearl flipped the cup revealed her findings.

"Flames and a devil, maybe a demon. Darkness and evil," Pearl whispered, her voice quivering with fear.

Amber's heart stuttered and hammered into triple time. Her maternal grandmother hadn't been afraid of anything. Ever. She was a bastion of strength and serenity. She only lost her cool when the sisters were acting like idiots. This was going to be bad, really bad.

Everyone started to chatter at once. The questions came too fast for Amber to ponder who said them.

"What else do you see?"

"That's not everything is it?"

"What do you think it means?"

Amber slapped her hands on the table, startling them into silence. "Let her talk." She waved at her grandmother, who nodded in thanks.

"I'm not getting anything else, and it's making me nervous. The only thing I do know for certain is nobody, and I mean nobody, goes out alone. We go in pairs or as a group. We need to keep rested, so sleep if you can. Meditation wouldn't hurt, either. Now," she clapped her hands, feigning enthusiasm, "I suggest a game of cards to pass the time."

Amber jumped up to grab the cards and scorepad, and they launched into a lackluster game of rummy where low score wins. They didn't get nearly the total distraction they needed, but it helped ease their mounting tension.

Amber flipped her cards onto the table. "That's zero points for me," she crowed triumphantly. "I win. Take that." She jabbed her finger toward Hazel. "I beat you." Hazel was the family champion at cards. Nobody ever caught her cheating, but they often jokingly accused her of it. She couldn't possibly be lucky enough to win every time they played, but she rarely lost.

The lights snapped off, and the kitchen went black. The only light was from the full moon streaming in through the bay windows around the table. They gasped in unison.

"I guess the waiting is over," Hyacinth said, pointing out the obvious.

"It might be a power failure," Amber suggested, knowing she was wrong.

Pearl snorted derisively. "This is it." She rose from the table and hurried to the pantry. She was back in seconds with a cookie tin. "Eat these. I made them yesterday. They're energy balls. They've got turmeric, ginseng, and matcha powder in them to bolster your strength."

"Remember to stay close. Don't even go to the bathroom without a partner." Amber looked each sister in the eye until they nodded agreement.

"Great, now I have to pee," Hazel groused. She nudged Lazuli to let her out from the back of the table. "You're up. You might as well come with me."

"How did he manage to cut the power?" Amber wondered out loud.

"Probably off the property," Pearl answered. "Not that it's going to do him any good. The generations of magic practised here will fuel our supernatural defenses. He's not getting past those wards."

Amber recalled the number of times unwanted visitors had been turned away, like the time they hadn't let Kody in until somebody vouched for him. With luck, those wards would hold against Keres and his cohort. Though, they'd never been intended to protect against true evil, and he'd gotten past the wards in the shop by using dark magic to crush the floral bouquets into dust.

Her heart sunk, and she was twitchy and uneasy. Dread pulled at her. It mixed with a weird elation for getting this over with and ending the nearly crippling fear which bound them all. This could go so many ways. It could end now, or it could blow up in their faces. She shook her head; strong emotions were never easy, especially when they countered each other.

"Should we pull the shades or keep them open for the moon's strength?" she asked when everyone was back in the kitchen. She popped an energy ball into her mouth. Chocolate, caramel, cinnamon, sage, vanilla, and half a dozen other flavours danced on her tongue. Delicious. A ripple of energy flowed through her.

Wow! There was strong, white magic in them. Gramma Pearl must have cast a seriously powerful spell on the treats. She could easily get addicted to them. She stuffed another one in her mouth the second she finished the first.

"Go easy on them. Save them for when you need the boost," Pearl chided gently. "The body can only stay in a heightened state for so long, and you know it."

"Yes, Gramma."

Hazel set a few candles on the table, and Amber snapped them to life with a flick of her fingers.

"Damn, I wish I could do that." Hazel laughed.

"You've got your own skills. I can't control water. There's no way I'd ever be able to pull water from the earth or change the way it flows just using my mind. Do you have any idea how impressive that is?" Funny how no matter what she was capable of, there was always a lingering envy for the skills she didn't possess. It was rare for a witch to be able to control all four elements—earth, air, fire, and water—and with that ability came an enormous responsibility. Amber wouldn't wish that duty on anyone, though she did have ancestors who possessed the entire set of skills. Pearl had limited ability to do so, but with her skills spread so wide, they weren't as strong as a single power might be.

They sat, waiting. Nerves tingling. Senses on high alert. They scanned with their minds, using every molecule of their psychic skills to search for Keres. Hazel tried finding Keres using a location spell and pendulum, but the pendulum swung wildly, refusing to settle on a particular spot on their map.

"Oh!" Amber straightened in her seat and stared out the window. "He's out there. He's close. On our property and coming closer."

His voice exploded into her mind. "Get ready, witches. I'm coming for you. I'm tired of playing nice. I'll get what I need if I have to kill you all."

She blanched. "By the Goddess, he's beyond evil. He's coming. He spoke right into my mind." She shivered, the violation stealing her will, threatening to render her weak and useless. She stiffened her spine and pushed back, throwing up the best mental wall she could muster. She'd keep him out if she could.

Lazuli mustered a breeze and snuffed the candles. "Now what?"

"Now, we wait." Amber's voice trembled. "No sense buying trouble. He'll be here when he gets here, and we'll fight him all the way back to hell."

Chapter Thirty-Nine

They waited and waited. Ten minutes passed. Then twenty. Then an hour. Amber's nerves were stretched to the limit. She felt like she'd explode from the tension or be compressed to death by the emotions she struggled to contain.

The kitchen door blew open, the deadbolt tearing apart the door-frame. The door slammed against the wall, bounced back toward the frame, and went still, half open.

Without a word, they rose from the table and stood together in a group, backs together. Three facing the open door, Hazel and Lazuli facing the two other entrances to the kitchen. In unison, they kicked off their shoes and slid out of their socks. When push came to shove, they could all pull strength from Mother Earth and bare feet facilitated that drawing.

Three tense minutes later, Amber spoke. "He's not coming in. He wants us outside."

"I still don't know how he got past the property wards," Hazel hissed.

"He must have found something when he was in my head. I don't know what or how, but he was in there for a reason."

"I thought he was looking for the object you keep seeing," Laz whispered.

"Yeah, me too." Amber breathed deeply and rolled her stiff shoulders. Her entire body ached with tension. "I'd rather not face him, but we're going to have to. The unending strain will weaken us. Let's do this." She touched each member of her family's mind, reassuring herself they still had contact.

Words were tough to cast, but strong emotions would come through loud and clear. In a pinch, they could communicate without words, which could give them an advantage.

"Mother Goddess, protect us in our hour of need. Give us strength to get through this and to end this peril to our family. As I will it, so mote it be," she prayed aloud.

They strode outside, strong and defiant, to stand with their backs to the house, facing their enemy head on.

"He's in the meadow," Amber declared. "I can feel him now. He must have found a way past our defenses when he was in my head. When this is over, we'll have to rebuild the defenses."

Taking the lead, she strode across the lawn, down the stone path that wandered through a forest of pines, spruce, and poplar trees, and toward their picnic meadow. Everyone followed, moving in unison without question. They'd have greater strength if they acted virtually as one, and they'd need every bit of their strength.

Fresh scents of evergreen, moist earth, and exhilarating night air invigorated her as she moved forward. The pathway was dark, the towering trees blocking the full moon's light. She moved with confidence. She'd been running this path since she was a toddler. Night in the meadow was a time of peace and tranquility. It was a slap to the face that Keres had chosen this beautiful place for a fight.

Trickling water from the creek running along the north side of the meadow reminded Amber they were almost there. Stepping out of the forest and into the manicured meadow was like stepping into daylight. The moon was at her peak, flooding the opening with light, illuminating the dark man standing there. Amber studied him dispassionately. He was still filthy and unkempt, as was his friend, who stood half a step behind and to the left, looking dazed and half unaware of his surroundings. Keres wore dark clothing and a western style duster jacket, the long sides held back by the hands on his hips. A belt knife hung dangerously at his hips. Darkness surrounded them, like he sucked in all goodness and light, leaving an empty void.

Her sisters lined up beside her. Pearl took the left end of the line.

"What do you want?" Amber demanded, hands on her hips.

"You know what I want." He stared down at his nails, buffed them on his sleeve, and looked back up at her. He was the picture of disdain and dismissal. If he wasn't so dirty, he'd look like a bored billionaire.

"I know you raped my mind, and you'll pay for it," she countered. She dropped her hands, keeping them loose and relaxed as if she were at equal ease. She wasn't. She felt like she'd burst like an over-inflated balloon. There was no chance in the universe she'd show her tension. "Beyond that, I don't give a rat's ass what you want or what you think we have."

"You'll care by the time I'm through with you. You've got what I need, and I'll get it if I have to kill every one of you." Magically amplified, his voice thundered through the night,

Chills skittered across Amber's skin, lodging in her heart. Beside her, someone gasped. His arrogance fueled Amber's anger. "Just how, exactly, do you plan to take it?" *Whatever it was.* She wished she had a better clue of what he wanted. A spell? The wrapped item in her visions? Something else? Unless he told them, they'd never know. Suddenly, she realized he had no intention of telling them specifically what he wanted. He was enjoying feeding their fears.

"Are we going to do this or what?" She shrugged as if she didn't have a care in the world. "It's late. I need my beauty sleep."

A gust of wind buffeted her body, rocking her back in place. Shit, he was powerful. "Is that the best you've got? Laz, if you please." Her sister raised her right hand and palm out sent a gale of wind back at him. She swirled it around him, tearing at his long jacket.

Water sluiced up out of the dry grass, soaking their feet. It rose to ankle height. Whitecaps formed, growing stronger by the minute until they struggled to stand. Hazel pushed back. She entwined her fingers with Amber's for extra power, and the water receded.

Keres skills were phenomenal. One person rarely held all that power. How in the world did he acquire such strength?

A hawk swooped across the night sky, squealing accusingly. Its mate followed, echoing its cry. Clouds skittered across the moon and blew away, and the clearing flooded with light once again. The ground heaved beneath their feet; Amber stumbled forward three feet before regaining her balance. Behind her, the soft sound of shuffling feet said her sisters staggered as well. She kept her eyes forward, but her peripheral vision showed them stepping back in line.

"Cynth?" Amber didn't look at her oldest sister.

The ground rippled in a wave from just in front of them, toward Keres. He dropped to his knees. His accomplice fell onto his backside and stayed there.

Keres leaped up, screaming. "Bitches. You'll pay for that."

The ground shook, and a geyser of water spurted up in front of the women, showering them in icy water. Keres wobbled almost imperceptibly. Expending vast amounts of energy was draining. There was only one of him, and there were five Hawk witches. Even if they were weaker individually, they might prove more powerful as a group. Hope surged in her chest.

"Had enough yet?" she taunted. Unchecked emotions would disrupt his control of magic. She was terrified, and she forced herself to remain calm and pushed forth a casual negligence.

"Bitch."

"I am not a female dog, but I thank you for noticing I am female." She winked and stepped forward, hoping her trembling knees didn't buckle.

He hissed.

An owl screeched nearby, the sound raking down her already tense nerves.

"Really, my boy," Pearl called out. "Can we just get this nonsense over with? My tea is getting cold."

A small burning bolt of yellow fire flashed from his left hand toward Pearl. Hazel extinguished it with a tiny spurt of water. Apparently, he hadn't fully mastered fire, though he had an excellent grasp of the other three elements.

They battled back and forth. Water for water. Earth against earth. Air pushed air. He didn't cast fire again. On the ground beside him, Keres' friend sat motionless. Keres must have him under magical control.

Amber laced her fingers with her sisters, knowing they held strong in a connecting line. She fed power to her family as they fought. She didn't throw fire, though she dearly wanted to. She wouldn't risk setting the meadow or the forest alight or worse, killing someone.

"Give it to me," he screamed, his voice cracking under the strain of his anger.

Amber laughed. "I'll give you nothing." Defiance against the man who'd raped her mind fueled her words. Deep down, the vindictive part of her wanted to end him, to snuff him like a candle. The civilized, compassionate woman in her knew it was wrong. Life, all life, even that of those who strayed into dark territory, was sacred to the Goddess. Never mind the rule of three. What you gave came back to you three-fold. And Karma, oh yeah, Karma could be a real bitch. The sanctity of life was the strongest of all rules, and she banked the urge to hurt him.

"Give it back to me. I can't revive her without it," he screamed.

The pain in his words hit Amber like a tsunami. She stumbled and righted herself. Revive her? Revive who? How? The questions tumbled around in her brain, knocking her equilibrium askew. Her head went light and she dropped to one knee when the realization hit that he was planning to try and raise his wife from the dead.

A shockwave of air slammed into her. She struggled to her feet and pushed against it.

Time crawled as they battled back and forth. Blow after blow. Amber felt the energy draining from her sisters. Moment by moment, they weakened from the strain of the battle, their emotions and unmitigated fear. They popped Grandma Pearl's energy balls until they were all gone. She pulled deep, pushing her strength to her sisters.

"Why did you blow the falls?" Amber demanded, trying to distract him.

Keres laughed. "I'm looking for the artifact your family stole from mine. I want it back. Give it to me, and I'll walk away."

"We haven't stolen anything." The possibility existed that one of their ancestors had taken something they shouldn't, but she was certain if they had, they had a damn good reason for doing so and until she understood what was going on, she wasn't handing anything over to him. Especially not after he'd attacked her, repeatedly. If it had the power to resurrect the dead, it was better off lost. She wouldn't tell him where it was, even if she knew.

A deer leaped into the clearing. Frozen, its white tail held high, ears flickering. It pivoted one hundred eighty degrees and fled back into the trees with a scream of terror. Amber's heart bled.

A picnic table to their left burst into flame and exploded without warning. Slivers of burning wood impaled Amber's arm and cheek. Everyone screamed and ducked. Lazuli dropped to her knees, clutching her thigh. Blood spurted from the wound. Hyacinth rushed to her side.

"It's bad," she shrieked. "Protect me."

The others hastened to stand between Keres and their sisters, presenting a physical barrier. Pearl struggled to put up a magical wall. The glow of her unseen power trickled across Amber's skin as the wall went up. It flickered, barely visible, and collapsed into nothingness.

Her earlier moment of near confidence faltered, leaving Amber shaking. What if they weren't strong enough?

A strange hum filled the air, the sound unearthly and wildly out of place. Swarms of wasps surged toward them, engulfing them, their stingers driving like knives into her skin.

"No!" she screamed. Hazel was allergic to wasps.

The swarm blew backward in the stream of water surging from the ground at Hazel's feet. Amber blasted a blowtorch of fire toward them. Incinerated, they crumbled to ash at her feet. Hazel groaned and fell to the earth, gasping. After feeding her strength to her sisters, the small blast sapped Amber's strength. She couldn't last much longer.

"Cynth!"

"Gramma, get over here. Put pressure on this." Hyacinth grabbed her grandmother's hands and pressed them against the still flowing wound on Lazuli's leg. "I've slowed the flow, but it's still bleeding." She raced to Hazel's side.

Only Amber remained standing. Gramma Pearl watched over Lazuli while Hyacinth poured her healing magic into stopping the swelling in Hazel's throat from the wasp venom.

Keres laughed triumphantly.

Amber's strength wavered as she tried to erect the protective wall Pearl had failed to erect. They needed help. Without thought, she called to Kody.

"Kody," her mind screamed. "Where are you?"

"Here." His answering mental response jolted her. He was close. He sent a picture of their house. "Where are you?"

She flashed him an image.

An engine roared in the distance. Trees crashed and thundered to the ground. Fear passed over Keres face. He stomped his foot, and the earth shook. Water surged again, the frigid shock of it coursing down on Amber's skin, threatening to break her control and drop the magic wall she struggled to maintain. Her knees buckled. She dropped.

Keres raised a hand, his palm wide open. Slowly, he closed his hand, making a tight fist. His laughter raked her nerves.

As if he were beside her, his hand on her neck, Amber felt her blood slow, her breathing falter. Despite her efforts to suck in air, blackness drew her toward oblivion. With the last of her strength, she threw a thought at Keres. "You'll never get it if you kill me."

His grip faltered for a second. Her vision lightened. He laughed and squeezed again. "With you dead, I have all the time in the world to find it."

"You'll fail," she gasped.

Keres loosened his grip, whirled around, and drawing a knife from his belt sheath, stabbed the other man in the chest. The man crumpled, and Keres laughed with glee as he licked the blood from the glimmering blade.

Blood magic!

No. Hell no!

How could he invoke such a terrible thing?

Stealing the life of another to fuel his power.

Amber's heart wept for the other man, even as Keres squeezed her neck again.

"No!" Kody shouted.

Amber felt his hands on her shoulders, then under the back of her T-shirt, gripping her waist. Strength flooded through her. She felt his energy, his magic, his love.

Her vision returned. Kody's power was backed by an unrecognizable, female strength.

"Screw you, Keres," she screamed, and with every bit of her power and Kody's, and the power aiding Kody, Amber braced herself. Quivering with dread, she banked the fear drowning her and stealing her breath; she rubbed her hands briskly together, building friction between them. Crackles of blue-orange light leaked from between them, arcing across the air like ball lightning as she lashed out. Electric blue and blood red fire screamed from her hands, flying across the clearing. Setting Keres clothing on fire.

Unearthly, deadly screams filled the air as his clothing burned. He dropped to the ground, rolling frantically to snuff the flames.

Amber leaned over and emptied her stomach onto the grass. She'd done that to him, burned him alive. It was the most heinous torture a witch could conceive. She crouched, trying to stabilize herself, but the remorse and exhaustion swamped her. She dropped to her backside, narrowly missing the mess she'd made and prayed to the Goddess for strength.

A surge of water exploded from the creek, dousing him and putting out the fire but failing to extinguish his agonized screams.

Remorse and guilt battered Amber as Kody knelt beside her and drew her into his arms. The screaming went on. She burrowed her head into his shoulder, sobs wracking her body. She'd done that. She'd caused his agony.

Motion to her left jolted her head up.

A small, grey haired figure sped past her. She followed the movement to Keres' side. A woman knelt beside him and placed her hand on his unburned face. He slumped and went silent.

"No!" Amber screamed. She'd killed him.

The woman hurried back. "Relax, child. He's not dead. I just took away his pain and put him into a coma. He'll need a doctor fast."

"You can do that?" Kody's voice cracked with disbelief.

"And a whole lot more." She laughed.

Amber stared back and forth between them, her mouth hanging open. Kody pressed one finger against her chin, urging her to close her mouth. "I've never seen anything like that," she blurted.

"Me either, and she's my grandmother."

"You, get over here," Hyacinth demanded. Kody's grandmother hurried to Hyacinth's side. "You're a healer?"

"Yes."

"Ease her throat. It's an allergic reaction. We need to stabilize her and get her back to the house. You deal with her, and I'll help Lazuli. Got it?"

"Wait. I have something." She raced for Kody's truck and came back with a duffle bag. She rummaged around inside and pulled out a roll of fabric. She untied the leather string binding it and extracted a small vial. She pulled its cork with her teeth and poured the contents into Hazel's mouth. Kody's grandmother placed her hands on Hazel's throat. Slowly, Hazel's breathing returned to normal. Whatever potion, or magic she'd used was powerful. Instant results. Amber wanted to get her hands on this woman's spell book.

"Back at the house, in the kitchen, there's a cookie jar full of round balls. Go get it," Amber ordered Kody. "There's an epi-pen in the downstairs bathroom. Bottom left drawer."

He brushed her lips with a hasty kiss and raced past his ruined truck and down the path.

By the time Officer Stone arrived, Lazuli and Hazel were stabilized. They hadn't needed the epi-pen; the potion had done its work. The others were weak and emotionally drained. The energy balls helped but not enough. They'd need serious refueling and rest to recover from this.

Amber trembled as she recounted the events for Stone. Tears ran down her face. "I can't believe I did that to him," Amber wailed. "I burned him alive."

"His burns are serious, but he'll live," Stone responded. She waved to the paramedics and Dr. Carter, who was working on Keres. "He'll be in the hospital for a few weeks before he goes to jail. He'll be under police guard the entire time. You have to relax and realize you had no choice."

"Easy for you to say," Amber snapped ungratefully.

Stone's eyes narrowed. "I'm going to let that slide and chalk it up to exhaustion and one hell of a bad night. The Witch's Council will deal with him. They'll probably bind his powers."

"I have his DNA, from under my cat's nails in my purse. Sasha scratched him when he kidnapped me. I forgot all about it," Amber declared. "Can the council use it?"

"I don't know if it's useful or not, but it can't hurt to have it."

Back at the house, they spent hours undergoing questions and filling out paperwork. Stone took the DNA sample back to the station
with her. The council would meet on the next New Moon.

Chapter Forty

"I can't believe Stone worked it to read that Keres managed to burn himself in a campfire," Kody stated, rubbing his hands soothingly up and down Amber's arms the next morning.

"The real explanation wouldn't be believed. What choice did she have?" Amber leaned into him and slid her arms around his waist.

He had her right where he wanted her. In his arms. "How are you holding up?" he asked.

"Okay. Not great, but okay. I'm definitely going to be talking to the therapist Stone recommended. I'm going to need help to get beyond this."

"I think that's a great plan. I may see her, too. I've got some serious adapting to do if I'm going to keep up with this family." He pulled her close and kissed her again, lingering over the sweet taste and inhaling the beautiful vanilla scent that was as vital to him as the air he breathed.

"Oh, quit it you two," his grandmother chided, coming into the Hawk family living room. "Haven't you hugged enough yet?"

"Not ever in this lifetime." Kody laughed and then frowned when Amber slipped out of his arms to embrace his grandmother.

"Abigail, I'm so glad you showed up. I needed that extra boost of power. I never could have ended it without you. Kody never told me you had magic."

Amber's glare burned Kody's skin. "Hey." He raised his hands in surrender. "I didn't know. I just thought she liked to garden."

"Men. They're so oblivious." Amber went back into his embrace.

He'd forgive her the shot to his ego. It hadn't been his fault he didn't know. He was just glad he found out in time to help. His knees buckled. She could have died; they all could have.

"How did you know I needed help? You were right there. Where were you hiding from me all that time? You certainly weren't at work." She looked up at him.

He kissed away the wrinkle in her brow. She looked much prettier without it, but she wasn't bad with it. She was, beyond doubt, the most beautiful woman he'd ever met, and he was head over heels in love with her. Even if her magic still scared him a bit.

"Don't try and distract me with kisses," Amber warned.

"Like this?" He brushed his lips across hers, revelling in their soft, sweet beauty. He could do this all day. He deepened the kiss, pouring his love into it, showing her the depth of his feelings for her.

She sighed happily against his mouth. He felt her lips curl up into a smile.

"Oh, get a room." Hazel shoved him gently on the shoulder, breaking the kiss. "You think you'd have enough of that by now. I heard you whispering all night. Yuck."

Amber blushed. "Yeah, we talked a lot. I barely got any sleep."

"Talked...right." Hazel laughed.

"Enough kissing," Amber decreed. "Answer my questions."

Kody tugged her with him and sat on the couch. Only when she was tightly nestled beside him did he even think about her questions. "Honestly, watching Hyacinth kill half the yard scared the hell out of me. All I could picture was your power; it could destroy the entire world if you set your mind to it. I couldn't deal with it. I took off."

"Yeah, I got that much."

He pressed his fingers on her lips. "I drove for a long time. Somehow, I ended up at Grandma's place. I started putting two and two together and realized she didn't just make teas; she was a witch." He glared at his grandmother. "Although, it took a long time to get her to admit it."

Abigail shrugged. "I've been hiding it for a long time. It's hard to break old habits. I'm just glad we got here in time."

"About that..." Amber prodded.

"I got the feeling, out of the blue, that you needed me. I tried to reach you psychically, but all I got was a frantic sense of immediate danger. I grabbed Grandma and bolted home. I broke a thousand traffic rules on the way, too. I'll probably have half a dozen auto-cam tickets in the mail next week," he said, feigning sadness, hoping for a sympathy kiss. Amber obliged.

"When we got to the house, you screamed in my head. You scared the living hell out of me, by the way. My truck will never recover. I took out a hundred trees on my way to the meadow. I figured the truck was faster." This time, the regret in his voice was real. That truck was his baby. Now, she didn't even run. The mirrors were gone, the bumper was rammed into the fan and radiator. The sides were dented and scraped clean of paint. He didn't care. He'd sacrifice a vehicle any day to save the woman he loved.

"What happens to Keres now?" Hazel asked, curling up in the plush chair across from Amber and Kody.

"Stone contacted the council. He'll be sent to a magical rehab hos-pital-slash-prison in Europe. He'll stay there until they're confident that he's no longer a danger to the world."

"But what about the artifact that he claims you stole?" Kody asked. "If it's as powerful as Keres seemed to think, won't someone else come after it?"

"Probably," Gramma Pearl replied, not alleviating his fears in the least.

"Then we should find it," Kody blurted, jumping to his feet, nearly throwing Amber to the floor. Why weren't they panicking?

"Relax. We'll find it, in time." Pearl said. "I've sent a message to the girls' parents. They'll have an idea how to deal with this. They'll talk to the council as well, see if anyone there has any ideas."

"He said he needed it to bring her back," Amber's voice cracked. "I think he wants to bring his wife back from the dead."

Anger ratcheted through Kody. "Jesus, it never ends." He slammed his right fist into his left palm. "We should have let him die." Even as he said it, he knew it was wrong.

Amber gasped. "No. It's not right to take a life. The council will deal with him. It isn't our place to choose who lives of dies."

"Then what do we do?" He pushed back his fear for Amber, for her sisters. He loved this family as much as he loved his own.

"We talk to the council. Find the artifact and put it into safe keeping, before someone else comes for it." Amber replied logically. "Until then, we carry on as best we can."

He sat beside Amber and pulled her tight. "I don't know if my heart can take this."

"You'll get used to living with magic and all the trouble, and the good that it brings," she reassured him.

"I hope so, because I'm not walking away." He kissed her cheek.

"Have I told you I love you?" she responded.

"Nope, not even once," he teased, though she'd declared her love more than once last night. She slapped his shoulder.

Amber pivoted on the couch to face him. By the Goddess, he was handsome. Strong, intelligent and magical to boot. He had a strong heart. He was kind and gentle. She'd never get enough of him. He was her dream man. She cupped his cheeks in her hands, loving the feel of his stubble against her palms. Rough and vital, it reminded her she was lucky to be alive.

"Kody Wilkins, despite the fact that your ancestor accused mine of being a witch just to protect herself from trial, I find myself in love with you." She kissed him.

He kissed her back and didn't quit until they were both breathless. "Amber Hawk. I love you right back." His nose was cool against her when he brushed them together. "I think I need to keep a tighter watch over you. I think I'll have to marry you just to keep track of what you're up to."

Amber laughed; a thrill raced down her spine. "Was that an actual proposal? If it was, it was rather pathetic."

Kody slid out from beside her and knelt on one knee in front of her, a soft smile on his face. Love shone from his eyes. She knew in that moment, he'd keep her safe, he'd protect her with his life, over and over again if need be.

"Amber Hawk, I love you. I think I have from the moment I first saw you. I cannot live without you. Will you please, please, please, do me the honor of becoming my wife?" Sincerity glowed in his eyes. He gripped her hand tightly between his. The tension in his palms betraying his fear she'd say no.

"Yes, Kody Wilkins, I will marry you."

He whooped with excitement. "Yay!"

Cheers of joy surrounded them. Everyone rushed to congratulate them. Group hug followed group hug. Even his grandmother got in on the act, as if she were already part of the family. In a way, she was. After all, she was a witch, too. As was he.

"One thing..." Kody's voice boomed out, startling everyone, especially Amber into silence.

"What?" Her brows came together in confusion.

"I'm not living in this house. I'm building our own. Your family would drive me nuts," he declared with a laugh.

Amber slipped between bodies until she was once again in the security of his arms. "I'm good with that, as long as you build it on Hawk land."

"That's a condition I can live with. But for now, I need you alone." He scooped her into his arms. "Where are your car keys? We're going home."

Laughing, she pointed him in the right direction and snuggled into his arms while he carried her to the car.

Love the novel you just read? Be sure to check out the rest of the series!

Your opinion matters. I'd love it if you would review this book on your favorite book site, review site, blog, or your own social media properties, and share your opinion with other readers.

Thanks in advance. Katie.

A Bit About Salem

The truth about the Salem witch trials is too many innocent people died. Were they witches? Perhaps. Most, for certain, were ordinary people. Several theories have evolved in the decades since the executions. Mass hysteria. Poisoning from rye flour gone moldy. A vicious land grab. Jealousy over healthy crops. I'm sure there are many more theories. As time passes, we get further and further from a truth we'll never be able to attain.

There were, however, some truths recorded at the time. Interestingly, none of the accused in Salem were burned, though one man was pressed to death. Witch burnings did, however, take place in many other locales, particularly in Europe. Nineteen people were hanged. Four died in jail. Of the twenty executed, five were men. Sources indicate over two hundred people were accused in Salem.

According to the Salem Award Foundation website, there are roughly 25 million people around the world who are descended from the Salem Witch Trials victims and the other participants in the trials. (Source: https://historyofmassachusetts.org/salem-witch-trials-victims/)

Various sources indicate that Wilkins is alternately spelled Wilkens. Hawkes is also referred to as Hawks. I've selected the most common versions for this story.

As a witch, Pagan and Wiccan myself, the entire history of witch trials and massacres worldwide, breaks my heart. I mourn for those who died by hanging, by pressing, by fire, and in prison. Persecution and prosecution without cause is always a tragedy. I'm optimistic that as we grow to learn more about others, and to accept others, tragedies like this will become a distant memory.

Disclaimer:

There is no Three Moon Falls, or Spruce Creek, nor is there a Three Moon Falls Lake. I've taken considerable liberty with the geography of Alberta in the creation of this narrative. The scenery depicted is an amalgamation of random mountain waterfalls, the Athabasca River, which I've canoed down on more than one occasion, and a number of small towns; not the least of which is Fox Creek, Alberta; the town where I spent my high school years.

About Katie O'Connor

Best-selling author Katie O'Connor lives in Calgary, Alberta, Canada. She married her high school sweetheart and is living her happily ever after. She is the mother of two grown daughters and is extremely proud of her five grandchildren.

Katie is the founder of The Write Chicks, a private romance writers' group set up with the sole purpose of supporting each other's writing careers. She was a 2025 Story Coach for the Alexandra Writer's Centre Society in Calgary.

Katie's career path has been long and twisted, with most of her life devoted to her family. Her jobs have included being a waitress, chambermaid, cashier, store manager, as well as a lab and X-ray technician. She's been a small business owner and is an avid quilter and crafter.

She's dabbled in writing since high school because something drives her to create stories, and swears it's impossible for her NOT to write. Unsatisfied with one genre, Katie writes contemporary romance, erotic romance, fantasy/paranormal romance, romantic suspense, and erotica.

She believes in all things magical, including dragons, fairies, UFOs, ghosts, and house pixies. But most of all, she believes in love, romance, and hope. If you need her, she'll be over by the coffeepot, eyeing up the cookies.

Where to Find Katie

Website: https://katieohwrites.com
Email:katie@katieohwrites.com
NewsletterSignup: http://eepurl.com/Q2nRr
Facebook:http://www.facebook.com/katieohwrites
Bookbub:https://www.bookbub.com/profile/katie-o-connor
Instagram:https://www.instagram.com/katieohwrites/
Goodreads:https://www.goodreads.com/author/show/5362469.Katie_O_Connor

Other Books by Katie

Their Christmas Heart
Their Christmas Love
Their Perfect Christmas
A Silver Fox Christmas Box Set
Heart's Haven:
Running Home
Building Trust
Saving Grace
Loving Winter
Heart's Haven Box Set
Three Moon Falls:
Fire Magic
Water Magic
Earth Magic
Midnight Magic
Air Magic
Stand Alone Books:
Carly's Heart
Matchmaker Christmas
Cupid's Charm
Gingerbread Dreams
Christmas in Silver Creek
Fake Dating at Half Moon Bay
Playing for Keeps in Half Moon Bay
Sleigh Bells Inn
Hearts in the Spotlight
To a Tea
Bulletproof Heart
Protecting Josie
Rekindled Fire
Winning her Love

Ticket to Her Heart
KO'd by Love